PRAISE FOR M...

BRANCH POINT

"A complex, exciting, thoughtful time-travel novel, with characters you'll care about—a terrifying reminder of just how close we came to losing everything once upon a time . . ."
—Robert J. Sawyer, author of *Far-Seer*, *Foreigner*, and *Fossil Hunter*

"A well-researched, deftly plotted novel about time travel, alternate worlds, and the perils of political extremism. This book gave me the chills."
—Allen Steele, author of *The Jericho Iteration*

"In the tradition of H.G. Wells. Clee's knowledge of history is encyclopedic, her interpretation of world events fresh and unexpected. The reader never knows what will happen next!"
—Julia Ecklar, author of *Regenesis*

Ace Books by Mona Clee

BRANCH POINT
OVERSHOOT

OVERSHOOT

Mona Clee

ACE BOOKS, NEW YORK

This book is an Ace original edition,
and has never been previously published.

OVERSHOOT

An Ace Book / published by arrangement with
the author

PRINTING HISTORY
Ace edition / February 1998

All rights reserved.
Copyright © 1998 by Mona Clee.
Cover art by Diane Fenster.
This book may not be reproduced in whole or in part,
by mimeograph or any other means, without permission.
For information address: The Berkley Publishing Group,
a member of Penguin Putnam Inc.,
200 Madison Avenue, New York, NY 10016.

The Putnam Berkley World Wide Web site address is
http://www.berkley.com

Make sure to check out *PB Plug*,
the science fiction/fantasy newsletter, at
http://www.pbplug.com

ISBN: 0-441-00509-8

ACE®
Ace Books are published by The Berkley Publishing Group,
a member of Penguin Putnam Inc.,
200 Madison Avenue, New York, NY 10016.
ACE and the "A" design are trademarks
belonging to Charter Communications, Inc.

PRINTED IN THE UNITED STATES OF AMERICA

10 9 8 7 6 5 4 3 2 1

Acknowledgments

To Brian Douglas Rush, without whom this book could not have been finished; Baron Michael de Ward, for his friendship, generosity, and unflagging assistance in locating rare research materials; and Mr. Phillip Shallcrass, Joint Chief of the British Druids' Order, for his invaluable help in preparing Chapter 7.

To Mary Fall Clee, for doing everything right; and Lawrence Clee, for instilling in me a love of science fiction and fantasy when I was but a wee babe.

Grateful thanks to my agent, Russ Galen; my editor, Susan Allison, a fellow Lovecraft fan; Laura Anne Gilman, for her support and excellent advice during rough times; and David McCambridge and Jim Webber—you guys know why.

Human beings and the natural world are on a collision course. Human activities inflict harsh and often irreversible damage on the environment and on critical resources. If not checked, many of our current practices put at serious risk the future that we wish for human society and the plant and animal kingdoms, and may so alter the living world that it will be unable to sustain life in the manner that we know. Fundamental changes are urgent if we are to avoid the collision our present course will bring about.

> —From the *World Scientists Warning to Humanity*, issued in Washington, D.C. by the Union of Concerned Scientists on November 18, 1992, on behalf of over 1600 scientists, including a majority of the living Nobel Laureates in the sciences.

OVERSHOOT

PROLOGUE

New Year's Eve, 2032

Hard as it is to believe at this late date, the human race has just pulled off the most excellent save in recorded history. Or so it very much appears at this writing.

There were many occasions when I had my doubts that the cavalry was going to get here in time. I often thought we'd finally managed to push our wretched old home planet past the point of no return. I was sure we had disrupted the ecological balance of the Earth beyond repair, and had destroyed our own civilization in the process.

Verily, by last spring we were down to the wire. The hands of the clock were fast closing on midnight. It did seem there was nothing left but for Butch and Sundance to bust out of hiding, take their medicine, and go to meet their Maker.

But we are clever. So very clever.

Many times throughout my life, I felt as if a great game were afoot behind the scenes of ordinary existence—an obscure race between light and dark toward a destination not yet clearly known, a gladiator's duel of whose workings I could only catch the briefest and most tantalizing of glimpses.

And now I find that I was right. I even played a role in that game, though not until the end did I come to know the players, and learn that I was one of them.

Hence this eccentric history.

My tale begins eight months ago, in late April of this year. In writing this account, I thought to present a slice of our daily life in my scribblings, to illustrate just how painful existence had become. There are, of course, times when it is still wretched, but—how shall I put this?—in the meantime the world has changed, and that makes all the difference.

The reason for our predicament was simple: Since the beginning of the Industrial Revolution, we humans had devoted our best efforts to building a great juggernaut of consumption and waste, which squandered the resources of the Earth and left it in ruins.

Within my own lifetime we had come to understand that we were conducting an experiment of global proportions on the very climate of our planet. We knew about the greenhouse effect, and knew what it might do to worldwide weather patterns upon whose stability our civilization depended. Yet our civilization also demanded everincreasing growth, and halting the burning of fossil fuels would have led to some rather dramatic societal disruptions itself. So we chose to gamble that our activities would not result in substantial global warming, or if they did, that they would not do us significant harm. We gambled, and we lost.

I wanted to chronicle every petty adversity with which life tormented the members of my house, as if by doing so I could somehow keep our successors—if there were any—from ever forgetting how dreadful it was. But I also wanted to jump back into the past, *my* past, and record certain peculiar and significant events I had witnessed throughout my lifetime.

I wanted to retrace, step by step, the twisting, winding path that led us into our recent difficulty—from which, such a short time ago, there appeared to be no way out. I wanted to get the perfidy down on paper, to tell it like it was, as we said back in the sixties.

Lastly, there were many questions I wanted to explore. Why, if there were a Creator, it had made us the way we were: possessed of brains powerful enough to contrive the destruction of all around us, but not of the common sense to refrain from such idiocy. I wanted an accounting, damn it. I wanted to know why we had been created in the first place, if all we were capable of was wanton destruction.

By last October it seemed as if the war to end all wars, the one that would put an end to war through our annihilation, was indeed imminent. Then the Green Man came, of whom you will hear much in these pages, and everything changed forever.

Until that time, my own vision had been so limited, I had never guessed that the ruin we inflicted on the Earth was not the last chapter of a dismal history of a soon-to-be-extinct apelike species—but only a difficult moment in an ever-expanding evolutionary path that is leading . . . somewhere.

This is not the end of history. We cannot possibly know where the path will ultimately lead. No matter! It is enough to know that it still leads and does not end. We will not know what final role we are meant to perform in this great drama of the Earth until millennia have passed.

When things were at their worst, there were still signs of hope, if only one had known where to look. Before the Green Man came, we had already begun to grow up; and therein lies the irony. The signs and clues were everywhere. I stumbled across them over and over again, but had never been able until the last days to weave them into a single, coherent image.

John Donne guessed the secret when he wrote long ago that no man is an island. The great philosophers, teachers, and mystics guessed it, and told us about it over and over again, in a thousand varied forms.

• • •

Here is a pattern. Aeons ago the invention of language set humans apart from the other animals and began to draw them together. The invention of writing quickened this process. When Gutenberg built his printing press, humankind—and the world—were changed forever.

In an eyeblink of geologic time, the children of Earth, scattered since Eden, began to come together again, and in doing so, began to transform.

Ideas changed. Once, slavery had been accepted the world over. But by the twentieth century, most peoples found the practice abhorrent, and viewed societies where it still existed not as the norm, but as troubling aberrations from attainable perfection.

Similarly, war was once accepted as a given in human affairs. War was inevitable; it was a necessary evil. The question was not whether a country would go to war, but only when and how. Then radio was invented, and brought the voice of war into our homes. Television followed, and brought the sight of it as well. That sight was often horrifying; and, again, ideas changed.

Once war was experienced only by its combatants, and the unfortunate people and animals who happened to get in their way. Now pictures of war intruded into the daily life of anyone who had access to a television set. War came to be regarded as unnecessary and evil. Countries that went to war were viewed as falling short of a standard human beings were supposed to meet.

There was an old saying that tyrants did their best work in the dark. Under the glaring eye of the television camera, the dark began to recede, and such work could no longer be so easily hidden, as it was in the past.

In Tiananmen Square, in the summer of 1989, tyrants were able to banish the cameras, and the world's outrage over the massacre of students there was not as violent as it would otherwise have been. But enough information about the killings leaked out through many of the other threads that had begun to bind the world together again (through telephone, fax, and the newborn Internet) to sully China's image in the eyes of the world for decades to come.

Two years later, in Moscow, would-be tyrants neglected to banish the cameras, and their attempted seizure of the Soviet Union was undone.

In the last decade of the twentieth century, the Internet exploded into public consciousness. Marshall McLuhan's global village was recalled; there was much speculation that the Internet was the first step toward the hardwiring of a global brain, and would unite human consciousness at last.

None of these devices, created by man, was sufficient by itself. To alter the basic nature of a species is a task of daunting proportions, and they simply were not powerful enough to do it.

But when considered together by certain individuals of intellect, they pointed to a pattern that could be studied. They artificially brought about states of mind in human beings that, however temporary, mimicked the results of a great leap forward in evolution.

Man might wait for the natural course of evolution to erase his failings, so that one day his presence on the Earth might not be inimical to the survival of all living things. But evolution is slow, and the capacity of humankind to destroy is swift.

All these toys of which I have spoken (the printed word, radio, television, even that benign, late-arriving leviathan the Internet) were not the answer to our woes. But in the twentieth century, and in the twenty-first—as in all previous centuries—there were watchers, who understood John Donne.

The watchers who lived in the last decades of the twentieth century and the early decades of the twenty-first recognized that we had run out of time. They watched the toys, and the toys gave them the key they needed to change the future.

Now, if you would, come back with me in time eight months, to the last week of April 2032, and see the world as it was such a short time ago.

— PART ONE —

Earth might be fair, and all men glad and wise.
Age after age, their tragic empires rise,
Built while they dream, and in that dreaming weep:
Would man but wake from out his haunted sleep,
Earth might be fair, and all men glad and wise.

> —Old Hundred Twenty-Fourth (1551)

Whatever befalls the earth befalls the sons of the earth.
Man did not weave the web of life; he is merely a strand
in it. Whatever he does to the web, he does to himself.

> —Attributed to Chief Seattle

Whoever desires to found a state and give it laws, must
start with assuming that all men are bad and ever ready
to display their vicious nature, whenever they may find
occasion for it . . . [Human temperament is] insatiable
. . . shifty . . . and above every other thing, malicious, in-
iquitous, impetuous and wild.

> —Niccolò Machiavelli

Have a nice day.

> —Annoying late twentieth-century saying

ONE

April 24, 2032

AT DAWN THIS MORNING, AS I LAY IN MY BED HALF
asleep, I decided to rise early and get a good head start on
my chores before the day got beastly hot. As I drowsed and
watched the sky gradually lighten, this ambition seemed
entirely reasonable to me. After all, it was only the last
week of April. It did not seem too much to ask that the
early morning air be sweet and cool. I momentarily forgot
that the year was 2032; I forgot that the gentle climate I
had once known was only a memory.

I rose and poured a cup of ersatz coffee from my ancient
minibrewer, which I had timed the previous evening to start
chugging at 6:00 A.M. sharp. Cup in hand, at first light I
went out on the deck of my house, which overlooks San
Francisco and the bay from its perch high above a Berkeley
ridgetop. Still groggy from sleep, I was startled to find that
the day was already hot as an oven. Then I realized that by
the time I finished all the work I had to do, I would be half
dead.

The sun had just cleared the East Bay hills, a glowering
orange globe every bit as malignant as that which had battered Peter O'Toole as he traversed "the Sun's anvil" in
that famed movie from my childhood *Lawrence of Arabia*.
The high-pressure dome that had been building over northern California for the past two weeks showed no signs of

having weakened during the night, and there was not a breath of wind anywhere. The air, trapped and stagnant in the sky above, had a rancid smell. Though the day was forecast to be clear of fog, I could not even see what was left of San Francisco, or the Golden Gate Bridge, for all the filth in the sky.

There it was—the world of the Overshoot. Greenhouse Earth, the greatest catastrophe in the history of civilization, which had crept up on us unawares, like a thief in the night.

I was overcome by a burst of rage. This ugliness, this pointless waste—none of it was supposed to be on my plate. Didn't I belong to the luckiest generation ever to walk the face of the Earth? Didn't I live in the greatest country in the world?

Impulsively, I threw my cup of coffee substitute with all my might against the wall of my house. Though we have very little money now, I did not care right then how much the gesture would cost me—how much the cup was worth, or how hard it would be to replace. I just wanted to break something and listen to it smash.

As I was sitting there on a deck sulking, Loki came up, took a gander at my broken cup and spilled drink, and said, "Christ, Moira, what do you think you're doing? We don't have that many cups left, you know!"

I turned a baleful eye on him. "It made me feel better," I said with a growl, in a tone of voice he has come to respect over the years.

He shrugged, and heaved a loud sigh. "Look, I'm going to make a run down the hill for provisions. Do you want to come along?"

"Yeah, why not?" I said. If I didn't shake off my pissy mood, I wouldn't get anything accomplished that day.

Usually I didn't go into Berkeley with Loki unless it was really necessary. Unless they could help it, no one else from the commune went either; the East Bay supercity was now as dangerous as any postapocalyptic burg from the old sci-fi cyberpunk literature that you could care to name. Loki, the streetwise hustler, could handle himself down there; the rest of us couldn't, not without him along. So I generally kept my visits to a minimum, to allow Loki to concentrate on his chores once he was down there, instead of on protecting me.

But it was getting to be time I went again. Loki couldn't get everything we needed by himself. No man, no matter how intelligent, has ever been able to master completely the art of shopping. Plus, Loki tended to splurge on unnecessary stuff if I didn't go along to keep a lid on his impulsive nature.

I'm a real tightwad these days, which is essential to our financial survival. All the scraps of money the six members of our commune can scrounge from savings, various and sundry surviving retirement plans, odd jobs on the Net, and so forth are deposited electronically to one account—mine—and used to buy supplies. Even as miserly as I am, the grand total is barely enough, and with each year that passes, its purchasing power shrinks, and we pull our belts even tighter.

A word about Loki, who is—surely!—my last lover on this Earth. Lyla Ferguson (you'll be introduced to *her* shortly) would give her eyeteeth to get her claws into him, since Lorenzo is nowhere near as good-looking, and legless, hostile George is confined to a wheelchair. Actually, that makes my day, even more than needling Lyla about Reaganomics, and how Mr. Ozone was right.

Loki's Christian name was Sven, but as a child he adored all the old Norse tales and legends, so when he emigrated from Norway in the early seventies and started college at crazy Cal Berkeley, he decided to take the name of the Scandinavian trickster for his very own. To keep it all in context, you have to remember this was during an era when hippie college students were routinely calling themselves things like Hershey, Peanut Butter, Bear, Prairie, Sun-

flower, and Tigger. But yes, I admit it, our commune is
made up of some very weird people.

The name Loki fits him, because he's such a sharp dealer.
Loki is a shrimp of a guy, despite all those Viking genes
he ought to have. He is an adventurer, a storyteller, a fan-
tasist, a raconteur, a con man, and a genius. All of which
is fine with me; a hustler of the first magnitude is exactly
what our commune needs to survive.

Back in the twentieth century, Loki made out like a ban-
dit when California real-estate prices were at their peak. In
the early 1980s he had a knack for finding the fixer-upper
that wasn't really that hard to fix. He would buy it for a
song and turn it over for a fortune. For a time he ran a
profitable appliance repair business. Then he bought a franchise and sold computers and made still more money. Then
he opened a gourmet roast chicken take-out place in Mill
Valley, in upscale Marin County, and made money hand
over fist. He never seemed to be able to hold on to his cash,
but he sure could get it in the first place. He still can. Since
it goes into my account, I hold on to it for him. Problem
solved.

When I refer to Loki as my lover, you must take what I
say in context. Loki and I are old as hell, and even if we
had any energy left at the end of a day, it's doubtful
whether (a) Loki could get it up, and (b) I could stay awake
long enough not to be rude. Though we had actually had
sex a few times when Loki first moved in years ago, of late
we have turned into two woebegone souls whose mission
in life is to keep each other company at night. We treasure
this companionship, this smidgen of creature comfort allotted to us in our golden years when most people have
none. We make the most of it; truly, we could write the
kama sutra of cuddling and snuggling.

Anyway, Loki had an energy-efficient scooter that he had
outfitted with a second passenger seat; this was our only
vehicle. He could pedal it all by himself on flat, downhill,

or mildly hilly stretches. But our house was up at the top
of the Berkeley hills, on Alvarado Road overlooking San
Francisco Bay, so we had to have the scooter's motor
power to propel our creaky bodies back up to the heights—
Withering Heights, that is, for that was what we had nick-
named our commune.

I collected the strap-on purse that went around my waist,
several string shopping bags woven by Rhiannon, and my
little hand-held electronic bank account debiter. We never
dream of carrying cash, and neither does anybody else. Despite the heat, I wrapped up in a hat, scarf, sunglasses, and
long sleeves to protect myself from the sun. Then I climbed
onto the scooter behind Loki and waited patiently while he
strapped me to him like I was a backpack; he is always
worrying that I'm going to fall off or something equally
stupid.

Under the gimlet eye of George, our Uzi-toting Vietnam
veteran watchdog, Loki keyed in the code that would de-
activate the electricity coursing through our fences and
front gate. He opened the gate just enough for us to edge
through, closed it quickly, and turned on the juice again.

As we sped off, I glanced back at my house and the
cluster of heavily farmed lots that surrounded it, still proud
as Punch of the whole mess, in spite of how rumpsprung
and careworn it looked. I loved the place, even now. I had
loved my home from the moment Roger and I bought it,
back in early 1991. I grieved for it later that year when it
burned in the three-thousand-home Oakland-Berkeley hills
hellfire, and I loved it all the more for the temporary loss
when it was finally rebuilt in all its splendor in 1994.

That experience had taught me there is a bright side to
almost every calamity. You see, all things considered, it
was a damn good thing the original house had burned up
in the fire, because back then the house was sixty years old,
and the annual maintenance costs had already begun to
reach for the stratosphere. They were enough to drive one

to a nunnery, or perhaps a condominium. But after the fire, the insurance company had to rebuild my house from the ground up, brand-spanking-sparkling-new, and this literally gave it a new lease on life. The reason this was an especially good thing was that by 2032 the house would have been more than a century old, and there would be no way our poor commune of aging, failing ex-yuppies and bitter Baby Boomers could have kept up with such a disintegrating monstrosity, no matter how cool the original hardwood flooring.

We waved at one of our neighbors, Mr. McClelland, who was sitting in the shelter of an old gazebo that used to enclose a hot tub. He was reading a book and balancing a shotgun across his knees, ever on the lookout for intruders. His place wasn't near as high-security as ours, but he made out okay. Then we went zipping past abandoned lots and houses as fast as we could go, slowing when necessary to steer through all the trash and debris in the disintegrating street.

As always, we tried not to be unnerved by all the faceless, dirty wretches who filed up the road, casting hard looks at the indescribable riches of the hill people. To them, our just-scraping-by existence was a dream of wealth and security. They really did think we were rich. And, by their standards, we were.

Of course, for the record, they themselves were pretty rich compared to the average sub-Saharan African in the year 2032. They could find abandoned lots, where people had never rebuilt after the fire, and throw up squatter camps. Sometimes they could go to the food bank down in the Oakland flats and get free food, even if it did taste ratty.

Yet, for people who did not have the good luck to live in one of the fortified dwellings in the Oakland-Berkeley hills, life was brutal, and hunger inescapable. Often, in the middle of the night, I heard screams coming from the road. None of us ever intervened in whatever rape, murder, or mayhem might be taking place. It would have been utterly futile; one of us might have gotten hurt, and besides, the next night there would have been other screams.

The gunk in the air had cleared somewhat, and I could catch glimpses of half-drowned San Francisco and Marin County as we headed down the hill. Twisting, winding Alvarado Road would take us within a stone's throw of our destination, the old Claremont Hotel—no longer a resort serving local yuppies, but now the East Bay's largest illegal flea market, known fondly as (yuk, yuk) Mad Mac's.

Illegal, true, but no cop would have dreamed of trying to shut it down. These days, "anarchy" was too weak a word to describe the state of Berkeley's streets. Few stand-alone shops could survive for long under such conditions, but even so, one of life's great truths remained unchanged: Despite the grim state of the world, thieves, muggers, dope dealers, hookers, petty criminals, big-time criminals, gang members, the unemployed, the homeless, the hordes of desperate immigrants who daily landed on our ever-shrinking beaches, and terrified ordinary citizens like me still needed to eat and wear clothing. And that meant they needed to shop.

The Berkeley Flea Market always reminded me of a scene from that old 1970s movie *A Boy and His Dog,* where all these postnuclear war tough guys who normally roam around the countryside killing and raping tacitly agree to check their weapons at the fortified entrance to the store and get along so that peace can briefly prevail, and they can take in an old, scratchy porno movie and chow down on some popcorn.

At the Berkeley Flea Market, people agreed to get along and leave the vendors alone so everybody could stock up on the necessities of life. In fact, a curious camaraderie often prevailed there; the market was a real social center. Once you had left its confines, street rules governed again and you were fair game; but anybody who stirred up trouble inside the market was banished forever, and that was a fate almost worse than death. The nearest similar market was in Fremont, a perilous land journey that nobody undertook on a regular basis unless they absolutely had to.

The sea had risen so much by 2032 that much of what we used to call the "flats" in the East Bay was under water. So were all the places I had loved to visit in my younger days—bookstores, cafés, bakeries, gourmet cheese stores, restaurants, movie theaters, craft shops, jewelry stores, art galleries, ethnic stores, thrift shops, wine bars, brew pubs, you name it. Nowadays the shoreline was only a few blocks away from the Claremont, at what used to be the intersection of Ashby and Telegraph. The only student at the University of California these days was the Little Mermaid.

Of course, the East Bay wasn't the only place so adversely affected. The sea had risen so much that a time traveler from the twentieth century would have barely recognized the Bay Area. For one thing, all our little coastal towns, such as Stinson Beach and Half Moon Bay, were gone. For another, the size of the bay had tripled when our levees were overwhelmed. The delta had turned into a huge inland salt lake, drowning suburbs along with orchards of fruit trees and many square miles of California's best land. Just thinking about it made me sick.

It was really sobering when you considered that so far we had pumped only enough greenhouse gases into the air to raise the average global temperature by five degrees Fahrenheit over its early twentieth-century level—and this was what we got. It was feared that the temperature was going to rise another four degrees by the year 2100; thinking about that *really* made me sick.

Whenever I went to the Berkeley Flea Market I remembered how all those old tyrannical twentieth-century advertisements used to cause otherwise perfectly sane people to live in fear of getting bad breath or BO. The Madison Avenue twits who wrote those ads hadn't known nuthin' about BO. I fantasized that some of them had moved to California and, even now, were shopping at the BFM with me. It would have been so perfect, so balanced, so karmic. Most of the market patrons stunk worse than people must have at any time in history since medieval London.

Not that it was their fault. I myself did not smell so bad, because I squandered part of my water ration on a daily washcloth bath. But I was one of the lucky few in the world who had a little extra water to squander. Folks who were less well off, which meant most Californians, were lucky if they could sponge off every couple of weeks. They had to depend on the public water supply, which was in chronic danger of collapse, whereas we had a backup, in the form of Loki's cleverly built cisterns and filters, which saved and kept pure what rainwater fell during the winter months.

Speaking of which, for years there had been this debate over whether global warming would make California hotter and drier, or wetter. The answer turned out to be—both! It rained like bloody hell during the winter, only to dry up and grow blisteringly hot in the summer. There was not enough money to build new reservoirs or redesign old ones, so basically they were used for flood control, and that made our water supply completely unpredictable. And, of course, more expensive. No matter what happens, it's always more expensive.

When the rain did its Noah's ark thing in the winter, the reservoirs filled up, and when they were full, we had floods. Every chance the managers got, they emptied the reservoirs as much as they could, because all that extra rain meant extra quantities of snow up in the Sierra Nevada. Even though the actual snow level had risen, there was still enough of the white stuff up there to cause massive flooding in the hot summer, when it all melted. The high country part of the old Yosemite National Park was choked with snow and inaccessible during the winter, and flooded practically all summer long.

While we're on Noah and his ark, let me say that I was a kid in the heyday of Joan Baez and her folksong-singing compadres, such as Odetta, to name one. Whenever I reflected on that old traditional spiritual Odetta had borrowed, "I've Got a Home in That Rock," I would go into a slow burn. ("God gave Noah the rainbow sign, no more water but fire next time"). I would resolve that after I died I would sit down and have a nice, long talk with God about breaking his promise to Noah—at least where California was concerned. We not only got the fire, we got the water, too.

The whole situation was, as we used to say, a bummer.

Loki and I checked our scooter with the market police at the entry point, along with his sawed-off shotgun and my ladylike TLG (that's for "tiny little gun," like Nancy Reagan used to carry). I'm still a damn handy shot. Loki and I hurried from stall to stall, fighting with the vendors, buying what I decided we needed, and debiting my account, all the while glaring at those nearest to us, lest any of them be tempted to swipe the stuff we'd just bought: floodlights for our nighttime yard work, coffee substitute, flour, sugar, batteries of various sizes, CDs, salt, vitamins, Geritol, aspirin, powdered milk, lightbulbs, disks for our old computer, razor blades and shaving stuff for the guys, and on and on and on. Loki's big haul for this visit was some spare parts for our generator; you can't count on PG&E these days (not that you ever could), and without the generator we'd be lost. As for me, I found an old issue of *Modern Maturity* from 2008 and bought it on impulse. You have to have a little fun.

Though I never told Loki (nobody needs a whiner these days) each visit when I first caught sight of the Claremont, it was a rotten moment, because I remembered how beautiful it had been in the old days. I remembered how happy we all had been when they managed to save it during the 1991 hellfire. Now it was an ugly, decaying wreck. Its bright white paint had long since peeled off, leaving the weathered boards bare. The grounds had been vandalized and stripped clean of anything of value. There was the smell of urine and sweat in all the big meeting rooms, where the vendors set up. The furnishings were gone, the panes of glass in all the windows broken, and the gardens a mere memory. The upstairs rooms were still used, I was told, for hard-core trade that I did not even care to visualize.

As always happened on a trip to the market, my stomach went into knots when I saw how prices had risen; despite the ingenuity of the two computer gurus in our commune (Rhiannon and Loki), and the ability of our one artsy-craftsy type (Rhiannon again) to make useful objects for trade or sale, our rapidly rising expenses seemed always about to overtake our modest inward-bound cash flow. It was very disheartening.

Something unusual was happening this visit, however. All around me, people were all jabbering about the upcoming presidential primaries and the November election. They were really excited; I hadn't seen anything like it in years.

We keep up with current events over the Net or from newscasts on our one television, when Loki can get it to work, so nothing about the election was news to me. But I'd had no idea people were getting so cranked up about it. They still seemed to believe, after all that had happened to us, that the outcome of the election could make a god-damn bit of difference.

In recent years the United States had had its share of men-on-horseback, of would-be dictators, of extremists who promised that, if they were only given the power, they would turn the clock back to the halcyon days of the 1980s. But this time around, there was a new guy in town, a hand-some young Republican candidate by the name of Julian

Imber, who had been compared to everyone from JFK to FDR to Winston Churchill.

The truly amazing thing was, Julian seemed to merit the comparisons. He was saying all the right things, he was making all the right noises about trying to get us out of the mess we were in.

We were going to make the hard choices that had to be made. We would admit the mistakes of the past and move forward. We were going to stand up and face reality head-on. We were going to acknowledge that the crisis facing civilization couldn't be cured overnight, or by the next calendar quarter, or by the time the next annual report was due, or even in twenty years, for that matter. Nevertheless, we were going to straighten up and fly right, starting now. Humanity was at war—at war with its own mistakes, at war with an environment turned on its head by our folly. We would fight that war and win it.

It all made bugles sound in my blood. This annoyed me greatly, because I'd gotten my hopes up a thousand times before in my life, only to have them dashed. I didn't particularly relish the prospect of being picked up and dropped on my ass yet again. Which was certain to happen, because our current plight was so dire, we were *way* past the point where ordinary political solutions were going to do us a damn bit of good.

Not that I had any brilliant alternative suggestions to offer young Julian. Not yet, anyway.

Still, I had to hand it to the kid. He made every intelligent proposal you could think of and still managed to get me excited. Halve CO_2 emissions this year, halve them again the next, no matter what the cost. Which made sense, because the only alternative was something unacceptable, like death by excessive heat. A Manhattan Project-type intensive drive to develop alternative sources of energy. A global Marshall Plan for the environment. (Ha! *I'm* old enough to remember! You didn't coin that phrase yourself, little Mr. Gopper, Al Gore did! But more power to you anyway.) One-child limits, free bicycles, sealed borders, and no ration coupons for the able-bodied unless they volunteered to serve on police forces, clean-up crews, rescue squads, and the like. He even said, with a wry little smile that won hearts everywhere, that the time had never been better to make use of solar energy. Yeah, I know his science was bad. He just said it for effect, to emphasize the importance of developing renewable energy sources. It's the thought that counts. And recycling. Recycling was really hot these days, as it were—and he was going to help the American public recycle everything down to belly-button lint.

He even proposed temporary martial law to help get matters under control in the country so we could get to work. That got a big rise out of what was left of the ACLU and the country's militia groups. Very strange bedfellows, you must admit, but these were strange days.

I listened in on the buzz and learned that one of our more extreme extremist groups was muttering that Julian ought to be taken out and shot like the mad-dog, dirt-kissing, Earth-worshiping pagan he really was under all that Republican cover.

Ahem. This particular group was originally Texas-based, and its members referred to themselves as the Blue Northers. Northers, because they held the previous century's Col. Oliver North in great veneration, and Blue Northers because they were from Texas, where blue norther storms can sweep through the state and lay everything low with a blast of cold in a matter of hours.

They scared the pie out of me. They gave new meaning to the word "paranoid." A Blue Norther could say out of one side of his mouth that our hideous environmental crisis had been engineered by Powers Unseen to bring down the United States—and in the same breath, argue out of the other side of his mouth that the pitiful, half-assed attempts by various nations to cooperate and deal with it were the precursors to the establishment of a totalitarian, atheistic world government. Blue Northers never lost arguments.

To make the situation even more droll, the Blue Northers had retained a nasty little Texas poodle of a lawyer, a woman who in fact had first been with the ACLU, but had evidently made it her life's mission to defend their right to freedom of speech, no matter how incendiary that speech might be. Each time a spokesman for the Blue Northers got up and suggested something like offing Julian, she would grab the mike and say the guy was only speaking in hypotheticals, that he had no intention of inciting anyone to violence, and he had every right to speak his mind. I used to be a lawyer, and it was people like her who gave us a bad name.

Julian, on the other hand, only laughed—and seized the opportunity to reassure the American people that he would not be intimidated by anyone who would use violence to subvert the republic. People liked that, a lot.

Okay, I'll cop to it. I liked Julian, too, which was kind of embarrassing and irksome, because I was so afraid he would turn out to be just another damn politician.

"Yeah, right," I felt like saying whenever he came on TV, "so where the hell were you thirty years ago when we needed you?" Of course, that was unfair, because he would have answered truthfully, "In high school." It wasn't his fault he hadn't been born until 1984.

As these thoughts went through my head, I must have gotten a faraway, halfway approachable look on my sour puss, because as Loki was bartering with a particularly obnoxious vendor over flashlight batteries, a clever huckster slipped through the crowd to my side. He looked to be pushing forty, which was not a good sign. Everyone his age and younger hates us Boomers, because they blame us for the world's present predicament (and not without some justification). We have a very sixties-style motto in our commune: Never Trust Anyone Under Forty.

"Hey, sweetheart," he whispered. "Yeah, you. You got money, I can tell it. You got spoiled back then, you remember how it used to be, huh? I got this new shit here. When you take it you remember all about yesterday, only it feels completely real, better than a dream. For a couple of hours. Or maybe you dream about your heart's desire, that you never got to have. Look, you don't have to pay me, this is a free sample. You come back here when you want more. Don't bother looking for me, I'll find you." He pressed a plastic vial into my hands and took off.

I was speechless and acted impulsively. I knew I shouldn't do it, but I glanced over at Loki, saw that he was still fighting with the vendor, and slipped the vial into my pocket.

When Loki rejoined me, I could tell by the look on his face that he had bad news. He showed me his tally of the day's purchases, and it exceeded by 30 percent the bill from the last visit. "And I was really cutting corners," he said.

I felt my stomach churn and turn over. "We're starting to dig into our principal in a really big way," I whispered.

He shot a glance at the people around us. "At least we *have* some principal. I don't think anyone else here does. Moira . . ." He paused, as if what he were about to say made him uncomfortable. "Moira, they've got some dope over there, real good stuff. I could get it for Lyla, but it will cost four hundred dollars."

Normally, I squelched his impulse buys, but Lyla was in a lot of pain these days. I wasn't sure I could win this argument, or that I wanted to. "Oh, well, what the hell are we saving our money for, anyway?" I asked. "A college education?"

"No, but we don't want it to run out before the last one of us is—taken care of," said Loki.

I thought about the plastic vial in my pocket. "What the heck. Go on, Loki, get the dope."

"Okay, boss," said Loki. He made an attempt at a smile, and opened his pack to let me peek in. "See what I bought? It's a present for somebody."

I inspected the contents and saw a nice, shiny campaign picture of cutie-pie Julian. "You shouldn't have," I said. "I'm past the pinup stage."

"Oh, it's not for you!" said Loki, and laughed uproariously. "It's for George."

"George?" I said incredulously.

"Yeah, he's crazy about Julian."

I shook my head. "Will wonders never cease? Well, if you're going to do that, I'm getting something for Rhiannon."

I went over to this stall that looked interesting. I saw some incense and grabbed it; incense was always a hit with Rhiannon. There were a lot of items that bordered on kitsch, and others that were just plain tacky and sentimental, like the tourist crap you used to find at San Francisco's long-defunct Fisherman's Wharf.

I had my choice of blue and green glass globes of the Earth, some inscribed with the words "Our Mother," and replicas of extinct animals, many with curious angel wings tacked on. Some of these even came with their own little base for burning a candle or other reverential offering. Or I could buy personal portable altars to fit any religious persuasion; pyramids that were supposed to boost your ability to achieve telepathic bonding with animals (presuming you could find an animal to bond with in the first place); or statues of redwood trees, whales, and the like. Most of these last were made of plastic and were downright ugly. But I found a surprisingly graceful wood sculpture of a dolphin— it was leaping out of the sea to touch its nose to the beak of a great, sweeping brown bird that might have been a pelican. I knew Rhiannon would love it. She was into birds in a big way. The sculpture wasn't cheap, but since Loki was bankrupting us anyway, I just said what the hell.

"Hey, Loki," I said when he returned with the dope, "are there any seeds in that stuff? Maybe Rhiannon can get some to sprout this time. God knows she can grow anything else."

Loki groaned. "Oh, no, now I really will have to finish the new greenhouse."

He wasn't kidding. If anybody with a 'scope spotted that stuff growing on our land, we'd be attacked and overrun for sure.

We retrieved our scooter and firearms and sped off up the hill. I couldn't make myself heard over the noise of the wind and the motor, so I waited until we got home to ask Loki about the vial. "Hey, listen, have you heard of some new drug that lets you relive past experiences? That really works?"

Loki paused before answering. Then he said, casually, "Why do you ask?" Then, of course, I knew he had heard about it.

"This guy tried to sell me some at the market."

Loki scratched at the stubble of his beard; he shaved only twice a week, to save water. "Yes, I do know about it, Moira," he said. "On the street, it's known as the *kehft*."

"Weird name. What does it mean?"

"Did you ever read any of the old novels of A. Merritt?"

"Never heard of him," I replied. I had once fancied myself an authority on science fiction, but that was before I met Loki.

"His best novel, *Seven Footprints to Satan,* was published just over a hundred years ago. In that book, the *kehft* was a green liquid that would give the drinker his heart's desire, whatever it might be, in the form of a dream that seemed absolutely real as long as he was under the influence."

"Cool. Then some sci-fi geek has cooked up this modern version, I take it."

Loki's voice was very stern. "I tried the *kehft* once. You stay away from it, do you hear me?"

"Well, aren't we bossy today? Let me get this straight. It's okay for you to try the stuff, but not frail little ol' me?"

"No kidding, Moira. Don't touch it."

"It's that dangerous?"

He nodded. "Yes."

"And just why is that?"

"Because it works. It absolutely works."

We observed a moment of silence. Then I said, "Well, it sounds like it would be a wonderful escape. . . ."

"It's too wonderful," replied Loki, his expression bleak. "A couple of more trips, and I wouldn't have been able to live without the stuff. I would have taken everything we had and sold it to get more of the drug. Then all of us would have starved to death."

I gave a snort of disgust. "At this point, is that really such a terrible fate?"

"I do not believe in suicide, Moira. Don't give that junk a chance to get its claws into you."

With that, he picked up our string bags—now bulging with purchases from the market—and strode into the house.

I waited until a judicious amount of time had passed, followed him, and stashed the *kehft* in my room, where I hoped he would never find it.

Finally I went out to the deck and cleaned up the mess I had made earlier. I knew I had to start my chores, but nonetheless I sat down for a moment and gazed pensively at the distant bay. It was a habit of mine to periodically take stock of my situation, to assess just how discouraged I should try not to be.

I was not a quitter or a whiner, but the times we lived in were truly ones to chill the blood. The members of my commune and I tried our utmost to hold on to what little we had and to keep our lives on a somewhat even keel. So far we had just barely succeeded, but there was no telling how much longer we could keep it up. Maybe a few months, maybe even a few years—whatever. The night was closing in. We weren't getting any younger or any richer, and times were getting way tougher.

I turned my mind to this with a vengeance. Most problems had a solution, if you only looked diligently enough. For obvious painful emotional reasons, we had avoided focusing on the nasty fact that, as members of our group started to die off, we'd have to locate and recruit reliable younger people to join us. Well, there was no use putting it off any longer, not if the youngest of us wanted to survive. I resolved to bring this issue up at our next meeting and force the others to face it.

Moving quickly from the micro to the macro view, I fretted big-time. The Earth was still heating up, and there was nothing I, or anybody I knew, could do about it. Of course, to be absolutely realistic, my friends and I didn't have to worry: We would all be dead long before the REALLY big crash and burn took place.

Unless there was a war, of course. That was a real threat to my personal well-being. I was aware, as was everyone, that the world could go up in smoke at any time. For years, every tinpot dictator who wanted some nukes had been picking them up for small change on the black market. Understandably, this state of affairs made the United States, Canada, Russia, and Western Europe very nervous. Over the past few decades, they had gradually found themselves to be islands of relative wealth, surrounded by a sea of desperate human beings—and their equally desperate leaders—who hated them, wanted their food, and had absolutely nothing to lose.

I took a deep breath. What if there were a war? What was the bottom line? Well, we'd go down the tubes, and so would most other species of life on Earth.

I strove hard to find some comfort. On the largest scale of all, I concluded, there was a glimmer of hope. I wasn't really worried about Ms. Gaia, not in the long run. I thought she would survive whatever horrible things we did to her, if only because the sheer weight of time was on her side.

She recovered from the meteor that supposedly smacked her sixty-five million years ago, and she would recover from us, though when she did, it was doubtful her climate would be particularly hospitable to human beings—a slight impediment to the prospects for rebuilding Western civilization.

To Mother Nature we were, after all, just another meteor; annoying as hell, but temporary. Over time, our home world would probably evolve a new dominant species, one that could thrive on a climate that resembled the inside of a Finnish sauna—although I thought if I were in charge, if I were Gaia, I personally would think twice about whether it would be advisable to cook up a dominant species again. I would probably choose to have lots of marmosets instead.

Meanwhile, here we sat, waiting for the other shoe to drop, with the joint getting hotter and hotter with every passing year. We were like lobsters in a pot full of water—and somebody had just turned on the stove. We were already scrabbling at the sides of that pot, trying to get out, but there was nowhere to go.

I became aware of a sour taste in my mouth. Throughout all of known history, members of the human race seemed to have a perverse, ingrained drive always to do whatever advanced the individual's short-term welfare, regardless of the effect on everybody else, or on the individual's own long-term welfare, for that matter. It was most odd; and it was not, after all, the sort of characteristic that tended to guarantee the long-term survival of a species.

This kind of behavior was so pervasive, so stupid, and so resistant to change, that I had almost concluded—for lack of any better explanation—that the fault lay not in our stars, but in our very genes.

It was just as if we had been hard-wired, from the very first, to be crazy as loons. It was almost enough (*cringe*) to make one believe in original sin.

I stood up, my joints aching, and headed back toward the house. Philosophizing was all fine and good, but I had a lot of yardwork waiting for me.

TWO

SOME REFLECTIONS ON THE PAST

AT THIS POINT, A LITTLE BACKGROUND, A LITTLE SETTING of the stage, would be in order.

My name is Moira Janelle Burke. I was born in San Antonio, Texas, seven years after the end of World War II. A midwave Baby Boomer, I was destined to enjoy the most prosperous era my country would ever know. When I was growing up, people like me had it all: my family owned a car, refrigerator, television, washing machine, vacuum cleaner, hi-fi system, a stand-alone freezer packed with frozen vegetables, and every labor-saving kitchen gadget that Sears, Roebuck could stuff down our greedy little gullets.

All fine and good. Yet until I was forty, there was never a day when I did not live in fear of the world being destroyed in a nuclear war. That fear darkened the entire first half of my life—and then it turned out I had been worrying about a lesser threat all along. Life has such a twisted sense of humor.

I was just a little tyke when Nikita Khrushchev banged his shoe on that podium at the United Nations and made everybody in America think they were going to die in a hail of atomic missiles—soon. I didn't completely understand what was going on, but I was smart enough to know I should be scared spitless. Every evening when Walter Cronkite or Huntley/Brinkley came on TV with the news,

I would flee outside into our big backyard in San Antonio. There I would climb to the top of our tall wild persimmon tree and escape temporarily from the specter of imminent atomic holocaust.

If the sky was clear, from the top of the tree I could see the city center, five miles away. Cozy in my perch in the sweet, cooling air, I would wait until a certain neon sign atop a downtown skyscraper winked on at dusk. The sign spelled out "Alamo National Bank" and never failed to reassure me with its solid predictability. No matter what they said on TV, it was not possible my world could be destroyed—not the dear, familiar world I knew, where evening came on gently, and those comforting, glowing letters always appeared when darkness covered the city, as regular as the sun coming up in the morning, and spring following winter.

In 1960 my father said he was tired of raking up all the leaves from my persimmon tree, and cut it down in a matter of minutes with a chain saw. For a week I walked around in a state of existential shock, or as close to such a state as an eight-year-old can get. So much for the dryad that must have lived in the tree, if my books of fairy tales and myths were to be believed—not to mention my eyrie, my refuse, my eagle's nest. How could he do such a thing, just because he didn't want to rake up leaves? It was not only destructive, it also felt wrong in a way I was then helpless to describe.

It dawned on me that my dad really liked to keep things under control. An exemplary product of twentieth-century Western culture, ol' Dad. Years later, by the time I finally left home for college, he'd cut down the rest of our other trees, taken out the lawn, and covered the backyard with concrete that required only a sweep with a broom now and then to keep it neat and clean. He had bought a few concrete urns in which my mother was permitted to grow flowers, so long as she disposed of them properly when they were past their season.

I mean, as the saying goes, you just can't let nature run wild.

The nuclear specter didn't go away. In 1962, two years after Dad cut down my arboreal refuge from the Huntley/Brinkley crowd, there came to pass that petrifying interlude in history known as the Cuban Missile Crisis. You know, when the Soviet Union and the United States bluffed each other to the very brink of atomic war. When, if events had gone a bit differently, the world would have been incinerated, and we-uns reduced to a load of crispy critters.

At the time of the Cuban Missile Crisis, my engineer father was employed in civil service at one of the many Air Force bases that ringed San Antonio. Thanks to those bases, that lovely historic city of Spanish missions, the Alamo, flamenco dancing, fiestas, the Paseo del Rio, and the best damn Mexican food you ever put in your mouth was on the Soviet Union's A-Number-One nuclear hit list.

Because San Antonio was such a prime military target, every day during the crisis we had air raid drills at my elementary school. We stockpiled water and canned goods there, and learned about civil defense. Watch one of those old black-and-white newsreels about the crisis sometime; I think you can still find them in video archives of the past century. If the newsreel shows schoolchildren crouching under their little desks during "duck and cover" drill, look for me. My classroom was filmed three times.

Even though I was still not old enough to fully understand the ins and outs of what was happening, I *was* old enough to observe the behavior of my elders. They were clearly scared shitless, so I was, too. By the end of the crisis, I was conditioned like one of Pavlov's dogs to jump out of my skin at the very sound of an air raid siren. Even when I was all grown up and practicing law in downtown San Francisco, I never failed to exhibit a nervous twitch when they tested the civil defense sirens each Tuesday at noon.

On my fifteenth birthday, in 1967, just before San Francisco's Summer of Love made the headlines, I seriously and fervently thanked God that I had been allowed to live that long without being nuked. I had tasted a drop or two of the world's sweetness; hell, *Star Trek* had even gotten renewed for a second season—what more could one ask for? I was, nonetheless, demanding of the Fates. I wondered how on Earth at this rate I would get to live long enough to get married or even to have sex. Or, to be brutally bottom-line about it, even to finagle some boy into giving me my first kiss, so I would no longer score so pitifully low on the Ann Landers purity test.

If only somebody had been around to tell me to kick back, smoke a joint, forget about The Bomb, and enjoy life while I could!—because starting at about age sixty, it was going to be all severely downhill, thanks to an obscure threat I couldn't yet see coming.

In April 1970 they held the first Earth Day, and some other daring high school seniors and I hitchhiked up to the University of Texas at Austin for a big rally and other festivities. Yes, we lied to our parents. But since I was already planning to flee to Austin for permanent cultural sanctuary the moment they handed me my high school diploma, I never under any circumstances passed up an excuse to go up there.

Originally, if the truth be copped to, I went up to the rally in search of some good parties. But, despite my youth, I was possessed of a few dormant brain cells. I remember sitting cross-legged in the sun on the grass in front of the University of Texas main building, drooling over this Viking-gened demigod with amber skin and waist-length red hair sitting next to me. (His name was Sigurd, Erik, or Jarl, I was certain.) When he saw fit to pass me a joint that was making the rounds of the crowd, I knew the ice was broken, and I was in heaven.

But I started listening to what the impassioned speakers at the rally were saying about saving the Earth before it was too late, and forgot all about the Viking. My dormant brain cells stirred uneasily in their sleep, and a couple of them flicked their switches to the ''On'' position. I began to feel that I was hearing something very important. And that I should pay attention. The people sponsoring the rally were so committed to what they believed that they had chosen to speak in spite of the fact that J. Edgar Hoover had the FBI watching them. The least I could do was check out what they had to say, and decide whether it was something I should be worrying about, too.

As I listened, I began to feel decidedly uncomfortable. This was crazy, I told myself. It was a beautiful day, and the world around me looked perfectly all right. Everybody knew that nuclear war would be the end of us if it ever happened, and the new dangers these Earth Day guys were talking about were very, very speculative, to say the least.

But the uneasiness just wouldn't go away. I was having my first inkling that Fate had just played a big joke on me—that, after all those years living in dread of The Bomb, I had squandered my youth being afraid of the wrong bogeyman.

THREE

APRIL 30, 2032

TODAY WAS MY EIGHTIETH BIRTHDAY, IF YOU CAN BELIEVE it. We had a celebration of sorts in the compound—not with party food like cake, booze, junk food, that sort of stuff, because even if it had been available on the market, it would have cost us a month's budget. Rather, whenever one of us makes it through another sweltering year, we drink a solemn toast with some of the filtered rainwater from our cisterns, and everybody prays like hell we'll have the luxury of doing the same thing in another three hundred and sixty-five days.

I got a couple of nice presents, though. You can always count on my dear, clever Loki to come up with something amazing. Somewhere (the flea market? the black market?) he had found an old T-shirt from the 1960s or 1970s. This particular T-shirt was all over the place back then; if you're old enough, maybe you remember it—a sarcastic parody, portraying a supposed panel from one of those romance/lovelorn comic books that were so popular at the time. A handsome, clean-cut young man has just said something to a blond girl with one of those overly ratted and sprayed motorcycle helmet-shaped hairdos. She's put a hand to her forehead, and there are tears in her lushly lashed eyes. ''Nuclear war?'' she cries. ''What about my career?''

The cool thing was, Loki had cleverly substituted the

words "Global warming" for "Nuclear war," and without even botching the shirt.

Rhiannon, my best friend, has owned a beautiful amber and jet necklace ever since she was a student. She always wears it, which is why it didn't get burned up with all her other things when some arsonists torched her old Victorian house in San Francisco ten years ago. Rhiannon has left me the necklace in her will, but since she is a decade younger than I, I probably won't get to inherit it. I'd rather have Rhiannon in any case. Anyway, she did something really touching. It was time to restring the necklace, and she saved out two small amber beads and two small jet ones. From those she made me a pair of earrings. You could barely tell the necklace was shorter. Let me say here that this was a most appropriate gift under the circumstances, since jet was formed nine million years ago when many of Earth's pine forests were submerged when the climate temporarily warmed and the seas rose.

At about eleven at night, when it had been dark for a goodly while, I left my room and went outside. It was still hot as blazes there, despite the lateness of the hour, and the fact that according to the calendar, the season was still supposed to be spring. Come late May or early June it will be even hotter, and we will have to switch our sleeping and waking times around, as we've had to do the past ten years. We sleep (as best we can) during the oven-hot days, and come out at night to plant, tend our garden, water the plants from the cistern, and so on.

There was a bright moon overhead, so I had enough light to guide my steps down our terraces of sprouting, drought-hardy crops to the big oak tree that stands near the edge of our property, by the road.

The terraces go almost to the very trunk of the oak, as every speck of land that can possibly support plant life in this wasteland of ours is used for food. But there is a small circle of dense shade around the trunk where it's just too dark even for lettuce, and there, for meditative moments, we have let stand the heavy decorated concrete bench my husband, Roger, bought from Smith & Hawken for my garden an aeon ago.

It's not all that safe, kicking back so close to the road, not with conditions as dangerous as they are now. I always keep my ears and eyes peeled for intruders, and take my beeper so I can alert George and his magnificent arsenal of firepower if anything happens. But Rhiannon loves the oak, and all of us together can't move that damn concrete bench, so that's where we relax, by the road.

In spite of the party, I was feeling rather overwhelmed. I had never been a quitter, but all I had to do was sit down and plot on a graph our increasing age and diminishing stamina, the skyrocketing prices in the market and our non-skyrocketing supply of cash, the capacity of our security system and the increasingly dangerous state of the streets outside our compound, and the conclusion was pretty obvious. Still, overpowering odds had always gotten my back up. I might end up starving, the street people outside might end up overrunning our place, or it might get so hot that we'd all die of heat stroke. But if Fate wanted the keys to my place, it would have to come right up and—to steal shamelessly from that old bumper sticker—pry them out of my cold, dead fingers.

I looked around at the garden, and stuck my lower lip out so far Rhiannon's pet cockatiel could have perched on it. Part of the problem was I couldn't stop thinking about the time I started gardening, right after Roger and I bought the place in the nineties.

Look, you, shut up, sit down, and don't laugh. At first the gardening was just for therapy. I really needed it back then. In 1989 I had finally gotten up the courage to fall in love for the first time in my life, at the advanced age of thirty-seven. Then the man I loved had been killed in a brutal massacre. I gave up my job as a lawyer, spent some time recovering up in Mendocino, and in an uncharacteristic moment of shattered nerves (or cowardice, more likely), declared myself no longer a contender in the game of life. I promptly married Roger, who was old and sedate, but who really cared for me, and had a lot of money besides.

I could have paid any number of landscape designers to come in and do the same thing. But I was hurting badly, and I wanted to grub with my hands in the dirt. I wanted to discover how you made life come out of nowhere. I wanted, no pun intended, to ground myself.

My very own spot of Earth here in Berkeley was so beautiful then. Over the years it was a haven for voles, moles, squirrels, raccoons, a fox, a pretty little bat, and even a couple of migrating ducks that returned every year. I had every kind of local wild bird you could think of. One magical morning I was outside wielding a watering hose tipped with a brass spray nozzle, when an iridescent hummingbird zoomed in from somewhere else in the Berkeley hills to cavort in the plume of spray. The bird looked like a living, darting jewel, and I held my breath, unwilling to move a muscle until it had finished the very last moment of its dance.

I bought a lot of fruit trees and practically killed myself digging the holes to put them in. I read up on compost and French intensive gardening. It was a while before my efforts were rewarded. For a couple of years I had no fruit; only a few Arctic Beauty tomatoes (one of the few that would grow in our then cool and foggy East Bay hills), a scattering of green beans, and a lot of large and embarrassingly phallic zucchini.

Then, on a cold morning one February, I went down into the garden to make my rounds. Not that I expected to see anything; the sky was overcast, it was freezing cold, and everything looked dead as a doornail. But all of a sudden I came to a stop in front of this apricot tree bred to fruit in chilly climes, like Washington State and the San Francisco Bay Area were in those years. To the casual observer, the tree was in your basic cryonic suspension. But as I examined it more closely, the skin on the back of my neck began to prickle, and my hair stood on end, because the newest shoots of wood had undergone a subtle change. They had deepened in color to a rich mixture of red and brown, as if they had veins through which blood had begun to course. The buds that would become leaves and flowers and fruit had begun to swell ever so slightly. The tree itself seemed to be drawing a slow, languid breath, as if it were about to stretch after a deep and satisfying night's sleep.

For me, it was like suddenly being able to read a foreign language that nobody else could. Nobody else I knew, at any rate. I walked farther along one of the garden's stepping-stone paths and looked at one of my perennial flower bushes, which looked raggedy and dead. At its very base, sheltered from the worst of the wind and cold, there were tiny flashes of new green shoots.

I went rushing around like a crazy person. Everywhere I went, if I looked hard enough, I could see signs that the season was turning, and spring on the way. I felt drunk with excitement, as if I had been given a privileged glimpse into a secret world.

Later that morning one of my do-gooder fund-raising acquaintances came over, a terribly nice lady who lived over the hill in Orinda and bought all her clothes in New York and Europe. I led her down to the garden, high heels and Chanel suit and all. For an experiment, I asked her if she could see any signs of life. Though she was polite, it was clear she thought I had lost my mind. She replied that she couldn't see anything, and courteously refrained from asking why on Earth I should care. Then I pointed out the change in the color of the apricot wood, and all the little signs that spring was coming. Wishing to be nice, she manufactured a great deal of enthusiasm from somewhere. She said what an interesting thing I had pointed out, and that maybe one day she, too, would like to take up gardening. But I could tell my experiment had not made the slightest dent in the smoothly rounded contours of her psyche.

I felt an odd chill go up my spine. She and I spoke the same language. I had used that language to describe my experience to her, but she simply didn't get it. She had eyes, and she saw the same slumbering garden as I did, but she couldn't *see* the secret world I could. When I spoke to her, it felt exactly like trying to describe red or green to someone who was color-blind.

I was sure, somehow, that I had always possessed this ability, lying latent and dormant somewhere in the depths of my psyche. It only required the right set of circumstances to bring it to life. But I had shown her the garden, and even explained what she was supposed to see, and she still couldn't.

But why couldn't she? I felt that uncomfortable chill again. If there were aliens among us, as all the tabloids said, I was very sorry for them. They must feel like this all the time: different and alone.

When I snapped out of my reverie, I found to my disappointment that the year was still indubitably 2032. I squeezed out several big, sulky tears. My little spot of Earth had once been so beautiful. And now look at it!

"Moira?" said a voice coming up the path. It was Rhiannon, clearly worried about me.

"Come sit down, please," I said, very glad to see her.

She was holding a clay pot. "Look," she said, "my mini barrel cactus has a flower."

Rhiannon shared my passion for plants and growing things. In this day and age, Rhiannon's little collection of cacti was quite an extravagance, even more than her pet cockatiel, which itself had cost us an arm and a leg, but I never, ever gave her any static over it. She was too valuable to the commune.

"That's nice," I said.

I must have sounded as enthusiastic as a wet dishrag. "Why are you moping?" she asked. "It's your birthday, not to mention Beltane Eve. Didn't you enjoy the party? Why are you sitting here in the dark?"

"The party was great. I'm just having a momentary dip in morale. Seriously, at the next meeting I really should broach an unpleasant subject—facing the fact that in the near future, we'll have to start recruiting replacements."

"For Lyla, surely," Rhiannon replied, her voice suddenly sad.

"Yeah. But after Lyla, I could be the next to go."

Rhiannon gave a broad grin and said, "You're too stringy, skinny and mean to die. You'll outlive us all."

"Don't be silly," I snapped, more pleased and warmed by her reply than I liked to admit.

Rhiannon thought for a long time. "Are you questioning whether it's worth it to go on, to keep struggling?"

"Not really."

I must have sounded less than convincing. "For me," Rhiannon said, "the point of going on is to *make* a point. I believe that every act has an eternal significance—a resonance, so to speak—above and beyond its effects here and now. The world may be going down the toilet, but I'm going to stay and fight as long as I can, just to resist."

I should clarify here that Rhiannon is our resident Glinda—the Good Witch of Withering Heights. As I mentioned earlier, her house was burned down ten years ago by arsonists; the rest of the story is that she was the high priestess of a Wiccan coven in San Francisco. While Rhiannon was out shopping for groceries one evening, some people sneaked up, poured gasoline all around the house, and bombarded it with a bunch of Molotov cocktails, or something equally vicious. The house went up like so much paper, along with everybody in it.

This sort of incident had become rather commonplace in our brave, new toasty-warm world. After all, the country was in the middle of a desperate crisis. And great catastrophes do tend to exaggerate the propensity of human beings toward religious and political extremism.

When I was younger, nobody ever talked about the environment or the Earth being sacred, aside from a few old Indians and the anthros studying them. Few people ever suggested that it was our duty to actually take care of the Earth. Anyone who saw the presence of God in rocks, trees, rivers, and beasts was either a kook, or an aborigine belonging to an obscure Third World native tribe whose beliefs were inevitably described by scholars as "pagan, primitive, and animistic."

However, when it became very clear in the early years of the twenty-first century that there was not just another Ford in our future, but the Overshoot, a.k.a. Hothouse Earth, everyone's tune changed dramatically. Suddenly, more eco-religious sects sprang up than you could shake a stick at, and all our Bay Area Wiccans and other assorted Neopagans suddenly found themselves in the curious position of almost being establishment.

In fact, around that time somebody estimated that there were more Neopagans in the country than Mormons, which was a hoot.

Everyone and his dog became an ardent environmentalist. Songs like "What Have They Done to the Rain" and Joni Mitchell's "Big Yellow Taxi" were hot stuff again, and were played everywhere. Anyone so foolish as to advocate further plunder of the environment ended up in the same pariah basket occupied by impolitely racist folks like David Duke and Mark Fuhrman back in the late 20th century.

Those of the intellectual persuasion re-popularized the venerable notion that the Earth, or Gaia, was made up of many complicated, interrelated systems, of which we—humankind—were an integral part. We had gotten the joint in deep trouble with our antics, and so, these guys reasoned, deep and mysterious forces were afoot that would change our consciousness—perhaps the very nature of our being—and thereby alter the impact we had upon the Earth. According to this viewpoint, the emergence of Earth-centered religions was not a case of the lunatic fringe going off on still one more ding, but strong evidence that humankind—as part of a self-regulating, homeostatic system—was modifying its own behavior, thereby minimizing its destructive effect upon the home planet.

Me, I had just been raised a nice little Episcopalian girl who didn't normally think about such things, but as the world got hotter and more unpleasant, the argument started to sound like there might be a grain of truth in it.

Of course, old beliefs die hard, especially religious ones. The Overshoot gave a big shot in the arm to religious doomsayers, who went about urging the rest of us to repent, for the judgment of the Lord was upon us.

It also gave a boost to various and sundry fundamentalist groups, some peaceful, some definitely not. For example, take the Dominionists, the religious equivalent of the Blue Northers. In about 2025 they really started acting up and getting attention. The hotter it got—and the scarcer precious resources got, which many greedy folks still coveted—the more they waved their Bibles, and the harder they jabbed their fingers at Genesis and insisted the Good Book Said Right There that we had the right to do anything with the Earth that we damn well pleased, and screw the consequences because the next life was all that mattered anyhow.

I have to say the Dominionists were a spunky bunch. The more people reviled them, the more defensive they got, and the harder they fought. Sometimes they couldn't make up their minds who they liked fighting more: rival fundamentalist groups, more temperate Christians, or any eco-religionists they could get their hands on.

Actually, Wiccans like Rhiannon were the Dommies' favorite targets, more so even than plain-vanilla goddess-worshipers, New Agers, or creation spiritualists. It was hard to go after the goddess-worshipers with any real zeal; they were mostly pudgy, matronly, Birkenstock-wearing, middle-aged women who looked so much like Mom that it was hard to get worked up enough to try burning them at the stake. And your typical New Ager didn't put up a good fight when accused of being a tool of Satan, but only fired up her aromatherapy equipment, took to her bed with a migraine, and attempted to recover inner balance and harmony. No fun at all to persecute. Even the creation spiritualists could trace their lineage to guys such as Matthew Fox, who had belonged to not one but two real churches, having first been a Catholic and then an Episcopalian. But pagans and Wiccans were fair game. Despite the era's fascination with Neopaganism, when the inevitable backlash came, they took it on the chin.

Of course, Rhiannon is not what people used to think of when they heard the word "witch." She describes herself as an adherent of a modern eclectic faith with philosophical roots in ancient, pre-Christian religions that venerated the Earth. She says she committed that description to memory early on, because in the good old days it always made door-to-door Bible-thumpers go away, complaining loudly that she used too many long words.

Truth is, people like Rhiannon never showed up in any of the old sensational horror flicks. Her idea of a magical act is not turning people into pigs, but picking up trash and litter on the beach (well, it was back when there were beaches, before the sea level rose). And that don't sell no movie tickets.

I cheered up, and seeing this, Rhiannon looked at me with this Cheshire-cat grin she always gets when she thinks she's done a good deed. She composed herself, back straight, eyes closed, hands resting on her thighs. I knew she was meditating, ratcheting her brain waves down to a level she called "alpha"; from there she would cast still another spell to protect our home and the people in it. She had told me once that she visualized the entire compound being surrounded by a shimmering, egg-shaped force field, through which nothing harmful could penetrate. It sounded cool to me; actually, to be honest, it sounded very *Star Trek.*

"Let all within the field be protected; let the power of anyone outside the field to do us harm be negated, but let no harm come to them," whispered Rhiannon. "Let a new day dawn from the night in which we find ourselves. Let the phoenix rise from the flame. I ask that all this be done properly, for the good of all people."

I wasn't about to shoot her down with one of my famous sarcastic barbs, because there were times when I had a sneaking feeling the stuff actually worked in some obscure fashion. I mean, half the world believed prayer worked. And this looked awfully like a form of prayer, no matter what label you gave it.

"You're stealing from the Episcopalians again," I said, when it looked like she was coming out of her meditative state.

She giggled. "How so?"

"You're praying for 'a happy issue out of all their afflictions.' I remember that from Sunday School."

She rolled her eyes. "No, we're both stealing from the same cookie jar."

"Nonsense. Episcopalians would never steal."

Rhiannon gave me a look of utmost seriousness. "Different religions are just different paths to the same understanding."

"Don't lecture, dear," I replied, "your academic side is cropping out again."

Rhiannon was a greater source of amusement to me than even Lyla Ann, which is saying a lot. Take her obsession with ethics, for instance. A Wiccan of her persuasion practically wouldn't blow his or her nose if she/he thought it would kill a resident bacterium. Her "Wiccan Rede" sounded as if it had been lifted straight from Saint Augustine. That ancient sage had once said "Love—and do as you please" (so very sixties!). Rhiannon's chums, in contrast, said, "An' it harm none, do as ye will."

Contrast? What contrast? All I can say is, thank heavens old Augie was long out of copyright, or my witch friends might have found themselves in deep bad karma.

Plus, putting on my former lawyer hat, Rhiannon's antics cracked me up no end. Whenever she found herself in a touchy situation, she felt bound by honor to cast only spells of protection, or spells to negate harm by others. She had a very good backup reason for doing no harm to others; she believed in the "Three-Fold Law," a Wiccan variation of the popular what-goes-around-comes-around rule, or the Biblical as-ye-sow-so-shall-ye-reap rule. Basically, it said that whatever good you did to others came back to you three-fold—and so did any bad. Therefore, just in case a mite of frail human malice or ill-will might sneak into her mental intent unnoticed and contaminate her spells, she always added what we lawyers used to call CYA clauses (that's for "Cover Your Ass"). Rhiannon never cast so much as a protection spell without tacking on a CYA or two, such as asking that the spell be proper, and for the good of all people. For that reason I always felt exceedingly safe around her—something I could never truthfully say about my fellow attorneys.

All this background notwithstanding, it had still never occurred to me that my roof would one day shelter a high priestess of the Old Religion, until Rhiannon was burned out of her house, and a common friend named Ian, one of the legion of unemployed stockbrokers in the Bay Area, begged me to take her in. Ian would have done it himself, but his own house was full of other deserving down-and-outers. I still resisted, mainly because I was a coward and afraid of being burned out too, until he read me the riot act.

"Moira, don't be such a chickenshit," said Ian. "Look, you owe me. Remember all the business I used to send your firm in the old days? *Take Rhiannon in.* If you catch her stirring up an eye of newt stew, you can kick her out. But I guarantee that won't happen. She's a vegetarian. You geezers up on that hill could use a comrade like her."

"Yeah, but she's a—you know, what if people find out? I mean, I don't know what sort of stuff she does, and if people walking by happened to see her, then—"

"You know what, Moira?" Ian's voice was very cold. "I got to know everyone in Rhiannon's group before the fire. Not one of them would have hurt a fly. The tradition they followed is so excessively ethical that other Pagan groups regularly poked fun at them. And *they're* the ones who got torched. It really isn't fair, and you ought to be ashamed of yourself."

On occasion vulnerable to peer pressure, particularly when the peer appeared to have firmly established himself on the side of the angels, I caved in and did the right thing. The irony of it was, the moment I laid eyes on Rhiannon, I realized that I had met her over forty years before, in Golden Gate Park. I had wanted her friendship then, but had lacked the courage to reach for it. But that's a story for much later.

"So," I said when Rhiannon was through meditating, "anything good on the Net?"

Sometimes it seemed Rhiannon spent half her waking

hours on the Net. She was not screwing off, understand; it was part of her job. Though we did possess an intermittently functioning television, the news there was always suspect. You were much more likely to get the real scoop on the Net. Plus, she got all sorts of odd consulting jobs that way.

Once she even befriended an old man dying of some terminal disease or other, and to our utter amazement, he left her a shitload of money in his will, so that we were able to get a new generator and refurbish our entire security system. And Rhiannon, who had brought home the bacon, got back on the Net and managed to acquire for an obscene price something she had always wanted—a pet parrot.

"A parrot?" I remember asking. "What on Earth do you want with a bird?" I was a dog person, myself.

"In legend the goddess Rhiannon had three magic birds," she replied. "Surely I get to have one, especially since my spirit guide is a bird."

"Oh, okay," I said. This vaguely rang a bell; back in my college days, I had taken a bunch of mythology courses.

"Remember how the Welsh saying went? 'There are three things that are not often heard: the song of the birds of Rhiannon, a song of wisdom from the mouth of a Saxon, and an invitation to a feast from a miser.' " She grinned, pleased at how clever she was.

"Well," I said, "to each his own."

"Look," she retorted, sounding a mite ruffled, "the big parrots are as intelligent as chimps and dolphins. Besides, a pet would help me stay psychically connected to the animal kingdom—what little of it is left."

She tried to hold out for a talking African Grey or a cuddly Umbrella Cockatoo, but there weren't any available (pets, natch, were a luxury few could afford these days). So she ended up with a small, utterly wild, ill-mannered young cockatiel, whom she tamed and wooed and loved and trained until you could have sworn there really were such things as familiars. It even talked, in a hoarse, gravelly voice that sounded like a cross between Lauren Bacall and Yoda from *Star Wars*.

Once it was paid for, the creature didn't cost us another red cent, either; as she worked in the garden, Rhiannon culled bits of seed from all our cereal plants (millet was a favorite) and she fed every single scrap of veggies from our dinner plates to the bird.

You think she named the bird Horus? Quetzalcoatl? Or gave it a name from any pagan pantheon that had to do with birds? Nope. She named it Tweety Bird—you know, for the little guy who used to hang out with Sylvester the Cat.

Anyway, as soon as I asked the question about the Net, Rhiannon looked pensive.

"Moira," she said, "I need to talk to you."

My stomach did a flip-flop. "Sure. Fire when ready."

She appeared to struggle for words and then said, "I think something is going on. Something really big."

I digested this. "Could you be just a tad more specific?"

"I'm not sure." She lowered her eyes for a moment and then resumed, her voice quiet. "You've known since I moved in that I was good with computers."

"Good? Jeez, you're a guru."

"Well, when I was about thirty, I was *really* good. I was a regular hacker."

"Thirty?" I yelped. "As I recall, hackers can't be more than twenty-five. It's a natural law."

She didn't laugh. "I eventually had to give it up when I started taking the implications of my religion seriously. I figured if there was anything to the Three-Fold Law, I certainly didn't want my mischief coming back to haunt me three times over."

"So why this confession decades later?"

"I'm still pretty good. I was fooling around on the Net

the other day, and so help me, I stumbled over something really weird. It was completely inadvertent on my part, Moira, I swear. I was out there in cyberland, feeling kind of lonely, doing a search for an old friend I hadn't talked to in years. He was a Druid guy I dated after my husband died, whose Internet handle used to be Green Man. Well, I ran smack into a message that should have been encrypted from hell to breakfast. But whoever sent it was in a hurry, or frazzled. The upshot was, they were careless, so I intercepted it.''

''Okay. So what?''

''At first the message didn't seem to be particularly sensitive, so I just blundered around, trying to return it to the sender. I planned to let them know anonymously that they'd better be more careful in the future. Well—this is the weird part. How can I say this? The message didn't *want* to be returned. The sending machine wouldn't take it back—I suppose to help avoid identification. The third time I tried to return the damn thing, it deleted itself. I got annoyed and frustrated, and finally hacked my way a few levels into the sender's security system. I was going to tell them off or something—you know, chew them out for being sloppy.''

''Bad, bad Wiccan lady,'' I said reprovingly. ''You're not supposed to get mad at people and chew them out.''

I was making fun of her, but she was too caught up in the story to notice. ''Once I got into the system, it thought I had a right to be there, and it gave me access to all its files.''

''That sounds way too easy.''

She lifted one eyebrow, just like Mr. Spock used to do on *Star Trek,* and said, ''But I'm way good.''

''And modest. You peeked, of course?''

She looked away, not meeting my eyes. ''Yeah. Hacker fever, you know. I was so curious, I couldn't help it. There are thousands and thousands of files and messages, Moira.

The one I intercepted appears to be the only time they've ever slipped up.''

"I'd certainly describe that as a prime case of serendipity. It was clearly meant to be. So what *is* going on?''

"I'm not entirely sure. I came to my senses after a few minutes and got out. Who knows who those guys are? I could have been putting us all in danger. So I didn't read enough to definitely answer any of my questions. But I think they're good people. I know this sounds bizarre, and I don't mean to be dramatic, but I felt like I was watching the last part of *The Empire Strikes Back,* you know— Luke's showdown with Darth Vader, the ultimate battle between good and evil.'' She put her hand to her throat and started toying nervously with her amber and jet necklace—a gesture particularly appropriate under the circumstances, since she'd once said it was supposed to symbolize humanity's eternal struggle to keep the forces of light and darkness in balance.

"Holy shit,'' I said, setting a new standard for originality.

"I want to get back in. I wish I could help them. I'm just afraid I might put us all in danger.''

"Look, Rhiannon, face it. If those guys are any good, they've already fingered you, and they already know who I am, because it's my name on the account.''

"Yeah,'' she said glumly.

"Based on what you saw, you *think* they're benevolent, right?''

She nodded. "But I can't be completely sure. You know that.''

I sighed. "Well, if we're toast, then we're toast. Exactly what is it you think they're trying to do?''

"There's an operation—or a project, or whatever—that they're calling 'Green Man.' That's why my flailing around in search of my old buddy snagged the message.''

"A project? What kind?''

Rhiannon avoided my eyes. "It appears to be an attempt to save the world."

I broke out laughing. I'm sorry, but after the buildup and all the tension, I couldn't help it. "Lotsa luck, dudes! Will somebody please tell them it's already been tried?"

She didn't crack the ghost of a smile. "This is different," she said quietly. "I'm not sure exactly what they're planning to do. I didn't have time to find out. But I have this feeling. . . ."

I sobered up real quick. These days, I no longer scoffed at Rhiannon's hunches, not ever. I'd learned.

She lowered her head and ran her hands through her long, white hair. "I think they're good people. I wish I could help. I want to help. I wish I could feel like I've done something, no matter how small, to strike back at—at the way things are. Do you understand how I feel? I hate standing by helplessly while the whole world slides into the abyss."

She was asking for my approval—to get back on-line, to contact this project, to get involved. "Rhiannon," I said, "you're the most ethical person I know. Agonize over it, like I know you will, and then do whatever your heart tells you to."

I'm not as brave as I sound. We're all so old, and our situation is so desperate, we really don't have that much to lose. It gives us a curious sort of freedom.

Suddenly, in the distance, I heard a sound like bicycle tires on crumbling asphalt. "Don't move," I said to Rhiannon. I reached for my gun and got ready to beep George; protection spells were all fine and good, but I liked insurance. The chance of some marauder getting through our swamp of fencing, barbed wire, electrified wire, and other assorted nasties was pretty unlikely, but you could never be too careful these days. My lifelong friend Aleta Mahoney had been killed some years before in a hail of drive-by bullets as she labored over a bed of quinoa grain near the road. I have never thought the shooting was random; whoever it was thought we were rich (as I guess we are, according to some people's frame of reference) and just wanted to hurt us.

I listened a moment longer and whispered to Rhiannon, "Get down behind the bench. The concrete will protect us if anybody starts shooting."

We waited. When I breathed, I made a sound like a wheezing bellows that I was sure would draw the approaching stranger straight to us.

The bike was coming slower now; the guy was having a hard time with the hill that peaked right in front of the compound. "Keep going," I whispered under my breath as he drew level with the main gate. But sure enough, when the bicycle reached the crest of the hill, the rider stopped. "Shit," I said.

Then, to my utter amazement, Rhiannon murmured, "There's nothing to be afraid of. Not this time."

There was a long pause, and then we heard him get off the bike, and swipe at the kickstand with his foot. His boots came crunching right up to the gate itself.

I peered over the top of the bench at the figure on the other side of the chain link and barbed wire. It was a she, not a he—an Asian girl barely into her teens. I gaped at her. Was she out of her mind, riding around on a bicycle at night by herself? She was risking robbery or rape—hell, she might even be risking death by barbecue, given how many people out there were hungry! In any case, if she had some special firepower that made her feel safe, I dearly wanted to know what it was.

She was carrying two sacks. She evidently knew our fence was electrified, because she didn't touch it herself. Instead, she crouched down in the driveway by this gap, right below where the gates meet, that is barely a foot wide. She took what looked like a thick, raggedy old towel out of one sack, and something small and wriggling out of the other.

"Go. Go!" she cried, and shoved the live thing through the gates. Then she wadded up the towel, swiftly blocked the gap with it, and was off on her bike before I could catch my breath.

"What in God's name is that?" I whispered. I hauled myself out from behind the bench, every eighty-year-old muscle and bone protesting, and walked toward the gate. Sitting there, looking confused and forlorn, was a young, very small dog with an excess of terrier in its ancestry.

I squatted down in front of the creature. "I don't understand!" I cried. "I just don't understand!"

The dog looked at me. I looked back. "The girl's trying to save her pet," Rhiannon said.

"Yeah," I replied. Once I focused on the situation, it wasn't so hard to figure out. "She's seen our place and thinks we're living high. She must have found the dog, God knows where, and taken it home. But her family, or whatever, can't afford the extra food. Probably they were planning to eat it, or sell it as a bait dog to a pit bull trainer; she doesn't realize we'll have to eat it. Or maybe she does, and thinks we'll kill it humanely."

"Oh, brave new world," said Rhiannon in a voice that was suddenly bitter as mine.

That got the wheels to turning in my head. I started thinking about how every one of the little pleasures that made life worth living had been stripped away from us in the past years. There were no clear, cool spring days anymore. No espresso at the corner shop—indeed, no corner shop, unless it was barred and bolted and as impregnable as Fort Knox. No street fairs with their silly little arts and crafts. No ice cream on hot days. No parks that were safe to go into.

Have I forgotten to mention that, in addition to being a tragedy fit to do the ancient Greeks proud, the Apocalypse was boring as hell, because there was nowhere to go, nothing to do, and no money not to do it with?

Anyway, I knew we couldn't keep this dog. The little meat it provided would be that much more protein for the six of us. The bones and the rest of the carcass could be boiled for stock, and afterward the leached bones could be crushed into meal for the garden.

But a world in which this scruffy little creature had to go into the soup pot, no exceptions made, was not a world I thought worth living in anymore. I had suffered enough. This one time, I wanted a little something back from life.

That was when I went over the edge. I put out my arms to the dog and called it to me. That dog was no fool; it knew a sugar mama when it saw one.

It came bounding forward, leaped into my arms, and snuggled there. I lifted the dog up, determined that it was female, and cuddled her in my lap. Her dark eyes, silver in the moonlight, gleamed up at me in utter adoration. She was mine until death did us part.

"You know we can't have pets that consume extra resources," said Rhiannon. "It's against the rules that you made! Moira, don't get hooked on the dog. I bet I can find you a bird!"

She did not sound in the least convincing. I think she herself would have died to protect Tweety Bird, and her powers of empathy were so advanced, she could tell I was in the throes of advanced doggie love.

And when you get right down to it, she was a witch. Modern witches positively bleed at the gums whenever an animal or a tree gets wasted. Rhiannon routinely poked fun at herself and her old deceased chums by referring to them as Birkenstock-wearing Bambi-Wiccans; and for that I was grateful. It is so much easier to tolerate religious people when they can laugh at themselves.

"I'll feed her from my food ration. No one else will suffer."

"You idiot! You'll starve!"

We heard the footsteps of one of our fellow old codgers shuffling toward us from the house. "Rhi? Moira?" a voice called. "Are you guys all right?"

"Yes, Father Lorenzo," I said. I always called him "Father" out of respect, even though he had quit the church long ago. He'd been a priest at that megachurch on Columbus Avenue in North Beach until it shut down. Father Lorenzo moved in with us, took one look at Rhiannon, hurriedly reevaluated his now pointless vow of chastity, and resigned from the priesthood. Verily, verily, this era in history should be renamed The Time of the Strange Bedfellows.

"Moira, are you really okay?" he cried.

"Yes," I said. But speaking further was the wrong thing to do right then; it primed the pump, and I began to sob.

Rhiannon put out a hand toward him. "We have a very tense situation here. Be careful."

Father Lorenzo gave the dog and me a stricken look. "Come up to the house," he said gently. "We'll get this straightened out." Now that my initial storm of emotion had subsided, I obeyed, heart sinking at the prospect of the battle I knew would ensue.

Rhiannon quickly summarized for him what had happened. Then her voice dropped to a whisper. Despite my age, my ears were still quite keen, so I could not help but overhear what she said. She might be a witch, but she did *not* know everything.

"Lorenzo, this is one of those times the rules should be bent. I really think she's close to the breaking point. The dog could bring her out of it. Besides, it's not like we have to put the dog through college or anything."

"But we can't feed a dog, even a little one—"

"She says she's going to feed the dog from her own ration."

"She can't do that! There's not enough for both of them."

"I'll pitch in some of mine. Besides, I just figured out a way to generate some more food for us. One of my friends on the Net posted a foolproof method for making acorn meal. We've been going about it all wrong; that's why it molded before."

"Lord God," said Lorenzo. "How I love you women. And the Net." He stopped short and looked down at her. "Of course I'll pitch in some of my ration, too."

He really had to, since he and Rhiannon were as good as married. "Come on," she replied, "we still have to put it to a vote."

Rhiannon and Lorenzo woke up Loki, George, and Lyla, and briefed them on the situation that now confronted us, with me clutching the dog to my bosom the whole time. The dog, no fool she, panted daintily, little pink tongue showing, and beamed looks of delighted interest at everybody in the room.

"I think we should make an exception in this case," said Rhiannon. "Moira is willing to feed the dog entirely from her own ration, but Lorenzo and I are going to contribute from our own resources. Of course, anyone else is welcome to do so."

George, ever supremely cantankerous, bless his heart, raised his hand. "Resources?" he asked. "Moira is a resource."

The dog cocked her head and looked at him with the appearance of extreme interest and admiration. Since George is such a crusty old buzzard, he doesn't get this look very often, from anybody. It shook him up.

"It is selfish for Moira to jeopardize the well-being of the commune by giving her rations to a dog," George continued, trying to ignore the creature. "She could die. Or even if she doesn't die, she would weaken herself."

Father Lorenzo shot me an apologetic glance. "Nice

logic, George, but sometimes logic doesn't cut it.'' The dog's head swiveled toward Lorenzo, and she trained her eyes on him in a manner that was positively winsome.

Lorenzo stammered, and I knew the heat-seeking missile had found its mark. ''I—I think we stand a better chance of keeping Moira alive with the dog than without it. Besides, you know none of us would have a home without her.''

An embarrassed murmur arose from the others. I didn't blame them; I was embarrassed, too. That was a real guilt trip. ''Now, Father,'' I snapped, ''that's not fair. In fact, it's blackmail. *I* wouldn't have a home without the efforts of everyone here. I couldn't farm this place by myself.'' I turned to face the others and said, ''Don't listen to his guilt trip. I know I'm being selfish. But I can't help myself. I just can't give up the dog. She chose me.'' I drew a breath and prepared to tell a real whopper. Except, on reflection, I wasn't sure it was a whopper at all. ''Guys, I really am prepared to starve for her.''

''I'll pitch in,'' said Loki, ever sentimental and generous. Actually, he had no choice if he wanted to stay in my good graces. He looked at the dog, who had begun to do her number on him, and tried to appear nonchalant.

When he said that, Lyla Ann turned and gave him a sugary smile. When she patted his hand—''What a dear, generous man,'' her look said—I wanted to go over and tell her to keep her mitts off him. And slap her, even if she was ill. Lyla Ann was not above using her sickness to get her way, believe me.

There wasn't much the others could do to stop me keeping the dog. Not that anybody really wanted to. I could see a lot of eyes tearing up as they watched me cradle the pretty little thing. In fact, the dog had done her work quite well; people were looking at her with downright hunger—for companionship, I mean, not food.

But of them all, skinny, button-eyed Lyla was the one

who really came to my rescue. I should mention here that Lyla is former Congresswoman Lyla Ann Ferguson, R-Bakersfield, once a staunch member of the Grand Old Party, an individual who had never in her wildest dreams expected to end up old, bitter, divorced long ago so the Hub could marry a girl half Lyla's age, helpless, penniless, bereft of medical care, and dying of very slow painful cancer . . . and in a hippieish, sixties-style commune with a bunch of liberals and other weirdos among her companions.

One day long ago, after I had called Lyla an elitist sellout token-woman bitch from hell, we had agreed henceforth not to discuss politics, but to stick to noncontroversial topics such as sex and religion. Lyla could still be a bitch from hell, but despite her illness there was no better worker in the commune (except Rhiannon, of course). Lyla could outlast the kind of bad times that flattened the rest of us, apparently out of sheer genetic cussedness. She was so tough, the bad times got tired of messing with her and went away.

"Listen, everybody," said Lyla Ann, "Rhiannon had a good idea about several individuals adopting the dog jointly and feeding it out of their combined resources. But I think I can expand on that notion and refine it a little."

Lyla Ann loved to one-up Rhiannon. Rhiannon's jaw clenched, and you could practically read her mind and hear her reciting the Three-Fold Law for dear life. "When I first joined the Junior League as a young bride in Bakersfield," went on Lyla Ann, holding center stage and loving it, "we used to take little dogs and cats around to old people in nursing homes. It did the old folks a lot of good; some of them used to tell me those visits were the one bright spot in their week. Scientific studies have shown that petting dogs and cats brings down the blood pressure. I say we should all pitch in a tiny bit of our rations to feed the dog, in exchange for which Moira will give us all visitation privileges. Any fool can see the dog will always be Moira's dog—it's bonded to Moira with epoxy glue, and that's that.

But Moira can just knuckle under and share. We're as pitiful as those geezers back in the nursing home; having a
dog would do us good.''

She strode up to me, hefted the dog in her arms, and
pronounced, ''Twelve pounds, maximum. We each give up
enough food per day to support two pounds of dog. Surely
we can do that. Any problems?''

There were no problems. Lyla Ann stroked the dog and
cooed to it and made silly baby-talk noises. You could sure
see her blood pressure going down. I started blubbering
again. Still holding the dog, Lyla Ann patted my arm of-
ficiously as if to say, ''There, dear, I've handled the situation for you; I do hope you're grateful.''

''Thank you,'' I said from the bottom of my heart.

Lyla Ann, the born fixer, basked like a tabby cat in sunshine. ''Oh, it was nothing.'' She quickly examined the
dog's underside and asked, ''What are you going to name—
her?''

I hesitated, and suddenly the perfect answer just floated
into my head. I looked at Lyla Ann with absolutely sincere
gratitude but let the devil sparkle in my eyes for just a
second.

''Hillary.''

FOUR

1970–77

I MOVED TO AUSTIN SHORTLY AFTER THAT FIRST EARTH Day rally. I had just celebrated my eighteenth birthday, was through, through, THROUGH with high school, and was ready to party all summer long and start my freshman year at the university come September.

After a single weekend of scarfing lotus blossoms in the counterculture capital of Texas, I decided I had found my own personal ecological niche. Hanging out in Austin was so much fun that I resolved I was not going to grow up, or even begin to take life seriously, until well past age thirty.

There was no reason to believe the future would be anything but glorious. I danced around my apartment in a 1920s-vintage house, my feet loving the touch of the worn hardwood floors, my body carefree in a halter top and shorts; I was the grasshopper frisking through eternal summer, while only foolish ants applied their noses to grindstones. I never gave a thought to the morrow. Forty was an inconceivably old age, which logic dictated I should reach one day. But in my gut I knew I would remain eternally twenty. Or maybe twenty-one.

However, in spite of my best resolutions, I read too much. I always had my nose in a book, and pretty soon I began to notice things that made me a tad uneasy.

In 1970 an international group of businessmen, statesmen, and scientists called The Club of Rome commissioned a study of population growth, food production, resource consumption, and pollution. It was published in 1972 as *The Limits to Growth.*

Let me just say that it did not present a pretty picture of the future. It did not inspire me to save my money and purchase an annuity for my golden years; quite the opposite. By the time I finished the book, I was so upset I dropped a lot of cash on some very good dope for right then and there. I felt powerless to do anything about the direful situation described in what I'd just read, and a little Colombian Gold was just what I needed to help me get over it.

The book sported a nifty introduction by the U.N. Secretary-General, U Thant, who gave the nations of the Earth approximately ten years in which to bury their differences and launch a global partnership to stop the arms race, improve the human environment, and defuse the population explosion. He said that if we didn't get moving within that ten-year period, the problems would have reached such immense proportions (and have gathered such momentum) that they would be beyond our ability to control. Poor U Thant; if he had only lived to 2030 or so, he could have written his own book, and it would have been titled *Told You So.*

Once I had read that book, I started noticing little stories about danger to the environment buried in the back pages of newspapers. I started paying attention to public television programs about the environment. Every time I turned around, whether it was a magazine article, a book, a newspaper, a TV interview, you name it, another worrisome eco story would appear. But curiously, I seemed to be one of the few people who noticed these things, let alone worried about them.

Remember 1994's *Jurassic Park*? Don't kid me; of course you do, unless you're too young to be taken seriously. Remember that most excellent scene in cinematic history when you're sitting in the dark theater equipped with Dolby sound, and you start to hear (or, actually, *feel*) a faint, insistent <<<Thud>>> coming from far away? You don't know what it is at first, and neither do the characters in the movie, with whom you are suddenly identifying with amazing intensity.

Then the guys look down at that plastic cup full of water. As the shock waves from each <<<Thud>>> pass through their car, they see the water in the cup ripple in response. Gradually, you all come to realize that a *Tyrannosaurus rex,* the evil King of the Dinosaurs himself (or actually, herself, in the case of Jurassic Park), is approaching.

Looking back, seeing the harbingers of ecological disaster shoot across my bow was a lot like watching those ripples in the water in the plastic cup. There were a lot of them in the seventies, more in the eighties, and just plenty in the nineties.

Nevertheless, it took people a very long time to even get it through their heads that (a) there was such a thing as an environmental *T. rex;* (b) not only that, it was making a beeline for them, and (c) during their lifetime, it might even catch them with their pants down, like the way the *T. rex* in the movie got that lawyer. . . .

(<<<THUD>>>).

Basically, humans are stupid, shortsighted, self-centered, greedy, and real good at denial. And those are just their good points.

The bottom line is, nobody took the greenhouse effect seriously enough in time for the nations of the world to make a concerted, coordinated effort to stop it. By the time everybody had proof positive, right in their own backyard, of just exactly what deep moose shit we were in, we had already pumped enough hydrocarbons into the air to change the Earth's climate in a most disagreeable way. And that change had so much acceleration and momentum built into it that by the time we really got a clue, we had overshot the point where we could stop it.

A few people saw the Overshoot coming long ago. Those people tried to warn others, but those others weren't willing, or able, to take them seriously.

Some folks might have listened, but the prospect of ecological collapse was too difficult to comprehend and too frightening to accept, so they stuck their heads in the sand and their butts in the air, like so many ostriches.

Still others lived out their lives centered totally upon their own little problems, and never even saw the freight train hurtling down the tracks until it flattened them.

A last selfish few (I won't name them; *you* know who you are) convinced themselves that even if the Overshoot came to pass, which they maintained was not at all certain, they personally could escape its worst effects. Since making the changes necessary to prevent it would definitely hurt them in the pocketbook, they proceeded, cold-bloodedly, to do their best to disable any attempts to deal with the coming crisis. It was okay to play dice with the future of the planet, they reasoned, because they had decided they wouldn't be touched, even if the rest of us fried.

They were wrong, and they may even be sorry now.

I was going to stop here, but I have this compulsive need to present the whole picture. There was one group of people besides the eco-freaks, the nature-lovers, the tree-huggers, the Lesbo-Dyke goddess worshipers, the eco-pagans, and the Democrats who took the issue of global warming very, very seriously.

This group was the insurance companies. With a few public utilities thrown in for good measure.

I would not lie to you. As early as the 1990's, the insurance companies were starting to take it in the shorts from all the violent storms that were smacking the U.S. There were hurricanes Andrew and Iniki; the almost-hypercane, Luis, which mercifully did not hit the States. There were ferocious winter storms that battered the east coast, and endless drenchings that turned the state of California into one mud slide after another or flooded the Midwest. In 1997 there was the rare Pacific hurricane, *Pauline*, which did for Acapulco.

By 1995 certain big insurance companies had forlornly concluded that all their calculations and projections about the world's weather were totally off course. Their financial losses skyrocketed into the billions, as droughts, floods, and storms hit the country with greater severity—and frequency—than had ever been expected.

Global warming might have been a looney-tooney, eco-fringey issue to Congress and most of Big Business in 1995, but it wasn't to the insurance companies, who sat by sucking their thumbs in angst, watching in horror as the red ink dried on their bottom lines. Trust me, nothing gets to a business person quicker than red ink *down there*.

In contrast, by 2032, nobody thought of global warming as a touchy-feely New Age alarmist notion anymore. There was so much red ink around, people had forgotten what black looked like. The insurance companies were just the first guys to get hit.

It doesn't get any more droll than this: by the mid-1990's the insurance companies had already begun to raise their rates in contemplation of further global warming. And they reportedly began to invite Greenpeacers and assorted other eco-hysterics to speak to their industry associations to explain to them what was going on. Talk about strange bedfellows . . .

FIVE

Our Little Bundle of Joy

May 15, 2032

A couple of weeks after my birthday I was once again sitting under the oak tree at midnight with Rhiannon, petting Hillary. This time we had Lyla Ann along; a little earlier, the men had had their turn with the terminally cute dog.

Here was my problem. I had to sit through petting sessions twice. If anybody else was going to get to fuss over Hillary and hold her on their lap besides me, I had to be there the whole time. Saying the dog had bonded to me was Lyla Ann's understatement of the new millennium. Hillary had decided the moment I picked her up that I was hers—lock, stock, and barrel. I belonged to her. I was her property. It said so, right there in the contract.

The little creature followed me everywhere; she would not let me out of her sight for a moment. As I went about my chores, the sound of her toenails on my once-expensive hardwood floor, the brick patio, or the concrete stairs accompanied me unfailingly, clickety-clickety-click. Even if I was doing something boring outside, she would not go lie in a shady spot under the tree and chill out. No, she stuck by me like a little guardian angel.

She even wormed her way onto the bed between Loki and me at night and insisted on staying there. As stubborn as she was winsome, she always got her way; Lyla Ann must have been like her as a girl, only not so pretty or so hairy. Once when Loki, in an exceptionally amorous mood, tried real hard to relocate her and snuggle up to me, she bared her teeth and growled at him.

So much for young love. Loki didn't hold it against her; she was so cute and flirty, she had him reduced to dog meat, too.

This devotion was very flattering and soothing to my soul. But said devotion presented problems of the strategic kind when the rest of the commune wanted to visit with the little wuss, whom they were after all helping to support. We finally got it worked out to where, once night had fallen, I would sit for half an hour under the oak tree while the boys fawned over Hillary and lowered their blood pressure, and the girls stood watch. Then it was their turn. Next night, girls went first, boys last. The night after that, we mixed and matched, to avert boredom.

Her unknown former owner had taught Hillary a grab bag of enchanting tricks. She would twirl around on her two back feet, sit up on her haunches like a squirrel or a real, live Texas prairie dog, and beg, or dance and feint and play catch-the-mouse with a tasty morsel ponied up by one of the suckers in the commune. She had a lot of border terrier or ratter in her. She was so vivacious, I was tempted to rename her Gigi, the Champagne Dog.

In no time she had the other members of the commune wrapped around her little paw, including George, which was a minor miracle. George is not the sentimental type. He has always been very aggressive and fighty, ever since Vietnam. He really enjoys his job as security chief and gun-toter; his dream is to come back in the next life as Steven Seagal.

At first George maintained that he had no use for Hillary. He said his first girlfriend, back in 1968, had owned "a yappy little dog," and that had been enough to last him a lifetime.

However, George found himself in a bind. Father Lorenzo, the prototypical "SNAG," or Sensitive New Age Guy (even if he did used to be a Catholic priest), made no bones about wanting to commune with the new dog. Loki, the only other man besides Lorenzo and George in the group, said loudly and often that he wasn't soft on animals, but he had to chummy up to the dog to keep me happy, and besides, he didn't want Lorenzo to look stupid out there petting the dog with all the women. Since Loki is George's best—actually, his only—friend (and role model and soul mate), George couldn't bear to be left out.

In 1970, at age eighteen, George volunteered to go fight in Vietnam. George has shown me a picture of his prize pickup truck, which his father had bought for him after George won a 4-H competition or something else equally quaint and redneck. It had a gun rack, an NRA sticker, lots of American flag decals, and an "America: Love It or Leave It" bumper sticker.

George got both his legs blown off by a land mine in Vietnam. It didn't turn him into Ron Kovic, or even Tom Cruise (damn, damn, damn!). It just made him mad.

Normally, you would not have picked someone like Loki to be George's soul mate in the sunset of his wheelchair-ridden life. But it made sense. Loki was quick-witted, charming, good-natured, and very amusing. Though admittedly he was a con man as crooked as a dog's hind leg, he was true-blue loyal to his friends, and that meant us. So, basically, Loki was everything George would have liked to be. Consequently George followed him around like a little kid tagging after his big brother. They cleaned their guns together. They talked about the many, many, many women they'd had in the past. (Yeah, right, both of you.) Loki brought George old copies of *Playboy,* or sneaked onto the Net using Rhiannon's computer and downloaded some truly eye-popping pics for George. They got out their prayer rugs and bowed in the direction of Southern California in memory of Ronald Reagan. They plotted how to make the commune's defenses even more intruderproof, and how to blow anybody who made it through into a million particles of bloody dust. George had a lot of hostility inside him that he'd stored up over the years, and Loki listened to him, let him get it off his chest, and directed it into truly constructive channels.

So George couldn't bear to be left out of any activity in which Loki participated. Loki kept up the bullshit about how he was only courting the dog to please me, all the while babying her and giving her bits of food and sending the rest of us into sugar shock from having to watch the spectacle. Before long, George was gruffly patting her on the head and giving her stray bits of roll or cracker, or perhaps a lima bean or two that had sneaked into his pocket at dinner. One time right after George polished off one of those Meals-Ready-to-Eat that we got dirt cheap from army surplus, he gave her the container to lick clean. When she turned up her nose at it, I swear he was hurt. Not that I blamed Hillary; I think that particular batch was left over from the old Persian Gulf War, and had never made its way to Bosnia to feed the refugees.

Anyway, you never saw so many adults hovering on the edge of real hunger come up with so many little tasty dog treats so quickly. After a mere two weeks at Withering Heights, Hillary had noticeably plumped out, whereas we all looked a tad leaner.

Well, anyway, moving right along, the moon was more than half full, so we had some decent light. Rhiannon and Lyla Ann had called a temporary truce in hostilities for the sake of Hillary and me, so it was actually promising to be a pleasant evening.

"I need to be cheered up," said Lyla. I knew she wasn't kidding. Her face was white and pinched, and even as late and relatively cool as it was, beads of sweat still gleamed on her upper lip. She had had a bad day with the pain. "Do tell me some witch jokes, Rhiannon, dear. There are so many.''

Rhiannon bared her teeth and said, ''Ha.''

''Then you have to promise to tell a Republican joke, Lyla,'' I said.

Lyla blinked. ''I don't know any.''

''I do,'' I replied. Heh heh, heh heh, heh heh. Gotcha.

''Today I heard a good Buddhist joke on the Net,'' said Rhiannon.

''Shoot.''

''What did the Buddhist say to the hot dog vendor?''

''What?'' asked Lyla.

''Think about this carefully, now. He said, 'Make me one with everything.' ''

Lyla wrinkled her brow. She was not really an imaginative sort, and her education in the liberal arts had been shorted at Chico State back in the 1970s.

I got it. ''Aarrgh, that's bad.''

Rhiannon giggled, quite pleased with herself.

''I don't understand,'' said Lyla.

''I'll explain it to you later,'' I said. ''Rhiannon, give her a witch joke.''

''Oh, all right. Why does a witch ride a broomstick?'' After a pause, during which neither Lyla nor I could answer, she said, ''Because Nature abhors a vacuum, and she'd look really stupid riding a mop.''

Lyla whinnied over that one like a prize pony.

''Here's another, Lyla,'' I said. ''Why is it good to have pagan friends?''

Lyla looked distrustful. ''Why?''

''Because they worship the ground you walk on.''

It took her a minute to get that one, too. She gave a faint, tinny laugh but seemed uncomfortable; I suspected she'd spent so many years trying not to offend the religious elements in her constituency in any way, shape, or form that by now she couldn't let her hair down.

"I do remember one Republican joke," she said gamely. "A kid is standing by the highway, trying to hitch a ride. First car comes up, and the driver asks him whether he's a Republican or a Democrat. When he says, 'Democrat,' the guy drives off—"

"Oh, for God's sake, Lyla, that's old—old as the hills!" I cried.

"Wait! Be quiet!" Lyla said with a gasp. There was an undercurrent of dread in her voice. "Somebody's coming."

We froze, and shortly heard the sound of bicycle tires crunching and laboring up our hill. "Oh, shit," I said, "not again! Battle stations!" I buzzed George to signal a yellow alert.

Lyla Ann clutched all twelve pounds of Hillary to her breast (or rather, all thirteen pounds, as I was beginning to suspect). "Moira," she commanded, "get down behind the bench with me. You have to, or the dog won't stay out of sight."

It was just like Lyla to let me know where I really stood in the scheme of things. "You, too, Rhiannon," I said.

She shook her head. "It's all right. The same girl is coming back to us."

Lyla made a funny sound that was riddled to the core with indignation and disapproval. "How can you possibly know that?" she cried. "I've had it up to here with all your hocus-pocus."

Rhiannon ignored the insult. "If it will ease your mind, hide behind the bench. There's no danger. Although—"

"Although what?" I asked with a hiss.

"That's odd," said Rhiannon to herself, sounding puzzled. But she didn't stir from her spot.

As the three of us stayed frozen in place, a bicycle cleared the crest of the hill and came to a halt. Just as if we were watching a rerun on television, we saw a slim girl's figure dismount and walk toward our electrified fence with a small bundle in her arms. What now? I wondered.

A cat, a bird, a snake? Or maybe a Chinese miniature pot-bellied pig, descended from the pet of choice in the yuppie 1980s?

This time the girl spotted us, sitting under the tree. She made a funny bowing motion and carefully inched her bundle through the gates, keeping it clear of the electrified metal. Then she hopped on her bike again and was gone in a flash.

This bundle did not jump up and run toward us the way Hillary had. But it emitted a loud noise, like the shriek of a jay.

"Oh, my God!" cried Rhiannon.

"Surely you mean 'Goddess'!" sniped Lyla Ann.

"I'll have you know that my religious path reveres the God also," Rhiannon said coldly. That was in fact true, and she was attempting to make a good save, but I knew what was really going on. In her youth she had been a Methodist, and under stress, she often reverted to the old ways.

Rhiannon dashed forward and scooped up the bundle. "Oh, no, oh, no," she cried. "Hillary was only a test." As she returned to the bench, I saw tears in her eyes. "It's a baby. They think we can take in a baby."

Lyla Ann's horrified eyes sought mine. A dog was one thing, but a baby was quite another. Lyla Ann knew we couldn't keep it, and she was appalled at what we would have to do.

"Hope springs eternal," I whispered. "What *is* it about people? Don't they know when to give up?"

"Oh, hush. What color is the baby?" demanded Lyla Ann. "Oh, let it be white. If it's white, we stand a chance of finding a good home for it." She examined the baby in Rhiannon's arms and then swore. "It's a little baby girl, and she's dark as sin."

"Lyla Ann! For God's sake!" I said, shocked.

Rhiannon bristled. "Even white babies have few takers

these days, Lyla, or do you enjoy kidding yourself?''

Lyla Ann began to puff up like one of the roosters on my grandmother's farm in East Texas when I was a girl.

"Look, you two old ditz-brains," I said quickly, "put a lid on it. No PC wars, not now. We need to hang together to figure out what to do."

"I was just being realistic," Lyla Ann said sullenly.

"We have to take it to the charity orphanage down in Oakland," I said. "We don't have the right kind of food for a growing child, let alone enough of it. The child has zero future here. We're nothing but six old people, trying to feed ourselves from a few acres of hardscrabble land. At least in an orphanage, there's a chance the kid may live to reach adulthood."

Rhiannon lowered her head, and I could see tears drop onto the baby's blanket. "Rhi," I said, "what else can we do?"

"Here," interrupted Lyla Ann, "let me hold her a minute." She took the bundle from Rhiannon and began to whisper stupid baby-talk nothings to it. I sighed, feeling utterly despondent. Lyla was a goner.

"Moira," said Rhiannon, "what if I gave up my place for the baby? Surely that would be enough?"

"No way! Rhiannon, are you out of your mind? None of us will live long enough to see the child safely grown, but if anyone should stay, it should be you, because you're the youngest. But you and the child still couldn't make it by yourselves, once the rest of us finally die."

Rhiannon let out a sob. "You said we should be talking about—replacements. Maybe this is the time to start."

"We'll deal with that later," I said, in as soothing a tone as I could muster. "A helpless baby is not a replacement for a working adult, and you know it. Right now we've got to find Loki and the others and figure out what to do."

Lyla glared at me accusingly. "You mean figure out how

to ditch the baby in Oakland and get yourselves safely back.''

''It's called survival, Lyla,'' I replied. I wished I didn't sound so cold, especially since right then I was so upset I wanted to throw up.

I turned toward the house, Rhiannon at my side. Lyla Ann followed along behind, dragging her feet, whispering and cooing to the baby. I had a feeling the story was not over.

The meeting was very short and very unpleasant. None of us wanted to do what had to be done, but there was no other choice. We didn't have the years left in which to raise a child. We didn't have the means. We didn't have the right kind of food, and we didn't have the extra money to buy it. The baby could not eat stray seeds gleaned by Rhiannon from the garden, like Tweety Bird, who weighed all of eighty-six grams and would never get any bigger. The baby was not a dog, which could be eaten if circumstances grew desperate beyond bearing, but in the meantime could be sustained by our table scraps. The situation was hopeless; we simply couldn't take the child in.

The next morning, when it was time to take the baby away, Lyla Ann was nowhere to be found. I think she was hiding in her room. Anyway, Loki borrowed George's best Uzi and went with Rhiannon on the scooter through the jungle of old Oakland to the orphanage. They got the baby there and returned safely. But judging from how quiet and subdued Rhiannon was all day, it must have been a pretty awful scene. I didn't ask about it; I didn't want to know.

Since Rhiannon wasn't using the computer, I logged on for a little while, to catch up on the news. The TV was being dysfunctional again, and would continue to be so until Loki could scam an appropriate part to fix it from Mad Mac's.

The news was always depressing, but I figured I already

felt about as bad as anyone could feel, so it couldn't make me feel worse.

Wrong. I encountered the usual downer stories from all over the globe, but there was one that literally chilled my blood. The Nile Valley, you may recall, had flooded quite some time ago as the sea level rose. That took care of most of Egypt's good cropland, and incidentally displaced millions and millions of people. Starving people are desperate, and a bunch of amazingly well-trained Egyptian commandos had managed to sneak a Chinese-manufactured nuclear weapon into the heart of Kiev.

Kiev was the capital of Ukraine, the onetime breadbasket of the Soviet Union. Ukraine was doing pretty well these days, comparatively speaking. It had lost some territory when the Black Sea rose, but it still had most of its good farmland, and had been very proactive in selecting appropriate crops for the warming climate. Ukrainians, like Americans, often had enough to eat.

Now the commandos were threatening to detonate the nuclear device if Ukraine didn't fork over a lot of food for Egypt, NOW. It was armed robbery, 2032 style.

A jolt of pure terror ran through me, thinking where this could lead—thinking about copycatters. I rushed away from the computer without even shutting it down, ran to the nearest bathroom, and this time did throw up.

I knew something was afoot when Rhiannon and Lyla Ann slunk down to meet me under the oak tree that night, ostensibly to play with Hillary, as had become our routine. Although these two were often at each other's throats, they seemed to find common cause at the oddest times. Tonight they both sounded like their nasal passages were all stuffed up, and they weren't keen on looking me in the eye. I couldn't wait to hear what they'd been cooking up.

"I've made a decision, and it's final," Lyla Ann said. She had that familiar bossy tone in her voice, and I knew,

God help me, that her mind was made up about something.

"I was very greedy and selfish yesterday," she said. "I'm very ashamed of myself, and I'm paying for it."

"What are you talking about?" I asked, a sharp edge in my voice. I was still spooked over the Kiev crisis and was in no mood for Lyla's posturing.

"I've been holding out on you. I should have spoken up last night, but I—hesitated."

She came to a stop again. "Please," I said, "do go on."

"I wanted to hang on to the last dregs of life, even though all I've got left is a few months. We all know I'm dying. I'm not going to be much good to anybody for very much longer. So I've decided to put myself down for the sake of that poor little baby. That way you and Rhiannon can go back and get it."

I was beside myself with fury. "Are you out of your frigging mind?" I yelled. "Killing yourself wouldn't do any good, because you know damn well we can't even get hold of the right food! And even if we could, killing yourself for the sake of one baby won't change anything! The world's too far gone! Why shouldn't you live out the last days of your life among friends? The hell with the baby! There are millions upon millions out there who will die no matter what you do!"

"Lyla, I told you, she's right," muttered Rhiannon.

Lyla withdrew her saber from the body of my conscience and turned, slowly and exquisitely, weapon raised and gleaming, to face her foe. "Oh, is she?" Lyla asked, ever so sweetly. "What do I recall hearing you say one time . . . ? 'Even though one can't pick up all the litter on the seashore, the Goddess is pleased when you pick up the single piece that lies within your reach'? Isn't that just what I'm doing, only with a human being, you pagan hypocrite?"

"Damn it, lay off her, Lyla!" I cried.

"No, I will not!" shouted Lyla. "I know exactly what I'm doing. I know there are millions of babies out there I can't help, but I held that one in my arms, and I can help *her*! I may just have one puny little vote left to me, but I'm going to throw it in the face of the powers that be.'' She smiled, as if suddenly warmed by a memory. ''Just like the time I cast the last deciding vote that overrode Slick Willie's veto.''

''Oh, fuck you and the horse you rode in on,'' Rhiannon said under her breath.

''Rhi!'' I exclaimed. ''Get hold of yourself.''

''Get off my case. I'm only human,'' she said. As dark as it was, I could see that her face was flushed.

''That's nice to know, dear,'' said Lyla Ann, never missing a beat. ''Now, then,'' she continued, addressing me in her customary brisk tone of voice, ''would you please convince Rhiannon to mix up the perfect potion to help me carry out the evil deed? I know she can do it.''

''I could, but like hell I will,'' muttered Rhiannon.

''Very well put, Samantha. Very ironic. Maybe you could get mummy Endora to help instead?'' Lyla Ann countered in a sugarcoated voice.

Rhiannon drew herself up and said coldly, ''Any good herbalist must know which herbs are deadly, if she wishes to practice her craft without killing people. Yes, I do know which plants are deadly, but I *avoid* them, I do not grow them!''

''So go out in the fields and gather some. I know you know which ones are poisonous—I heard you bragging about it when I first moved in here.''

Rhiannon threw up her hands in annoyance. ''Okay, fine! I used to know of a dozen places where hemlock grew wild, up in Marin County. But I'd need an armed escort to go get any of it.''

''Both of you stop it right now!'' I cried. ''Veto! You know the word 'veto'? I know you do, Lyla Ann, because you just said it. Well, you're both vetoed! Lyla Ann, read my lips: We don't have any baby food, or the means to get it.''

To my amazement, Lyla Ann hung her head. I looked to Rhiannon for an explanation, but she wouldn't meet my eyes.

''What,'' I asked slowly, ''is going on here?''

''I *said,* I've been holding out on you,'' Lyla whispered.

I was speechless.

''I have a lot of money hidden away in an account I never told anybody about. I was going to give it to you before I died, or access it if we really got in trouble. It's enough to buy plenty of formula and Gerber, until the baby can eat solid food. Rhiannon has even found someone on the Net who has a stash of baby food to sell. Once I'm gone, you can find an able-bodied adult replacement for me.''

A Republican and her cash are not easily parted, I said to myself. I didn't know whether to kiss Lyla, for trying to save the baby, or slap her for holding out on us, which was so against the rules it was barely forgivable, even under these circumstances.

''Even so,'' I said at last, ''we're all very old. Unless we're very lucky getting replacements, and our successors manage to keep this place, the baby will end as a street child anyway. Give it up, Lyla.''

''Nope,'' said Lyla Ann with a shrug, ''my mind's made up. I'll do it the hard way if I have to. It would just be nice if Rhiannon would be a sweetheart and make it easier for me. After I'm dead you can go get the baby, if it's still there.''

Rhiannon and I exchanged glances full of fury—at Lyla. With a deft flick of the wrist, she had us both right where she wanted us. No wonder the bitch had been reelected so many times.

I knew there was no use arguing with Lyla Ann when she was set on a course. ''Tell you what,'' I said, stalling.

"Loki will take Rhiannon back to the orphanage, and if the baby's still there, they'll bring it back. Just please don't go and kill yourself until they bring the baby home, okay? Don't kill yourself for absolutely nothing."

Lyla considered. She was much too practical to throw away her last dregs of life for nothing. "Okay," she said.

"There's just one problem," Rhiannon said in a low, furious voice. "I already asked Loki, and he refuses to take me. He's totally against the whole idea. And so is George."

"Oh, hang it all!" I said. The only person in the commune more stubborn than Lyla Ann was Loki.

"Rhiannon can drive and I can shoot," Lyla Ann piped up.

I felt my teeth clench. "You may be a lifetime member of the NRA," I said, hissing, "but we both know you're so sick that your hands shake and your aim is spoiled. Rhiannon and I will go."

Rhiannon glanced at me, and her eyes were unreadable. Not for the first time, it seemed as if I could hear her thoughts in my own mind, and suspected she could hear mine. Like Lyla Ann, she wanted more than anything to save the baby; but her convictions prevented her from killing Lyla, even for that worthy end.

She was caught between the horns of the devil's own dilemma . . . as it were. If the baby still lived, we could lie, say it was dead, and save Lyla—assuming we were good enough liars, that is, which we weren't. Or we could bring it home in the knowledge that Lyla would subsequently blow her brains out. Or try to, and miss, because her hands were so unsteady. Then we would have to finish the job.

Lyla took a deep breath and briefly let down her chirpy, bitchy facade. "Look," she said quietly, "I'm getting sicker. I'm not good for much these days. I hurt all the time. I just want a graceful way out. A good excuse—I just don't want to go for nothing."

"I understand," said Rhiannon, and began surreptitiously wiping at her eyes, as if we wouldn't notice she was crying. In an odd, twisted way, she and Lyla really cared for each other. Maybe opposites really do attract.

I couldn't sleep and sat out on the deck most of the night, brooding over the fix we were in. I ignored Loki whenever he came skulking out to see how I was, in retaliation for his being such a pigheaded bastard.

We could still get candles now and then, though they cost us dearly. Rhiannon insisted on having a few for the Esbats and Sabbats, and for meditation. All night long, I could see flickering light in Rhiannon's room, reflecting off the glass pane of her half-opened window, and I knew she was praying.

In the morning we set off toward the orphanage. Rhiannon was driving, and I was cradling one of George's many Uzis as if it were an autographed picture of Mel Gibson. "Brace yourself," said Rhiannon. "You're going to be repelled by what you'll see."

"Oh, shut up," I snapped. "I'm as hardened as any of us."

"Let me hear you say that two hours from now."

I have always specialized in famous last words.

The orphanage was housed in the old Oakland Children's Hospital. A large majority of the few surviving Bay Area charities had banded together, and were essentially running the human equivalent of an animal shelter. The orphanage was a dog pound for children and babies, nothing more, nothing less.

I couldn't fault the people who ran it; they were trying to stem the likes of a tidal wave with their bare hands. Hardly anyone anywhere had money for anything except for the bare essentials of life; and those were the lucky few. Most people in the Bay Area spent their lives scraping together enough food to stay alive, and enough money for a halfway safe place in which to eat that food. There was nothing left over for those who couldn't fend for themselves—the very old, the sick, the very young.

The orphanage stank to high heaven of baby shit and other filth. The din produced by hundreds of shrieking, frightened, crying children was enough to drive one mad. Indeed, I wondered how the charity workers held on to their sanity. There were few enough of them; from the look of things, they needed four or five times as many staff.

We went up to a frenzied-looking man at the intake station. My Uzi didn't seem to bother him in the least; he was used to such sights. Rhiannon introduced herself to him. "Yes, yes," he said distractedly, "I talked to you yesterday."

Even in this bedlam, it was understandable he would remember her. At seventy, Rhiannon was still quite striking, with her long, snow-white hair and her dark eyes. She had been even more striking in her youth, when her hair had been jet black.

"Yes," the man continued, "you came to drop off an abandoned baby. Or was it you who gave up your twins?"

"No. I dropped off the baby."

He focused on Rhiannon more closely and reddened. "Sorry. Of course you weren't dropping off your own children. You could be a grandmother. What do you want?"

"We've changed our minds. We want to adopt the child we brought here yesterday."

"Let me see, let me see," he mumbled. I stole a look around the room and shuddered. There were starving and sick babies everywhere, waiting to be processed—the flotsam and jetsam of the maelstrom that was the Bay Area. Right off the bat, I spotted one I was sure was dead, lying on an old piece of terrycloth towel. And another who looked sick enough to die, lying on a piece of newspaper.

My breath caught in my throat and I thought I was going to faint. That piece of newspaper bore a headline.

Rhiannon's whole attention was focused on the man at the intake station, who was pawing through a jumble of papers. I walked over to the newspaper, gritted my teeth, and turned the baby on its side so I could read the headline.

The baby was so hot to the touch, I knew it would die. I read the headline, backed away, and put my head between my knees to try to keep from passing out.

Kiev was gone. God in heaven, who was next?

"I can't seem to find my record of the child," the man said. "Did you see me write down anything about it?" he asked. "Do you remember?"

"I saw you write something on one of those rectangular cards," replied Rhiannon, pointing to the rat's nest of papers on his desk.

"Oh, yes." As he fussed on, out of the corner of my eye I saw a man approaching with something that looked like a body bag. Before my very eyes, he picked up the dead baby I had spotted and dumped it into the bag. Then he added two more I hadn't noticed. He touched the sick child, whose body covered the news of Kiev's death, concluded that it was still alive, and left it there.

I turned back to the man at the desk. I had to get back home and lie down, soon. "Please hurry," I said. "Just find the baby for us and let us get out of here."

"Just a minute," he said. He wandered off into another office, and returned after a few minutes. "I am told that the child died during the night," he said to Rhiannon. "I'm sorry." There was sympathy in his voice, but he would not meet her eyes. And some of his befuddlement had vanished—as if something had focused his wandering attention on the matter at hand.

"The child was perfectly all right when we brought it here," Rhiannon replied.

"Oh, it probably looked okay," said the man, again avoiding her eyes. "They can be sick and not show it, but once they do, you'd be amazed how quickly they go."

"I'll bet. The main ward's upstairs, on the second floor, isn't it?"

The man looked at her guardedly. "Why?"

"I used to be a volunteer in this very building, years ago. Back when it was a hospital. The second floor seemed like the logical place for a large children's ward."

"It's . . . changed a lot," he said, making an unsuccessful attempt to smile. "Oh—oh, dear." His gaze focused on something behind us, and we saw that a van had pulled up. It was full of kids roughly between ages three and five, who were quickly shepherded by the driver and another caretaker toward the intake station. By the look of many of them, they had lived on the street for some time.

"I'm sorry. I must deal with this," he said. "I'm sorry I can't help you ladies."

He dashed forward and tried to form the children into a semblance of a line.

Rhiannon turned with surprising meekness and appeared ready to go. When the intake guy, the caretaker, and the driver all had their backs turned trying to control the street children, Rhiannon fastened her hand around my wrist in a tight grip. "Can you climb a flight of stairs?"

I didn't want to, but I couldn't think up a good excuse to get out of it. She pulled me up a flight of steps just to the left of the front door. "I know this place," she said grimly. "I just want to see something."

Sure enough, the second floor had been converted into a single large ward, full of hundreds of dirty little beds and crying children, straight out of Dickens's London. "Follow me. Act like you belong here," ordered Rhiannon.

She walked slowly up the center aisle, looking to the right and left with sharp, inquisitive eyes, as if she had every right to be there. I trailed along in her wake, wishing that I had a tissue or a piece of cloth to put over my nose and mouth.

We weren't challenged until we were three-quarters of the way to the other end of the hall. "Hey!" cried a harassed-looking woman with a red face, "who the hell are you?"

"We are looking for a child we brought in yesterday," replied Rhiannon, her voice cold and businesslike. "We wish to adopt it."

"You have to check with the guy downstairs. You can't come up here without a requisition form."

"Oh!" Rhiannon said, feigning surprise. "Let's go downstairs, Moira. We must follow procedures."

That got the woman off our backs long enough for us to get downstairs and reach the front door. The man at the intake station saw us then and cried, "Hey, how come you're still here?" but Rhiannon grabbed my hand and hurried me outside.

"Get on the scooter and let's go. He won't follow us; the poor bastard's got his hands full."

Not until we reached the safety of the compound and had stashed the scooter and returned the Uzi to George did Rhiannon speak to me again. She was shaking like a leaf. "Moira, George says Lyla is asleep. I know we save the booze for holidays, but I really must have a drink. Let's sneak up to your room before we try to go talk to her."

"You've got it. I'm going to have several drinks. How come you're so sure I have a stash?"

"I've known you for years."

We crept up to the sanctuary of my room like schoolgirls avoiding the hall monitor, followed by Hillary, who always managed to figure out when I was home. Hillary jumped up on the end of my bed and went to sleep, and I got out some rotgut whiskey I had found at the flea market. It had come in an old Lucky's house-brand pint bottle, but the label was very worn, and I hadn't been fooled for a minute. This stuff was new and very, very rough. The cheap whiskey we used to get at Lucky's when I was younger would have tasted like the finest single malt Scotch in comparison.

Tweety Bird heard us come in and started calling for Rhiannon. She went next door to her room and returned with him sitting contentedly on her shoulder. I handed her the bottle, and she knocked back a couple of shots. Then I did likewise. "That was awful," I said. "You were right, I absolutely was not prepared for it. Nothing could prepare one for that hellhole."

Rhiannon was still shaking, though not as much as I was. "So what was it that got to you?" I asked. "I thought you were the hardened one."

"I had a hunch," she replied with a shudder. "I can't prove it, even now. Even if I could, I'm not sure I could blame them for what I think they're doing. But how it sickens me! How could we have let ourselves come to this?" She put her head down and began to cry. Tweety Bird regarded her with that goofy look that cockatiels have, and nibbled daintily on her cheek.

I let her get it out of her system. "Tell me the hunch."

"Lyla gave me the idea," she whispered. "There are so many children, they cannot find homes for all of them. If they're lucky, they may be able to place a tenth of all the ones who come in. I think they're euthanizing the ones they know they can't place."

I started feeling sick again and had some more whiskey. Upon leaving the orphanage, I had seen nothing on the premises so clichéd as an oven-shaped building that could be a crematorium, or a smokestack belching stenches of questionable origin. But overnight, the baby had vanished. As far as we could prove, it had never even existed.

"Why do you think that?" I asked.

"I had a good look at those children on the second floor. They must be the ones that make the first cut. Did you notice anything unusual about them?"

I felt ashamed of myself. I hadn't really paid attention; I had been focused only on myself. "No," I said.

"Every last one of them was white, or very close to it."

I drew in my breath slowly. It was clear the orphanage couldn't handle the mountains of human castoffs who arrived on its doorstep each day. It was also clear that the orphanage was the last stop, that there was nowhere else on Earth for those unwanted babies and children to go. It took no rocket scientist to realize that the people running the place only gave beds to the few children they had a prayer of placing in foster homes.

I wondered what I would do under the same circumstances, and could not come up with a more workable answer, sick as it was. "People are disgusting," I said. "What are we going to tell Lyla Ann?"

She sighed. "Just what the man told us. The baby died."

I was fast getting drunk, but I didn't care. "Rhiannon, can you handle more bad news?"

"Why not?" she said. "I have a lot of practice." So I told her about Kiev.

She listened in complete silence, her face growing tighter and tighter. I poured us each another shot of whiskey. When I had downed mine, I began to cry, partly from nerves, partly from fear. "Well," I said, speaking the unspeakable, "what's next? L.A.? Have we really screwed the pooch this time? You think our Republican hunky-babe can save us from this one?"

Rhiannon closed her eyes. "Perhaps," she said, her voice low and urgent. "Perhaps, Moira. We just cannot give up hope."

"I don't plan to. They don't call me a mean little old lady for nothing."

She bit her lip, while Tweety Bird climbed up to the top of her head to get a better look at the room. Cockatiels are very smart birds, but his interests did not extend to global politics.

"Remember when we watched *Jurassic Park* on your old VCR, after I first moved in?" she asked. "Remember how the Jeff Goldblum character was always saying how ingenious life is? He kept going, 'Life finds a way,' or something to that effect."

"Sure, I'll buy it. Life always finds a way. The only question is, can our particular brand of life—*Homo sapiens*—find a way that works for us? And, like, quick? Otherwise, we've gotta hand Gaia over to the tarantulas and the other hot-weather boys."

We split the last of the whiskey. "I have some news for you," said Rhiannon. "I heard from the Green Man people again."

"You looked them up again?" I asked.

"No, they contacted me. They managed to track me down."

I stared at her, trying to figure whether she was scared, but this particular time I couldn't read her at all. "Well, we knew that was a possibility. It must have been child's play for guys like that."

"I've been mainly corresponding with what appears to be one man. After a few exchanges, he said the strangest thing—that I didn't sound like Moira Janelle Burke. He wanted to know what had happened to you, and who I was."

A chill took hold of me, and for a moment I felt very afraid. "Of course you don't have any idea who he is."

"No. I'm not that good, unfortunately."

"Jesus," I said, "it could be anybody. I managed to meet a lot of people in eighty years, you know."

"Well, I tried to throw him off the track. I said the account was very old, it came with the house, and I was just using it."

"What did he do?"

"He seemed to accept that answer, for now. I decided to be straight about how I mistakenly intercepted his message, so he wouldn't get paranoid. I said that I had read a few of his files, then realized I had no business being there, and had gotten out. I said I wanted to learn more about Green Man, and help if I could. He seemed dubious, but asked me to wait, and then somebody else joined him on-line and sort of began to interview me."

"What did you tell him?"

"Everything I could, without compromising our safety any more than I had. The funny thing is, that second guy I told you about really warmed up when I told him about my religion."

"They're Wiccan?" I exclaimed.

"No . . . I really don't think so. All I know is that for some reason, the second guy let down his guard when he heard that."

We must have passed out on my bed from booze and emotional exhaustion. When we finally woke, it was dark, we were hung over, Tweety Bird was perched on Rhiannon's stomach, asleep, and Lyla was pounding on my door, demanding to know where the baby was.

We persuaded her not to kill herself immediately by promising that we would aggressively search for a replacement for her, baby or otherwise. Following that, I had a long, headachy talk with Rhiannon, in which I had to play hardball.

There was no question Lyla was going to kill herself at some point, I said. Rhiannon could either help her go with dignity, there being no medical doctors around, or she could force Lyla to shoot herself and make a mess of everything.

Eventually Rhiannon knuckled under, though it went against every fiber of her being. She had a few seeds of a lethal herb hidden away, she confessed to me, and made her plant them in the garden. And so we waited.

— Part Two —

The wonders of inanimate nature leave Americans cold.
... The American people see themselves marching
through wildernesses, drying up marshes, diverting rivers, peopling the wilds, and subduing nature.

—Alexis de Tocqueville, *Journal,* 1836

The industrial society sees the universe as a mechanical
system. It sees the human body as a machine, life as a
competitive struggle, and calls the waste of scarce resources "progress." And it will sacrifice *anything*—the
planet's health, our children's future—in its quest for
unlimited economic growth.

—A State Green Party platform, 1996

Scientists first raised alarms about climate change in the
late 1980s, but the international community has taken
few concrete steps to address the problem. The world is
gambling, in effect, that problems in the future will not
be serious enough to warrant inconvenience in the present. With each passing year, the future gets closer and
that bet gets bigger.

—*Time* magazine, July 8, 1996

SIX

1977

AS THE YEARS PASSED, I WORKED HARD TO BECOME THE most professional student the world had ever seen. Actually, it was easy. A big bureaucracy like the University of Texas had a hard time just keeping track of its forty thousand students, let alone forcing them to do things like graduate before the turn of the century. If the school admin types really started zeroing in on you, you could always confuse them by doing things like switching majors for the umpteenth time, or dropping out of school for a year. It all worked for me.

In the summer of 1977, the local Lion's Club sponsored a contest for the best essay by a college student entitled, "The Turbulent 'Sixties—What Went Wrong." I sent in a short piece about what went right, and to my amazement won the $2000 prize. By fall I was feeling itchy, and rich besides; I decided I wanted to do something really exciting for a change.

Like magic, like synchronicity, an ad appeared in the student newspaper, the *Daily Texan*. A local travel agency was hawking an unbelievably cheap round-trip airfare to London that would take effect in mid-October 1977.

What a no-brainer! There was all the money in the bank; clearly, there was my destiny. I was still eligible for railway discounts, if not youth hostels, having reached the advanced age of twenty-five. So I resolved to get wild and take the whole semester off.

One of my major life goals was not to spend the rest of my life as a provincial hick from Texas; to avoid that wretched fate, it clearly behooved me to travel abroad, and invest in some cultural furnishings for my mind. And if a stray party or two happened to come my way, all the better. Not to mention lots and lots of cool British shops full of cool British stuff.

Some other students had told me that there was this great YWCA on Great Russell Street, right across from the British Museum in London, and that was supposed to be affordable and safe. That was good enough for me. I hopped my plane, landed with a mammoth case of jet lag, and groped my way painfully through the snakes-and-ladders maze of the London Underground to my destination.

The YWCA was, in fact, a haven. It had a bed that allowed one to lie in a horizontal position, and unlike the 747, it was not constantly in motion. That was all I needed. It took about a day to recover.

When I was in *compos mentis* again, I was overjoyed. I had finally reached my cultural mecca. I was now in the fabled land of Shakespeare, the Brontës, Jane Austen, Dickens, H. Rider Haggard, and Sherlock Holmes. Mostly British by ancestry, except for some stray pesky German genes, I had at last come home.

I hit all the big sights in London. As I did so, I got a big shock. It slowly began to dawn on me that people there were really not fond of tourists, especially Americans. (Though on more than one occasion, it seemed the Brits actually *liked* visiting Germans, which made no sense at all, considering what the Germans had done to them in World War II.) This really offended me, because I wasn't behaving anything like an ugly American. I wore no brightly colored Hawaiian shirts; I did not flock with other Americans and talk loudly in an obnoxious Texas accent about the strange local customs; and, gimme a medal, I did NOT complain about the food, not even once.

Or the liquid refreshments. For example, once I was dying of thirst after a marathon of walking and sightseeing. I went up to a kiosk, thinking I could buy an ice-cold drink to pour down my parched gullet. Now, anybody raised in Texas knows that the only thing that really quenches a bad case of dehydration is ice water, or in a pinch, cold sody pop. But this concept was foreign to the British. When I paid for a cup of "lemonade" and got some stuff that resembled warm 7UP, I protested loudly, and asked for ice.

"I'm afraid you'll have to go back home for that, luv," chirped the *Masterpiece Theatre* type slinging the swill—definitely more Downstairs than Upstairs. To either side of me, people rolled their eyes. I even heard a snicker. What a typical American, the spectators seemed to say—coming to London and expecting to find things exactly as they were back home.

Or take the foot-crunching day I spent at the magnificent British Museum. Exhausted yet culturally enriched, I went into a pub across the street that was named, appropriately, the Museum Pub. My feet were on fire, and my very hip joints ached, so I ordered a beer. "And exactly what kind do you mean, dearie?" was the barkeep's response. Hell, I didn't know, so I asked for a pint of bitter (I'd heard that phrase somewhere). This was not good enough; he still asked me more incomprehensible questions. I finally told him to give me anything alcoholic he felt like recommending and keep the change, and I ended up with a mug of unleaded dark beer with extra octane, some No-Nox additive, and probably something special to clean my engine, too.

All this coldness and brusqueness took its toll. Within a week, I realized I was lonely. I was totally without friends or acquaintances in, as Dr. Watson once described it, the great wilderness of London.

Yet it was quite clear the British were not the least bit warm and fuzzy, or inclined to ease my Yankee pain. I plaintively wondered what had happened to the generous, spunky Brits of Winston Churchill's war years; to the cultured, erudite folks I had seen described in dozens of British novels since my earliest childhood. It seemed they were nowhere to be found these days; it was a mystery worthy of Sherlock himself.

Anyway, I figured there had to be an answer to the problem somewhere. The Brits might seem to be one of the coldest peoples on the face of the Earth, but they had to break down and be human sometimes; otherwise, how could there be more new Brits each year? I thought that I could crack this nut, if I only put my mind to it.

Before long, I hit on an answer. The problem was tourists. Or rather, the problem was that *I* was a tourist.

So I would stop being a tourist. I would not do the things that "everyone did" while in London; I would do the things I really wanted to do. And I would stop giving a damn about what anybody thought of me in the process.

I went to the theater as often as I could, which sometimes was twice a day. I sought out museums, bookstores, and funky shops that really appealed to me. These were inevitably off the beaten path. I tried being friendly when I could, but if people were jerks, I shrugged it off. I was only there for a short time, which was diminishing daily; I didn't need them. Even if nobody ever gave me a kind word, I knew I could skim off the cultural cream from their snooty city and take it home with me.

It worked like magic. More often than not (though usually after a brief period of prickly standoffishness) the people I ran into did respond with friendliness. Even if they said something faintly rude or condescending, if I brushed past it and continued to ask questions about the museum display, or whatever, they usually came around.

Old guys were particularly nice. Once I asked "Were you in the war?" we soon became fast friends. By 1977, few young people on either side of the Atlantic seemed to care about what happened in World War II, and the old warriors were delighted to find a girl who was interested to hear about it. They usually rounded out their monologues with a story about their favorite brave Yank GI, and on an odd occasion I was even asked home to dinner with themselves and the wife.

I went to pubs that didn't have to deal with swarms of touristy people like the Museum Pub. This strategy worked like a charm. I could order a beer or two, not be humiliated, and be left to read a book in peace.

I had a feeling this was all leading up to something. On my very last day in London, I had a most unusual encounter.

I stumbled onto a place I hadn't been before in Bloomsbury, near the University of London, where a lot of students seemed to hang out. It was a pub called The Green Man. The wooden sign over the door depicted, literally, the head of a grimacing, green-colored man who had tendrils of vegetation billowing from his mouth, ears, and eyes. Said vegetation cleverly curled around to form his beard, mustache, even his eyebrows. He was very strange and very intriguing.

Being close to the university, the pub was the sort of place where one brought a book, so I felt completely at home. I ordered a pint of beer, with a view to whiling away the afternoon with a beat-up old tome I'd found in a secondhand shop. It was a most curious novel called *The Goat-Foot God,* by someone named Dion Fortune. I had paged through it a little, and it looked way weird. But I had just seen *A Midsummer Night's Dream* at the Olivier Theatre, and was open to reading a book that appeared to be about the Greek god Pan.

It was a tad offbeat, true, but I had not traveled thousands

of miles to put up my feet at Denny's and read the latest
Western by Louis L'Amour.

The day was warm, and all the outside tables were full
except one in a shady corner. As I went to claim it, I noted
that an unattached male was sitting at one of the neighboring tables. This looked sorely promising, even if he was
British.

I put on my sunglasses (the better to examine the chap
surreptitiously) and sat down, positioning my chair so I
would be able to talk to him if something developed. I
opened my book, sat back, and proceeded to scope out the
situation.

He was perhaps five years older than I, of medium build,
with dark brown hair, a pleasant face, and startling blue
eyes the color of the sky in Austin. He was studiously pe-
rusing a bunch of papers and flyers, an egghead as ever
was.

I decided to be a good girl and pretend to read my book
for a little while.

The book was really far out, sort of mythological and
occult. It started pulling me in right away, and for several
minutes I forgot to spy on him.

When I looked up, I saw that he was looking at the cover
of my book with an expression of intense interest. He raised
his head, our eyes met, and I literally felt a physical shock,
as if I'd swallowed a large gulp of fiery Mexican mescal,
including the worm. He gave me a sheepish smile, which
made my head swim.

Until that smile, I would have been tempted to call him
nondescript—excepting, of course, those remarkable eyes.
But the smile, and the personality behind it, transformed
him into a really gorgeous man.

I gave him the tiniest timid smile in return and went back
to my book.

This impasse continued for quite some time. Out of the
corner of my eye I saw him sneak a look at me several

times, but he was evidently too shy to speak up, especially since I'd caught him in the act of spying on me first.

I couldn't concentrate any longer on my book; it might as well have been a copy of *Reader's Digest.* By this time my guy had his head down again and was pretending to pore over his papers. I could read the title of one of the flyers, upside down: It said *The Green Party.*

This was intriguing. Green Man, Green Party. Green was clearly the color of the day. Not only that, it also gave me the pretext I needed to speak to him. "Excuse me," I said, "I hate to sound like an ignorant American, but I am one. What does the name of this pub mean? Who is the Green Man?"

He looked up and gave that smile again, his relief clear. Not only had I broken the ice, it also was clear I had asked a question he knew the answer to. He was delighted to enlighten me. "Well, that depends on who you ask. There are a lot of different opinions," he replied. "If you'd like to hear them, I'll tell you. But I warn you, I'm doing graduate work in medieval history and mythology, and I do tend to run on a bit."

Oh, man, I said to myself, nice-looking, and he's really interesting, too . . . now I understand why I've been having such a piss-poor time in London; Fate's been making me save all my good-luck credits for a last big blowout.

"You're at the University of London?" I asked. My heart was going wham, wham, wham, exactly like in a Silhouette romance novel.

"Yes," he replied, "University College."

I couldn't think. I fell back on my well-honed flirting skills and said breathlessly, "Oh, I adore mythology!"

"Do you really? Then we have something in common."

I swallowed. You don't know the half of it, honey chile. "I come from the only state in America that has its own valid body of mythology," I said, miraculously keeping a straight face.

I was shining him on, but in a good-natured way. "Which state is that?" he asked.

"Texas."

He looked at me incredulously for a moment and then threw back his head and laughed out loud. *Nice voice,* I said to myself. How I'd like to put a guitar in his hands. Or myself in his hands. "Well done!" he said. "I could certainly make a good case that you're correct. The Alamo's a wonderful story."

"San Antonio's my hometown. The local Daughters of the Republic of Texas maintain the Alamo like it was a shrine or something. They call it 'the cradle of Texas independence.' They're pumping up the mythology as fast as they can."

He laughed again, and I pressed on. "So, what are you going to do when you've finished your studies?"

"Become a writer—and a successful one, I hope."

"Have you published anything?"

"Not a lot, just a couple of books of children's fantasy."

"What do you mean, just a couple? Jeez, that's two more than most people have published."

"It's one thing to publish. It's quite another to make your living at it."

"Oh, I see," I said. There was a short pause. "So, who is this Green Man they've named the pub after?"

He said, quite seriously, "An ancient symbol—perhaps even an archetype."

Thank heavens I'd read Carl Jung during my University of Texas course-surfing! "An archetype or symbol of what?" I countered.

"Most likely—in modern times, that is—of mankind's relationship to the Earth."

"You mean it used to mean something *different*?" I asked. As I continued to gaze at him with avid interest, he proceeded.

"Actually," he said, his voice waxing enthusiastic,

"carvings of Green Men are found on churches all over Europe, not just here in Britain. Some people think he's the representation of a forest god, a holdover from older pre-Christian pagan religions. The more mystically inclined take another approach. They believe he used to represent a pagan god—probably a fertility god, and the instinct to reproduce—but has changed in modern times.''

"Into what?''

"Well, if these people happen to be Jungians, they believe that archetypes are unconscious images of human instincts. As our many assaults upon the Earth continue and danger to the environment grows, human beings develop new instincts—and therefore new archetypes for symbolizing them.''

"For the purpose of what?''

"Of responding to the peril,'' he continued. "The archetype's purpose is to mobilize us to stop ravaging the environment before it's too late. In other words, the Green Man is a—what do you Americans call it?—a wake-up call.''

It had been five years since I'd read *The Limits to Growth* and that other Paul Ehrlich book about population, but I hadn't forgotten either one of them. I could almost buy into what this guy was saying—and it disturbed me.

He must have seen the look of worry pass across my face, because he hastened to say, "But other scholars believe the Green Man is just a mythological character with no particular modern resonance—you know, Jack in the Green, Robin Hood, the May King—in another guise.''

I must have looked like I was struggling to keep up with him, which I was, a little. He gave me a self-conscious grin and said, "Sorry. I can't help lecturing. I'm writing my master's thesis on Green Man imagery.''

"No, it's fine,'' I replied. "I'm a professional student—I plan to keep on taking courses at the university back home until they kick me out! Look, I didn't really understand how the Green Man can have an old meaning and a modern meaning. When you're talking about a myth, isn't the older meaning the only one that's really valid?''

''Oh, no, not at all!'' His interest and enthusiasm—and especially his gorgeous white teeth that flashed whenever he smiled—were wonderful.

This encounter was a real stroke of luck. Even in reputedly intellectual Austin, conversations of this caliber were hard to come by. What passed for café society at the university usually meant talking about the latest redneck rock act on that PBS show *Austin City Limits.* And on top of it all, the guy was so good-looking!!

''Pretend it's the year 1200,'' continued my captive scholar. ''Can you imagine any of the men who were working on the churches and cathedrals at that time, carving images of the Green Man, concluding that he was the symbol of an imperiled Earth?''

''No,'' I had to agree, and laughed. ''They probably didn't even know what 'imperiled' meant.''

''Exactly. The Green Man must have had an entirely different meaning to those people. But you see, if a myth doesn't change with the times, it ceases to be of any value. If it stops evolving, if it stops reflecting the concerns of a changing civilization, it ceases to be a myth. It just dies. That's why your Joseph Campbell wrote of the 'hero with a thousand faces.' He has so many because he's always changing with the times.''

Just before leaving for London, I had seen that fabulous new movie *Star Wars.* ''So Luke Skywalker is just his thousandth-and-first face?'' I asked.

My new friend absolutely beamed. ''Right!''

I felt very proud of myself. ''So what's an example of an old myth that's still alive?''

''King Arthur,'' he answered promptly. ''Every time England is in danger, they drag him out of mothballs. Every time a new writer gets hold of him, they reinvent him, so the story's as fresh as ever. I've even heard that some American writer is working on a book that retells the Arthurian saga from the point of view of the women involved.''

''A feminist King Arthur? Far out,'' I said.

''Or take Robin Hood. As with Arthur, no one's even sure he was a real person. But during the Middle Ages, he was so popular that the bishops used to complain that people skipped their sermons to see the latest Robin Hood play. Seven hundred years ago, his story was already changing to fit the times. First he was a Saxon peasant, rebelling against the Normans right after the Conquest. Then he was the son of an earl, fighting for the rights of the common man during Richard the Lionheart's absence from England. Then he was supposedly alive in the year 1322, a liegeman of the Earl of Lancaster, involved in a rebellion against King Edward II. Errol Flynn turned him into a swashbuckling romantic. Today there are at least two proposals for Robin Hood television series floating around in the British film community. One's for a comedy, in which a feminist Maid Marian leads the band of Merry Men.''

Wow. He even had connections to the British film community. ''Far out!'' I said again, doing my best to run the phrase into the ground.

''The other's a straightforward retelling of the myth, only in 'Aquarian Age' terms. Very modern.''

''Aquarian Age? You must be joking!'' I cried. ''How is that possible?''

''From what I've heard, there's quite a mystical overtone to the proposal. Supposedly this Robin is not only a Saxon fighting the Normans, he is also the spiritual son of an ancient Celtic deity, Herne the Hunter, or to use an even older name, Cernunnos. Robin's duty is to keep the forces of light and darkness in balance. He opposes evil sheriffs, abbots, and sorcerers, all in a day's work.''

My brain was on overload. ''Oh, wow,'' I said, to buy time. ''This is incredible.''

The guy grinned and gave a little shrug. "I think so."

"All right," I said triumphantly, "explain Frankenstein. Is he a myth? He seems like one, but where on Earth did he come from? I can't begin to think of any earlier mythical figure that Mary Shelley used for her model. He can't be a myth if he's brand-new."

"Oh, yes he can," the guy said with a laugh. "The Industrial Age desperately needed a Frankenstein myth, but there wasn't one, because the Industrial Age had no precedent in history. So Mary Shelley made it up out of whole cloth. There you have it, a brand-new, invented myth for the modern age, and as full of life today as King Arthur."

It was a slam dunk. "I'm convinced," I said. "So you hang out at this pub because it's called the Green Man, huh?"

He shook his head and gave me that sheepish look again. "The real reason, I must confess, is that the pub is quite convenient to the university."

"But what a coincidence!" I said, hoping to tweak him a bit. "You're so interested in mythology . . . and 'The Green Man' is a hell of an unusual name for a pub, you must admit."

Ooops. Judging from his expression, I had clearly proven myself ignorant. He laughed, but in a nice way. "To an American, I'm sure it is. However, there are more than thirty pubs in London alone with that name, and many more in the countryside."

"Oh," I said. "Green Men all over the place, everywhere you look, hmm?"

"I'm afraid so."

"So tell me, if the Green Man's pagan in origin, what's he doing on churches all over Europe?"

"That's a very good question. No one's sure. But I must say the fact certainly amuses our many British pagan groups."

I was silent for a moment, musing. He had said something else that puzzled me. "Why would Robin Hood have anything to do with the Green Man?"

"Because there's a school of thought that believes that Robin Hood, Jack in the Green, the King of the May, and the Green Man may all be different names for the same legendary figure. You know, the forest king, the man in the greenwood, the wild spirit who lives in the wildwood. Perhaps even Herne or Cernunnos."

A piece of the puzzle slipped into place with a click. "In that TV series you were talking about, Herne and Robin Hood are different characters, but they may really be different aspects of the same mythological figure?"

He nodded. "Possibly."

"But you're not sure."

"No one can ever be sure."

"Then the series will change the myth and screw it all up."

He shook his head. "There is no truth or falsehood in mythology. A myth is like the result of a great projective test—like the Rorschach—but given to an entire people, rather than an individual. Myths reflect what's going on in the collective mind of a society at a given time. Myths can change—and they should."

My head was spinning. "Yowza." I sat back and toyed with my glass of ale, which was now perilously near empty. "So Robin Hood probably wasn't a real person after all. Not with all this baggage he's carrying."

"He may have been, but if he was, over the centuries his story has gotten tangled up with many other legends."

"What do *you* personally think the Green Man is?" I asked.

"Well . . ." he began, and gestured to his papers, "since I'm doing a lot of work for the Green Party in addition to my studies, the thought of him as a symbol of our relationship to the environment is quite appealing. We're thinking about using a Green Man as a logo on some of our publications. He'd make a great mascot, don't you think?''

I looked up at the wooden sign over the door of the pub. Something about the Green Man depicted there was starting to bother me. ''You know, at first I didn't look closely, and thought he was smiling or grinning, but the longer I look at him, he starts to look as if he's choking. As if he's being garroted like in that gross scene in *The Godfather*.''

''You're very perceptive. Isn't that exactly what's happening to the Earth?''

<<<THUD>>>

Whoa. He was right. And that really freaked me out.

It upset me so much, I didn't even want to think about it, because this was not a movie, this was real life. But I couldn't close my eyes and pretend I hadn't heard about such stuff.

I regrouped. ''I've never heard of the Green Party. I don't think we have one in America yet, or if we do, it's got to be out in California. Is it British?''

''European. It's gaining a lot of momentum in Germany, where they have a much more serious pollution problem than in Britain. But we've got a thriving branch of the party over here, too.''

''Germany . . .'' I said. ''The worse the problem, the greater the response to it. Could this possibly be a hopeful sign?''

''I think so,'' he replied.

''I mean, back in Texas, not too many people are that concerned about the environment. If they hear bad stuff about it, they just tune it out.''

He threw back his head and laughed out loud at that. ''May I ask your name?''

''Sure,'' I said. Gettin' somewhere at last! ''Moira Janelle Burke.''

''Miles Earnshaw.''

"Nice to meetcha, Miles," I said.

At that moment, my stomach, which was empty, gave a loud growl. I was mortified, except it gave Miles the excuse he needed to take the next step. "Would you like to have dinner with me?" he asked.

We ended up in Soho at a tiny Indian restaurant that made curries so fiery they could take off the roof of your mouth. I'd had no idea food that good was available in London. As I would learn years later in San Francisco—stick to the tiny little ethnic dives, and you'll have the best food in the city.

When we were finished eating, Miles said, "Tonight's Halloween. I've made a commitment to attend a gathering out of town. How would you like to go for a drive in the country and take in some local color?"

Metaphorically speaking, my jaw hit the ground. I had just been asked on a major, open-ended date—one with no safe, discernible boundaries. And by a relative stranger.

I hadn't told him yet that my plane left in the morning. I had an out if I wanted one. "Well, just what sort of thing do you have in mind?" I asked, taking a sip of yogurt drink to quench the fire in my throat.

"Going to the ancient Celtic site at Avebury, near Stonehenge, and sitting in on the Druid New Year celebration."

It was fortunate I had just swallowed. Otherwise I might truly have choked, or have spewed the table with a mouthful of perfectly good *lassi. "What?"* I croaked.

"My Aunt Cecilia lives in a little town near the Avebury site. We can go with her."

I was on the verge of being seriously freaked. "Why on Earth is she attending?"

"She's a Druid. She's organizing it this year."

"Oh, is she?" I said weakly.

He shrugged, as if it were the most natural thing in the

world to announce to a new girlfriend that one's aunt took
tree-hugging with the ultimate possible seriousness. "She
invited me out, and I'd planned to drive to Avebury later
this evening. If you want to come along, you'd be quite
welcome."

Holy Christmas, I thought, what have I gotten myself
into? "Miles, are you a Druid, too?" I asked.

He shook his head. "Oh, no—Church of England, but
rather open-minded."

"Open-minded doesn't begin to describe it," I replied.

He laughed. "Being Anglican works for me, but other
paths work better for other people. It's not, as you Americans say, all that big a deal, though your religious fundamentalists would doubtless disagree with me."

"But how can you participate, if you're a Christian?"

He gave me a rueful look and replied, "I forget how
'uptight' even liberal Americans are about religion. Moira,
lots of Christians attend the holiday festivals at Avebury.
People from a dozen religious paths attend. No one is refused entry because of their particular creed. All that's required is that you revere the ancient site and want to take
part in the ceremony."

I took a deep breath, held it, and exhaled. "I don't know
about this . . ." I said dubiously. "I mean, what kind of
stuff do the Druids *do*? You know . . . do they do weird
stuff?"

He gave me an amused look and laughed again, though
charitably. "No, Moira. It's possible that in Roman times
they sacrificed human beings, but one must remain skeptical; we get those tales from Julius Caesar, who was hardly
an unbiased source. Considering that he and later Romans
completely obliterated the ancient Druids, there's quite a
possibility that he made up tales of human sacrifice to justify his actions."

"Yeah," I said, desperately searching for common
ground. "And besides, didn't the Romans sacrifice animals

all the time to read their entrails? They weren't exactly members of the ASPCA.''

He gave me a reassuring smile and said, ''I keep forgetting how easily spooked Americans are by matters mystical.''

''We are not!'' I said indignantly. He looked at me with both eyebrows arched, and I added, ''Well, maybe we are.''

''Several years ago, your famous science fiction author Ursula LeGuin wrote an essay,'' Miles said. ''It was called, 'Why Are Americans Afraid of Dragons?' and was reprinted over here in an anthology for writers of children's books. Naturally, because of my interest in children's literature, I read it.''

I considered. ''One obvious answer is that dragons are very scary.''

He nodded. ''So is fire. So are most powerful things. So what should we do—turn our backs on them?''

Point well scored. I conceded, and changed the subject. ''So what's all this about the Druid New Year? It's only October.''

''Druids celebrate ancient Celtic holidays. The ancient Celts ended their year with the onset of winter. They didn't call it Halloween, but 'Sowen.' ''

''How do you spell that? Like you say it?''

He really chuckled at that. ''We're talking about the Celts! Surely you're joking! No; try S-A-M-H-A-I-N.''

By this time, nothing was too strange for me to deal with. ''Okay,'' I said indulgently.

''Summer was over, the crops were harvested, the animals that wouldn't live through the winter were slaughtered for food, and the whole productive cycle of the earth was ended for the year. A logical time to end one year and start another, wouldn't you say?''

It made sense. ''Yeah, or on a more upbeat note, you could start the New Year in March or April, when spring comes.''

He took a bite of some extremely hot lamb curry and grimaced. "Some people do celebrate it then. Either way, you don't get January first, do you?"

"Nope. Okay, Miles, level with me. What's the deal with your aunt? Does she cast spells?"

His eyes danced. "Only the good kind. She says magic should be treated with the same respect as a loaded pistol. We also have frequent debates where she goads me to prove that it's all that different from prayer, and I always lose."

Oh, my God, I said to myself, I'm lost in a madhouse. But it's fun. At least I think it's fun. Out loud, I asked, "Are there Druids who cast the bad kind?"

"I'm sure there are, but she wouldn't have anything to do with them."

"She brews up herbal remedies, that sort of thing?"

He nodded. "Oh, sure. Though she's the first to take antibiotics when the going gets rough. So—shall we go?"

I shook my head. I was chicken. "I don't know."

"On the other hand, we could skip Avebury and do something tame like go to the ballet."

With a funny knot taking shape in my stomach, I said, "My plane leaves for Dallas tomorrow morning, Miles."

"Oh!" he exclaimed. And then, with a quick save, "Well—change your reservation."

I was really tempted, but it would have cost another hundred dollars. Or so I told myself; in fact, I was backing away from this big time. The money didn't really matter. The truth was that I was getting massively scared. Scared of becoming massively crazy about a complete stranger. Scared of getting involved with what might be a weird environmental sect. Scared that the Druids might be crackpots. And even more scared that they might not be.

"It would be expensive. And I'd have to pay more hotel bills and that sort of thing . . ." I stopped short, because it sounded like I was begging to move in with him.

"My aunt could put us up overnight."

"I don't know . . ."

Miles considered, and then said firmly, "Look, I know you must be nervous; you barely know me, but I assure you, I'm perfectly harmless. What if we just run out there for the evening? The distances here in Britain aren't anything like the ones you must be used to in Texas; we can be at Avebury in a little over an hour, say hello to my aunt, observe the ceremony, and I'll drop you back at your lodgings a little after midnight."

I thought hard, and decided I would never in my life get another chance to do something crazy like this. "Well, okay," I said, feeling rather shaky. "I'll go. How do you say Halloween in Celtic again? Sowen, like sowin' the crops?"

"Yes, except remember that the Druids also follow the British tradition and call it Calan Gaeof, which means 'Winter Calends,' or the first day of the quarter of winter."

"Jeez," I said with a groan. "The inmates have taken over the asylum. How will I ever keep this straight?"

SEVEN

OCTOBER 31, 1977

THE DRIVE OUT TO AVEBURY TOOK HARDLY ANY TIME AT all, or so it seemed. I made forced, lighthearted chitchat with Miles, but I was frantically apprehensive the whole time. I didn't know what the hell I had gotten myself into, and could not decide whether I was being open-minded and adventurous, a paranoid mess, or a complete fool who deserved to die and disappear and never be heard from again. I had not even had a chance to leave a note at the YWCA telling them who to blame if I ended up the victim of an occult Satanic ritual murder.

The rolling landscape of the Salisbury plain slid by and I barely saw any of it, for all my fretting; the next thing I knew, we were on the outskirts of Avebury, and Miles was pointing the car up a graveled path to an incredibly picturesque-looking cottage.

"This is Aunt Cecilia's house," he announced. I was speechless; it really was a cottage with a thatched roof, straight out of a fairy tale. There really *were* houses like that in the world; I mean, Beatrix Potter could have lived there, or perhaps a hobbit or two. I was reassured beyond belief to see a multitude of carefully pruned rosebushes surrounding the place, a bunch of chickens scattered about, hunting for bugs, and a little Yorkie dog parked near the front door.

"She's probably inside cooking," Miles said. "They always have a group dinner before the ritual, like one of your American potlucks."

I stared at him, still speechless. Druids and potluck suppers? Well, and why not? In this crazy world anything appeared possible.

As we approached the front door, I heard the sound of leaves crunching around the side of the house. As I watched, an enormous pink pig, weighing many hundreds of pounds, ambled into the front yard, paused, and looked at us thoughtfully.

"Miles!" I said, gasping.

"That's Popeye," he said, and rapped on the door.

"He's loose!"

"No, he's not a farm animal, he's a pet. They're very intelligent, you know, more so than dogs."

I swallowed a couple of times. "No, as it happens, I did not know that."

I heard footsteps approaching the door from inside the house and willed myself not to faint dead away. I had no idea what the woman who was about to open that door looked like, but I was ready for anything. Even Margaret Hamilton, Ding Dong the Witch Is Dead, right down to the pointed hat and green face.

The door stuck a little, and I heard her tug. I closed my eyes for a split second and rubbed the palms of my hands on my pants. When I opened my eyes, I saw a short, well-padded little woman in her midforties, with Miles's brown hair and blue eyes. She seemed very friendly and very ordinary—the sort of woman you'd expect to run into at the farmers' market.

"Hello, dear," she said, and reached up and hugged her nephew. "You've brought a friend along?" Miles introduced us, and we shook hands. She either didn't notice, or was too polite to mention, that my hands seemed to have recently spent time in a deep freeze.

"Come in," she said. "I'm almost through with my cooking, and then I'll get cleaned up, and we'll go into town for supper. I take it friend Moira would like to join us. Would you like to attend the ritual also, my dear?"

"Uh, yes," I said, far too brightly.

We followed her through the house, which was predictably tiny and cozy, and full of all sorts of interesting artifacts I wanted to stop and examine, but couldn't without being rude. Auntie was something of a pack rat, it did appear.

I wondered what she was cooking for the potluck. Yorkshire pudding, perhaps, or bubble and squeak, or shepherd's pie, or some tasteless English mutton stew.

"Company!" shrieked a high-pitched, childlike voice from the kitchen. "Whee, company!"

I looked at Miles for reassurance. "What the hell?" I whispered under my breath.

"That's Cecilia's Congo African Grey parrot," he said. "They're very intelligent—in many ways they're as smart as a five-year-old child."

"Oh, yes," chimed in Auntie, "they're right up there in the brains department. African Greys actually use language, rather than imitating sounds. My Ezekiel is very smart, even for a Grey."

"*Ezekiel?*" I demanded. A Druid with a parrot named after a prominent Biblical figure? Holy moley.

She shrugged, and grinned much like Miles. "It's easy for the bird to say."

As we approached the kitchen, I smelled something very interesting. But I couldn't begin to identify it, not in the context in which I was encountering it. "What on Earth are you making?" I asked.

"Chili con carne," she replied. "I've a new recipe from an American cookbook. I followed the directions exactly, and do you know, it's as spicy as a good curry!"

I stammered for a little while and finally managed to say,

"Chili? You're cooking chili? I'm from Texas!"

"Chili!" screamed Ezekiel.

"He's just learned a new word," said Cecilia, rather proudly.

We entered the kitchen and I saw a sleek, beautiful gray bird with red tail feathers sitting on a perch by one window. "Company!" he screeched, looking at me with great interest.

Cecilia guided me toward the stove. "If you're from Texas, then you can tell me if I've got it right. The only chili powder I could find came from a Middle Eastern store in London, and I'm afraid it must be much different from what's available in America."

"So long as you could find powdered cumin, you can't go too wrong," I said.

"Oh, that's readily available." She spooned a bit of the chili into a small bowl and handed it to me. "It's hot, do be careful. What do you think?"

I blew on it and tasted it. It was remarkably close to what I might have cooked up at home, except that the chili powder was definitely not Gephardt's and was not made in San Antonio. "I'm told chili powder varies from Texas to New Mexico to Arizona to California," I said sagely, "so this chili powder must be even more different from what's available in my home state. But it's good."

"Some of the members of my grove don't like spicy foods," said Cecilia. "I was thinking of serving it with rice. Is that appropriate?"

I couldn't restrain a bit of embarrassed laughter. "It's not really authentic, but heck, do what makes them happy."

"Or I thought of serving it with a bit of sour cream."

"Oh!" I exclaimed in horror. "That's an abomination. They do that in *California*."

"Karafornya?" said Ezekiel, testing the word.

Cecilia and I snapped out of it in time to see Miles laughing like his stomach hurt. "You women are like two peas in a pod,'' he said. ''The world's not going to come to an end because of how you serve up the chili! Give me a bowl of it right now, I'm famished.''

Cecilia and I exchanged knowing glances. The details of culinary science were in fact very important.

''Miles,'' she scolded, as she dished out bowls for all three of us, ''make yourself useful and ladle the chili into those ovenproof dishes I've got stacked over there. You can help me carry them to the automobile.''

Miles wolfed his chili and complied, like a good nephew, while I took advantage of the distraction to examine the kitchen and its contents. I was no longer afraid of Cecilia. I was fascinated by her, her house, her bird, and her kitchen. I had the strangest feeling of contentment.

The sun was setting, and lit up the kitchen with a warm glow. There were bright, airy, magical touches everywhere. Austrian crystals in the shape of stars hung suspended in the many windows, catching the light, sometimes sparkling, sometimes reflecting patches of rainbow colors on the walls. There was a vase that displayed a great handful of ripe wheat, as if it were a dozen red roses. Beneath the windows, which had many panes of venerably aged glass, there was a wide wooden sill, on which a jumble of treasures was exhibited: rocks of many different colors and shapes, seashells, birds' eggs, feathers, a variety of small incense burners, small china figurines of animals, pots of living herbs, bundles of dried flowers and herbs, an ancient Roman coin, several candles, a large sprinkling of acorns, and a sprig of mistletoe. I was enchanted.

I took a chance and approached Ezekiel on the perch. ''Hi, there,'' I said.

He responded with a wolf whistle, much to Miles's delight.

''What's with all the animals?'' I asked Miles.

''They're her pets.''

''She likes animals, huh?''

"Given how many pets she has and what she paid for them, I would think she rather did," he replied.

"She doesn't—uh—use them or anything, you know?"

Miles rolled his eyes dramatically and then shut them, as if weary. Me, I shut my trap. My only consolation was the impression that he had been asked such stupid questions before.

"Miles, dear," called Cecilia, "if you'll put all the provisions in the boot, I'll gather my things. Let's hurry, I've promised to be there at half past seven. Then we've got to drive out to the great circle by nine o'clock, before the others arrive. Bring lots of warm jackets, it's going to be cold."

"Yes, Aunt," said Miles.

"Why does she have to be there so early?" I whispered as Cecilia retreated into a far bedroom.

"She's the priestess of this particular order."

"What?" I started to yelp the word but caught myself. "That little tiny woman? I know you said she was a Druid, but you mean she's their leader or something?"

Miles gave me a wry look. "Why are you so surprised? We've heard of women's lib, even over here. In fact, the Druids have archdruids, just like we have archbishops, and while most of them are older gentlemen with heavy black reading glasses, a couple are women. Surely, Moira, you're not against women being priests?"

I was checkmated. "No," I said hotly. "But Miles, I want you to know you are blowing my mind to pieces, and I will have my revenge. I am going to faint sometime in the course of this evening, and you will have to pick up the pieces."

Miles gave me a distinctly fetching look and replied, "Don't worry, I'll resuscitate you."

I felt my face turn scarlet. I had the hots for this guy something awful, and frankly was beginning to be scared to death. I was in way over my head—guywise, religious-wise, you name it.

The potluck was held at a house in town, and resembled the suppers they always had before a vestry meeting at my Episcopal church back home. The crowd was older, al-though there were a few long-haired people in their twen-ties. It was a diverse group; some of the men looked as if they might be financial types right at home in the City; others appeared to be teachers, university professors, farm-ers, a Fleet Streeter or two, and assorted brainy technical types. With a couple of notable exceptions, the women did not generally belong to the British equivalent of the Junior League. Their style of dress and hair tended to the Earth Mother; there was much talk of gardening and herb lore as liberal quantities of port, sherry, and hors d'oeuvres were served.

However, when all was said and done, there was no com-mon thread binding all these people together, other than the fact that they were all having dinner together on Halloween before attending a Druid ritual. I couldn't explain this to save my life, even though I had this weird feeling that the lack of other factors in common was very significant, and a key to understanding—something. Something elusive, and perhaps important.

The conversation was animated and full of real laughter, not the hip laughter with an edge to it that I had so often encountered in the hip bars of Austin and pubs of London. The other people, though generally older than I, were all very polite and made sure to include me in ongoing con-versations—a courtesy I was not accustomed to in the United States.

When it was time to eat the main dinner, the guests ob-served a rather interesting custom: They ate the food in complete, solemn silence, and placed a plate piled high with goodies before a chair that remained empty throughout the meal.

Miles explained to me before we ourselves sat down at the table that at Samhain the Druids remembered loved ones who had passed on and that the silent meal, or "dumb supper," was a gesture of respect and reverence toward them. The plate of food and the empty chair were provided to honor the spirits of those dead ones; and he assured me the food was not wasted, but was fed to the animals afterward, or composted.

On this droll note, Cecilia, Miles, and I left a bit early, to prepare the site for the ritual. On the way over, I found myself chirping away about how wonderful everybody was, and how silly it was for anyone to think Druids were weird.

Cecilia and Miles both began to look worried. "Moira, dear," said Cecilia at last, "I must say something. You must not idealize this group of people. It is like any other group of human beings in the world—it has its good apples and its bad ones. Every religion attracts what you Americans call 'nuts,' and alternative religions are no exception. William Butler Yeats may have been a famous British occultist, but so was Aleister Crowley."

"Yeats! I know him. Who's the other guy?"

Cecilia gave a sort of shudder. "He's been referred to as 'a flawed magical genius.' I can't abide him, myself. He liked to call himself 'the Great Beast.' But do some reading, and make up your own mind."

"We Brits specialize in producing rather twisted civil servants," put in Miles, arching an eyebrow.

"But all those guys at the potluck seemed so nice," I protested. "Was I wrong?"

"I think they are nice, all of them," Cecilia hurried to say. "You must remember, though, that I organized this particular grove, and put in a great deal of work to sustain it. I run a good group, if I do say so myself."

"Cecilia's the one everybody in our family turns to in times of difficulty," Miles said. "She's our Rock of Gibraltar. But not every grove leader is like her, or every Wiccan coven leader. People are people.''

I thought for a moment, and admitted to myself that I could think of more than one flaming twit at my church back home in San Antonio. "Okay, fair enough," I said.

When we drove up to the ritual site, I asked Miles, "Why don't they do this at Stonehenge? That seems like the more natural place.''

"Too many tourists," he replied, wrinkling his nose. "Believe me, they're happy to let the tourists have Stonehenge, and be left alone here. Avebury is a bit older, and larger, so it's better for rituals.''

"And the original Druids built it?''

"No." He shook his head. "The pre-Celtic peoples of Britain. The Druids just appropriated it.''

I nodded. "So the Druids were invaders themselves.''

"Yes, or rather the Celts were," said Miles.

"Miles," I said hesitantly, "explain something to me. All those people at the potluck were so—different. There was no common pattern that I could see—I couldn't say, 'Oh, Druids, they're the Earth Shoe-Birkenstock crowd,' or 'Druids, they're the animal rights crowd or the eco-freak crowd or the business community.' ''

"You're right, they do come from all walks of life.''

I started to ask whether I was overlooking a common bond that drew them to the ancient site, but Miles and Cecilia tore out of the car and hurried to get ready for the ceremony.

The Avebury henge was a huge monument, consisting of a circle of raised earthworks and ditches perhaps a quarter mile in diameter. It was so big that it actually enclosed the town of Avebury. We entered the henge from the south, passing by a great portal stone, and proceeded to what Cecilia called the "southern inner circle" of stones. Only a few of the original stones were standing, the rest having been systematically destroyed or buried from medieval times on by zealous personages with a bug up their butts. Of the few that still remained, many had names such as Devil's Chair, Devil's Brandiron, Devil's Den, and Devil's Quoits. The people who had named the stones, not to mention the stones themselves, had been in something of a rut.

"Jeez," I said sourly, "it makes you wonder how any ancient monuments have survived anywhere. Why can't people leave history alone? They don't like Pharaoh Akhenaten and his monotheism, so they erase his name from all the Egyptian obelisks and confuse the rest of us. They don't like all the old standing stones, so they blow 'em up or bury 'em. No wonder you can't get a job these days in archaeology."

Archaeology was one of the possible majors that had really appealed to me back at the University of Texas, but I hadn't pursued it, because you really couldn't get a damn job.

Miles replied, rather archly, that at least one of the spoilsports had met an interesting end. In the fourteenth century, he said, the locals were in the process of digging a deep pit in which to bury one of the Avebury stones. As they got ready to drop the stone into the pit, it slid in prematurely, and a guy who was a barber, complete with a genuine pair of medieval barber's scissors, tripped and slid in along with the thirty-five-ton rock. He didn't see the light of day again until 1938, and even then could get no peace. His skeleton was moved to a London museum, and the whole kit and kaboodle, the barber included, were blown to smithereens during a German bombing raid on the city.

Anyway, Miles and Cecilia quickly unpacked a large amount of newspapers, straw, and kindling wood from the trunk of the car. A pile of timbers had previously been set up in the middle of what was left of the circle of stones. Cecilia put a large metal cup of water on a lightweight wooden table she had placed next to a large, grooved pillar, which a sign said marked the site of an obelisk stone that used to stand at the very center of the circle. Lastly, she changed into a long white robe with a hood, placed a small sickle-shaped knife in the belt of the robe, and poured us all another generous shot of sherry to sip while we waited for the others to arrive.

They were not long in coming.

Now, I was used to church services being a real pain in the ass. You went to church, you sang some hymns with cool-sounding language that dated back to the time of Henry VIII or his kid Elizabeth, and you recited stuff from the *Book of Common Prayer* that sounded equally poetic. But then you settled in for a long, boring sermon, followed by a long, boring Sunday school session taught by the guy who owned the local Carrier Air Conditioning franchise. Then, finally, the reward: You got to go to the parish hall and have coffee and flirt with the boys.

Well, Cecilia's Druids were solemn enough, but I kept having this weird feeling that everybody was there because they wanted to be, not because their parents made them go. And I could certainly understand that; these clever Brits had succeeded in figuring out a way to dress up and party on Halloween, even though they were supposedly too old for such stuff! It was right on.

Cecilia lit the bonfire, which shortly was raging away, and bustled around giving everybody their very own candle, including Miles and me. It was really cold, but I didn't care, being bundled up, and enthralled by what I was seeing.

Miles whispered to me, "The ancient Celts believed that on Samhain, the boundary between the world of the living and the world of the dead flickered and faded and grew thin—so that any visions that come are stronger than at other times of the year."

Then he hushed up, because Cecilia had begun to chant.

"We are gathered here, within this sacred place, to witness the merging of time. Past, present, and future are one within this circle, and we are made whole by recognizing our place within the chain of tradition. We are spiritual seekers, bound together in one eternal quest—the quest for light. In this holy place, while our Ancestors walk among us, we call upon the flowing spirit of our faith.''

Long and low, the group began to chant a word: Awen. "It means spirit, or inspiration," Miles whispered.

My hair stood on end.

Cecilia rose. "We gather here in peace," she said, "to celebrate the festival of Calan Gaeof, the Winter Calends, the first day of the coming winter. Let us call now to the four quarters in the words of the traditions met as one within this sacred circle, that our Ancestors might know the old ways are not forgotten.''

Now my skin got into the act, too, and began to prickle.

Miles nudged me as an elderly, bearded fellow got up. "I know him. He's a lifetime member of the local Anglican Church," said Miles. "See, he's facing east. He's calling the eastern quarter, but he's going to use very Christian terminology.''

He did, and I was bewildered.

A professorial-looking woman got up next and called the southern quarter, using language that was unfamiliar to me. "She's quite the student of American Indian shamanism," Miles cued me.

Next, a young woman with bright red hair, whom Miles described as Wiccan, got up and called the western quarter, asking a goddess and a god to attend her. The names she used were Celtic—Cernunnos and Rhiannon. At least I knew who the former name was: Miles and I had already hashed him over at the pub. As for Rhiannon, all I could think of was the Fleetwood Mac song.

Lastly, a Druid I recognized from the potluck stepped forward to call the northern quarter. "Listen carefully!" Miles commanded.

"I call to the city of Falias to the north, to the Spirits of the Earth, the Black Raven and the Brown Bull, to Moirias the Green Man, Guardian of the Stone of Destiny and the Gates of Night.''

I gasped out loud. ''What the hell? He said 'Green Man'!'' I said hissing. ''And then he said my name!''

''No—Moirias, not Moira.''

I was overcome by a pronounced shudder. ''Well, it is way too close for comfort. I am not reassured at all.''

''The ancient Greeks used the word *moira* to describe something like fate or destiny,'' said Miles, freaking me out even further.

''So, who the hell is Moirias? Is that still another name for the Green Man?'' I whispered. ''Tell me!''

Miles spoke slowly, as if choosing his words with caution. ''Moirias is a Welsh name. It means, as close as I can translate it, 'He who is full of purity and greenness.' ''

''Goddamn it! My name is another name for the Green Man! What does all this mean?''

Miles took a long time to reply. ''I don't know,'' he said in utter seriousness. ''This is disturbing. Perhaps we all are the Green Man—or must be.''

''Oh, damn it,'' I whispered fiercely at him. ''I don't understand what is going on, but I am now, truly, going to faint.''

Having gotten my mind totally blown, I must have subsided into something like a reverie then, at Avebury. I watched, detached, as one by one, people went up to the altar Cecilia had set up, and placed on it such things as photographs of loved ones who had died, to celebrate their lives, remember them, and mourn their passing.

Then there came prayers to bless a newborn child, and a recent marriage, and other prayers for those who had died during the year. A tale was told of the festival of Calan Gaeof, and of the death of the Celtic sun god, whose spirit did not die, but left his body in the form of an eagle, to be reborn in human form at the winter cycle, thus beginning anew the cycle of the seasons.

Then the last prayer of all broke through my mental stupor: It was a prayer to heal the Earth. For some reason I found myself listening to it apprehensively.

A man in a long white robe whom I had not seen before intoned, in a voice as rich as polished wood, the following words: "Our ancestors held that both Spirit and the universe are eternal, but in dark times, both may be overwhelmed by fire and water. As we have grown in understanding, so has mankind, like the Great Spirit, developed the power to destroy by fire and water. But, like the Great Spirit, we may choose to use our power not to destroy, but to create and sustain. I pray that Spirit grant us the wisdom to nourish and sustain our Mother, the Earth, as she nourishes and sustains us.

"May we always sow more than we reap. May we recognize our kinship with all of Earth's beings: with the stone ones who define this circle, the green ones who give us food and medicine, the feathered ones who carry our prayers to the heavens, the furred ones who are our guardians and guides, the scaled ones who slide between the worlds—all who grow or walk upon the Earth, who crawl beneath it or fly above it, all who swim in her rivers, lakes, and oceans.

"I swear the oath our ancestors swore: If we break our covenant with Mother Earth and the creatures that the Great Spirit has made, may the ground open up and swallow us, may the waters rise up and overwhelm us, and may the heavens fall and crush us. So let it be."

People in those days were fond of talking about "altered states," and that's what I must have experienced at that moment. I had a sudden, overwhelming vision of the medieval barber, struggling to bury one of the devil's stones, suddenly being swept beneath it and crushed. For a mo-

ment, I felt as if I were that barber, watching for a split
second all those tons of rock descend to crush me. Then
the meaning of my unwelcome vision became clear to me:
We *had* broken the covenant, and I was going to pay the
price, as was everyone in the circle with me, and everyone
on Earth.

With the force of a hammer blow to the head, I became
vividly aware of the feel of the Earth beneath me. I was
conscious of it as a spirit, a creature, a living, half-ghostly
thing. I sensed the water moving in rivers like blood
through veins, sensed green growing things breathing in
and out, like lungs. I sensed a great web, of which I was a
part. I thought I sensed consciousness, or something eerily
like it.

Yet the Earth was also like a great beast that was sick
and in pain, its breathing labored, its blood gushing from
many wounds, its lifeforce faltering. With the impact of a
rain of fists, I felt its anguish, its fear and anger, and its
will to struggle and survive at any cost—any cost whatsoever, no matter if the survival of my own species might
be forfeit.

My mind screamed silently, over and over, as I saw a
picture of one possible future Earth unfold before me.
Again I imagined myself, and all mankind, falling into a
pit of our own making, like the medieval barber, and being
crushed by the implacable weight of the sarsen stone we
had so foolishly dislodged.

It was so very real, I could not convince myself, no matter how hard I tried, that I just had a hyperactive imagination. Or that I was overemotional, or too excitable.

On the first day of winter, the veil between the worlds
had indeed thinned, as the Celts believed, and I had had a
vision of future years to come.

After that, I was so frightened I wanted one thing, and
one thing only: to get away from Avebury, from the Druids,

from Miles, and from the very memory of that horrible vision.

A door had been opened, across whose threshold I was terrified to go. No matter what the cost, I would turn my back on it.

In Texas, where I grew up, only three categories of citizens had "visions": saints, evangelists, and crazy people. I definitely did not belong to either of the first two, and so I had to belong to the last.

I was quiet and withdrawn when the ceremony ended. My hands shook, and I felt chilled to the bone. Miles was very concerned, but I didn't tell him what had happened to me; I only said I was very tired. As the ritual concluded, the other men and women were solemn and reverent in demeanor, but soon warmed to the cheer they knew lay ahead. Putting the fire to practical use, they passed around large quantities of sherry and cider and began to roast chestnuts and marshmallows. Druids clearly knew how to have a good time—better than I.

Miles sensed I was in trouble, so he quickly said our good-byes and bundled me into the car for the drive back to London.

I talked little, and pretended to doze, though my mind was racing furiously. When Miles asked if I felt ill, I seized on the excuse and said I felt a touch of the flu coming on.

By the time Miles dropped me back at the YWCA on Great Russell Street, I think he realized much more was wrong with me than fatigue or illness. We exchanged addresses, but he'd caught on that I only wanted to get away from him, and that he would probably never see me again; it showed in his face.

"Please do try to write," he said. "I'd really hoped I'd get to know you better. Are you positive you can't stay a few more days?"

"I'd love to," I lied, "but I have to get back. School, you know."

Of course, that was a load of bullshit. But he didn't add to my discomfort by pointing it out. "I haven't met many girls like you," he said wistfully.

"Thanks," I replied.

"Is there any chance you might be able to come study in London for a while? You American students seem to come across so many opportunities to study abroad."

"Maybe," I said, seeing a way to stall him; I would sound agreeable and run like hell. "I'll really look into it."

"I'd be glad to help." He took out his wallet and gave me a card. "Here's my address. Please write."

I said, "I'll really try."

So we said good-bye. I didn't write, of course.

Years later, when I got access to computerized newspaper databases at my law firm, I started checking up on Miles, and the possible future with him on which I had turned my back. He published a lot more books. He produced and directed excellent but obscure films and television productions. Eventually he married a very rich New York socialite, which really got me to scratching my head. He was even elected to Parliament at the end of the century. From everything I could tell, he led a full life. I lost track of him in 2020, around the time things started going completely haywire on the planet. But as it turned out, I did see him one last time, toward the end.

When I was safely on the Braniff jet going home, I sat down and had a long, confused talk with myself. I was still trying to make sense of the petrifying events at Avebury.

I wondered whether I was crazy. Had I smoked so much dope in college that now I was seeing things? Or was there something *else* going on that I ought to screw up my courage and pay attention to?

I had always felt pretty confident that there was a firm boundary between fantasy and reality. But I wasn't at all sure that it lay where most people thought it did.

Middle America seemed to have its feet planted firmly on the ground when it came to deciding where the everyday world stopped and far-out, woo-woo hokum began. However, no sooner did I take comfort in that thought than it occurred to me that middle America often played fast and loose with the definition of things fantastical, as long as middle America already happened to approve of them.

Nobody had yet scientifically proven the existence of God, but the polyester crowd habitually went to church and worshiped Him anyway. The same Ohio burgher and his matron who sneered at the New Age crystal rubbers could become downright credulous where guardian angels were concerned, and on occasion could be spotted in air-conditioned shopping mall stores that hawked plaster cherubs and angel tarot cards. No, the standards of middle America were going to be no help in figuring out whether I was looney tunes.

I remembered I had a great-grandmother in East Texas who regularly said she talked to deceased members of the family. In many places she would have been locked up, but East Texas tended to tolerate the local village eccentric, and besides, the place itself was southern gothic and eccentric enough to scare William Faulkner. Clearly a predisposition to weirdness was already lurking in my genetic heritage.

Suddenly an old, faded memory started nagging at my brain, demanding to be heard. The damn thing would not leave me alone. It had something to do with fantasy versus reality, but I could not nail it down. I kept finding myself on the verge of recapturing the memory, only to have it slip away again—very *Twilight Zone.*

Then, with the mental equivalent of a popping flashbulb, the thing crystallized and snapped into focus. I was stunned, because I hadn't thought about it in almost twenty years, and probably would never have remembered it again, except for the shock I'd gotten at Avebury.

Suddenly I was no longer on the Braniff plane; I was in

a beautiful park in San Antonio, Texas. I was six years old.
I was all dressed up in a costume, and was playing the role
of my favorite fictional character at the time, Robin Hood.

The skin on the back of my neck prickled. All those
years ago, I had played at being Robin Hood—one guise
of the Green Man.

It happened like this. At five years of age I had gone
through a Zorro phase, brought on by watching every single
episode of the black-and-white Guy Williams TV series. In
my games, I role-played the caped crusader from old California every chance I got. My mother had even made me
a black velvet coat, which she secured with a piece of my
grandmother's old costume jewelry. A fake rubber sword
and a pair of red rubber boots rounded out the costume.

At age six I had tired of Zorro and graduated to Robin
Hood. In my imaginary plays, I was always Robin. Forget
second-fiddle Maid Marian; gender considerations simply
did not bother me. Zorro's rapier had been traded for a bow
and a set of suction cup-tipped arrows from the local five-
and-ten-cent store. I had a green cap, a green shirt, and
green pants. For some reason, the red rubber boots stayed;
I made a very Christmasy-looking Robin.

My mother had taken a playmate and me to San Pedro
Park in San Antonio, which had hundreds of venerable oak
trees, and natural, crystal-clear springs that bubbled straight
out of limestone rock. The sky was a bright, piercing blue,
smog was unheard of, and the day was crisp, cool, and
exhilarating.

Texas had recently undergone a long drought, during
which the springs in the park had dried up. But recently
the rains had decided to return, and so the springs had come
back. Now the park was green and sparkling again, a wonderland for a child of six.

The central role of Robin Hood being taken, I had gen-
erously allowed my playmate to be Maid Marian. I had
given her a spare set of bows and arrows (I had a collection

of them by then), and we were shooting at various targets that we pretended were the evil sheriff of Nottingham and his henchmen.

I recall wishing fervently, as I got ready to fire one particular shot, that I had a real bow and some real arrows, not that crummy plastic stuff from the dime store. I was standing looking up at a steep little hill, atop which grew a small but determined live oak tree. The oak, I decided, was a particularly bad henchman about to jump Little John. I fired right at his black heart and missed, my arrow disappearing over the top of the hill.

My aim was good, I could tell that, but rubber suction-cupped arrows just didn't perform like the ones on TV and in the movies, and consequently I often missed the sheriff's men. Leaving my friend behind, I went trudge, trudge, up a scrabbly path to the top of the hill.

Where there was no arrow to be found.

Puzzled, I climbed back down, wondering if I had somehow managed to shoot the arrow all the way over and past the little hill. I began to search the ground everywhere. Though I had read nothing of chaos theory (the old *Classics Illustrated* comic books were about my speed back then, and besides, chaos theory was still in its infancy, or perhaps not even yet a twinkle in a theoretician's eye), I nevertheless knew intuitively that a relatively small error in the trajectory of a rubber-tipped arrow early in its flight could amplify into one hell of a course change by the time the arrow fell to earth.

My friend had stayed behind. She was either lazy, or thought that the grunt work of looking for arrows should fall to the player who had scammed the role of Robin Hood for herself.

I rounded the hill, and for a moment had the park all to myself. The sunlight sparkled on another crystal stream, which poured into a deep, clear pool wherein tadpoles and small fish could be glimpsed. The wind blew gently, the leaves in the oak trees whispered, and I felt like a very small speck in a very big world—a world that was fairly bursting with mystery and promise.

My mother had read me a lot of fairy tales. So it seemed perfectly natural to find that there were dryads in the oak trees, a water nymph in the deep pool, and a being made of sparkling light that played in the branches of the oaks, disguising itself as sunshine. They liked me, and said hello. I said hi back. The stream flowed, like crystal-colored blood through veins of white limestone, the oaks breathed, and the wind patted my cheek, as grown-ups always did upon encountering a pretty child.

Then I saw the arrow, in the middle of a little clearing. Not my arrow, but one crafted by hand with a straight wooden shaft, several brown and white feathers, and a sturdy arrowhead made of slate or flint.

Up till then I'd thought I had a fairly good idea where reality ended and play-pretend began. Nobody had laughed at me yet and told me that spirits did not really live in the trees and pools in the park, or float upon the breezes, but were only products of my imagination. Still, I was a pretty level-headed kid. Fairy tales were one thing—they were written in books, and books were a respectable source of authority—but dime-store arrows transmuting into gorgeous hand-made arrows in midflight were quite another.

I knew that this magnificent arrow was not the one I had shot into the air. But it *was* exactly the arrow I had wanted, and it lay exactly where mine should have landed. Surely this was crazy. Or was it?

As I stood there, I grew less and less certain that I did know where the real world stopped, and the world of make-believe began.

I knew for sure that I wasn't Robin Hood, but I also knew that if I pretended to be Robin Hood, for a short time I certainly felt as if I were the fabled outlaw.

Here I had wished very hard for a special arrow, and apparently I had gotten one, through a mechanism not yet clearly understood. Maybe some obscure sort of magic had been at work. Maybe, under such circumstances, fantasy could become reality. Then, like a revelation from on high, it dawned on me. A clue! Didn't they always sing on *Walt Disney's Wonderful World of Color* about "when you wish upon a star"? If Disney said it, then that was proof that sometimes dreams really could come true.

I picked up the arrow. It was quite real, and had a good, solid feel in my hand. My brain still searched frantically for some way to fit this occurrence into what I understood of the world. Finally I realized there was only one course of action left to me: inquire of the highest authority. I would ask my mother to untangle it all at the earliest possible moment.

I turned to go. Several yards away, a flash of orange plastic caught my eye. There, against a stone, was my rubber-tipped arrow.

That should have explained everything, but I almost left the thing where it was. I felt as if someone, or something, had brushed my own arrow aside like a fly and given me a magic arrow in its place.

Yes, it was a coincidence that I had shot my plastic arrow toward a spot where someone else had happened to lose a real, handmade arrow; it was coincidence that mine had gone astray, and coincidence that I had happened to stumble upon my new treasure. But I felt it was quite significant that all these coincidences had happened *just so*.

It was too bad fifteen years would have to pass before I could wander into an encounter with Carl Jung and the concept of synchronicity, during my University of Texas liberal arts course surfing days; I really needed the help back then.

With a jolt, my memory of the park dissolved, and I came back to myself and the humming engines of the Dallas-bound Braniff jet. At that moment, a realization dawned on me.

The memory had scared me. I was a coward.

Miles had been absolutely right; Americans were very much afraid of dragons, me first and foremost. Miles had opened a door for me that led out of mainstream life, into a world where the imagination was free to roam, where people wrote books, where myth and magic could be part of their daily lives. He had offered me passage back into a childhood place, where the boundaries between the ordinary world and the world of the mind were not graven in stone.

And I had been scared to death. I was still scared, and was running away for all I was worth, like a child afraid of the dark.

I just couldn't handle it.

I turned my back on that possible future. I slammed the door and bricked it over, just like Montresor in *The Cask of Amontillado.* I denied the *Twilight Zone,* backed hurriedly away from the *Outer Limits,* and ran with all my might toward a conventional, mainstream life.

I did so with my usual thoroughness. Not long after that, I got the notion that I ought to go to law school.

EIGHT

MAY 22, 2032

THIS WAS A FRIGGING BITCH OF A DAY. IT DID NOT GO
well at all.

I slaved in the garden for hours in the heat, and at the
end of it, I hurt like hell all over. God, how I hate weeds.

The little bastards suck up the extra carbon dioxide in
the air twice as fast as the plants we WANT to grow, that
we NEED to grow. You have to uproot every last stinking
one of them, without exception, or they'll take over a la-
boriously terraced bed in a week. You don't dare take a
break, no matter how bad you feel; you don't dare leave
even a little one sitting in the dirt, because you are too tired
to pull one more of the wretched stinkers; give them a
week's head start and they'll own the place, and you'll wish
you were dead.

To make matters worse, our bees didn't do so well this
year. I suspect a lot of them may have gotten poisoned from
all the crap out there in the water, in the soil, you name it.
See, we have to keep our own bees, purchased at exorbitant
cost, because there are no longer enough wild bees and
other pollinating critters to service food crops—anywhere.
You got no pollinators, you got no food from your food
crops. Got it, duh? Consequently bees are worth their
weight in gold these days. (If you want to know what to
blame, try all those pesticides that went into all those nice

middle-class lawns starting in the previous century.) Today I examined as many of our trees as I had the strength for, and the fruit set this spring was piss-poor, to put it mildly.

There are plenty of obnoxious insects, though. God, how I hate them. The infinite variety of biting, stinging, itching, buzzing little bastards that used to be confined to the tropics in civilized times but have now invaded America.

There was a stupid song we used to sing back in grade school, about the boll weevil, that now must apply to every insectoid pest in the Western Hemisphere. "The boll weevil is a little black bug, from Mexico they say, come to try the Texas soil, and he thought he'd better stay, just a-lookin' for a home, just a-lookin' for a home." How was I to know, sitting in my little starched dress, trilling away with the other six-year-old cherubs, that that song was describing one of my major future miseries to a T?

When I was growing up in Texas, yeah, we had boll weevils. We also had roaches the size of chihuahuas. When I moved out to California, leaving those guys behind almost made up for losing good Mexican food. But now I have the worst of both worlds. Still no good Mexican food, or food of any kind, for that matter, but those cursed roaches had migrated to California and planned to stay. When I came in from work, I wanted to check the Net to see if anyone knew of a voracious, small, furry animal that liked roaches . . . and get one.

Surprise, surprise, Rhiannon was already on-line. I was about to ask her to do a big-time search for biological pest controls, when I caught sight of her face. Right then I knew the day was about to get worse.

"Jesus H. Christ, what is it?" I asked. "Green Man?"

She nodded.

"So, what's wrong?"

"I'm scared."

I felt as if a cold, gray cloud had just wrapped itself around me. So she really had blundered across some psychos on the Net—and they knew who we were. Great.

"Care to enlighten me?" I snapped.

"They do mean well," she said absently.

"Indeed? That's nice to know."

"They are both very emotional. They have an important decision to make in the near future, but they are divided about the morality of making it. One feels that our situation is so desperate, any action that will better it—eventually— is justified. The other believes that they are perilously close to playing God, and is all but paralyzed with indecision."

"Rhiannon, why is this *our* problem?"

Rhiannon blinked at me. "They've asked for my advice."

"So, you don't have to give it, let alone get mixed up in this any more than you already are. We have enough problems to deal with here."

"Moira!" she said with a hiss. "Stop thinking about yourself for a second, please! Stop being so self-centered!"

It was like a dash of cold water in my face. "Oh, all right, if you insist," I replied. "What's the deal? Tell me what's going on."

"They have something they believe can rescue us. *Most* of us, that is, from all of this." Rhiannon waved one arm slowly, as if to encompass the very world around us. "Either they are crazy—or they can do exactly what they say they can do. If the former is true, then I am wasting my time, but I am doing no harm. If the latter is true, then I am advising two men who hold in their hands the powers of life and death, one of whom is willing to unleash those powers if our situation grows desperate enough. In that case, I must be very careful what counsel I give."

I was dumbstruck. After an extended silence I managed one word. *"Counsel?"*

"They ask me a lot of questions. They seem to want reassurance that what they're thinking about doing is right."

The whole situation suddenly seemed extremely insane to me. "Rhiannon, how can two guys you've met over the Net have the power to destroy the world? Come on."

"Not to destroy the world," said Rhiannon. "To change it. And there aren't two guys, there are many, many people, all over the world. All linked up, all working—together. I just happen to be talking to the ones who started it all."

"Or so they say." I was skeptical, yet at the same time, a cold premonition began to inch its way up my vertebrae.

"Remember, Moira, how I told you at the start that there were thousands of other messages relating to Green Man? That I only intercepted one message?"

"Rhiannon, I don't know about this. I'm getting scared."

"If these men are fakes, which they could be, despite the messages, then I'm having extended discussions about ethics with people who can't do any harm anyway. If they're not fakes, then maybe I'm helping. They seem to want my help, so—on the off chance they can do what they say they can—I'm helping."

"How can they possibly get us out of the mess we're in? It's too late!" I said. "We're too far gone. I'll drop dead of surprise if godlike Julian can even do any good once he gets elected! Even if every last person in the world suddenly got in the boat and rowed in the right direction, it would still be a toss-up whether we could pull our asses out of the fire in time!"

Rhiannon regarded me gravely and said nothing.

The chilly feeling in my spinal cord intensified, and I started to gasp but could not. My breath would not come. "Just how do they plan to make us all get in the boat?" I asked in a voice that sounded thin and frantic.

"Change us."

"HOW?"

She shook her head patiently. "I don't know yet. That's not really important. The question is not how they could do it, but whether they ought to do it."

I retreated from the room, my spirits in complete disarray. I ran to my room, fished out a new tiny bottle of rotgut Loki had picked up for me down at the Claremont, and took it out to my perch under the oak tree. I drank all of it, but afterward my nerves were still shot. I was scared to death and utterly demoralized.

NINE

JUNE 21, 2032

OH, GOD. I DON'T WANT TO WRITE THIS, BUT I MUST, OR I will not be able to be at peace with my soul, let alone sleep, despite any potion Rhiannon can give me. Lyla is gone, and she did not die easily.

She had been maintaining for a very long time. The cancer caused her continual pain, but it was not unbearable. We had all prayed that she would have one of those spontaneous remissions the medical profession always used to talk about.

Last week, her pain intensified exponentially. She was a brave, bitchy soul, a real fighter, and it did more violence to my heart and soul to hear her scream than anything in living memory. To see someone like Lyla Ann Ferguson reduced to a weeping, pleading piece of suffering flesh, with no dignity left, no sparkle, no rapier wit, no arrogance—with nothing left at all—was the most horrifying thing I have seen in my life.

Rhiannon did everything in her power to ease Lyla's pain, but it had progressed to a point where nothing except real narcotics would have done the trick. At last Loki slipped away, to a shadowy black market far more sinister than Mad Mac's, and returned with a small amount of morphine, a dose of which we promptly gave to Lyla.

It bought us all a few hours in which to gather our frightened, scattered wits about us. We met outside, while Lyla enjoyed a brief haven of rest.

Rhiannon's face looked like a death mask. "The herbs aren't anywhere near full grown," she said. "I can't use them to put Lyla out of her misery, not for at least two more months."

I had guessed that already. From our library, I had brought down my yellowing, half-century-old copy of *Final Exit.* "Then we'll have to use this," I said.

Rhiannon hid her face in her hands and started weeping. "Yes, we must," said Loki. "We cannot afford any more morphine. When this batch is gone, she will be in agony again."

I looked at Father Lorenzo. "What do you think, Father?"

He spread his hands apart in a helpless gesture. "The Church forbids suicide as well as mercy killings—though I have never been made to witness another's pain of this intensity. I wonder if the men who made those laws had ever seen someone die as Lyla is dying! I will not stand in your way if you try to free her from it. Perhaps you and your book are the instruments of God's will. Once I would have thought myself justified in saying you are about to commit a mortal sin; now I cannot say that in good conscience."

I looked at George. "When I was ten I had this dog named Jerry," he said, his voice raspy, like a metal shovel being raked over concrete. George always sounded like that when he got emotional. "He got run over, but not completely. His hindquarters were crushed, but he was still alive. So I bashed his head in with a hammer and buried him. Funny thing was, anytime I went out to the grave, I knew Jerry wasn't mad at me. Jerry loved me when he was alive, and he loved me when he was dead, because I helped him die easy. There's no reason God would want somebody to keep on hurting like she's hurting. What's the point? Go to it, Moira, and if God has something to say about it, He can damn well speak to me.''

Had the situation not been so horrifying, I would have fainted with surprise to hear George speaking in the least iota like a sensitive New Age guy. As matters stood, I took it as a sign that I was doing the right thing.

"Okay," I said. "Who'll help me?"

The cowards, they each and every one of them ducked their heads. Then, predictably, Rhiannon looked up first. "I will.''

Father Lorenzo, having been shown up as an almost-coward, said, "Me, too."

"Yeah, and me," said George.

Loki regarded me with a stricken look. For quite a long time he could think of nothing to say. Then he said, awkwardly and most inaccurately, "Lord, please let this cup bypass my unworthy lips.''

"You went out and got the morphine," I replied. "So, okay, you can have a walk this time. Give me what's left of it.''

He nodded, stiffly. "Here." He put a plastic Baggie with a syringe and a vial partly full of liquid into my hand. I examined it, and determined there was enough for what I had in mind.

So all the rest of us, except Loki, went up to Lyla's room.

She woke up when we entered. "I was starting to feel so good, and I really slept," she cried, "but now all I can think about is when the pain's going to come back!''

"Hush, my dear," said Rhiannon. I gave her the morphine, and with expert fingers, she filled the syringe. It was a megadose. She did not bother to clean the needle; there was no point in doing so. She shot Lyla up on the inside of her left elbow, and sat back while the drug took effect. With her eyes, she signaled me to get my own preparations ready.

Rhiannon had given Lyla so much of the shit, it made

her giddy right away. "Oh, God bless you," Lyla said after a couple of minutes had passed. "I can tell the pain isn't coming back. I knew you wouldn't let me down, Rhiannon. Whatever that stuff is you brewed up, it's wonderful."

Rhiannon flushed. Lyla was so far gone, she thought she had Rhiannon to thank for the respite from pain, not Loki. As I watched, Lyla began to cry, mumbling about how wonderful it was not to hurt anymore, and how precious life was if you weren't in pain.

I dashed out of the room, the better to collect a rubber band, a thick plastic bag without a trace of a hole, a torn sheet, and the will to do what I had to do.

When I returned, Lyla was high as a kite, and maudlin. She was clutching Rhiannon's hand. Although her eyes were darting back and forth and she didn't seem to be able to focus her vision upon our witchy friend, she was talking intently to Rhiannon.

"I want to say something," Lyla whispered. "I don't think I'll die now, I feel so much better, but just in case I do, I want this to go on the record. You're misguided, Rhiannon. You've been led astray somehow. You call yourself a witch, and you should be damned for that, but I know in my heart that you are one of the most Christian women I have ever met. I cannot believe that God would send you to hell for what you've done. You are a good person, Rhiannon. Surely God looks at what one does instead of what one says. No matter what, when I get to heaven I will make sure that there is a place for you there, too."

Had our hearts not been breaking, it would have been exquisitely funny. In her delirium, Lyla seemed to think there was the equivalent of a House subcommittee in heaven, before which she could plead Rhiannon's case and obtain a pass for her through the pearly gates, despite her evil pagan witchery.

Rhiannon wept and wept, silently, the tears running

down her face like a waterfall, her eyelids red and puffy as pillows.

"We always fought," said Lyla, "but it was all in good fun, at least I hoped you knew that. Hell's bells, sometimes you were all that kept me going. We'd argue, and I always stood up for what I believed, and you did, too. Neither one of us gave an inch. I really admired that about you, Rhiannon. You weren't like Moira, who sits on the fence far more than she ought to. You were a real friend, and I always knew I didn't have to walk on eggshells around you, because I always knew you could take care of yourself. You were tough, like me. We should have been sisters."

Rhiannon gave a harsh, gasping sob, which made Lyla look even more distracted. "Is something wrong?" she asked.

Rhiannon squeezed Lyla's hand, very hard. Rhiannon couldn't speak. Somehow I managed to find my voice. "Everything's okay, Lyla," I said. "Rhiannon's fine."

Lyla didn't seem to take it in entirely that I was the one who had spoken. She looked confusedly in Rhiannon's direction and said, "Speaking of Moira, she is a saint, for having given us all a home, but between you and me, I never could understand what Loki saw in her. He and I were much better suited for each other. As old as Moira is, she's still pretty, but I was much more independent, and I think more intelligent. Oh, well, I know the truth. Men don't like uppity women like me. Not the Republicans, and not even the *Democrats,* in spite of all their feminist mealymouthing. Bill screwed around on Hillary every chance he got, didn't he—and with what? Bimbos! My husband was the worst of them all—him and that goddamn campaign worker."

The others looked at me, and I lowered my eyes, feeling my own tears begin, and my face turn scarlet.

Lyla gave a deep sigh. "Oh, I'm feeling sleepy again. It will be so nice to have a nap. I'll wake up and feel so much better. Rhiannon, I know you'll go to heaven, and someday I'll see you there. I'm so glad you tried to save the baby.''

Her eyes closed, and she fell into a deep, drugged sleep.

Rhiannon totally lost it. She groped her way into a far corner of the room and started sobbing her heart out. George, the erstwhile warrior, sat motionless in his wheel-chair and would not meet my eyes. Father Lorenzo crept over and put his arms around Rhiannon, and silently rocked her back and forth.

My stomach tied itself up in knots. They were all basket cases; it was up to me, and me alone.

My hands started trembling, more than they normally did because of my age. I felt dizzy with fear and dread. I scanned the directions in *Final Exit* one more time, said a prayer to God, and added one to Rhiannon's god and god-dess for good measure. In any case, my prayers were re-turned unopened and unanswered—the abyss responded not—and I had no choice but to proceed.

Lyla Ann was so far down, I did not think she would feel any pain. And even if she did, it would be nothing like the pain the cancer had given her during the past week.

I gritted my teeth, tried to ignore my pounding heart and my wish to throw up, and fastened the plastic bag over her head. I secured it firmly around her throat with the rubber band, so that no air could enter. Then I bound her wrists and hands with a long strip of cloth torn from the sheet.

Then I sat back and waited. I wished one of the others would have the presence of mind to come over, gag me, and tie my hands together. Otherwise I might lose my nerve, try to free her, and leave her just as sick as ever, only with brain damage from oxygen deprivation on top of it all.

I had never killed anyone before. Yet I knew I had to see this thing to the finish, no matter how painful it might be.

I knew, with my mind, that the struggle I was about to

witness would only be Lyla's dying body, her autonomic nervous system putting up a last-ditch fight. The ANS is incredibly robust and vigorous and hates to die, or where would we be today? I knew that Lyla—the being, the woman, the creature inside the flesh that was Lyla—was not suffering, in fact was not even conscious.

And yet it was a dreadful thing to watch.

As her body used up the oxygen, it began to gasp for air with the most horrid, rasping spasms. Her body twitched, fighting for its own life, though her consciousness was drugged and absent. Her body could not move its hands to the plastic bag, nor to the rubber band. It could only gasp, with increasing desperation, as the life-giving gas ran out and the shadow of approaching death drew ever closer.

George wheeled out of the room. Rhiannon, the consummate witch, she who was used to balancing the powers of light and darkness, of life and death, merely hid her face in her Christian lover's shoulder, and wept for her breaking heart. Lorenzo endured, because that was what he was trained to do.

I saw it through, to the last. I made myself do it.

The dying took forever. I never glanced at the clock, and did not know how long it lasted in real time. In the time that governs the heart, it took an eternity.

At some far distant point in time, Lyla finally and mercifully lay still. I sat, weighed down with limbs of lead for a long time afterward, so I could be certain she was dead. Then I took off the plastic bag and the rubber band and the binding around her hands.

A human being, no matter how sick, is still alive. I was overpowered, looking at Lyla's dead body, by the sense of total absence I saw. It was not so much that she was dead, but that she was not alive. There was a limp, gray, contorted, aged body on the bed in front of me. It was ugly and repulsive. But none of that mattered. The important thing was, there was NOTHING inside it. No resonance.

No grief. No residue of past passions, past battles, past griefs. Simply—nothing. The void. The unmaker of universes. The absence of light, spirit, and gods.

Everything that had made Lyla herself had fled. I hoped, from the deepest recesses of my soul, that she had gone to that heaven in which she could still join subcommittees and do what she thought was right.

TEN

1978–85

THERE IS A SAYING THAT TEXAS IS SO CULTURALLY ISO-lated and provincial, everything happens five years later there. Well, I think that was a fair statement. By early 1978, the sixties, which had come late to Texas like everything else, finally started to fade.

They faded very quickly. It was like somebody had turned off a faucet. One moment everything was normal, and the next it seemed like everybody interesting I knew had suddenly left town; the only people I knew in Austin who were as old as I was were aging hippies—who at last were starting to wake up and realize how hard a life without money could be when one was no longer pristinely young.

I started worrying about money, too, because over the years, prices had been slowly inching up, and Austin was no longer the cheapest paradise in the world in which to live. The eighty-dollar apartment, if it could still be found, was now two hundred dollars. The barbarians were truly at the gates, as my lovely city on the Colorado was slowly being discovered by the outside world. Before the change was over, the city and its environs would be known as Silicon Gulch, and would be as expensive to live in as Houston.

It's cute to be poor and live in a hippie apartment in an old house when you're very young. Cash flow is not a major concern; when you're a kid you don't even need clothes, just a bike, a halter top, a pair of short shorts, and some Famolare sandals—and you're adorable. It's cute to be poor at twenty-two; but I was beginning to suspect that at thirty-two it would be distressing, and at forty-two downright embarrassing. I started having this uncomfortable feeling that I had to stop drifting like a jellyfish and do something constructive with my life, other than simply enjoying it.

Then, to make matters worse, punk rock arrived on the scene.

To my horror, punk soon wiped out almost all traces of the sixties in Austin. Suddenly all the guys in bands started looking like Mick Jagger with too much eyeliner; people with icky hair and bad attitude were in, and people with long, flowing tresses wearing tie-dye were getting called dinosaurs by jerks in passing cars.

All the punk bands traipsed through Raul's, this club on Guadalupe Street a block from the university: the Skunks, the Next, the Standing Waves, Terminal Mind, the Explosives. I muttered surly things under my breath whenever I caught a glimpse of one of the invaders, yearned for the good old days of Woodstock, and had a horrid premonition of what it would be like to turn into a Boring Old Fart some years hence.

I could see the handwriting on the wall, and so, when at last my dreaded thirtieth birthday drew ominously near in the Lone Star State, I decided I should do something important with my life. So I settled on a doubly valuable career, one that could be put to socially conscious good uses, such as sticking up for the poor or protecting the environment, or in the alternative could be counted on to make money. After watching too many episodes of *The Paper Chase* I finally did, in a moment of insanity, apply to law school. Worse yet, I got in.

At the time I thought the sixties had simply been obliterated by the passage of time, and now it was every man for himself. But they hadn't been; that decade had wrought deep, long-lasting changes in our culture. Many doors were now open to me that would have been barred shut the year JFK was shot.

In the early seventies women made up only a small fraction of the students at the University of Texas School of Law. By the time I started classes there, in the summer of 1980, women made up almost half the student body. By the time I graduated, they were slightly in the majority.

Years later, Jerry Rubin was credited with saying, "The sixties didn't die, they just came indoors." If he really did say that, he knew what he was talking about.

I had recently started to get a clue that it really did matter who held the reins of power, in society and in government. It was all fine and good for people like me to squander their youth in the pursuit of knowledge and pleasure, but at some point we had to put away childish things and take some responsibility for the state of the world.

In 1976 a bill passed Congress to form Redwood National Park in northern California. I'd never been to California, but I watched the controversy with interest from afar; I had always loved fights, as long as I didn't have to participate directly.

Seems a lot of California timber company loggers got very upset at the notion that the last 2 or 3 percent of virgin redwood groves remaining in the United States might be protected from their chainsaws for all of perpetuity. The loggers, some of whom had mortgages, and the rest of whom paid rent, were understandably distressed at the threat to their livelihood. But they did not think the problem fully through. They fought the park bill tooth and nail, doubtless with encouragement from their employers. They never stopped to think that, given how few old-growth stands of redwoods were left by 1976, chopping down every last one of them would have only postponed the loggers' inevitable job loss by a period of months, or a few years at the max.

I wondered about this a lot. What did they teach those guys in high school up there in Fort Bragg, California, anyway? Anybody with a brain could figure out it was time to start learning how to repair television sets. Or maybe computers, the wave of the future. At any rate, to get out of an industry that was dying.

Well, the loggers cut down an especially big virgin redwood, cleverly carved it into the shape of a Georgia peanut, and trucked it all the way across the continent to Washington, D.C. But President Carter signed the park bill anyway.

I took note that it occasionally did make a big difference which elected official was minding the store. In the 1980s, when I finally got to see those massive redwoods Carter had saved, I realized that the game was often played for some pretty big stakes.

When I was finally finished with law school, I accepted a job with a big firm in San Francisco and refugeed to the West Coast. My ancient Datsun 510 and I crossed the border into California on New Year's Day 1984, and our lives were never the same afterward.

San Francisco was like fairyland to me, no tasteless play on words intended. It was an alien world, and one that had its warts. But it was wonderful nonetheless.

For starters, it took most of the assumptions and preconceptions I had acquired during my life in Texas and turned them on their heads. Where to begin? For the first time in my life I saw that each day, in the weather section of the paper, there was a pollution count listed! Very, very strange; more proof that I had emigrated to Mars.

San Francisco was a Lucullan feast that never ended, for someone of my background. Whatever thing you got interested in, there was more of it in San Francisco than you could ever do. Name your poison: interesting used-book stores that actually *smelled* like book stores; cooking; hiking; artsy-fartsy literature; artsy-fartsy art; New Age thought and pseudothought; environmental politics; city politics; jewelry making; wine and wine tours; film; music; et cetera, et cetera, et cetera. The rule probably held true for sumo wrestling and bondage/domination, though I never checked out those particular areas of interest.

London and New York had the Bay Area beat, hands down, for serious theater, but you could always get cheap plane flights to those cultural ultrameccas, and besides, those towns came with their own drawbacks—such as cold weather, waxed toilet paper, a lack of fresh vegetables in the winter, or gang rapes in the parks.

I had truly studied The Law in the hope of doing something to aid the distressed ecology and environment, but I soon found that all the big firms that paid big salaries to poor graduates with massive federal student loan debts were on The Wrong Side. There was an environmental law group at the firm I eventually joined in San Francisco, but they did most of their work for Exxon. So I decided to cut my losses and specialize in tax and financial planning. I could always give lots of money to worthy environmental organizations, and the ASPCA, too.

By 1985, the year I turned age thirty-three, all the available evidence indicated my love life was not destined to be happy, at least in this incarnation. Heaven knows what awful thing I had done in the previous one to deserve this fate, but it must have been a doozy. I had run from Miles like a true chickenheart. Now I had gotten myself mixed up with two men at once, both of whom were terrible mismatches. One of them only wanted me for a fling, and the other one wanted me to marry him.

The twenty-year-old was this yummy guy spending the summer with my firm as a law clerk. He came from a rather prominent family on the East Coast that thought very well of itself, so my private name for him was John-John. I knew from the beginning that this affair was going to self-destruct come September, because to young Mr. Fine Old Family/ Harvard Law, his time in California was just a sun-drenched summer diversion with a *faux* Farrah Fawcett. At first I thought this arrangement would suit me just fine, because if the affair wasn't going to last, then it meant I didn't have to worry about getting committed. Only thing was, I was getting to the age where I could actually consider the thought of settling down with one guy without breaking into a rash.

John-John was gorgeous. Usually I couldn't stand red-heads, because they were so pasty white and had freckles, but John-John had dark, coppery-red hair and olive skin. Besides that, he was indefatigable in bed, and though relatively untutored, he was most inventive.

I latched onto John-John thanks to an amusing and for-tuitous set of circumstances. At twenty he was the youngest summer clerk at our firm. (Most people don't even get out of college these days until at least twenty-two, often later.) All the women law clerks who were interested in matters social had set their sights on what they considered to be Big Game: midlevel associates, and in one case, a young partner. None of them paid any attention to the kid, lucky for me.

My other fella, Roger the widowed partner who was around sixty, was the nicest old guy I had ever known, but face it, he was slowing down. All that talk about "the more snow on the roof, the more fire in the grate" is just prop-aganda. If I had only had Roger for a boyfriend that sum-mer, I would have been climbing the walls in frustration.

But I figured out during John-John's very first week in San Francisco that he constituted the golden opportunity of a lifetime for summer fun and leisure. He had been let out of the cage of family responsibility for a wee bit, and desperately wanted to make the most of it. For three short months he didn't have to behave. He didn't have to worry if something "just wasn't done." (His imitations of his mother frequently ended in stomach pains—mine—from all the laughter.) He didn't have to worry about the *Social Register.* For once in his life he wanted to have fun and get it all out of his system. And I was there to help.

All summer long we pretended we didn't know each other at work, only to meet afterward at one of San Francisco's thousand and one delightful, obscure ethnic restaurants, or our respective apartments. One time we spent an entire weekend in a rented house right smack on the ocean in Mendocino, and never once left the premises (I had told Roger I was going to work on an article for a scholarly legal journal that weekend.) *Cosmopolitan* magazine would have been so proud of me; and yeah, the whole thing looked so great on paper.

But then John-John went back East to school, there was no one else in my life but Roger, and I found this state of affairs to be grossly unsatisfactory. Of course I was attracted by Roger's secure position in the community, his confidence, his worldliness, and his cushion of investments and savings that insulated him from financial worries. Roger was the sort you could take to the opera, the symphony, or to the finest restaurant in Paris, and hold your head high. But he no longer had the fire of youth.

So, during that September of 1985, I found myself in a period of serious life-force withdrawal. Roger had gotten trained to seeing me only every other weekend (my fault! my fault!), so I had a lot of downtime on my hands.

One lonely Saturday night, just as I was starting a good wallow in my own misery and self-pity, what should turn up on *Showtime* but my old friend Robin Hood! About thirty seconds into the first episode, my hair started standing on end and didn't stop until I had seen the whole series. This production owed nothing to Errol Flynn or any other

early twentieth-century swashbuckler; it bore no resemblance to any other cinematic attempt to capture Robin
Hood. It *had* to be the series that Miles had raved about so
long ago. It was nothing less than Miles's ancient legend
and archetype, brought to life again after the passage of
many centuries.

Miles must have been beside himself with joy whenever
he finally saw it. I almost wondered if Miles, or maybe
Miles's Druid aunt, had had a hand in writing it. It was
riddled with mystical concepts, such as Robin's task being
to hold the powers of light and darkness in balance; I hadn't
seen anything like it since *Star Wars* and all that talk about
the Force. The forest god Herne the Hunter, a.k.a. Cernunnos, was Robin's guide and teacher, and spoke of Robin as
his son. The series had "Green Man" written all over it.

A recurrent pattern in myth is that when a hero falls,
another is raised up to take his place. The first Robin was
dark, brooding, and intense; when he was killed, the second
Robin, called by Herne to take his place, was golden-haired,
boyish, and possessed of remarkable beauty. The first
Robin might have been the spirit of England, fighting for
freedom, but the second one was Luke Skywalker, catching
up the fallen master's light saber and continuing the struggle; he was the brave young successor who, all too often
in the real world, did not appear to carry on the work of a
fallen John Kennedy. He was, simply, Hope.

Hope, this year wearing the guise of the Green Man.

I couldn't stop calling up from memory all the serious
things that Miles and I had discussed that afternoon in London. And now I abruptly found myself living in an era
where the ancient archetypes of Cernunnos and the Green
Man had suddenly returned, alive and kicking, to the cultural consciousness.

Returned? Hell, they even had their own TV show—so
eighties! This was a very small harbinger, but a harbinger
it definitely was. For the first time I began to wonder if I

might be witnessing the beginning of some strange, subtle shift in the wind, that Shakespearean tide in the affairs of men—the sort of thing that would have sent Miles into a frenzy of excitement.

As it developed, my nose was good. Something was definitely afoot, although I would not figure out what it was for years to come.

— PART THREE —

. . . in the sea of life enisled,
With echoing straits between us thrown.
Dotting the shoreless watery wild,
We mortal millions live *alone*.
The islands feel the enclasping flow,
And then their endless bounds they know.

But when the moon their hollows lights,
And they are swept by balms of spring,
And in their glens, on starry night,
The nightingales divinely sing;
And lovely notes, from shore to shore,
Across the sounds and channels pour;

O then a longing like despair
Is to their farthest caverns sent!
For surely once, they feel we were
Parts of a single continent.
Now round us spreads the watery plain—
O might our marges meet again!

Who order'd that their longing's fire
Should be, as soon as kindled, cooled?
Who renders vain their deep desire?—
A God, a God their severance rules;
And bade betwixt their shores to be
The umplumb'd salt, estranging sea.

—Matthew Arnold, "To Marguerite"

A human being is a part of the whole, called by us "universe," a part limited in time and space. He experiences himself, his thoughts and feelings, as something separate from the rest—a kind of optical delusion of his consciousness. This delusion is a kind of prison for us, restricting us to our personal decisions and to affection for a few persons nearest to us. Our task must be to free ourselves from this prison by widening our circle of compassion to embrace all living creatures and the whole of nature in its beauty.

—Albert Einstein

Behold, they are one people and they have all one language; and this is only the beginning of what they will do; and nothing that they propose to do will now be impossible for them. Come, let us go down, and there confuse their language, that they may not understand one another's speech.

—Genesis 11:6–7

ELEVEN

JUNE 23, 2032

GOD HELP ME. LOKI'S VERY SICK. HE'S GOT THE FLU; HE probably caught it on that trip to the black market to get Lyla's morphine.

He locked himself away in the room he and I share at the first sign of illness, hoping he wouldn't give it to the rest of us, though even so it may be too late. There's no telling how long he was contagious before he started feeling bad. I leave food and stuff at his door, and sleep on a couch downstairs. Thank God the plumbing in there is still functioning. When he gets too weak to come to the door and get it, I'll have to go inside and care for him, wearing one of those doctor's face masks that Loki, with great foresight, picked up at Mad Mac's long ago.

I was hoping he just had a stray bug that would go away soon, but Rhiannon found out something on the Net that terrifies me. The authorities always try to keep this sort of thing quiet, because more panic is the last thing we need right now. But when she finally got on the Net last night (there had been an equipment failure), she found out in short order what this Flu Thing is. Understand, she hadn't been on the Net during the last crisis days with Lyla, so she didn't find out about the flu in time to warn the rest of us not to go out, because we might catch it.

It's not what we used to think of as flu season when I

was young, but the viruses don't seem to care anymore. They do what they want, whenever they want. The climate's screwed up, and so masses of people are migrating all over the place and ending up where they have no business being. Viruses mutate, or whatever it is they do, all the time these days.

Here's what Rhiannon found out. There have been a lot of new varieties of swine flu showing up in China and Southeast Asia in recent years, because of the ongoing migrations. New people move through villages, looking for a safe haven somewhere, anywhere, and come in contact with the local pigs. The people are run down and starving, and many of them are sick. Somebody with the flu sneezes, and some of the virus finally ends up sitting next to some swine flu virus already in the porker's gullet. The two viruses exchange DNA, and a star is born—a brand-new genetic combination, never before seen on Earth. The viruses undergo what Rhiannon describes as an antigenic shift—that is, the antigens turn into a form that's entirely new and unique. A human being's immune system has no ''antibody memory'' of this new virus, and so the person essentially has no immunity to it. The result is a pandemic.

This was the process that led to the great flu pandemic in 1918–19. No one remembers it today, of course, although my mother used to talk about it when I was a little girl. Something like twenty million to forty million people died worldwide, and that was when there were a lot fewer people, and transportation between population centers was a lot slower and less frequent. Plus, Rhiannon says that it happened a lot of times in the eighteenth and nineteenth centuries.

It used to be, before everything broke down, that the health authorities could be counted on to monitor Asian hot spots, detect the emergence of a new virus, and quickly prepare a vaccine.

Until about the time I reached sixty, nobody took the flu

very seriously. Each November when I was working at the law firm in San Francisco, we dutifully lined up at work and got our flu shots. We would then complain loudly that the place on our arm where we got the shot felt sore and warm, or that we had a headache and felt giddy, and usually got a free half day off work out of the deal. It was all a big laugh. Nobody ever dreamed of dying from the stuff in his or her lifetime.

Rhiannon says this new flu is popping up all over the West Coast and that it's deadly. I'm very, very frightened.

JUNE 25, 2032

Loki could hardly crawl to the door to get his food and water. He rapped on the door and ordered me to listen to what he had to say. He could barely talk, he was so weak. He told me that if he died, which he was afraid might happen, that he wanted Lorenzo, the strongest of us, to use the mask, drag his body outside to our small landfill, and burn it. He tried to joke that the prospect appealed to the Viking in him, and that it would be a fit way for him to go. I agreed, and then I started sobbing. He told me to stop being such a sentimental woman, that he'd rather have a funeral pyre like Odin than end up as compost for another damn apple tree.

Brave words. I'm afraid I'm going to lose him. And so quickly, without warning. How can this be happening to me?

What will become of the rest of us without him? We can't handle ourselves at Mad Mac's the way he could.

I'm older than he. It's not fair that he should die first and leave me all alone.

JUNE 26, 2032

This morning Loki didn't answer when I knocked on the door. I donned one of the surgical masks, some gloves, and an old robe we could burn, and went inside. None of us is a doctor, and Rhiannon couldn't get an answer over the Net as to whether these precautions would do any good, because the Net is down today. Lately it's been down as much as it was during its early heyday in the 1990s, which is a hell of a goddamn lot.

I went into the room, not knowing what I would find. It was hot and close and smelled sickening, so I opened the windows to air it out. Sometime during the night Loki had apparently thrown up, and soiled himself, too, without being able to get to the bathtub. So he was lying on the bed covered with filth. He'd dragged in his food from the previous day but hadn't touched much of it, so it had spoiled. He was delirious, and hadn't drunk any water at all, that I could tell. I have never had a strong stomach—I would have made a terrible nurse or doctor—and so I went to my chest of drawers and hit my stash of whiskey a couple of times before I could get over my gag reflex.

I went back into the room and mopped up all the stuff on the floor. What I would have given for anything like Lysol, from the old days! Then I removed all of Loki's clothes and stuffed them into an ancient Hefty bag from the basement. I cleaned him off as best I could, having only some precious hoarded paper towels, cheap harsh soap, and water. Then I worked the soiled bedclothes out from under him, put them in the Hefty bag, and handed it all through the door to Rhiannon for burning.

I was so freaked out that I flushed too many paper towels down the toilet and choked it up. Then I started crying, and was on the edge of real hysterics until I dug into my cheap whiskey stash again. Then the tears turned maudlin, and I kept going back and forth to the handbasin for water to try to cool Loki's fever.

We had a few aspirin tablets in the house, and at one point he became halfway lucid and I successfully got him to sit up and swallow a couple, for all the good they would do. He was as hot as if he had been roasting in an oven. He felt very light and frail when I helped him up to swallow the pills. That was when I knew I was going to lose him.

The day was so hot, I sweated like a pig under my mask, and in my gloves, but I didn't dare take them off. Even though opening the windows helped a little, the room still stank, and we had nothing in the house to make it smell better, not even some incense to burn. Air fresheners were a thing of the remote, decadent past.

My own reactions disgust me sometimes. I loved Loki. I knew perfectly well Loki lived in his body, and it was failing him, dying out from under him, and yet I could hardly make myself take care of him, I was so sickened by the smell and the mess and the humiliation that he should come to this, at the end of his life. If there had been anybody I could have paid to clean up the mess, I would have paid that person.

I tried to make him comfortable, but he was probably too far gone to notice. I could see him burning up like a candle before my very eyes. Shortly before midnight he died, without ever having come back to consciousness enough to really recognize me, or for us to say good-bye.

That's the way the world ends. That's the way lives end, with people whimpering, vomiting, and shitting all over themselves.

Rhiannon ordered me out of the room. She made me strip off all my clothes, the gloves, and the mask, and give them to her to be burned. Then she led me forcibly into her room, and stayed with me while Lorenzo, the only able-bodied man left, wrapped Loki's body in plastic and dragged it outside to be burned. His head bumped once on the stairs on the way down, in a macabre way that reminded me of that scene with the dead Yankee in *Gone With the Wind*.

We planned to leave Loki's room open to the not-very-fresh air for several weeks. Rhiannon said she would try to find out on the Net how long before it was safe to live in such a room again, where someone had died from this virus. She brewed me up a sleeping potion that must have had witchy magic in it, in addition to herbs (or maybe she had her own booze hidden somewhere). It put me out and sent me into a long, dreamless sleep. But when I awoke, it was hard to see a reason for going on with life. I stayed in Rhiannon's room for several days, thinking I must have caught the flu, too. But as it turned out, I wasn't sick—I only had a bad case of despair. At length I got up and resumed my chores and duties, because there was nothing else I could do.

TWELVE

1985–89

I FINALLY HAD AN ATTACK OF GUILTY CONSCIENCE, AND cut loose poor Roger, the aging partner. I leveled with him, and told him I wasn't in love with him and couldn't marry him. My life would have been much easier married to a guy with his kind of money, but I wasn't ready to settle for a solid, comfortable, secure relationship yet, much less perpetrate a fraud.

Before I settled for comfort and security, that dreaded fate, I wanted to be madly, passionately in love, the way I could have been with Miles had I not choked at the wrong moment like the sorry piece of chicken poop I was. Even though I was starting to get a tad long in the tooth, at least with respect to the dating meat-market, I hadn't entirely given up hope that my prince would come. There was still plenty of time left, or so I calculated, in which I could choose to capitulate to the ugly realities of life and settle for something less than I really wanted.

Besides, the late eighties were a wonderful time to be young (or relatively young) in San Francisco, with plenty of money to spend. Sure, the country was piling up monetary debts that would come due in the nineties, and was engaged in a whole-hog wrecking of the planetary life support system that would flatten us all starting in about the year 2020, but if you didn't know dipshit about things like that, it was a glorious time to be alive.

The economy was still booming, and the recession of the 1990s was still far off. Every six months we junior attorneys got enormous raises, as our West Coast law firms attempted to keep up with wildly inflating New York salaries.

Whenever we got to interview prospective new associates, the firm encouraged us to take them to the best restaurants—Amelio's, Ernie's, Masa's, Chez Panisse, the Pierre at the Meridian, and Le Trianon. We bought toys. We had the latest computers, cars, compact disc players, cellular phones, and VCRs. We dressed well. We flew to other cities to see our yuppie friends from law school who had joined other firms. We talked business for five minutes, and again chowed down *gratis* on the corporate credit card of yet another hapless law firm. It was pretty obscene, but we were smack in the middle of it and were having a great time. We didn't ever think the pigeons would come home to roost.

However, all good things must come to an end. In early 1989 my years of partying and spending were suddenly and abruptly curtailed. Fate decided to slap me hard. Fate decided that it was finally time for my comeuppance.

In February, Aleta Mahoney (my office buddy and fellow Cosmo Girl) and I got wind of the fact that our firm was going to host a visiting law professor from Beijing for a few months. The guy's name was Li. He not only taught law in Beijing, he was also on some prestigious Chinese board of trade. Since our firm had opened an office in Beijing several years before, and was desperately trying to position itself as a legal powerhouse in the rapidly developing business world of the Pacific Rim, it went for this professor like a trout for the bait. Money was no object; the firm rented a luxurious apartment on Nob Hill for its visiting Eastern dignitary. It provided him with a posh office overlooking the bay and a munificent (if temporary) salary, all in the hopes that he would go back to Beijing absolutely glowing, and tell everybody about us.

Aleta and I had recently seen a rerun of Greta Garbo in *Ninotchka* on cable TV. We thought it would be a real kick to take a humorless Communist and introduce him to the decadence of San Francisco . . . sort of like having a kid and discovering Christmas all over again. Plus, I had really gotten into cooking, and I was dying to see what he would think of all the incomprehensible culinary offerings in San Francisco's Chinatown, and what dishes a genuine native Chinese might prepare from them. So after he'd been at the firm for about a month, we went to see him, certain that he was lonely and neglected and ready for some fun.

Around eleven-thirty one morning, Aleta and I put aside our work and headed up to the luxurious partner-level office on the building's top floor, where they had sequestered the professor.

I composed myself and assumed a respectful air, as would fit one about to pay a call on a distinguished Chinese scholar—most likely an aging scholar, given the length and breadth of his résumé. The door was open, so I stuck my head into the office and saw one of the firm's senior partners in conference with a stranger seated behind a desk.

Thank God I had a moment to recover. This was no graybeard, no drab Communist Party functionary. This was one of the most gorgeous men I had ever seen in my life.

As I watched, he concluded his meeting with the partner, rose, shook hands, and led the other man to the door. His manners were flawless. As was his thousand-dollar fawn-colored Italian suit, which exactly matched his skin, and set off his startling, slanted, cat-green eyes to atrocious advantage. I was certain he was only half Chinese; I was already dying to learn what the other half was.

I barely had the presence of mind to turn to Aleta as she caught up and say, "Dibs. I saw him first. Try to move in and I'll kill you."

Aleta shrugged indulgently, and then got a good look at Li. "That's the Chinaman?" she gasped.

"Don't use that word!" I hissed. "Don't you know it's politically incorrect?"

"Well, I was caught off guard."

We peered inside the office again. In contrast to the visiting professor's person, the room was a bloody mess. There were books, newspapers, and magazines everywhere, on every subject imaginable, as well as mounds of computer printouts and a new fax machine. And a brand-new computer! The firm had a couple of cutting-edge 386-SXs, and from the looks of the machine on our visitor's desk, this was one of them. I was jealous—after all, I was here first.

The senior partner edged past us, giving us a distinctly strange look on his way out, and then there was Li, in our faces, his hand extended, trying to say hello.

It was a rout. Aleta clammed up and left me holding the bag. I mustered as much self-composure as I could (which was not much) and shook Li's hand. "My name is Moira," I said, "and this is Aleta. We are two senior associates with the firm. We came to welcome you to our practice and to invite you to lunch."

"Aleta, Moila," he said, "my name is Li." I almost gasped. All the "flied lice" jokes I'd heard in my life weren't just the product of rampant anti-Chinese racism; the guy couldn't pronounce the letter *r* to save his life, and couldn't say my name right. (However, for sanity's sake, I will mostly continue this narrative as if he could render his *r*'s correctly).

"I would be delighted to have lunch with you," went on Li, undaunted. He glanced at his watch—a real Rolex— and said, "I have no lunch plans scheduled for today. Are you free? If you are, where would you like to go?"

A Rolex, not to mention the Italian suit? The Chinese Commies were funding him big-time. Evidently they did not want him to appear threadbare and materially embarrassed in front of the money-grubbing capitalists of the morally bankrupt West.

I looked to Aleta for help and got absolutely none. "Well, actually," I said, thinking fast, "we had a couple of ideas. The largest Chinese settlement in the United States is only a few blocks from here. We wondered if you would enjoy a visit to Chinatown. Or, there is an amusing new restaurant nearby that is pure San Francisco whimsy. It's called the Fog City Diner."

"The diner, please," replied Li. "To me, such a place would be foreign and unusual. Although another time I would like to see your Chinatown."

"Would you?" I breathed. I could almost hear Aleta making gagging noises behind me, at what a ditsy airhead I was fast becoming. "I've become very interested in cooking since moving to San Francisco," I said to Li, "but I just don't know where to turn in Chinatown, or what to buy, it is all *so* unfamiliar. Perhaps you could help me? Maybe you could give me a tour sometime?"

"I would be delighted," said Li. "Tomorrow, perhaps?"

"Sure!"

"Moira, you said you have moved *to* San Francisco? Where did you live before you moved here?"

"Texas."

"Texas!" exclaimed Li. His eyes fairly glowed. He made a six-shooter from his hand and said, "Bang, bang. Hi-yo, Silver! I have seen films about Texas."

It never fails. Foreign men just love us Texas gals.

At that moment Aleta gave a stagy gasp and clapped her hand to her mouth. "Oh, my God," she said, "I feel *so stupid.* Raynor, the partner, wanted me to sit in on a conference call with him, and it may last through lunch." She glanced at her watch. "Oh, shit, I'm five minutes late! You guys go on without me. We'll go out for drinks sometime this week, I promise."

She took off like a shot. Aleta was a gallant, generous lady. She also knew a lost cause when she saw one.

Li was half French; that was where he got the green eyes. Given how gorgeous he was, his mother must have looked like Catherine Deneuve.

She had been a nurse in French Indochina during the 1940s, before the French rout from what became North Vietnam and South Vietnam. Stationed in Haiphong, she refused to return to France and safety even when hostilities first erupted between the Communist-backed Viet Minh and the French in 1946. The fighting went on until 1954 when, for her humanitarian pains, she got captured by the Commies and thrown in prison.

Apparently her case attracted some international attention, much like that of the female American soldier captured during the Persian Gulf War who it later turned out was molested by the Iraqis. By the time her local jailers had finished with Li's mother, the Chinese—who had backed the rebellion against the French—had some cause for concern. Even the Chinese could be vulnerable to public opinion at times, and the prospect of world attention being devoted to the plight of a beautiful Frenchwoman being assaulted by lots of Viet Minh prison guards was not at all appealing. The Chinese quickly sent a diplomat to Fix Things. In the course of trying to comfort the French-woman, apologize for the humiliations she had suffered at the hands of the Viet Minh, and get her not to make an international incident of it, the diplomat himself fell in love with her, proving that even emissaries of brutal, totalitarian regimes can turn into wild cards given the proper circumstances.

Yes, he was Li's father (since Li was not born until 1957, that much at least was clear). She also fell in love with him, which is understandable, under the circumstances; he certainly was doing a damned good imitation of a knight in shining armor coming to the rescue. For the next year she fought with her government, and he fought with his, and eventually the governments got tired, went away, and let them get married. According to Li, she and his father were still both alive and well, although slowing down, and lived in a nice house in Shanghai.

I went to lunch with Li. And dinner. And lunch again, and dinner again, and then to bed a lot.

We were both good facsimiles of each other's dearest fantasies—that was the deal. He was the Miles I had let get away, but even more foreign and exotic. On my part, I was blond, from Texas, a smart lawyer, and in his book looked like a Hollywood movie star. (Well, so make allowances; check out the Chinese cinema of the period sometime.)

I soon learned that the key to understanding Li was the role his mother had played in educating him and shaping his personal ideology. From his babyhood on, she had filled his head with ideas of what a great country China could be if it ever embraced the 20th century along with the rest of the world. She told him all about the democratic and quasi-democratic nations of the West. Daringly, she invited many intellectuals and scientists to ostensibly "diplomatic" gatherings at her home, so that Li was exposed from boyhood to a remarkable variety of ideas, many of which strayed far from the official party line. Heaven knows how he even got enough of a security clearance to visit San Francisco, but maybe his diplomat father helped balance the score.

When he was a teenager, Li resolved to fit in, be a good boy, and gain his regime's confidence. Then he would get out, see the world, and make up his own mind about everything that mattered.

Having escaped temporarily from his stifling culture, Li enjoyed the freedom of San Francisco with the fervor of a political prisoner who'd just spent twenty years behind bars. He wasn't jaded about anything. Everything he encountered was new and wonderful to him. He wasn't bored, hip, or cynical like all those folks down south in L.A. For him, every day was like Christmas morning. Which made sense. He was spending half a year on a world circling Alpha Centauri; on another planet, you can let yourself flower with impunity.

His office was such a mess, because for the first time in his life he could read anything he wanted. He spent a sizable part of his salary on magazines, especially newsmagazines. He bought a small TV and, with rapt fascination, watched the first months of 1989 roll by, uncensored. The phones worked over here, and that pleased him so much, you'd have thought he'd hit the jackpot at Vegas. He was in love with his fax machine. The first thing he'd do when he was introduced to people was ask them for their fax number, and then send them faxes.

He read voraciously—anything he could get his hands on was fair game. Books on computers, on the development of technology, on international relations, on China (from the perspective of foreigners), and on the environment. Once he wandered into a New Age bookstore and came out with a bunch of books by scientists discussing the nature of God; I couldn't get him to pay any attention to me the entire next weekend.

He read an *awful* lot of stuff about the environment. This really puzzled me. I didn't think the Chinese even knew the meaning of the word ''ecology.''

Americans were certainly starting to pay attention to the environment and its problems, though actually doing something about them was another matter indeed. By 1989 there was growing concern about local environmental problems, such as toxic waste, and global problems, such as the ozone hole over the South Pole.

There was even significant alarm about the prospect of global warming, since 1988 had been a bitch of a hot summer all across the country. However, people who expressed too much concern about the greenhouse effect were still routinely ridiculed, especially by those who had a vested economic interest in ignoring that potential problem.

Either that, or they were labeled "New Age worshipers of Satan" by someone on the religious right, who would then thunder about how it said in the BIBLE, in GENESIS, that mankind had a God-given right to exercise as much dominion over the Earth as he pleased, and anybody who said different was in league with Satan. Or (presuming the speaker could handle multisyllabic words) was an animist tree-worshiper intent on sacrificing people at the altar of environmentalism.

This maneuver worked for a long time. For years it reliably discredited the hapless targets, sidelining them with the UFO folks and the crop circle crowd.

Not until 1995 would the influential U.N. Intergovernmental Panel on Climate Change finally come out and say that the climate was warming and that human activities were responsible for it.

Now, that's where *we* were back in 1989. Where was China in that year? Don't even ask. I simply found it beyond all reason that (a) there could exist such a creature as a Chinese ecowarrior, and (b) I had managed to locate and fall in love with him.

One day I surveyed all the books on ecology in Li's apartment and finally asked, "Why are you so interested in this stuff?"

Li considered. "Because I am a patriot, and China stands to suffer a great environmental crisis in the future."

"Yeah," I said, "but nobody else Chinese I've heard of is particularly concerned about it."

"On the contrary," he hastened to assure me, "many of our scientists are worried about the depletion of resources in China, as well as increasing pollution. They realize that if the global climate were to warm even slightly, our food supply could be devastated. If sea levels rose a couple of feet, countless millions of our people who live in coastal cities and near rivers could be displaced, and die as refugees.''

''You're kidding. They actually realize this?''

''Scientists do, yes. As things are now, every spring floods bring disaster to eastern China. But if the average temperature were to rise even a little, the snows of the Tibet-Qinghai plateau would begin to melt, too. The source of the Yangtze River is in that western region; as the snows melted, water levels would rise along the Yangtze's central and lower reaches, displacing and killing millions more.

I looked at him, nonplussed. ''Well, I am aware that China's been dealing pretty well with its population explosion,'' I said, feeling a mite stupid, ''but in all honesty I've never pictured your scientific establishment lining up to join the Sierra Club.''

''You are correct,'' Li conceded, ''our concern for the ecology is relatively recent. But those of us who are truly educated learn quickly. Surely you know the story about the time Chairman Mao tried to get rid of the sparrows in Beijing?''

''Nope, 'fraid not,'' I said. ''I don't think that one made the *San Francisco Chronicle*.''

''Chairman Mao believed the sparrows were a nuisance to public health. So he asked all the people in the city to take to the streets and bang on woks and pans to frighten the birds. If the birds were forced to stay aloft, they would eventually drop dead of exhaustion. This was done, and many of the birds died. Soon there followed a plague of caterpillars, not only in Beijing, but in the surrounding countryside. They devoured all the crops, enveloped the city's trees with their webs, and rained down upon the people passing by on the sidewalks. So Mao halted the campaign to wipe out the sparrows, a little wiser and sadder.''

''Well, well,'' I said sagely.

''Let me show you something,'' said Li, in his best law school lecture voice. He grabbed a pen and a stray piece of paper and drew a graph with one vertical axis on the left and one horizontal axis at the bottom. He labeled the vertical axis "Money in savings account" and labeled the horizontal axis "Passage of Time." It was marked off at ten-year intervals. He sat back, surveyed his artwork, and looked pleased. "This is how the law of the compounding of interest works in capitalist countries such as the United States. I put in a dollar, and at the end of the year I have a dollar and ten cents. The next year I start with a dollar and ten cents, and that amount compounds."

"Good grief, Li, I know that," I said under my breath, "they teach it in law school." But he was so enthused, he didn't notice the sarcasm in my voice.

He then drew a curved line from left to right, which first tracked the horizontal axis, but soon turned steeply upward and became almost vertical. "Do you see how the increase in the amount of money in my savings account is relatively slow at first, but then the amount begins to rise very quickly, and as we reach the fifth decade, the growth curve has become almost vertical?"

"Li," I replied patiently, "of course I see it. I deal with financial issues every day. I *am* familiar with this concept."

"Of course you are. That is why I chose it. But this curve does not just describe the compounding of interest—it is also an illustration of the principle of exponentiality. Had we not taken drastic measures in China to forestall exponential growth, our population would have mushroomed out of control, and this very year the populace would be facing mass starvation!"

"Ah—I see where you're going," I said.

"This curve applies to many other things as well—to world population, pollution, industrial production, consumption of resources, and production of heat-trapping 'greenhouse gases' such as carbon dioxide. All of these are growing at an exponential rate."

"Since China is trying to industrialize," I said, "surely

the authorities don't want to hear there's a downside to it.''

"Of course they do not. But I cannot stand by when the danger is so great. Moira, a cowardly man might be silent in the face of official disapproval, but a true patriot could not be, even if speaking out cost him his life. Do you not agree?''

Of course I did. "Yes," I said reluctantly.

"China—and the world as well—must act soon if we are to prevent disaster. But the Chinese government does not wish to face facts because, as you say, they have made industrial development into a god. The West does not want to listen, either, because its people are spoiled, and would resist any reduction in their standard of living, no matter what the future cost. Yet don't you see the danger that lies ahead for all of us if these trends are allowed to continue?''

I nodded. "I certainly do. But frankly I don't have a clue how anyone could overcome the kind of opposition you describe!''

"Here is the core of the problem," said Li, slipping back into professorial mode. "When you are dealing with exponential rates of growth, change can occur so swiftly that you can overshoot the limits of stress that your system can bear before you know what has happened to you. You can overload your system to the point of collapse and leave yourself no time to act, simply because at the end of the curve, the rate of growth is breathtakingly swift!''

"Give me a good example," I said. "I do better with examples.''

"Certainly! Consider the balance between food production and population," he replied, not missing a beat. "No matter how advanced our farming techniques may become in China, there will be an ultimate limit to how much food can be produced; the only rational debate concerns where the limit lies, not whether it exists in the first place. If population is allowed to grow at an exponential rate, eventually our food-production system will no longer be able to keep up with the increase." With one forefinger, he tapped the place on his graph where the curve went vertical. "In the twinkling of an eye, you can move from a situation in which people have barely enough to eat, to a state of massive famine. You can move from one situation to another before you have time to prepare because, where the curve turns vertical, the rate of increase is incredibly fast. Then the entire system collapses."

I felt a chill wind at the nape of my neck. I knew any minute I was going to start remembering the English Druid's curse, and the vision I had had of being crushed by a great sarsen stone, so I hurriedly stuffed a lot of mental blankets over the picture.

Not that it did much good. Let me say that Li was beginning to strike me as a man with a mission. I had a feeling he'd keep bringing up this topic for the rest of his visit. I also had a feeling it might be harder to seduce him into staying in America than I'd estimated.

"My mother told me a story when I was a child," Li continued. "It is a riddle that she learned in school in France when she was young. Suppose I have a handsome pond, with attractive plants and many fish. Suppose also that I have a water lily in the pond that *doubles* in size every day. If it ever grows so large that it covers the pond entirely, my fish will die, and all my other plants will be choked out."

"Okay," I said, afraid there was going to be a punch line that would upset me.

"Now pretend that if I don't keep my water lily under control, it will cover the pond in thirty days. Think carefully, Moira: In the early days, there appears to be no problem. Even on the twenty-eighth day, the water lily still only covers one-quarter of the pond. I, who am stupid, still think I have plenty of time in which to act—to correct a problem that I am only now beginning to perceive. But on the twenty-ninth day half the pond is covered, and I suddenly

find myself with only a single day left—the thirtieth day—
in which to save my pond. Because of the rapidity of exponential growth as it approaches a fixed limit, I have in-
advertently let the water lily's growth overshoot the
capacity of the pond and my capacity to act. If I cannot fix
the problem at once—if I need more than a day's lead time
to do what is necessary—I've lost everything.''

He jabbed at the graph with his finger. ''We are subject
to many fixed limits. All the problems I mentioned could
be put on this graph together with the water lily. These
problems are growing exponentially, and if we don't do
something about them, we will suddenly overshoot the capacity of the Earth to sustain us, and we will—what is that
American phrase I heard the other day?—we will 'crash
and burn.' ''

I did feel rather upset; my intuition had been right on.
Only through an effort of will did I refuse to relive my
dream of the great, crushing bulk of the sarsen stone falling
toward me in the pit, blotting out the light, and then my
life.

''Li,'' I replied, ''you wouldn't stand a snowball's
chance in hell in the U.S. Senate selling this scenario, let
alone China. God help you, but nobody anywhere wants to
hear it.''

''It is quite possible,'' Li added with academic thoroughness, ''that this crash-and-burn will occur in our lifetimes.''

''Ugh,'' I said. The U.S. Senate wasn't alone—*I* didn't
want to think about it either. What could I do, anyway?

Shit, I had wanted to get him to go to the Elite Café with
me and try their good Cajun cuisine—especially the black-
ened redfish, which was still pretty trendy, even in 1989,
though it had been even trendier a couple of years earlier.
Now I didn't feel like eating much at all.

''What if we just ordered in some Chinese food?'' I
asked.

Li rolled his eyes and tossed the graph onto a pile of papers. With a deep sigh, he went over to his apartment computer (on loan from the firm), sat down, and began to monkey with it in a desultory fashion. "Sometimes I feel like giving up," he said.

As for me, I felt ashamed of myself. Coward, coward, coward—that was me. I had never been one to man the barricades or get arrested at nuclear power plants. Unfortunately, I had the uncomfortable feeling that any minute I was going to get maneuvered into a position where I had to take a stand on a very unpleasant issue. I didn't like it at all. I didn't want to get involved.

I calmed my fears by promising myself that I would start giving money to Greenpeace. Greenpeace had plenty of people who weren't afraid to be activist, and I had plenty of money. That was what you called complementarity. I could give them money, I wouldn't have to get behind any barricades, and we'd both be better off. "Would you prefer Italian food instead?" I asked Li.

THIRTEEN

JULY 4, 2032: 10:30 P.M.

ON THIS HALLOWED AMERICAN HOLIDAY IT WAS SO deathly hot that during the day we all slept in our extra-deep, insulated basement, which has one tiny, ancient window-unit air conditioner connected to a special vent to the outside, to keep us from cooking like so many tough old chickens in a Crock-Pot. It's horrible to have to use up so much expensive electricity for the air conditioner, but on days like this we have no other choice, and we figure we break even, since no one is upstairs using lights, the computer, and assorted other stuff while they're busy sleeping in the basement.

The thing that really worries us on days like this is whether our crops will survive, even though we grow the most heat-resistant varieties available. We have a carefully constructed drip watering system that wastes as little water as possible, but even so, our water is limited, and on days like this the plants expire it as fast as they can suck it up. The fruit trees fare a little better, thank heavens, since we have a long, hollow, aluminum tube with a pointed end to which we can affix a hose. We drive it into the soil and pump water to the tree's roots way underground.

We rarely even use the house toilets anymore, to save more water. I mean, there is a limit to how many times you can go in a house toilet without flushing; after we had reached that limit a number of times, we realized we had to do something drastic. We bought a chemical toilet for a hefty price from a guy on the Net, but you don't have to flush it, and we calculate that we broke even saving in water costs in about six months.

At 10:30 P.M. it was still boiling hot, but at least the sun had been gone an hour and a half. As usual, Rhiannon, Lorenzo, and I were sitting under the oak with Hillary, contemplating with dread the long night of hard work that lay ahead of us. George was up in the house, fussing over his beloved collection of security apparatuses. He hadn't been very social since Loki had died and he'd literally lost his only close friend.

I was still grieving and traumatized to bloody hell, but I have always tended to reach out to people when I'm hurting, not turn inward, like George. So I wouldn't have missed moping with Lorenzo and Rhiannon and petting my dog for anything.

We didn't talk much, because we were all still pretty shell-shocked. First Lyla, now Loki. We had gradually shouldered the work Lyla had been able to do, but with Loki gone, there were only three able-bodied people left in the commune. We had no idea how we were going to get all the farming done, at our ages.

"Every night since Loki died," remarked Rhiannon, "I've been working magic to bring us help. I don't know what form it will take, but I'm doing my best."

"Well, you'd better hurry," I said sourly. Lorenzo gave me a reproachful look, but I didn't care. Rhiannon was lucky I hadn't said something really caustic about her hocus-pocus bullshit. We were just plain screwed, and that's all there was to it.

"You have to give it time, Moira," she replied.

I started to make a nasty remark about how if things went well, she took the credit, and if they went poorly, she had only to say that her magic needed more time, or better conditions, or more mojo, and she was off the hook. She had it set up so she could never be wrong, or her magic be shown up as bunk. But then I realized I would sound exactly like Lyla, and that shut me up fast.

At that very moment, I thought I saw a flicker of movement across the road, behind some scraggly juniper bushes. I moved my hand slowly and closed my fingers around my gun. "Don't act startled, but I think one of our little friends is across the street."

Lorenzo moved his own hand to his pants pocket and hit the beeper for George. There was another movement, and then something like a long stick of bamboo protruded from the bushes, with a piece of whitish cloth dangling from it. "What the hell?" I whispered.

We sat still as statues for several moments. "It's the universal signal for surrender!" Lorenzo exclaimed.

"Oh, bull. Nobody's under attack except us," I retorted.

"People always used to wave white flags in movies when they wanted to parley," said Rhiannon. She looked thoughtful and then stood up decisively. "I'm going to see what's going on." With that, she started walking toward our gate.

"You get the fuck back here now!" I cried. "If anything happens to you we are finished. Do you hear? Finished!"

"It's all right," said Rhiannon.

"Oh, goddamn it," I said with a hiss, "stop her, Lorenzo!"

He shook his head. "I know better than to try. Besides, I trust her intuition."

"You're idiots, both of you!"

Rhiannon approached the gate, stopped, and waited. Before long a figure emerged from the juniper bushes, still holding the white flag. "It's okay," I heard Rhiannon say. "Come over and talk to me."

The person proved to be a very young man—short and skinny, pale-skinned like a ghost, but wiry. I tried to estimate whether I could plug him from where I was sitting before he did something to Rhiannon. But to my amazement, he came up to the electrified fence, put down the piece of bamboo with the flag, and got down on his knees. He started babbling thanks to Rhiannon, and crying like a five-year-old.

"Told you," Lorenzo said to me.

Rhiannon leaned down and asked him if it would be okay if her friends came over, too. "Yes, ma'am, whatever you say!" he cried.

So we went, me dragging my lower jaw on the ground behind me.

His name was Beto. He had been watching us for a long time, he said, and had figured out that two of us must be sick or have died, because he hadn't spotted them in a long time.

Beto spoke a funny sort of 2030s street patois. It's hard enough for me to understand, let alone to try to faithfully render in a document like this. So I'll just translate; I haven't the patience to deal with it.

"I was hoping you needed help," Beto said, trembling. "I have this girlfriend, Ciel—her name means 'heaven' in Spanish—and she's pregnant. We don't have any place to live, so we hang out in buildings downtown. It is dangerous and she has gotten raped three times. If you will let us come live with you, I will do anything you tell me. I am not very tall, but I can work hard, as hard as all the rest of you put together. I can do business on the street to pay for all the stuff babies need when it's born. Please, let us come stay with you here, where it's safe. You won't be sorry."

Lorenzo and I just stood there with our mouths open. The offer was very attractive, but how could we be sure that he was really on the level?

"My vote is to trust him," said Rhiannon.

At that, Beto threw himself at her lower legs, wrapped his arms around them, and began to cry even more buckets.

"Thank you, ma'am, thank you, thank you," he said. Repeatedly.

It appeared he thought Rhiannon was the boss. Given that she seemed to be the only one capable of making a decision at that point, maybe he was right, and she was in charge.

With a whirring sound, George swept down the path toward us in his wheelchair, his Uzi fully armed and ready. "Stop," said Rhiannon, "everything's okay. Beto is going to come work for us."

"Like hell he is," said George, giving Beto a baleful look. "He's bad news—just look at him."

"No, no!" said Beto. "Please, let me go get my girlfriend. She's almost about to have the baby. If she has it on the streets somebody will kill it. My friend is guarding her, but I've got to get back quick, before he goes off or something."

"George," Rhiannon said firmly, "we need help; here it is."

"Hmmpf," he said. It was clear he didn't like the idea. He glared at Beto a few moments longer. "Go get the girl," he said finally. "There had better not be anybody else with you. I'll open the gates for a second to let you in, but if you've got any friends who plan on coming in with you, I'll mow you all down, including the girl, like so many gooks." He patted the Uzi. "You know what this is?"

Beto nodded. "Good," went on George. "I'm not afraid to use it. I killed plenty of kids like you in Vietnam—not that you have any idea what that was—and I can still do it if I have to."

"Easy, George," I said. The whites of Beto's eyes were showing, literally, and I didn't want the boy to lose it. "Beto, how soon can you be back here? We have a lot of work to do."

"Three hours," he said. "Ciel can't walk so fast."

"We'll be here all night, working. Do take George with

the gun here very seriously. He knows how to use it, and when he thinks he's in the right, he doesn't mind killing people at all.''

Beto nodded, and took off running down the hill, toward Oakland, all the ruined old buildings, and his girlfriend.

"This is an ultimatum," George said when Beto was gone. "If you're going to make it harder for me to do my job, then I need better equipment to do it with."

"Ultimatum?" I retorted. "Sounds like a stickup to me."

George just shrugged. "I've had my eye on this high-powered laser-targeting rifle for some time now. With it, I could hang out on the deck up there and plug anything on this property. You people get your sorry asses in trouble down here, and I won't have to waste time wheeling down from the house to save you."

"How much is it?" I asked.

"A lot. You compromise our security, it's going to cost you."

That was that. I said okay, and he went back to the house to hop on the Net and order his treasure.

The rest of us, we just worked like sons of bitches. We had recently planted collards, turnips, and soybeans, and my task that day was to cull the excess sprouts for a stew we would make just before dawn. Since the plants covered several terraced beds near Aleta's grave, this was a big undertaking for an oldster like me.

We have limited garden space, so we grow only those crops that will give us the highest concentration of nutrients possible per given area of dirt. That means no tomatoes; no lettuce (not that lettuce stands much of a chance these days what with all the blasted heat); and worst of all, no asparagus.

We grow mainly fourteen crops, all selected for efficiency in providing us with critical nutrients in a small space (we only have about a thousand square feet per per-

son, max, of usable garden space to work with): collards,
filbert nuts, garlic, leeks, onions, parsley, parsnips, potatoes,
peanuts, soybeans, sunflowers for seeds, sweet potatoes,
turnips, and wheat. All heat-resistant varieties developed
over the past couple of decades, of course. When we first
set up the commune, we consulted every book we could
get our hands on from the back-to-the-land movement of
the 1960s. One book, in particular, was our gardening bible.
It was called *One Circle* (a title that tickled Rhiannon no
end) and had been published back in 1985 by a group in
Willits, California. Willits was in Mendocino County,
which, along with Humboldt County, was where all the
hippies went (at least those who wanted to remain hippies)
when the sixties were over. It was from this book that we
culled our selection of crops.

We also get a lot of helpful hints over the Net, since
there are communes like ours all over the world these days,
trying to be self-sustaining and get by on practically nothing.

Beto returned right on schedule, with an exhausted,
frightened, and noticeably pregnant girl in tow—I guessed
she was about six months gone. ''Frightened'' is not a
strong enough word, actually. She looked so unnerved that
a single harsh word would send her into a dead faint. I told
George to stand well in the background and keep the Uzi
inconspicuous; I didn't want the girl miscarrying right in
my front yard if she caught sight of it.

George dutifully opened the gate with his remote, allowed the two youngsters to slip inside, and closed it again.
Rhiannon descended on little Ciel like a woman with a
mission.

According to the Wiccan scheme of things, women pass
through three stages in their lives: Maiden, symbolized by
the new moon; Mother, symbolized by the full moon; and
Crone, symbolized by the waning moon. Rhiannon was definitely Crone these days, but she could slip back into

Mother mode like a greased eel threading a pipe. That's definitely what she was doing now. She put her arm around Ciel, hugged her, whispered reassuring little things to her, and patted her tummy to gauge how far along she really was.

I was finally convinced that Beto was for real, and that he truly loved Ciel, by watching his face as he watched Rhiannon baby the girl. In a matter of seconds it became clear he adored our resident witchlet as well. He'd gone down on his knees in front of her during the first encounter, like she was the Virgin Mary or something; heaven alone knew how he might abase himself now, given the chance.

"I'll take Ciel inside and give her a bath," said Rhiannon. "We can put Beto and Ciel in Lyla's old room, if that's okay, Moira—it's nice and private. Ciel, we're going to give you something to eat, and put you to bed for a nice long nap."

She took Ciel, who by now had begun to sob with relief, up the path toward the house. Beto squared his shoulders and stepped forward. "Ma'am," he said, "show me what work to do, and I'll do it. The Lady"—he said the word so reverentially, it deserves to be capitalized—"won't be able to finish the work she was doing just now, so I'm going to do it, and as much more as you can give me."

"Deal, pardner," I said amiably.

"And here," he said, putting a wad of bills into my hand. "This is all I could lay my hands on. It's yours."

I looked down. It wasn't much, but every little bit counted these days. "Thank you, Beto. We'll use it to buy things the baby needs. That's only fair."

He grinned with delight. I set him to weeding out the greens, and made sure he knew to save every one for the morning's stew. Then I sat back and took a much-needed breather.

• • •

The Lady, he'd called Rhiannon. I sure wouldn't forget to tell her about that. She'd expire with delight, I thought, as that was how she referred to her Goddess.

I looked up the path and saw Rhiannon and Ciel go into the house. Feeling on the verge of tears myself, I said a prayer of thanks to whatever God or gods or goddesses might be listening. It could have been just coincidence, Beto dropping into our laps like this, but if Rhiannon's spell-casting weren't responsible for this most blessed turn of events, then coincidence was going our way big-time. Considering that coincidence had not been anybody's friend since the turn of the millennium, I could almost believe we had Rhiannon to thank for our good fortune.

FOURTEEN

APRIL 30, 1989

LI WAS BORED SILLY WITH THE ROUND OF SOCIAL EVENTS
to which the firm subjected him—cocktails at this or that
partner's house in Pacific Heights, a private showing of
Chinese antiquities at the De Young (as if he wanted to
spend his time in California studying things Chinese!), an
afternoon of golf followed by dinner with the boys at the
Olympic Club. So whenever he didn't have his nose buried
in print media, he prevailed on me to escort him to various
funky, nonmainstream parts of San Francisco. Since there
were a lot of those parts back in those days, we were pretty
busy.

We did all the south of Market clubs, even though we
were way too old for that sort of foolishness. We went to
every variety of Latin-American restaurant in the Mission
District. We went to every non-Chinese ethnic restaurant
on Geary and Clement. We got a book and went on a dozen
charming, obscure walking tours of the city that I had never
heard of. We also went to the Condor Club to pay homage
to Carol Doda, who reputedly brought topless dancing to
California on June 19, 1964; Finocchio's to check out the
female impersonators; the "Beach Blanket Babylon" re-
vue; the Museum of Russian Culture, with its framed and
mounted cigarette butt once smoked by Czar Nicholas II;
the Filthy Fortune Cookie Factory in Chinatown; and City

Lights Bookstore and all the postbeatnik espresso joints in
North Beach.

We toured the Castro. Li tried to appear very cool with
respect to all the male couples holding hands and otherwise
engaging in PDAs, but People's Republic Chinese have a
real streak of Puritan in them, and I could tell it was a
struggle for him. He never realized that the local boys (1)
figured him out instantly, and (2) cut him a lot of slack
because he was just a poor, ignorant foreigner. This last
would have enraged Li, since in his heart of hearts he considered *us* to be poor, ignorant foreigners, and himself the
emissary of an ancient and far more noble civilization.

We also spent a lot of time at the public library, where
Li took maximum advantage of our society's free access to
information. He read all the old hippie revolutionary hand-
books from the 1960s. He read books on spycraft, the CIA,
the KGB, police interrogation methods, secret societies,
conspiracy theories, computers, and a lot of stuff on high
finance, paired with true crime narratives dealing with
money laundering. Not to mention a ton of books on
China—as if he were trying to see his country as others
saw it, and thereby learn where it really stood in the global
scheme of things.

Thanks to him, I started learning a lot about China, in
which I had hitherto had little interest. To keep up with
events back home, Li read all the American papers at the
library, and a lot of Chinese papers that he picked up at
international newsstands and in Chinatown.

On April 15, while I was preoccupied with getting my
taxes in, he said, "This is bad news. Hu Yaobang has died
of a heart attack."

"Who?" I asked absently.

"Hu," he said. "Hu Yaobang."

"Who was Hu?"

Li was not the type to go for Stupid Grade School Humor, so I didn't point out to him how silly this conversation was getting.

"He was the General Secretary of the Chinese Communist Party from 1981 until he was deposed in 1987. For comparability, what if I asked you, 'Who was Jimmy Carter?' "

"Okay, sorry. Other than that he's dead, why is it bad news?"

"He was greatly loved by students and reformers. There will be demonstrations in Tiananmen Square."

"You're kidding! That would be the first time, ever!"

Li gave me an exasperated look. It never ceased to amaze him how little Americans knew about the most populous country in the world. "Not at all. Students have demonstrated many times in the Square. On May fourth, 1919, there were massive rallies protesting the portions of the Treaty of Versailles that affected China. In 1976, when Zhou En-lai died, there were demonstrations so fierce that when Deng Xiaoping was blamed for them, he was removed from power."

"But he's back now. Isn't he China's chief leader now?"

"Yes. In fact, he is the one who chose Zhao Ziyang to replace Hu Yaobang as General Secretary in 1987."

"Wait, fill me in on this. I'm lost," I said.

"Certainly. In late 1986 there was a new outbreak of demonstrations in many cities, demanding political reform. Hu Yaobang was accused of being too soft on the students and on bourgeois liberalism, and was forced to resign. That is when Zhao Ziyang became General Secretary, and Li Peng became Premier."

Li continued to monitor the course of this situation in the days that followed, growing more and more worried about it. A week later, students began boycotting classes. Then the government published an editorial condemning them, and students from more than forty universities marched to Beijing's Tiananmen Square, outside the ancient Forbidden City, to protest. The trouble went on, always in the background, always present, always threatening to erupt and spoil Li's day. I wished the students would just sing "Give Peace a Chance" and go home.

I continued to go more and more bonkers over Li. It was an unlikely romance, defying all expectations—but then, those are always the best kind. Though we were worlds apart in any of a hundred ways, our personalities fit like yin and yang where it mattered. Hell, Li was just plain *fun,* even if he does sound prissy now and then when I try to get him down on paper. He was interested and enthusiastic about everything. He did not know the meaning of the verb "to whine." He was smart, but not arrogant; argumentative, but never mean; proud, but not pompous or pretentious.

I finally broached the subject of getting married so Li could stay in the country. He looked like he was going to accept, but then got cold feet and said it would look like he was using me. Then I pointed out that he'd said he had a shitload of dough in Swiss banks, courtesy of his mother's family (who wanted the cash to be available if she or her children ever fled the country and needed cash). So, if we got married, it would look like I was using him, so we were even. I suggested he keep his money, but donate a wad to the ASPCA in my name to show good faith. He was about to write a check, when we both broke up laughing at ourselves and instead agreed to save the cash for a honeymoon in Europe.

Yet it was never meant to be.

Near what would be the end of his visit, we spent a magically beautiful day in the Haight. There had been a pounding rainstorm the night before, which had washed the city clean and blown away every last trace of smog. The sky was achingly blue and bright, the sun golden, the air sweet and fresh and cool—the kind of day we took for granted in 1989 but never have now.

We meandered up and down the main drag, as well as side streets and tiny, quaint alleys, until I was quite lost. By early afternoon we had polished off some sandwiches in a little café and were ambling aimlessly along a sidewalk, no destination in mind, just getting high on the warm sunshine. Suddenly Li caught sight of a thrift shop that had a window full of a lot of American cultural debris. He came to a point like a Labrador and headed straight for it. We were almost there when I turned my head and caught a glimpse of something fascinating.

I found myself peering down a long, dark passageway between two buildings. At the end, glowing in the butterscotch sun, was the most exquisite little garden I had ever seen. "Li! Look here!" I called. I thought he would like to see it, because I had the notion the Chinese were really into gardens.

"In a moment," he replied, sounding hypnotized; the gadgets in the thrift store window had already cast a spell over him.

"No, come look now, just for a second."

With an air that indicated he was being a very good sport, he came over and stood beside me. Then he seemed to forget all about the thrift shop. "I have never yet been able to visit Europe," Li said in a hushed voice, "but this looks like pictures I have seen of Italy and France." He headed straight for the garden.

"Wait, it might be somebody's house!" I cried.

"No, it's not. Didn't you see the sign?"

I craned my neck, and saw I was standing directly beneath a hanging wooden sign. It said, "The Green Man."

I gasped, as if I had received an invigorating electric shock. "Oh, no," I said fervently. "Not him again."

"Is this a nursery for plant material, perhaps?" asked Li, looking puzzled. "What does the name mean?"

"Oh, it's sort of mythological," I muttered. Li strode

forward, all eyes and ears and curiosity, and I followed timidly.

The garden filled an enclosed courtyard that was, at the most, twenty by twenty feet square. I felt myself begin to drink in its beauty. Truly, Li and I had walked across time and space into a sunny corner of Tuscany a hundred years earlier.

The walkways were brick, each set lovingly in place by hand. Beds of flowers and herbs were laid out with elegant simplicity, and since the courtyard was too small for more than a couple of in-ground trees, there were numerous small trees in pots, all apparently very happy. There was a tall, skinny eucalyptus tree with funny rounded leaves that smelled divine when you pinched them, and half a dozen tubs full of little lemons and limes and oranges. A lion's-head fountain was set prominently into one of the stone walls, and it worked. Dotted about the garden, positioned in and around the plants, were copies of ancient Greek and Roman statues. Lastly, there was a huge center planter spilling over with brightly colored Iceland poppies; decorating the side of this planter was an excellent rendition of the Green Man himself, complete with a grimacing face, and an avalanche of carved green leaves for beard and hair. He was either made of concrete, dyed to look a weathered, ancient green, or he was copper, and had been allowed to turn green with age.

"Ah," Li mused, "this must be the Green Man to which the name of the shop refers."

"No kidding," said I.

I heard a faint meowing sound, and looked down to see a beautiful cat with amber eyes and thick, cream-colored fur wrapping itself around my ankles; it seemed very sure of its privileged niche in the universe. I inhaled deeply, and smelled sandalwood incense in addition to the fragrance of the garden. "Is this a shop?" Li asked, sounding puzzled.

"Yes," said a voice nearby. "Would you like to come

in?'' I turned, and saw a man standing in a doorway wreathed with vines.

Li also turned and stared at the guy, open-mouthed. This fellow was as eccentric, as Haight-Ashbury, as it got. He was quite broad and tall, and rather well fed, with a long mane of red hair and a curly, cascading beard; very Ghost-of-Christmas-Present. He had on a billowy dark green blouse, belted around his waist in the best medieval fashion, and sported a breathtaking Celtic knot medallion on a chain.

I pulled a genuine Texas hick-from-the-sticks act and gawked at the guy as if he were a giraffe. Li kept staring at the guy with a fascination so avid that I truly would have grown concerned, had I not been personally certain of Li's sexual preference.

Li gestured to the various growing plants and inquired, ''You are an herbalist, it would seem?''

''Why, yes,'' said the long-haired guy. ''Are you?''

''I have studied the properties of many herbs. I am a visiting professor of law from Beijing.'' Ka-baam! They were off and running. It was soul mate city. I hadn't known until then that Li was into herbs, but when I thought about it, herbs were a very Chinese thing to be into.

They fussed over this plant, then that, and compared notes every step of the way. The shop owner would explain the attributes of a particular herb—medicinal, culinary, astrological, you name it—and then hang on Li's every word as Li imparted to him any and all sagely Chinese wisdom he possessed on the subject.

By the look of it, they would need half an hour just to get through the stuff growing in the garden. When I stuck my head into the shop and saw jars upon jars of dried herbs, I knew I was in for the long haul. Once Li got really interested in something, there was no tearing him away.

So I had the interior of the shop to myself, and time on

my hands to poke around. It was quite dark. Some light
came in through a lovely stained-glass window that bore
the words "The Green Man." It was embellished with an
intricate design with lots of leaves and flowers that the sun
set ablaze with color.

Other than that, oddly, there was no light in the tiny
shop, except for a candle burning in a far corner, in front
of a curious assortment of statues: a Buddha, a graceful
Quan-Yin, a bust of Apollo, a rather fierce Indian repro-
duction of Kali, an Egyptian cat with an earring in one ear,
and a small Virgin of Guadalupe, like you could get all
over the place in the Mission District. An altar? I wondered.
If so, it was a very eclectic one.

The shop was exceedingly quiet and peaceful. There was
no radio playing in the background, in fact, no taped music
of any kind—not even that repetitious soothing stuff you
always heard in New Age shops. Instead, on the far side
of the shop, there was a stand with a large ceramic bowl
full of plants and large rocks over which water burbled, no
doubt with the help of an aquarium pump.

I felt myself beginning to relax. That accomplished, I
began to snoop around. Of course, I made a beeline for a
big jewelry display case in the middle of the shop. Once
there, I gazed in fascination at the goodies I saw inside.
The guy must have been on the wholesale buyers' list of
every manufacturer on the planet that made museum repro-
ductions.

Most of the jewelry was designed to be worn around the
neck as a pendant. There was a silver replica of the Aztec
god Quetzalcoatl. (All right, coming from southern Texas,
I knew about him, okay?) There was a replica in brass of
the Celtic god Cernunnos, from the famous Gundestrup
Cauldron, that I would have sent anonymously to Miles, if
I'd only known where he lived. There was an exquisite
silver copy of the little snake goddess from ancient Minoan
Crete, which I recognized, having had a few courses in

women's studies back at the University of Texas.

In another corner of the shop I saw the guy had taken a big branch of manzanita—that western tree with rich, dark red wood as smooth as jade to the touch—and festooned it with all sorts of fascinating decorations made from nature, such as dried flowers and many tiny shells, each suspended by a silken thread. There was even an abalone shell the size of your thumbnail. He had air plants, mistletoe, Spanish moss, dried berries, some few blue jay and peacock feathers, tiny bright beads and glass Czech crystals, a bit of amber and carved jet beads, and a little leather pouch holding frankincense or myrrh.

While I was admiring the display, a woman emerged from the back of the shop and said hello in a most pleasant fashion. I smiled and tried not to stare, which was hard since just the sight of her took me right back to my carefree hippie days in Austin.

She was fair-haired, freckled, pleasingly plump, and wore her hair coiled and pinned up in a big fat braid on the back of her head. Her long, flowing dress was made from one of those cool Indian-print bedspreads like you used to get at Pier 1 Imports back in the 1960s. On her left hip she balanced a chubby, red-haired baby.

One look at her, and I was certain this woman baked all her own bread. People always asked what had happened to the hippies, and while I couldn't speak for all of them, a few had clearly remained in the Haight and turned into Earth Mothers.

''Can I help you find anything?'' she asked.

''Oh, no, thanks,'' I said. ''I'm here with a friend. He's talking to the guy out there about herbs.''

''Oh, wow,'' she said, her tone implying they would be at it for a long time. I saw her go up to the two men, greet Li, and speak briefly to the red-haired guy. Then she gave him a light peck on the cheek and took off briskly, as if to do an errand.

Awww . . . I thought. How cute.

Still, the boys would not come in from play. I retraced my steps to the doorway of the shop and positioned myself in the vicinity of Li's left elbow. He reached over, squeezed my hand absently, and kept right on with the conversation.

Oh, Lordy, I said to myself. They had graduated from herbs and appeared to be discussing one of Li's most passionate interests, the environment.

"The rainstorm last night really damaged my poppies." The shop owner was speaking. He cast a woeful glance at his garden and sighed. "Their petals are so delicate . . . most of them were just beaten into the dirt."

Li considered, every inch the meticulous Chinese scholar. "Over the past ten years, then," he asked, as if he were a doctor examining a patient, "would you say the weather here has become more unpredictable?"

My ears pricked up. Where was this conversation headed?

The shop owner gave the question serious thought. "Most definitely. They're saying that last summer, 1988, was one of the hottest in our country's history," he replied. "We appear to be starting a drought here in California, yet when the few rains do come, they're ferocious. They used to begin in November and continue through March, but they were gentle. Now—it's as if the weather has gone mad."

I'd often wondered if I were telepathic, or psychic, or clairvoyant, or had a sixth sense, or something weird like that. For some reason, when I heard the red-haired guy say that, I felt really creepy—as if someone had walked over my grave.

"This disruption," said Li, "it makes you angry?" That question really puzzled me. Why would Li be so interested in this guy's emotional reaction to the weather?

"Very! Some people say that we will end by destroying the balance of nature; I'm afraid they may be right."

Li didn't miss a beat. "The weather patterns you describe seem consistent with the climate change predictions made by certain Chinese scientists who have modeled the effects of projected increases in atmospheric greenhouse gases."

The shop owner looked astonished. "Your scientists have access to such information? They know of the greenhouse effect?"

For a moment, Li looked just a mite condescending. "Oh, yes. A nation's scientists must have access to reliable information, if they and their government are not to be embarrassed in front of the global scientific community. My government simply does not make that information available to everyone."

"I see," replied the other man. "My apologies. Tell me, can you do anything to influence your government?"

"No, Arthur," replied Li. So they were already on a first-name basis! "Can *you* do anything—American though you are?"

"I do what I can to make a difference when the opportunity presents itself, no matter how small it may be. A group I belong to attempts to use magic and weatherworking to alter probabilities and affect the flow of random events. But the tide is not yet with us, and any impact we have is as yet very small. You see, people are very much afraid of facing the idea that we may be in the process of altering the climate of our planet. They don't want to think about it. If forced to do so, they often respond with ferocious hostility and ridicule."

Hearing this speech, my eyebrows arched higher and higher, until they were in danger of nudging my attractive Farrahesque hairline. But Li didn't appear in the least perturbed. He looked about, and waved a hand to include the garden, the shop, and the cat, which was now sacked out on a stone bench in the sun. "Let me ask you a question: All this—why do you love it so?"

Arthur appeared quite startled. "I don't know what you mean," he said. "I have always had a garden and kept animals."

"Why?" asked Li. "Did anyone teach you to value them?"

"No," he said uncertainly.

"Can you remember a time when you did not value them?

"No," said Arthur, and gave a hesitant laugh.

Li lowered his voice confidentially and said, "When I was a boy I spent a summer studying at a Tibetan monastery. As the son of a diplomat, you see, I had access to certain unusual and fortunate opportunities. The monks there embraced what I would describe as a veneer of modern Buddhism, overlaid upon a much older spiritual tradition—one that, like yours, emphasized magical practice and ritual, as well as what you Westerners would call shamanism. Perhaps it is a coincidence, but those monks also had a passionate love of the natural world, which they imparted to me—"

"I have studied shamanism also, following a Native American path," Arthur broke in.

"You see," said Li, with a note of triumph in his voice, "there is a pattern here. You and I speak a common language, though we are strangers. We share that language with the monks, whom you have never met, as we surely do with thousands of others, scattered across the Earth. This is a curious brotherhood, you must agree. What is its nature, and where does it come from?"

Arthur appeared to think furiously. "I read an essay once, by a writer drawing upon a poem by Lord Byron, 'The Isles of Greece.' "

"I am not familiar with that poem, though I have read Byron and all the great English poets," replied Li.

Arthur knit his brow, and I could practically hear the gears grinding inside his head. "Ha!" he said. "It goes like this:

> 'Earth! Render back from out thy breast
> A remnant of our Spartan dead.
> Of the three hundred grant but three,
> To make a new Thermopylae!' "

"Ah," said Li, "I understand the classical references."

"Anyway," Arthur went on, "the essay proposed that in every era, there exists a 'saving remnant'—a few people on whom falls the responsibility of rescuing civilization in times of peril. Could that be your brotherhood?"

Li regarded him intently. "Perhaps. One thing is clear enough, though: If only a few scientists can see what lies ahead, we are doomed. Everyone must come to realize the danger we are in. Everyone in the boat must row together, or we are done for."

Arthur nodded. "As we Americans say, 'We're all in this together.' We are all connected, we are all part of one another, and part of the web of life on Earth. Yet so many people don't seem to get it. I'll never understand why; it seems perfectly obvious to me."

"During my time in America I have read books of poetry, literature, and religion," Li stated, nodding. "The Englishman John Donne wrote, 'No man is an island.' "

"That line is quite famous," Arthur replied. "Poets and mystics have always said that sort of thing. From time to time it has seemed to me that perhaps the insight is spreading. After all, next year will be the twentieth anniversary of the first Earth Day. But barring a miracle, I'm afraid that most of mankind won't catch on about the danger we're in until it's too late."

He fell silent, probably because Li was regarding him with a ferociously curious look. Li murmured, "Perhaps the task of your saving remnant is to make everyone aware of the danger we are in—to make everyone feel it as you feel it.'' He grinned. ''Now if only someone could just wave a magic wand and make it so.''

''Magic can assist the process,'' said Arthur, quite serious, ''but much more is needed. Perhaps if enough warnings were shown on television here in the West, people would start to awaken.''

''Television?'' exclaimed Li.

''Oh, yes! Years ago, young Americans protested the Vietnam War and put an end to it. Do you know why they were able to do so? Because the rest of the nation saw the war in all its horror on television. Television brought the war into their living rooms, and they didn't like what they saw one bit. If it's the year 1914 and World War I is starting on the other side of the globe, that atrocity is easier to ignore than if the year is 1968 and you see Vietnamese children being napalmed while you're eating your dinner. Television can draw us together—artificially—and give us a heightened consciousness of our place in the world, and our relationship to each other.''

Li looked intrigued, and Arthur hurried to hammer his point home. ''Here's another example. On that night back in 1969 when the American astronauts first landed on the moon, some huge percentage of the Earth's population watched it happen on television. The whole world came to a standstill and held its breath as human beings achieved the impossible. And do you know what else happened? All over the world, wherever the television images could penetrate, the crime rate dropped. People were too caught up in wonder, in oneness, to go out and commit as many crimes as usual.''

''The next night the crime rate went back to normal, did it not?'' asked Li.

''I'm sure it did. But if you can bring about a temporary

change in the behavior of humanity, you have taken the first step toward making a permanent one.''

Li clasped his hands together. ''Yes!'' he said. ''Television. That's how it could begin.''

''How what could begin?''

Li gave another grin and said, ''The 'great leap forward' that we need.''

Arthur picked up on the Chinese irony and laughed uproariously.

''Television would be of little help in China or the Soviet Union, where it is controlled by the state. However, I have learned how to use the fax machine in my office,'' Li went on, all serious again. ''My standing within the party is such that I could easily get access to a fax machine in China. Just think, in a matter of an instant, I could communicate with anyone in the United States. The fax machine is a very powerful tool; it, too, could be a beginning.''

Arthur chuckled. ''Oh, forget faxes! You need to get on the Internet, my friend, through one of your universities, or a scientific institution.''

Li paused. ''I have heard much whispering about this Intelnet back home,'' he said, watching Arthur like a hawk. ''However, access to it is limited to government officials, and to the privileged students and faculty of some universities. In any case, no one but the younger students knows how to use it. Tell me what you know.''

I practically collapsed with giggles. Because Li really did pronounce his *r*'s as *l*'s, he had just made a great pun. Yet he had no idea what he'd even said! Given Intel's prominence in the microchip industry, he had pretty accurately described the larval Net.

''Gladly,'' replied Arthur. In spite of all his flower-growing, he seemed to be quite the technophile. ''Imagine a network of telephone lines that links most places on the Earth. Now imagine thousands of computers hooked into those phone lines, further linking the world together. That's the Internet.''

''I see,'' said Li. ''How is it better than a fax machine?''

Arthur looked very pleased with himself. ''I can't possibly tell you. You'll just have to experience it for yourself. Surely your friend here can arrange a session for you—perhaps at the University of California, over in Berkeley. You cannot imagine what it is like, Li. You can talk to anyone in the world, whenever you want, just by sitting down at a keyboard. You compose written messages before you get 'on-line,' as it is called. When you send them, transmission is practically instantaneous, and—this is the beauty of it—the cost is next to nothing.''

''Would a man using the Net be less obvious to a Party spy in the office than a man sending a fax?'' asked Li. I could fairly see the wheels turning in his head.

''Probably,'' replied Arthur. ''But here's the important part. I just read a statement by one of the original architects of the Internet that I can't get out of my mind. The man said, 'The Internet may alter what it is to be human more than any technological development since the capture of fire.' I think he knew what he was talking about. Suppose for a moment that the Earth were alive. Each telephone line would be like a separate neuron, and all of them together would be something like a giant planetary brain. Perhaps one day, because of this evolving network, we will be able to leapfrog over our current primitive stage in evolution, and the peoples of the Earth will be one.''

Li was silent for a very long time. As last he said, his voice full of conviction, ''Perhaps that is the analogy I need. However, I have serious doubts. You assume, Arthur, that if most of mankind was linked together by this Net, men would come together and act as one—permanently. They would grow to value another's welfare as if it were their own. You assume that the Net would destroy selfishness and make violence next to impossible—whether it be

directed against other men, or against the Earth. But I fear
you are wrong."

"Why?" asked Arthur.

"The early Marxists tried to build a society to which
each man would contribute according to his means and abilities, and from which each man would take according to
his needs. It was assumed that once a political system was
established that told men the right thing to do, THEY
WOULD DO IT. But they did not. These early Marxists
were great dreamers but great fools. You, too, are assuming
that once men are made to *see* what is right, they will do
it. I fear that men are so flawed, mere knowledge of the
truth is insufficient to result in lasting change. More is
needed."

"Such as what?"

"I don't know—yet. Perhaps they must be enabled to
feel it, as you say, 'in the gut.' "

"How would you possibly accomplish that?"

Li shrugged. "Perhaps it would make more sense to
scrap the present version of mankind and start over, as any
good engineer would do when a machine is too poorly designed to be reclaimed."

"Well," Arthur said after a long pause, "I hope you are
wrong, with all my heart."

I went back into the shop, wanting a moment of peace
and quiet to absorb what I had heard. So I started to devote
my attention to the selection of books and pamphlets that
the shop offered. The shop had literature from all over the
place. There was the *Green Egg,* a journal out of Ukiah,
California. The *Pagan Muse and World Report,* published
in Mountain View—just to the south of us, in Silicon
Valley. Apparently the title of the latter was a play on *U.S.
News & World Report.*

"Aaargh," I said under my breath. I picked up a copy
of *Magical Blend,* a slick magazine featuring far-out articles by some pretty major writers. Oddly, it was published

in Chico, an undistinguished town whose local cuisine reputedly emphasized those two unique American foodstuffs, Velveeta and Spam.

I found a book called *Drawing Down the Moon,* about modern paganism in America, by one Margot Adler. She proved to be the granddaughter of the great psychologist and contemporary of Freud, Alfred Adler. Next to it was an intriguing pamphlet titled *Neo-Paganism and the Race to Save the Earth.* Lastly, there was the Reclaiming Newsletter, out of Marin County, whose guiding light appeared to be a woman of high moral principle who was devoted to saving the environment. She advocated taking a sack when you went to the beach or the park and picking up some of the trash. You couldn't pick it all up, but by picking up what you could, you made a statement and a teensy change in the state of the world. She was named Starhawk and referred to herself as a witch.

Slowly it percolated through the limestone layers of my Central Texas aquifer brain that the writers of all this literature, not to mention the red-haired store owner and his lady, were not just eccentric—they were also pagans, like Miles's aunt.

The question logically followed, What brand of pagans? You could read all about them in the press these days. Eco-pagans? Techno-pagans? Druids? Witches? New Age crystal-rubbers, perhaps? I wished Miles were there to help.

I allowed myself to wonder briefly whether I would find dead animal bodies if I poked around in the back of the shop while the guys yakked on. But I couldn't get too worked up over the possibility. I recalled the cream-colored cat outside; the last thing on that fatty's mind had been concern over any imminent dedication to the powers of darkness. Plus, I couldn't quite visualize the guy who was busy pissing and moaning to Li over his battered garden and spouting John Lennon-type philosophies taking a sacrificial knife to the cat. Maybe to one of those ridiculously expensive jewel boxes of Sheba cat food, if the can opener wasn't working—I could tell he spoiled that imperious feline—but that was the extent of it.

My brain befogged from a tad too much new input, I sat down cross-legged on the floor and resolved (a) not to be judgmental and (b) to wait patiently for Li to rescue me.

Li didn't come. But before long, the cat did. It spotted me and sauntered over for a nice, long, sensual petting session.

We were still so ensconced when Li and Arthur came into the shop. "I want to show you this book," he said to Li, and shot me a look of concern, as if to ask, "How are you bearing up, civilian?"

"Nice cat!" I exclaimed nervously, teeth flashing in my best Texas prom-queen manner. I stroked the cat's fur so hard it growled in protest. "He's a lovely cat. So sweet, so companionable. Where did you get him?"

"This is Moira," said Li.

I grinned again, hysterically. "Hi!"

"A lovely name," said Arthur, "with so many resonances." He regarded the cat solemnly. "Her name is Astarte," he said, subtly informing me of my mistake in gender. "I found her abandoned in an alley and adopted her."

"How nice!" I exclaimed, again showing too many teeth. "That was very kind of you."

"Here's that book I mentioned," Arthur said to Li. He burrowed into a shelf beneath the cash register. "*The State of the World, 1989.* I think you will find this very useful in your research."

Li accepted the book as if it were made of solid gold.

"Take it," said Arthur. "I can get another. And get Moira to show you some of the used-book stores around here. You'll find many more books like that. After she's through introducing you to the Internet, of course."

Clearly, I had just been drafted.

"Thank you," Li replied. He asked me, "Are you ready to go?"

Was I ever. "Sure!" I piped, at my perky best.

"I am very grateful," Li said to Arthur. They shook hands.

"Excuse me," I said, breaking into the otherwise jade-smooth flow of their good-byes. I had to say speak up, or a golden opportunity was going to slip away forever. "I want to ask Arthur a question. I know this is going to sound really stupid, but I don't know anybody else to ask."

"Okay," said Arthur.

My heart in my mouth, I said, "Ummm—I've only met a few pagans in my life. You, and a bunch of people I met at a Druid ceremony near Stonehenge in England back in 1977. Long story, actually. Anyway, pagans get a lot of bad press. If people think about them at all, they think they're Satanists. On the other hand, based on the Druids I met, and you, and the literature on your bookshelf over there, pagans seem to be pretty okay people who are really into nature and environmental protection. I guess what I'm asking is, are most of you really like that?"

I thought that if Arthur burst out laughing, I would die of mortification. He didn't, though. While I sensed a hint of amusement in his voice, he replied to my question very seriously. "You want the whole lecture?"

"Uh, sure, okay," I said. Uh-oh, I really meant.

"I can't speak for other pagans, but I can certainly give you my opinion. There are probably as many different pagan paths as there are Christian sects, but I would say most of them incorporate a special reverence for the Earth. As far as being okay people, well, a group of pagans is going to be like any church congregation you might care to pick. It will include plenty of good folks, but it will also have its contingent of screwed-up kids, screwed-up adults, ego-tistical assholes, needy, unhappy people, power politickers, and in-groups and out-groups."

He paused, and I saw an opportunity to get in another good one. "Are Satanists considered pagans?"

He did laugh then. "Ask three pagans and you'll get four answers. There is usually an ongoing debate in the pagan community about just that question. What makes it so funny is that we don't believe in a Satan to start with. He's really a Christian invention—so we're arguing over whether to include as 'pagans' people who may believe in something we don't even think exists.

"Also, it's not that clear whether Satanists exist. Depending on how you define the term, they either do or they don't. For example, there are guys out there who read LaVey's *Satanic Bible*. Or who run around turning their crosses and pentacles upside down and putting on bad theater they call black masses. But apparently they're so wrapped up in rebelling against Christianity, they're practically Christian themselves. I don't spend my time rebelling against Christianity. It's another valid spiritual path that many hold dear, so why on Earth should I put it down? So—whatever those guys call themselves, are they really Satanists? Who knows?

"Then there are others whose main belief seems to be that all human action stems from self-interest. They believe it's okay to further their self-interest whenever possible but, while having no set moral code, acknowledge that others also have a right to further their own self-interest. 'Do what thou wilt' is their motto. They're often passionately opposed to restrictions on personal rights and the freedom of the individual."

"Wait a minute," I said. "They sound like Libertarians."

Arthur laughed. "I wouldn't be surprised if some of them considered themselves Libertarians, or agree with the party on social issues. They're very eighties people—depending on how they dressed, they'd fit right in on Wall

Street. Robert Ringer, *Looking Out for Number One,* you know. Michael Douglas, greed is good.''

''Sheesh,'' I replied.

''Here, this will blow your mind. Somebody pointed out the 'Nine Satanic Statements' in LaVey's *Satanic Bible* to me once and asked me if they looked familiar. How well read are you?''

''Well enough.''

''Listen to this: 'indulgence, not abstinence; vital existence; kindness to those who deserve it, not love wasted on ingrates; vengeance instead of turning the cheek; responsibility to the responsible, not concern for psychic vampires; man is just another animal, sometimes better and sometimes worse than the others; and so-called sins all lead to gratification.''

''That's only seven,'' I objected.

''So, I forget the rest. Do they ring any bells?''

''Yeah.'' Right then I felt like a very slow 286 computer with an overstuffed hard drive. Where, oh, where had I read something like that? ''Wait a damn minute!'' I finally exclaimed. ''That's straight out of *Atlas Shrugged.* He ripped it off!''

Arthur grinned. ''Actually, it's said LaVey 'condensed' the nine statements from Ayn Rand.''

''Oh, for crying out loud!''

''Anyway, to wind up, as with any group of people you could name, there are always a few disturbed people running around calling themselves Satanists or whatever. You know, your basic sadist or fucked-up kid—like the boy in the paper recently who really just wants to torture cats, but says he's a Satanist because he wants an excuse, and knows it will shock his parents even more; or the nut down in the Texas Rio Grande Valley who kills a college student, and then says he did it because he was into Santeria.''

''I've heard of Santeros!'' I said. ''See, I'm originally from Texas. They sacrifice chickens by cutting their throats and draining the blood for their rituals. It's been documented.''

''Yes, so I'm told.'' He nodded. ''I'm not a Santero, but I do have to point one thing out. According to what I've heard, the chicken is not tortured, but killed quickly. It is then roasted and eaten for dinner after the 'service.' Do you eat chicken?''

''Uh, yeah,'' I said. ''I do.'' Before he could nail me, I added, ''Only I get Foster Farms to do my dirty work for me.''

He grinned. ''Anyway, the question still is, Do Satanists exist? Well, if there were an all-powerful evil superbeing, I doubt he'd have a lot of followers. Hanging out with him strikes me as a real good way to end up dead. So if that's how you define Satan, there probably aren't many real Satanists. Does that answer your question?''

Whew! Was he long-winded! ''Yeah, you sure did.''

''I'm glad,'' Arthur replied. Somehow I got the feeling he'd given this speech before.

''We'll say good-bye, then,'' said Li, and they shook hands.

''Blessed be,'' replied Arthur.

I steered Li back onto Haight Street and into the very first sidewalk café we found. There we reached a mutual agreement that an onion tart and a whole bottle of Cakebread Sauvignon Blanc to split between us was in order. For a while we ate and drank in companionable silence. I was still trying to sort everything out.

At first I thought it was great that pagans were so concerned about the environment. Somebody had to be. However, an unpleasant realization gradually began to settle over me, like a gray blanket of smog. The more I thought about it, the more depressed I got.

Say the word ''pagan,'' or even better, ''witch,'' and

your average sound-bite-educated Joe would immediately
get a mental picture of a hideous old woman with sickly
green skin, a wart on her nose, and bad teeth. Or a gorgeous
bimbo babe like Elvira, Mistress of the Dark, down in L.A.
Or a certified kook.

It was all fine and good that pagans were among the first
to rush to the environment's defense, but if environmentalism got to be perceived as a favorite pagan cause, it
would suffer a major black eye PR-wise. There were plenty
of Darth Vaders around who could be counted on to make
the most of that black eye.

Li and Arthur were right: Everybody needed to get into
the boat and row together. Pagans, the Rotarians, the 4-H
Club, the Girl Scouts, you name it. The churches had to
stop fussing over matters that weren't of life-and-death importance. Congress had to stop spending all its time on
things that were relatively low on the survival priority list.
Otherwise nothing was going to happen.

I became aware of Li's fingers on my arm, shaking me
to get my attention. He asked, "Here is the question I cannot answer. Let us say that I believe that all men are brothers. And that I have always seen myself as a part of the
whole of creation—along with the trees, the air, the other
animals, and the Earth under my feet." He paused, and
gestured with his hand to include everything around us. "It
is as obvious to me as the fact that I possess five fingers.
It is so obvious that I never question it. My studies have
told me that mystics and religious teachers have believed
much the same thing since the beginning of recorded history. Yet so many people do not perceive the world in the
same way I do, I cannot explain it! Their perception is alien
to mine. Why, it is as if I can see a color they cannot! Why,
Moira—why is this so?"

I shrugged. "Solve that question," I said, "and all our
problems will be over. One guy goes into a redwood forest

and sees the handiwork of God. Another goes in and just sees board feet!''

''Surely there is an answer somewhere!''

I thought hard. I really tried—I racked my brain to come up with something that would help. But I was too tired and jaded.

Then it happened. You can take the girl out of Texas, but not Texas out of the girl. The significant quantity of wine I had just consumed must have affected my thought processes, not to mention my judgment, because I suddenly began to remember bits and pieces of conversations I had overheard as a kid, and I began to giggle helplessly. I was, as we used to say in high school, simpled.

''If they're color-blind, it must be genetic.''

Li gave me a stern look, as if to remind me we were having a serious conversation. I didn't care. ''My mother's people, back in East Texas, thought family accounted for a lot of the way folks behaved,'' I informed Li. '' 'The Cunninghams are all crooked as a dog's hind leg,' they'd say. Or, 'Everybody in the Gribble family tipples, it's in the blood.' Or, 'The Walkers all have a mean streak a half mile wide.' They thought everything had to do with family. It's gotta be genetics, Li.''

Li stared at me, speechless, for an extended period of time. I thought he was angry that I had been so flippant with one of his precious ideas, and I began to get defensive. ''Oh, chill out,'' I said with a growl. ''I was just fooling around.''

''There is a gene in mice that controls nurturing behavior,'' he said, a faraway tone in his voice. ''If the gene mutates and becomes disabled, the mice will actually sit by idly while their young starve to death. If something caused this mutation to occur in a large number of mice, the species would die out very quickly.''

I stopped laughing. ''Where did you hear this?''

''I read it in a scientific magazine just the other day,''

Li replied. "So the question is this. Let us say I perceive that 'all is one.' I perceive myself as a small piece of creation, made of the same building blocks as the trees, the animals, the birds and the fish. As I *am*. Your 'Woodstock' song is right, Moira: We are stardust. We are billion-year-old carbon. Everything on Earth is made of the stuff of exploding stars."

"Yeah," I said, "that's right on."

"Do I possess a mutated gene that is relatively new to the human race, which allows me to be one of the first to perceive that truth, that strange color that others cannot see? Or do I possess an older gene that has somehow escaped a disabling mutation—a mutation that clouds perception and causes a sort of spiritual blindness?"

I just looked at him with my mouth wide open. He was as serious about this as it got. "You're saying you think we have a cussedness gene?" I said at last.

"Either that, or a benign 'perceptual gene' that has been damaged."

"That would explain a lot of the variation in human behavior. People who have the right gene and are exposed to an environment that nurtures it turn out like Mother Teresa. People who don't have the right gene or the right environment are like James Watt."

"Who's that?"

"Ah-ha, there is something you don't know! He was Secretary of the Interior under Reagan. He once said, 'If the troubles from environmentalists cannot be solved in the jury box or at the ballot box, perhaps the cartridge box should be used.' "

"Cartridge box?"

I made a pistol with my hand and said, "Bam bam bam!"

Li shuddered. "Moira, how long will it be until your scientists have completed that Human Genome Project?"

"I haven't the faintest idea."

"Oh, never mind," he said with a wave of his hand. "It should be simple enough to find out. Moira, this is very important: I must see the Intelnet with my own eyes."

"I'll do what I can to help. Several guys at work have relatives who are at Cal, either students or professors. It shouldn't be hard to scare up somebody who can help."

"I have read that the Intelnet was invented by persons in your defense program," Li went on, "and designed so it could not be controlled by any one person. This is a revolutionary idea! It may truly be one of the important pieces of the puzzle."

I felt icy little fingers on the back of my neck as my woman's intuition kicked into high gear, and something began to dawn on me. I was starting to understand a lot about my strange new boyfriend. He very likely was a spy—as it was turning out—but his goal wasn't to overthrow *my* government.

"Arthur's basic idea is correct," Li went on. "If he were here right now, he would say that faxes, the television, apparently even the Net—all these things are like devices that enable the blind to regain a small portion of their sight. Now you have added another key to the mystery—that the blindness we speak of may be genetic. If we have somehow lost the use of an important gene, these devices could mimic its effects, by cultivating in us an artificial understanding that we are all part of one another." His face suddenly clouded. "However, I cannot escape my initial conviction that the help they give would be too weak, and too temporary, to be of any practical good in the long run."

I had no idea why, but suddenly my head began to swim, and I felt as if I were floating in the deep void of space. I was adrift in an alien sea, without compass or guidance, without direction. Something of grave importance was about to happen, though I did not understand it. Yet I was the pivot on which the event would turn; I was the linchpin. Without me, nothing would happen. I was terrified.

I found that I was ripping into shreds the napkin that had come with my wine. I tried to speak, but could not catch my breath. With a determined effort, I swallowed, and said in a shaking voice, "In that case, your answer is obvious, isn't it? It's perfectly plain what you have to do."

"No, it isn't," replied Li.

And he thought he was so smart! "Perhaps all those things like the Net and television are not what you need, not in themselves," I said. "But they *point* to what you need. You want to reconnect people, but television is too weak? So go out and get a better connector!"

Li seemed thunderstruck. "Where?"

"For crying out loud, I don't know. Find one. Or make one. You've already got the goddamn answer. All you need now is to find a good engineer."

Li regarded me silently for what seemed like an eternity. "Very well," he said at last. "That shouldn't be difficult."

I put down what was left of my napkin, and commandeered what was left of the sauvignon blanc. I poured it into my glass and guzzled it like Kool-Aid. The most curious feeling of contentment stole over me. I felt as if I had just experienced not the fifteen minutes of fame that everyone was supposed to enjoy in this modern world, but fifteen minutes in which I had been privileged to play an obscure but vital role in the course of history. There was meaning to the universe. There was a pattern, hidden somewhere beneath the seeming chaos of events. I had played my part in the design, known that was what I was doing, and done it well.

FIFTEEN

AUGUST 12, 2032

BETO WAS AS GOOD AS HIS WORD. HE WORKED LIKE THE proverbial dog. Never in all my years on the planet had I ever seen anybody drive himself the way he did—not even at my old law firm back in the 1980s, where billing three hundred hours a month was a mark of valor. He toiled like a madman, which brought home to me, better than any number of words could have done, just how desperate a life he and Ciel had led before we rescued them.

This being the Berkeley hills, most of our acreage did not consist of level ground, to put it mildly. Years before, we had made rows and rows of terraces, using boards and rebars, in which to grow our food crops. These terraces were in various states of disrepair, but Beto tackled them in nothing flat. He went out during the day (with George's Uzi for protection), scavenged a ton of usable boards from deserted houses, and replaced all the rotten ones. And that was just for starters.

The porous hoses in our jerry-rigged drip-watering system were old and patched many times over with duct tape. Beto disappeared into the wilds of Mad Mac's and managed not just to find new ones, but also barter for them—and on top of that, to trade stuff for them that cost us next to nothing.

How did he do it? Ever the good street hustler, he chatted

up a tough old hardware vendor and eventually found the guy's weak point. That hard-bitten geezer had a prime collection of antique Teenage Mutant Ninja Turtle action figures, so Beto deduced that he was into nostalgia. Beto tried various angles and got him talking about food. Eventually Beto observed that the guy—who was getting a little fuzzy around the edges with advancing age—would grow positively weepy whenever he started talking about his childhood. He particularly idealized the apricot preserves his grandmother had made when he was a kid.

Well, *we* had apricots, put up from the now-venerable tree I planted in the early 1990s when Roger and I bought the place. We had apricot preserves! My jaw on the ground in disbelief, I gladly parted with six jars, and in return we got half a dozen new hoses—brand-new, never used, still bearing their original Orchard Supply Hardware packaging label.

Not one to rest on his laurels, Beto next went for the basement stairs—the ones that went down into the underground room where we slept when it was really hot. They had been getting more and more rickety for years. One day Beto heard Rhiannon going down them. Given that he hovered protectively around Rhiannon as if she were his sainted mother, he noticed right off that the boards were squeaking, and hopped on the project immediately.

I could go on and on. Every day he worked in the gardens beside Rhiannon, Lorenzo, and me, doing as much work as the three of us put together. Ciel was so overly pregnant that she couldn't do any hard physical labor, but she knew how to use a needle and thread, as well as my ancient sewing machine down in the basement, and devoted herself to mending everything in sight, even George's underwear. In return, he almost got to a frame of mind where he could accept her presence with good grace.

For a brief time, it seemed like everything was coming up roses. Or rather, to be more precise, collards, filberts, garlic, leeks, onions, parsley . . . and all the rest of that jazz.

There was one bad incident, however, when Beto brought up the possibility of bringing his sick grandmother to Withering Heights. He said he was afraid something would happen to her. She had a place to stay, but the old man she was living with was at death's door, and when he died she would have nowhere to go.

Rhiannon, Lorenzo, and I kept an open mind, but to our great astonishment, George would have none of it.

Intentionally or not, Beto mentioned his grandmother when all of us were assembled at the dinner table. Maybe he knew George would shut him down, and was hoping the rest of us might overrule him. But George put his foot down, and said to the assembled company, but especially Beto, "We can't take on any more people who don't produce anything, son. You do enough work for yourself and your girlfriend, but we're still going to be on tight rations when the kid is born. I have kept my mouth shut so far and gone along with the team, but I am dead set against this. If you can show me how you can pay extra money for your grandmother, or how you can get enough work out of her to justify the rest of us pulling our belts in even more, you do that. But we're not taking on any charity cases, not if I have anything else to say about it."

Beto got pissed, and said something pithy in street patois about George riding around in his wheelchair all day looking busy but doing nothing. That didn't help matters one bit. George left the table in a fury, and later, when Rhiannon, Lorenzo, and I got him alone in his room, nothing in the world could have budged him. Fortunately Beto didn't get to hear this part of it.

"You let that woman in, and pretty soon every piece of human trash in the flats is going to be up here!" George yelled. His voice was quivering and the muscles in his face were working. I had never seen him so angry, or seen his selfish streak quite so pronounced. "Who knows how many uncles and aunts and cousins he's got? They'll come in here and take over and pretty soon we'll be out on the street. He should be glad we're giving *him* a place to stay, not to mention the girl and a squalling brat.''

"George," said Rhiannon, "it's his grandmother. Try to understand. How would you feel?"

"It doesn't matter how he feels! This is a war, just as much as 'Nam ever was. If we take too many people on board, we sink.''

"How can you be so hard-hearted?" I asked.

That made him mad. George didn't like to be put in the role of the bad guy. "I'm just being practical. The old woman is sick, and I know how the rest of you operate. You might swear on a Bible now that you wouldn't go spending our hard-earned money on medicine and pain-killers and things for her, but the minute she was under your noses and blubbering, you'd do it. We'll bankrupt ourselves. Better never to let the temptation get started in the first place. Moira, we can't take in every stray cat, and you know it. You let her in, it's over my dead body!"

"Stray cat!" exclaimed Lorenzo and turned away. Yet George had a point—an ugly, awful point that we could not really refute. We were in the same boat as every other "have" in the world: rowing for dear life with one oar, and whacking at the hands of people trying to climb in with the other.

"George," said Rhiannon, her voice full of reproach, "how can you be so cold?"

He glared at her. "It's called survival, lady." He spat and said, "I always thought it was a shame they didn't draft women. Then maybe some of you would understand."

I attempted to assert what little authority I had, as host of this jolly shindig. "George," I said sternly, "in the past, our group has always tried to get along, and to live by majority rule. Now the rest of us don't want to close the door on letting Beto's grandmother come live with us—"

"I do!" he bellowed. "And if you don't like it, I can go live with old McClelland down the road. He's offered me a place there more than once!"

Well, that shut us all up but good.

I tried to finesse the matter, and later told Beto that whenever one of our number had very serious reservations about a step the commune should take, we usually abandoned the whole idea; it was the old notion that the team pulled together, or not at all. I could tell Beto didn't take it well.

"Yes, ma'am," he said, "I understand." It always made me uncomfortable when he called me "ma'am," because it made me feel even older than eighty, and it did not somehow feel politically correct to me.

"Are you sure?" I asked. "I'm sorry."

He nodded, but his face turned rock-hard and rock-smooth, so I could not reliably read his reaction. It might have been sullen, or angry, or humiliated. I couldn't tell. His eyelids lowered, shading his eyes and any expression in them from my view.

"I wish we could help your grandmother," I said lamely. "I'm sure George does, too. But we have to draw the line somewhere, or none of us will survive."

He nodded, but I knew very well it wasn't over.

Perhaps as a strategic move, Beto did everything he could to cover himself with glory. He undertook so many creative home repairs it would tire me even to list them. Best of all, he succeeded where even Loki had failed. The last time the television broke, Loki hadn't been able to connect with anybody at Mad Mac's to diagnose the problem correctly, let alone fix it. Beto did. And so we had wheels again, as it were, just in time for the 2032 Republican National Convention. Beto looked quite pleased with himself.

It was a done deal that gorgeous young Julian would get the nomination, even before the festivities began. He had no opposition worthy of the name, and even if he had, the

Repubs hadn't had a candidate like him in living memory, and would have been crazy to run anybody else. Neither had the Democrats; our current incumbent president was a tired old guy who should have been out playing golf, if only there were still golf courses. He was only running for a second term because the party wouldn't let him quit. He didn't have a prayer.

None of our political parties held actual conventions in real places where people showed up in person—not anymore. It would have been prohibitively expensive, not to mention prohibitively dangerous. It was all done with elaborate real-time teleconferencing in a studio, using Net hookups and what-have-you. You could follow it over the Net, or if you were really well off, hook up your television to the Net for the best seat in the house. The scattered delegates could even send commands over the Net that would set off individual clapping, cheering, and booing sounds in the studio where the candidate was speaking.

"Oh, he looks just like the young Robert Redford," said Rhiannon with a sigh after we had finished dragging the television into her room and hooking it up to her computer. Now, this description was not altogether accurate. He did have that cute cleft in his chin and blondish hair, but to my mind he was MUCH better-looking than Redford. His hair was curlier—it made gorgeous thick ringlets all over his head—and there was the most luscious olive tint to his skin, like a suntan that didn't fade come December. This may have been because he was one-eighth black. Whatever. All the genes in the salt shaker fell out just fine this time, thank you very much.

"I just love this guy," continued Rhiannon, waxing into soap opera mode as we watched the tube. Understand, Beto had managed to pull off a major coup and score some halfway decent jug wine down at Mad Mac's, and we had all been imbibing some of it and were feeling festive.

George gave a disgusted grunt at all this carrying on. He

was crazy about Julian himself, but she was laying it on a little thick.

"Hey, Julian's a winner!" protested Rhiannon. "I can't help getting all worked up about him. You can make fun of me all you like, but this is the first politician in years worth getting excited about. If anybody can still make the political system work to save our candy asses, he can."

"That's scary," I said, still in a quirky mood to throw cold water all over everything. "If he can't, that means we can throw said political system out the window."

Rhiannon considered. "Fair enough, I guess. But look, people, he's got the magic. Didn't a television commentator once contrast merely good speakers, versus inspiring ones? For example, if people heard a speech by Al Gore or Adlai Stevenson, when it was over they'd say, 'How well he spoke.' But if they heard JFK or Martin Luther King, Jr., speak, the people would say, 'Let us march!' Julian's got what it takes to motivate people. I watch him, and I think he really is the right cheerleader to bootstrap us out of this mess! And don't think I'm alone! People on the Net, all over the country, come unglued just talking about him!"

I crossed myself, ostentatiously. "I hope to God you're right."

George gave a loud sigh. "Don't get yourselves all bent out of shape, kids. Somebody'll come along any minute and blow his brains out. Jesus knows there are enough wackos out there."

Rhiannon caught her breath. Then, quite deliberately, she sketched a banishing pentagram in the air before her.

She was quite serious about it. I lost all impulse to poke surly fun at her, and raised my own hand in an ancient gesture to ward off evil—palm outward, with index and little fingers raised like horns. It came very easily to me; it was also the "Hook 'Em Horns!" sign so beloved of University of Texas Longhorn fans back in my lost twentieth-century youth.

"Amen," I said, hoping somebody was listening.

SIXTEEN

MAY 13, 1989

IT TURNED OUT THAT THE YOUNGER BROTHER OF ONE OF my fellow law firm associates was getting his Ph.D. in computer science at Cal Berkeley. Armed with an introduction, I promptly called up said brother, named Jim, and asked if it would be okay for him to introduce Li to the Internet. I guess I had the notion there would be a problem, because Li was from Red China, but Jim actually laughed out loud when I asked. So over to Cal we went the next Saturday afternoon.

The Internet had begun life in the sixties as the defense-oriented DARPANET, Jim explained when we got there, but its defense functions had long since been spun off to somewhere or other. Therefore the CIA would not care if we logged on and let Li check out a few newsgroups. I had no idea what newsgroups were, but I gave a knowing nod so I wouldn't look completely ignorant.

Jim's passion in life was computers (a most peculiar malady, epidemic among members of my generation of the male persuasion). So he was delighted to volunteer to spend half of his entire weekend showing a visiting Chinese professor what the Net was all about.

We went to Jim's office on campus. Eyes shining, Li sat down on a stool at Jim's right side. Jim logged onto his computer, with Li staring at it all the while like it was the

Holy Grail. I, forgotten already, pulled up a stool and sat to Jim's left.

I didn't own a computer and had not considered buying one. My secretary did all my word processing, and that arrangement was just fine with me. In terms of knowing what Jim was doing with his keyboard and all those funny commands he typed in, I might as well have been on board Klaatu's flying saucer in *The Day the Earth Stood Still.*

If I'd had an inkling how important the Net would be to our poor struggling commune forty years in the future, I would not have been so churlish about having to watch the boys slobber all over Jim's 386SX computer while ignoring me. If I'd had any idea that I was watching the birth of a vast human linkage without precedent in the history of the world, I would have been a little more attentive. After all, if I'd been able to travel back in time and watch the first Bible roll off Gutenberg's press, you can bet I would have shown a little respect.

If I'd had the slightest clue about the eventual contribution of the Net to the survival of our very civilization—an indirect contribution, but one that was real enough—I probably would have been salaaming in front of that ugly box right along with the guys.

Well, Jim finally got to the end of his sorcerous Unix-based invocation of the damned Net. He even managed to get an incomprehensible-looking menu listing of arcane choices to stop scrolling by at the speed of light, and hold still on the screen. "Now," he announced, his voice fairly shaking with excitement, "now I'm going to send a message to my neurosurgeon friend in South Africa."

Lah de dah, I thought. They fussed on and on while this feature of the software rebelled, and then that one. "Gosh, it's temperamental today," said Jim, and Li nodded in his patented sagely fashion. Jim composed an E-mail message, tried to send it, and got a bizarre error message on the screen. He cursed, rebooted his computer, got back on the Internet, and tried again.

This went on for some time until he cried, "Ah-ha!" and I knew he had finally succeeded.

To be fair, the Internet was still in its infancy. Delays and frustrations were to be expected and forgiven. Hell, the Net could still behave like that in the late 1990s! When I finally got on the Net myself years later, via a certain infamous ISP that was fondly referred to by its patrons as Netcrap, the delays and frustrations could still drive the most patient of people stark, raving mad.

Finally I could stand it no longer and snapped at Jim. "The computer is attempting to transmit your typed-in message over a telephone line, am I not correct?"

"Uh, yeah," said Jim.

I pointed to the phone, currently encumbered by a large, rectangular Hayes modem. "That *is* a telephone, am I not also correct?"

"Yeah," Jim said again. He clearly didn't understand what I was driving at.

"Why don't you turn off the damn computer and pick up the damn phone and *dial* the number in South Africa and just give him your message in person?" I cried. "I understand you want to communicate with your buddy, but I fail to see the value in persisting in doing it the hard way!"

Jim and Li exchanged a brief glance. It said, in no uncertain terms, that The Little Woman Simply Did Not Understand. I wanted to explode.

"Moira," said Jim, gently as if he were speaking to a psychiatric patient, "the Net is still getting off the ground. You have to be patient."

"You're telling me."

"In time, every computer on the face of the planet can be linked to every other computer, via the Net. I will be able to log on and leave a message for anyone in the world who has a computer and a modem, at any time, and sooner or later they'll get it.''

''I can do that right now. All they need is a telephone and an answering machine! Forget computers, they're *expensive*!''

Jim and Li exchanged another knowing look. ''I understand,'' said Jim. ''We are only now beginning to explore the vast possibilities of the Internet. The Internet can link people together all over the Earth in a way that's simply never been possible before.''

''Ever heard of writing letters?'' I retorted. ''I know they take longer, but what's the damn hurry?''

Jim thought about that one. At length he spread out his hands in a helpless gesture and said, ''This is different. I can't put it into words for you, Moira—I'm not good at that sort of thing, like Li is. I can only tell you that this is a whole new ball game. It's different, in a way I can't express.''

Something inside me responded to the conviction I heard in his voice, and I settled down somewhat. ''I don't know a damn thing about computers,'' I said. ''Are you sure you can't explain to me exactly how it's different? Try!''

Jim thought for a moment, his brow literally furrowed. ''When I finally got through to my friend in South Africa,'' he said, ''the message was transmitted almost instantaneously. I can write him a letter while I'm not on the Net, attach it as a file to a short 'hello' message, and send the whole package in a matter of seconds. He'll get it within hours, or often within minutes. Communicating with someone on the other side of the world is much faster than snail mail, and much, much cheaper than talking on the telephone.''

''Snail mail?'' I asked. ''What's that?''

''The postal service.''

''Oh!'' I suppressed a giggle. I'd never heard that term before, and it was pretty right on. ''Okay, so people who

are actually able to use computers can talk to their friends
all they like at very little cost.''

Jim pointed to a big, thick, three-ring binder. ''Those are
the hard copies of my correspondence with the guy in South
Africa. Of course, in time I'll just keep all the letters on
disk. There's no real reason to keep printing them out, except I'm still not weaned away from paper.''

It was packed; it must have been the length of *Gone With
the Wind*. ''Holy Christmas,'' I said.

Jim fiddled with the keyboard some more. ''Let's check
my mailbox, see if I've got anything.'' His fingers went
clickety, click, and he cried, ''Hey! Here's something back
from Pieter already!''

He pulled up the letter from the guy in South Africa,
muttering, ''He must be having insomnia again. I think it's
the middle of the night over there.''

The letter popped onto the screen, and Jim chortled with
glee, as if it were Christmas and he'd gotten a present. Li,
too, looked all goo-goo-eyed. ''He says he couldn't sleep,
just like I thought,'' said Jim.

''And he's a neurosurgeon?'' I said. ''Great.'' I craned
my neck to see the screen. Pieter thanked Jim for an article
on something incomprehensibly technical, promised to send
him another one equally incomprehensible to normal people, and made a couple or two remarks about the political
situation in his neck of the woods—it was, you will recall,
a stormy time in South Africa in that era. He closed with
a computer joke that I didn't get but that sent Jim into
giggles. Quickly, Jim fired back another joke.

''He'll still be on-line, so he'll get it right now,'' Jim
explained. ''Now let's check out Usenet.'' He typed more
arcane commands, we waited awhile, and then a whole new
print menu sprang up. ''These are all newsgroups, or ongoing discussion groups. Here's one that discusses developments in computer science. Think of it as a permanent

bulletin board hanging in a hallway somewhere in cyber-space.''

"Cyberspace?" I echoed, rather faintly.

Jim waved his hand at the air in the room. "Oh, an alternate kind of space where electronic-mail messages and bulletin board postings exist."

Woo, woo, woo. My head was starting to hurt. "Okay," I said, "and then what?"

"Pretend that anybody who walks by the bulletin board can tack up an index card on which he's written a message for the others to read. Or maybe he's commenting on a message someone else has already posted. Then other people can comment on his message. You get enough discussion about one topic, and it's called a 'thread.' "

"Producing an almost instantaneous synergy of minds all over the world . . . as many minds as wish to participate in the dialogue," said Li. He had a faraway look in his eyes, and his voice sounded positively reverent. "This is revolutionary! Think of the problem-solving capability of such a system. Suppose you have a political question you wish to explore. You propose it to the newsgroup. You ask for input and suggestions. Immediately, the power of many, many minds is applied to the problem."

"So how's that different from posing a question to a bunch of university professors?" I asked.

"Think of the time it would take to locate them, to get them to meet with you, to get them to read what all the others had said," Jim spoke up. "And then you'd only hear what a bunch of professors had to say, not intelligent lay-men who happened to be interested in the question, too. The pace of inquiry would be as slow as molasses in January, just like academia is, with six-month lags between papers, and rebuttals to papers, and debating that goes on for years. This stuff is almost instantaneous, because every-body gets involved and jumps on it at once. It's fun, and people get so excited about debates, sometimes you get hundreds of messages a day.''

''And how many newsgroups are there?'' I asked.

''Oh, thousands. The number grows daily.''

I experienced a distinct shock. ''Wow . . . there must be something for everybody out there in cyberland.''

''Oh, sure,'' said Jim. He thought, and said, clearly intending to be helpful, ''Suppose you had a question about dating? There is a newsgroup that discusses dating. You could post your question there, and sit back and listen to what everybody had to say.''

He meant well, but it was *so* condescending. ''I do think about other things besides dating,'' I retorted. ''I am thirty-seven years old, not a teenager. I'm an attorney with a very good law firm, okay? Can't you think of something less sexist?''

''Well, I only meant, maybe if you had a question about the problems of older straight women trying to date in San Francisco or something—''

''Kid,'' I said, ''stop while you're ahead.''

Li wasn't listening to either of us. ''Is there a discussion of the student prodemocracy movement in Tiananmen Square?''

''Oh, of course!'' Jim said, almost stammering.

''Last week General Secretary Ziyang made a statement that was almost supportive of the students, and I had hoped the demonstration would end,'' said Li. ''But today I read in the newspaper that the student leader Wu'er Kaixi has called a hunger strike. Where would I find a discussion of it?''

''Here, let's have a look!'' Jim's hands went roaming over the keyboard again, working more occult magic.

I had to put my two cents in. ''Li, I hope those kids wind it up soon. They're going to get their butts kicked!''

To my utter amazement, he exploded. I'd never seen him so mad. ''Moira, I explained that they are trying to establish a tradition of democracy in my country! Would you silence them?''

"No, I just meant that they're dealing with a really nasty regime, and if they aren't careful, they could get hurt."

Li drew himself up in a huff. "As I told you, Chinese students have always risked their lives to save China. The youth of my country are not cowards."

I rolled my eyes. "Li, whether the students are peaceful or not, the government's going to get tired of the bad PR and will squash them like bugs!"

"Yeah," piped up Jim. "Gorbachev is supposed to visit in a couple of days for that big conference, isn't he? But the square is full of student protesters. If they're still there when Gorby arrives, it will be pretty embarrassing."

"Deng Xiaoping will never fire on the students," Li stated.

I rolled my eyes and sighed loudly. "How can you be so sure?"

"Remember the Tiananmen Incident in 1976? Following the death of Zhou En-lai? Deng Xiaoping himself was blamed for it, and he lost his position as acting premier and chief of staff. He has been, as you say, on the other side of the desk."

"So you really expect him to be magnanimous now?"

"He cannot be anything else! Ten years before that, in 1966, Deng was a victim of Mao's Cultural Revolution. He was designated 'China's Number Two Capitalist Roader,' second only to President Liu Shaoqi, who was shortly murdered by Mao. Deng's son, Deng Pufang, was then a brilliant student of physics at Beijing University. He was beaten and tortured by the Red Guards to give evidence against his father. He refused, was clubbed senseless, and was put in a room on the fourth floor of a building, from whose window he either fell or was pushed, breaking his back. Despite all his father's efforts, today he is a permanent wheelchair cripple. He has written that the philosophy of humanism, which can restrain the worst atrocities of which human beings are capable, is notably absent in Chinese tradition. How could Deng Pufang's own father fire on the sons of other fathers?''

Li paused, as if recharging his batteries. ''Look, honey,'' I said in my most conciliatory tones, ''Deng Pufang's statement is the reason I think the students should be careful. People *are* capable of the most terrible atrocities—all people, even his own father.''

My lover looked over at me, his face hard, and said, ''Even someone like Deng can change. His son has become one of China's first voices for humanism. Moira, can't you believe that a man can change? Or that the world can?''

''Yes,'' I replied. ''In principle. I'm just not sure either has changed on this particular occasion. Anything is possible.''

''No! The students in Tiananmen are China's future; they will not be shot, like the students at your Kent State.''

I shook my head. ''I still think they ought to finish their studies and work to change the system from the inside, like the sixties protesters did.''

Now Li exploded with temper. ''It will take too long! We are talking of China, not the United States! Moira, change MUST come to China now, even if it means blood will be shed!''

I was flabbergasted. ''I'm not trying to make you mad, Li. I just didn't know how strongly you felt about it. When I was a kid I thought this sort of demonstration was cool, but then you learn that it's kind of silly, and there are better ways to get what you want. Besides, my government killed only four students, but I'm afraid that yours wouldn't think twice about killing four thousand! I just think the students ought to be careful.''

He went absolutely ballistic. ''They have the courage to stand up for what they believe. They are willing to die for it. Yet you call them silly! For shame, Moira. Have you no backbone?''

''Sure I do,'' I said, ''but if there's a way to get what I want without taking a bullet in the head, I prefer that way. What's the deal, anyway, Li? Do you know those kids?''

''Many of them are my students,'' he said stiffly. ''I should be there in the square with them, not here, thinking of nothing but my own pleasure.''

''Oh, stop it!'' I snapped, trying to ignore the feeling that my stomach had just turned to ice water. ''Now you're being silly.''

''I am not!'' he retorted.

''Li, when you came over to the States for this visit, no one had any idea that a protest was going to erupt in Tiananmen Square. You might as well reproach yourself for not owning a crystal ball. All right?''

I turned to Jim, who looked remarkably uncomfortable at having to witness our domestic argument. ''Found anything?'' I asked.

''Here we go—bingo!'' he replied. ''A Usenet group about Chinese culture, with a big, long thread on Tiananmen Square.''

Li practically threw Jim out of the chair, hunched forward, and stared at the monitor. ''These are the addresses of the parties who post messages, are they not?'' he asked, never taking his eyes off the screen. ''Am I interpreting the addresses correctly? Are some of the posters sending messages from inside China?''

Jim bent forward. ''Sure looks like it.''

Li ran a hand through his hair and said in an agitated voice, ''All this time, I have been overlooking a tool of great importance. See this post here—does it not appear to originate from Beijing University?''

''Sure does,'' Jim said.

''And this one—and this—they are all from Chinese universities!'' cried Li. ''How could I have overlooked the

Internet? How could I have been so blind?''

I gave a loud sigh. "Li, cut yourself some slack. Until recently there was practically a law that you couldn't be into this computer and Net stuff unless you were under twenty-five, or worked in a university computer science department. Ordinary people don't know how to do this stuff. The attorneys don't even have computers at work, and we're a hot-shit law firm! We're over thirty. We don't do computers!''

"I do," Li stated, looking me right in the eye. "Starting right now." He leaned forward to pore over the screen again. "Look at this! There are comments from a dozen countries. The eyes of the world are turned on Tiananmen Square—the course of the future is described here, as it happens! Jim, Jim, am I able to reply to any of these messages?''

"Sure, to all of them," Jim replied with an amiable shrug.

Li sprang out of his chair, walked to the window, looked out across the Cal campus, and returned to fix Jim with a look of great intensity. "Would it be possible for me to visit you here each day? During lunch, perhaps, or after work? To keep abreast of developments in the square and to send encouragement to my comrades?''

"Well, sure," said Jim. "Anytime. I'm here late.''

Li grasped his hand and shook it, hard. "Thank you, thank you! I will catch BART every day at five P.M. and meet you here. Tell me, is it possible to save any of these messages?''

"Yeah, you just download them and save them to a floppy.''

"Please, show me how!''

So Li was going to head over to Berkeley after work each day? Great, I thought.

Jim picked up some five-and-a-quarter-inch floppies from a neighboring desk. He showed Li how to post his own replies to Usenet messages, and how to copy them to disk if he wanted to save them. Then he showed him how to post original comments of his own to the newsgroup. As soon as Li got the hang of it, he was off in his own private world and forgot about us both.

Sensing that the situation had become really heavy, Jim tried to lighten things up for me. "You know, Moira, you can make a lot of friends over the Net. I've met lots of people by reading science groups that interest me. Lots of times I'll send e-mail directly to one of the posters who's said something interesting. That's how I met my friend in South Africa."

Li surfaced briefly from his reverie, nodding absently at this, as if to say, "How very nice." He thought for a time, and once again put on the manner of the erudite Chinese sage who had just solved a riddle. "I believe this Internet could become the most efficient mechanism on Earth for bringing kindred minds together—almost instantly," he pronounced. "In the future, armed with this machine, no man need ever be alone. Whatever your passion, whatever your mission in life, you will find others who share it on the Internet. You will find companions quickly and easily, and vast distances between you will become meaningless."

Then he went back to his newsgroup.

I always wished Li would not refer to "man" and to "men" when we had this sort of philosophical discussion, but this time I put my quibbles aside, because I had begun to feel tingly patches of gooseflesh begin to rise up on my arms.

In that moment my disdain for computers and the geeky people who worshiped them simply vanished, as if it had never been. I realized, in my heart, that Li was onto something very big.

"Is there a newsgroup devoted to saving the environment?" I asked Jim.

"I'm sure there is. I just haven't looked for it."

"Are there ones devoted to particular churches, where you could post suggestions about the socially conscious actions you think they should be taking?"

"Again, I'm sure there are. There is probably one for bird-watchers—or for doll collectors, or anything else you can imagine. You hang around Usenet long enough, there's no telling what you'll stumble across."

A shadow of my old impatience returned. These ivory tower types could be so dense sometimes. "Well, Jim, do you think there might be a master list of all the Usenet groups somewhere, one that you could even print out for me?" I asked.

"Oh, yeah!" said Jim, as if the thought were a revelation to him. "I'll get hold of it, and mail it to you at the law firm."

"Thank you," I replied. "I'd really appreciate it."

"No problem."

I had one last important piece of business to take care of. "Tell me, Jim," I said, "is there a software program that can look up the names of people using E-mail, anywhere in the world?"

"There are a few," Jim replied. "Some are better than others. Security isn't all that good right now, though I expect it will get a lot better in the future, as more people get on the Net. If you know someone's Internet name, or handle, you can often find out what his or her legal name is—and vice versa."

"Can you help me try to locate somebody?"

"Well . . . I could try."

He seemed reluctant, so I asked why. "This software isn't really legal. But it's been passed around so much, I guess it doesn't matter. Here, I'll set up the query, and you put in the person's name."

With apologies to Li, he pounded some more keys and brought up a different-looking screen. Mentally crossing my fingers and toes, I impulsively typed in Miles's full legal name.

"It takes a while," Jim said. "This computer is a 386, but it could be faster. I can't wait to get my hands on one of the new 486's. Talk about power! And speed! Those things'll go like a drag racing car."

Good for them, I said to myself, watching the radiant eye of the computer and listening to its hard drive grind away.

Then, to my astonishment, a name appeared on the screen, complete with an e-mail destination, and a real live address. Judging from the location of the latter, I had fingered Miles.

"Who is that?" demanded Li.

"An old boyfriend," I said. "You'd like him."

"Hmmpff," said Li. I didn't get many chances to make him jealous, so I didn't hesitate to take advantage of this one.

"He's really into environmental protection, too," I added. "You guys would have a lot in common."

"How close a boyfriend was he?" Li demanded.

I laughed, and rolled my eyes. "Oh, for God's sake, we only had one date. Keep your pants on."

Mollified, Li sat down at the terminal. "Then I shall introduce myself."

"What?" I cried. "You're not actually going to write him?"

"Are you planning to?" Li asked.

"Well, I wasn't sure. I hadn't made up my mind. Actually, probably not. I was just curious."

"Then there's no reason I shouldn't. I've never sent an e-mail message yet. I might as well start somewhere. I'll simply mention that a mutual friend said he shared my interest in the environment, and take it from there."

"Be my guest," I said with a sigh. Li had a new toy, just like his fax machine at work, and he was determined to use it. He would probably have sent an E-mail to Richard

Nixon if the old guy had been on the Internet, too, and I had come up with the address.

My brain on overload, I excused myself and went out to find some coffee and give my poor aching IQ repository a rest.

Well, there was no doubt about it. I had to admit the handwriting was on the wall, in a number of ways. I would have to pray that this Tiananmen thing didn't mushroom. Otherwise, Li might not stay put, which would be a disaster, since my mind was made up that he was the guy for me.

Also, I was going to have to get a computer. The future was calling, and I couldn't afford to be left behind, thirty-seven years old or not. But with Li around to help, learning to master that monster wouldn't be nearly as hard.

SEVENTEEN

SEPTEMBER 5, 2032

THIS GREENHOUSE EFFECT THING HAS A MIND OF ITS OWN. It has what we used to call "attitude" back in the old days—a downright mean and malicious attitude. Yesterday's caper was the quintessential example of a malignant Fate adding insult to injury.

Tornadoes? In California? Naw . . .

When I moved to California in the 1980s, I realized that I was moving to the land of earthquakes, floods, mudslides, and big-time fire danger, but I consoled myself with the fact that I was giving up hurricanes on the Texas Gulf Coast, and vulnerability to tornadoes whenever I ventured north of Austin.

We still have earthquakes. We have even bigger floods and mudslides now, thanks to our screwed-up climate. We have wildfires you wouldn't believe, because the state gets unbelievably hot and dry in the summer. And now on top of it all Southern California get hurricanes and we have tornadoes! Goddamn it, it's not fair. Not fair!!

Yesterday afternoon I was outside gardening, and a weird, heavy rainstorm came up, even though it's way past the season for such foolishness. The wind hopped around and changed direction constantly and generally acted schizoid. We even had thunder and some lightning, things you almost never used to see in California.

Then everything got real still. Rhiannon burst out of the house and called to me, "Moira, is something strange happening?"

I was, by now, very suspicious. But I kept telling myself, "No, it CAN'T be! No matter what has happened to the climate, there are limits, and this is still California!"

To my horror, I looked up and saw a genuine tornado funnel cloud. The cursed thing was flying straight toward our property. With a shriek, Rhiannon threw herself into a huddle on the ground beside me. Beto came out of the house just in time to see the monster in all its glory, screamed in terror, and fainted.

"Seems to me your Goddess is in one of her dark moods," I shouted to Rhiannon over the freight-train imitation the wind was making.

Rhiannon's normally pale face had turned downright ashen. "That's the most hideous thing I've ever seen," she cried.

The damned thing looked like it was going to keep on moving and leapfrog right over our turf, and I hoped we would get off scot-free. I hoped it would be content merely with scaring the holy bejesus out of us. But it changed its mind in midleap, did a little dip, and neatly and cleanly collapsed one of the metal water-saving cisterns we had mounted on cinder-block supports next to the house. Then it hopped away again, touched down several blocks down the street, and completely obliterated another secured compound like our own.

When we had recovered from our fright, and realized we were somehow going to have to do the impossible—replace the cistern—I asked Rhiannon to get on the Net and find out how many tornadoes there had been in California in the past few years. I wanted to know whether this was a one-night stand or whether, realistically speaking, we had more such encounters to look forward to.

You can guess what answer she came up with.

Then I roused Beto, and we went into the house to check on Ciel, praying that she hadn't seen it, hadn't panicked, and wasn't delivering the baby prematurely at that very moment. Thankfully, she had been in a sound sleep and had missed the entire thing.

We were all very glum at supper that night. Losing the cistern put a major dent in our ability to save drinkable rainwater through the dry season, which was a necessity, given how unreliable water from the East Bay Municipal Utility District had become. Beto said he could put out the word and try to buy a big used metal container that we could convert into a cistern, provided nothing toxic had been stored inside it. Rhiannon said she would post want ads all over the appropriate places on the Net. But, brave efforts aside, this was a major setback.

We turned on the television, which was still working, thanks to Beto. Young Julian, borrowing shamelessly from the legacy of Franklin Delano Roosevelt, had begun having "fireside chats" with the American public, and here he wasn't even formally elected yet.

He repeated yet again the same litany that had catapulted him to the threshold of the presidency. Sure, he sounded like a broken record, but that was the only way he could drum the formula into people's heads.

We would all sacrifice—we had no choice. Times were desperate, we were desperate, and only a global effort comparable to that of the Allies in World War II was going to save us from disaster. We did not face the Nazis this time, but a hostile power far more deadly and terrifying: an environment turned on its head by our own folly and selfishness.

No matter how much it hurt, we would sacrifice. The hour was so late, there was no longer any alternative. We would turn all available resources to immediately developing clean alternative sources of energy. Gasoline would be as hard to come by as gold bullion from Fort Knox. We would have one-child limits, free bicycles and public transportation, no air conditioners, and sealed borders. Everyone would be required to serve on public emergency task forces to deal with the crisis. Not one more molecule of CO_2 was going into the air if he could help it. If people didn't like it, then we would have martial law, because these changes HAD to take place, or we were all going down the toilet.

I think he put that last a bit more elegantly. But we all got the general picture.

When the chat was over, George sat back in his chair, gave a faint imitation of a rebel yell, or something to the same general effect, and said, "The boy's got balls—but he's a dead man walking."

"Don't say that!" Rhiannon hissed, half begging.

"Shit, lady, he gored everybody's ox with that speech. It's just a question of who'll be the first to take him out."

"He's telling the truth!" Rhiannon cried. "We're lucky if we've got one chance left at this point! So he's goring somebody's ox? Well, damn it, the boat is sinking! What good are possessions, or power, or wealth when it's a hundred and twenty degrees outside and you're about to die? Surely people understand that by now!"

"People," replied George, "are incredibly stupid. Still."

Rhiannon threw up her hands in disgust. The news came on then, with word of what appeared to be the beginnings of Kiev-style nuclear highway robbery, this time involving several Arab capitals versus Tehran. Tehran was still the capital of a militant, Islamic fundamentalist country, but it was quite prosperous compared to its fellow Moslem states. And so it goes.

"I'm not going to listen to it! I can't stand it!" Rhiannon cried, fleeing the room for—I was certain—the sanctuary of her computer. I was reminded of the many times as a child when I had fled the bad news on Huntley/Brinkley for the eyrie of my long-dead persimmon tree.

I got up, turned off the television, and wondered what to do with myself. George wheeled away, muttering something excessively cantankerous. I had about made up my mind to go raid my stash of expensive rotgut when Beto said, hesitantly, that he had to talk to me.

I knew what it was about, even before he started in on me. "I know what you already said about my grandmother. Still, I was wondering if you could talk to George. The old man she was staying with died, and she has no place to go. I'm afraid that something is going to happen to her if she's stuck outside very long."

Shades of the *Twilight Zone* episode where the guys in the bomb shelter had to chase off their neighbors with a shotgun! I had never been good at chopping people off at the knees, for all that numerous other lawyers in my old firm seemed to enjoy it immensely.

"I wish I could change George's mind, Beto," I replied. "So far I haven't been able to. He feels very strongly that we can't take on another person who can't work. George has been a good sport whenever we've made other decisions; this is the only time he's really insisted we go along with what he wants. We have to respect his wishes. At least we could help Ciel and the baby."

Looking back, I could try to count the ways in which that was the wrong thing to say, but I'd be here until the next century. It wasn't my fault I wasn't any good at finessing the unacceptable.

Beto walked away without another word. Given that he had nowhere else to go and was completely dependent on us, he must have been incredibly angry to do that.

I went to Rhiannon's room, sat down on her bed, and told her about the incident. She was looking frazzled and distracted, and I had to repeat my tale of woe before she could really focus on it.

"I was going to mention something to you," she said when I had finished. "I saw Beto down by the gate this morning talking to three boys on the other side of the fence. They looked like they were having quite an argument."

My blood ran cold. "Could you tell what it was about?"

"Of course not. I could only read body language. The three of them seemed to be pressuring him about something, and all the while he kept shaking his head. The three finally walked away, looking very angry, and one of them shot the finger at him."

"This has something to do with the grandmother, I know it," I replied. "Do you think George would really bolt if we let her in?"

Rhiannon thought about it. "In this case, yes. Whatever his good points, George has always been one pigheaded guy."

"I'm not worried about Beto betraying us. He's a good kid. I'm afraid we'll lose him. What will we do then?" I asked.

She sighed. "I'll do my best to talk to him."

"He really cares about you and respects what you say."

She nodded. "And, whatever the argument was about, he stuck to his guns and didn't give in. That's why they went away mad."

"Okay," I said. "Do what you can. If we lose him, we lose him, though it would be a shame. He'd certainly be easier to replace than George."

"I'd rather not replace either of them," said Rhiannon, and turned back to her keyboard with a distracted air, the lines of her face falling into a frown.

"Now what's up?" I asked her. "More of the same? What's the latest from our friends the Illuminati?"

"Oh, stop it," she said, sounding agitated. "Don't make fun of this. It's no laughing matter. They're getting close to the point where they need to make a decision about putting Green Man into effect. One of them has been for it all along; he says there's no reason to delay, that they should go ahead now before a war forces their hand. The other says they should wait awhile longer, and be absolutely sure that we can't save ourselves under our own steam."

"Before what?"

"Before they act. The weird thing is, I don't think either of them is an American, but guy number two wants to see if Julian can make a difference before, as he puts it, they 'unleash the whirlwind.' "

"Jesus," I said under my breath. "These people are crazy, Rhiannon."

"I don't think so. Before you came in, number two had just quoted Robert Oppenheimer to me. Did you ever hear what Oppenheimer was reported to have said at the Trinity site when they exploded the first atomic bomb?"

My knowledge of pre-Moira history could be a bit fuzzy, and I had to admit I hadn't.

"Upon seeing the mushroom cloud, he repeated a line from the Bhagavad Gita: 'I am become Death, destroyer of worlds.' He says he knows how Oppenheimer felt."

I felt the gooseflesh rise on my neck and the back of my arms. "Then the first guy responded. He told number two not to be such a child, that whenever decisions were made that affected the future of humanity, somebody would suffer. He told another story—about the time Robert Oppenheimer went to see Harry Truman, and told the president he could not live with himself because he had blood on his hands. Truman listened to him calmly, reached into a drawer, and said, 'Would you like a handkerchief?' "

The two of us sat silently for some time, just looking at each other. Then I got to my feet and said I was turning in. Rhiannon knew I'd had enough and let me go. I went back to my room, drank as much of my rotgut as I dared, and tried to quell the rising tide of dread that was eating at my soul.

EIGHTEEN

The Gate of Heavenly Peace

We can afford to shed a little blood.

> —Deng Xiaoping, before the Tiananmen
> Square massacre of June 3–4, 1989.

JUNE 5, 1989

THIS IS STILL ANOTHER ONE OF THOSE CHAPTERS I WISH I didn't have to write.

The protest in Tiananmen Square did not die down. It worsened, daily, until it seemed inevitable that it would end in disaster and somehow take Li away from me—as it did.

I went over to Berkeley with Li every day after work. At first I only did it so I wouldn't be left out of a very important event in his life. But gradually I found myself being drawn into the drama being played out on the other side of the world, as if it were taking place right in the city of San Francisco.

When it all started, I did not know a single one of the protesters in the square. It made no difference to me, practically speaking, whether any one of them lived or died. Yet with every newspaper article I read and every bit of televised coverage I saw, they became more and more real to me.

In addition to the newspapers and television, every day I took BART to Berkeley after work and stared at a computer screen with Li and Jim, watching the Usenet messages from China scroll by. Each message was like a Lilliputian thread, deftly cast and fastened around my heart. Print, television, and the insidious Internet—they all combined to drag me out of my complacency and isolation, and thrust me into a world of dread and empathy for people I had never even met.

Thanks to these technological sorceries, the students in Tiananmen Square became as real to me as my friends and neighbors. I cared about them. They were real people, defying a dictatorial government, who might pay for their rebelliousness with their lives. I lived in daily fear of what was going to happen to them.

They *were* my neighbors, of course. They were other pebbles on the same beach—like me, parts of a single continent.

My feeling of kinship with them was not constant. It fluctuated with the current that gave it strength. At times the experience of connection, of brotherhood, was hard to hold on to. But it persisted. In the end, the old media and the new Internet combined to mimic in me, fleetingly, the original effect of a set of damaged but very crucial genes.

May 14 was the second day of the hunger strike. That evening, twelve of China's most famous writers and scholars went to Tiananmen Square to present emergency appeals to both the government and the students. But their efforts failed on both counts, and the situation deteriorated further.

May 15 saw the third day of the strike. Mikhail Gorbachev (in the full splendor of his pre-1991 coup power) was due to arrive in Beijing for the first Sino-Soviet summit in thirty years. The only problem was, the square was full of angry students. The embarrassed government canceled its plans to welcome Gorbachev to China in Tiananmen Square.

On May 15, many rank-and-file workers from the city

began to take part in the protest, supporting the students' cause; in fact, so did some of the soldiers. In that brief window of time, showing support for the students seemed to be on the correct side, politically speaking, and safe in the bargain.

On May 18 the hunger strike entered its sixth day. The few reformist leaders in the Chinese government found themselves in a grave predicament. They were duty-bound to support the student protest, but knew full well that this course of action might lead to their own fall from power, and the elevation of their hard-line colleagues. That was just what happened; on May 18 the government laid plans to declare martial law.

The next day, the moderate General Secretary of the Chinese Communist Party, Zhao Ziyang, was removed from office. All over the city, rumors ran thick that the People's Army was going to invade. This was all but unthinkable; the People's Army had entered Beijing only once before, in 1949, along with a triumphant Mao Zedong. The Army was supposed to be the "people's army," just as its name proclaimed. The people, still believing this, came out of their homes and pleaded with the troops to go back, and at first they did.

Protest fever spread. Workers organized, and formed the new Independent Worker's Union right in the square.

By May 19 the hunger strike had lasted a week. As tensions mounted, someone leaked word of a government plan to impose immediate martial law. The student leaders called off the hunger strike, and declared a mass sit-in at the square. In the evening, Premier Li Peng called for "firm and resolute measures" to end the turmoil, a prelude to what was coming.

Even so, as the days passed and the students stayed in the square, Li and I began to hope that the storm would pass. The students got away with one thing after another, without significant government retribution. On May 20 the government did formally declare martial law in Beijing, but an army advance toward the city was blocked by large numbers of students and ordinary citizens. No crackdown followed, and on the twenty-third, the troops pulled back to the outskirts of the city.

At that point the striking students established the Defend Tiananmen Square Headquarters, naming a fiery young woman, Chai Ling, as commander in chief. Another group formed the Alliance to Defend the Constitution, which promptly decided that the students would end their occupation of the square on May 30. A resolution to that effect was announced at a press conference on May 27 in the square, and Li and I breathed a sigh of relief. But the students were divided, and began to squabble among themselves. Chai Ling and her faction rejected the resolution to end the occupation of the square, and stayed.

On May 30 a group of artistically inclined students unveiled a ten-meter-high statue of the "Goddess of Democracy" in the square. The aesthetic value of the piece might have been questionable, but as propaganda it was a potent slap in the face to the hard-liners who now ruled China. That was when Li started calling to book a flight to Beijing.

I did all I could to persuade him not to go, that there was nothing he could do, this late in the game. He merely shook his head adamantly and said, "Moira, I know too many of them to stand idly by. If there is fighting, or if the protest is broken and the government tries to hunt them down, I can help. I can hide them, and help them get out of the country, if need be. I must be ready to go at a moment's notice."

In retaliation, I got out my plastic and charged a full-fare return ticket from Beijing to San Francisco, usable anytime. I had it messengered to my apartment, and over his protests, put it in his luggage.

To conduct these Internet vigils, we usually got to Berkeley and reached Jim's office by six in the evening, San

Francisco time. So by the time we got on-line, it was sixteen hours later in Beijing, or ten o'clock in the morning on the following day.

On June 2 we were still at Jim's as it neared 10:00 P.M., or two in the afternoon on June 3, Beijing time. Still another hunger strike had been declared, and Li had begun to verge on panic. Then, in consternation, we learned that earlier in the day the troops had received orders to reclaim the square "at any cost."

Using information gleaned from the Usenet postings, we pieced together the story. Early in the morning, army units had tried to get to Tiananmen Square but had been blocked by students, workers, and residents of the city. By the time Li and I decided to log off and get some sleep, the troops had been ordered away from the city.

It seemed safe enough to go home and get what rest we could. However, both Li and I were too uneasy to do so. There was a cot room on the floor, since Jim and his students often pulled all-nighters, and we decided to nap there, grab some coffee around six o'clock in the morning, and get back on the Internet. Fortunately, June 2 was a Friday, so we didn't have to worry about calling in sick.

What we didn't know was that while we slept, a full-scale military assault was already under way.

Early the next morning we groped our way over to the student union and grabbed some coffee. By that time it was ten o'clock at night in Beijing. In horror, we saw a newspaper headline: At nightfall, the government had ordered people to stay away from Tiananmen—whereupon a crowd of several hundred thousand people had gathered in the square. Five thousand military police in full battle gear had burst out of the Great Hall of the People on the western side of the square, only to be surrounded and stymied by the crowds. Soldiers outside the square then began firing their weapons, using tear gas, and beating anyone in their way.

We raced back to Jim's computer, got on Usenet, and with growing fear read about the massacre as it unfolded.

Troops and armored personnel carriers converged on the city. The students and workers fought back with barricades, rocks, and Molotov cocktails. Many people were killed or wounded, including bystanders, on the western approaches to the square. Along Chang'an Boulevard, hundreds of people died when the army found its path blocked.

At eleven o'clock in Beijing that night, a single armored personnel carrier made it into the square and was set on fire. Student leaders camped in the square learned that armed troops would move on the square within a few hours. By midnight nearly forty trucks carrying soldiers were slowly advancing toward the square from the west, and a thousand troops approached from the east. By three in the morning on Sunday, June 4, the square was surrounded, trapping several thousand students and supporters inside. The troops shot into crowds on the outskirts of the square. By five in the morning, demonstrators began to leave at gunpoint, and control of the square was passed over to the soldiers, tanks, and riot police. And at six, army units rolled over tents in the square, many with students still lying exhausted inside them. Skirmishes continued throughout the day, and many more people were killed.

The Usenet messages often contradicted each other, but they were all chilling. None asserted, like the Chinese government, that no one had been killed; they only disagreed on the number of the dead. I kept copies of the printouts Li made. Here are some of them. You will, I trust, forgive the imperfect English.

It is incredible. We were too innocent. People were too kindhearted. The students love peace so much, even in the last moment they still did not give up their hope. They had dreamed of democracy, freedom. . . .

They had dreamed of the happiness in the future. They had dreamed of having a people's government. They had dreamed of the protection of people's army. But all the sudden, all beautiful dreams were broken by the white smoke of tear-gas bomb, the fire spurted from muzzles and the huge shadow of tanks. The Chang'an street became a river of blood. . . . June 4, 1989, the history will remember this day for grief. . . .

The TV and radio that are all controlled by the dictators are still roaring "suppress the counterrevolutionary rebellion." They even lied that "no one is dead in Tiananmen Square." There is not any newspapers since the slaughtering. A lot of people listen to VOA and BBC in the evenings to get some news. Beside of this, people pass news on the streets. The messages talking about how people are killed come along continuously. . . . The situation right now is unclear. No government leader has showed up after the insane act. A government speaker was showing on TV last evening but his false smile cannot cover the weak of his heart. . . .

> —from a Beijing University student

When Deng Xiaoping–Li Peng regime gave the order to fire at patriots in the name of revolution, the whole world was stunned. The day of June 4, 1989, witnessed the most barbarous, most inhuman suppression in the modern Chinese history. . . . The nation is in a most critical crisis, with its best sons and daughters being slaughtered. We can no longer keep silence.

> —from a statement by six Chinese Communist Party members at Virginia Tech, renouncing their party membership

This is the darkest day in China's history, the ugliest time through human civilization. . . . This is the death throe of the frenzied Deng-Li regime. As all of them have dirty bills in hands, they have no choice but to fight to death. Thus the people have no choice either but to fight until they overthrow the most rotten government in the world history.

—from a Chinese student in Shanghai

By the end of the day, Li had cried out all his heartbreak and was exhausted. We went back to his apartment and fell into an exhausted sleep. When I awoke early Sunday morning I heard him on the telephone, booking a flight to Beijing for that night.

I couldn't sway him, no matter how much I begged and pleaded. He told me to keep for him what possessions he had acquired during his stay in San Francisco, and promised to let me know that he was all right as soon as he was able—and could say so truthfully.

When a week had gone by, I got Jim to help me locate people in Beijing on the Internet. I started frantically E-mailing everybody I could get hold of with a Beijing address, asking if anyone knew what had happened to him. As he was a teacher, I had hopes that at least one person I E-mailed would know and would be brave enough to tell me.

On June 16, I finally got a reply. The sender had somehow managed to anonymize his name and address, so neither Jim nor I had the ghost of a clue who it was. The message said that Li had been arrested for aiding Tiananmen refugees fleeing the government police and would certainly be tried and sent to prison. It closed by asking me to stop sending messages to China, because in the wake of the massacre, everyone was suspect. Merely receiving messages like mine was enough to render an innocent person

suspect in the eyes of the government; if I continued to
bombard people in Beijing with queries, I was only expos-
ing them to danger.

For years afterward I periodically checked with Amnesty
International to see if they knew anything about Li. They
didn't. As far as I could tell, he was either dead, or had
dropped off the face of the Earth.

NINETEEN

JUNE 18, 1989

NEEDLESS TO SAY, I GOT NO SLEEP ON THE FOLLOWING Friday and Saturday. As a result, I spent Sunday morning wandering around my condo like one of the living dead. I was frantic with grief, but I was so tired I couldn't concentrate on anything, not even cleaning the place or doing the laundry. I needed something to occupy my mind—to take it over so I could stop thinking of Li every waking moment.

So I went to work, even though it was Sunday. I hoped I could force myself to concentrate on something abstract, like a client's tax problem. There would be a few professional acquaintances at work, so I would be forced to exercise restraint, behave professionally, and not be in the least tempted to pour out my tale of woe yet again.

I tried to get into my work, and ended up taking care of a few loose ends. But in the end, I couldn't stay focused on the law any more than on my laundry. When dusk fell a little after 8:00 P.M., I retrieved my car from the Embarcadero parking garage and started home. Or so I thought.

Before I had driven very far, it dawned on me that I was afraid to go home. Nothing awaited me there but empty rooms, which would soon be filled with the ravings of my outraged, anguished mind.

I headed out California Street, picked up some food from

a little Chinese take-out place, and drove toward the Golden Gate Bridge. I wasn't sure what I'd do: maybe walk out to the bridge, or go to the Cliff House for a drink and watch the sun go down, or stroll in one of the wooded areas that overlooked the ocean.

The moonlight sparkling on the water was entrancing— and strangely comforting. The light got colder and whiter the higher the moon rose, until the whole bay seemed enchanted. I drove farther into the park, until I reached a lookout point, wooded with cypresses bent over by the wind. There I stopped again, and watched as the moon slowly lit up the vast black stretch of the Pacific to the west of the Golden Gate.

Why all this made me feel better, I didn't know. I felt empty and melancholy, but the grief that burned me like so much acid had briefly receded, and by that point the mere absence of great pain felt a great deal like pleasure.

It was a stupid thing to do, but I decided to go for a walk. I left my car, crossed the drive, and began hiking up a trail that led into a denser stand of forest to the west of the Presidio buildings, which promised occasional ocean views. I gave no thought whatsoever to my personal safety; I wasn't exactly thinking clearly at the time.

The trail kept going upward, and I thought I remembered from a picnic years ago that it eventually led to a high forested bluff that overlooked the ocean. I had no intention of hiking that far; I just wanted to find a tree to sit under where I could stare at the moon and continue to enjoy my bout of unexpected tranquillity.

I found a good tree and plunked down with my back planted firmly against it. I could see the moon through the branches overhead, and I took several deep, long, calming breaths. The tension that had held my head in a vise for the past few days began to dissipate.

As I continued to sit there with the tree propping me up, and the moonlight turning the forest all white and spooky,

I had the most eerie feeling that the calm and comfort pouring into my heart were coming from somewhere outside
me. I mean, I had been a complete and total mess for the
past few days. There was no way I was personally capable
of generating peace of mind and a quiet heart, not through
meditation, mind control, or any conceivable amount of
New Agey crystals.

All my years of singing in the girls' choir had not combined to make me a religious person. Still, the impression
persisted that the influx of serenity I was experiencing came
from something other than myself. It was quite bizarre; the
feeling was something I couldn't shake. Maybe it was because the moon was so very, very old. The moon had been
through meteoric bombardment, and besides that had
watched humanity go through a lot too. But it was still
shining away, enigmatic and serene as ever. It was a role
model to emulate.

At length I decided to stop trying to dissect the experience with scalpels, and just accept it. I didn't care where
the help was coming from, so long as it kept coming. Whoever instructed people not to look gift horses in the mouth
had had the right idea.

Eventually I attained a somewhat unsteady state of confidence that I could actually make it back to the car, drive
home, and get a wee bit of sleep that night. I stood up and
walked back onto the trail. Then I came to a horrified standstill, because two very large, hairy, grubby men were coming up the path straight toward me.

Since the early 1980s a lot of homeless people had taken
up residence in the park. Probably 99 percent of them
would have been as scared of me right then as I was of
them. Those 99 percent were poor, sick, helpless, mentally
ill, or living in the grip of a substance abuse demon. They
needed help even more than I did, which was a truly frightening thought.

But—politically incorrect as it might be to breathe such

a notion openly—that still meant 1 percent of the park's
denizens were bad news. There were predators in the forest;
there was no doubt in my mind that two of them were
standing before me that very moment. And they were glad
to see me.

When they first spotted me, they stared as if unable to
believe their good luck. Then they broke into a run, heading
straight for me. I could see them scoping out the area on
either side of the trail, getting ready to head me off if I
tried to go around them.

I had worn my jeans and tennis shoes that day, and I
was in good health and good shape, so the playing field
should have been reasonably level—or so I thought. I spun
around and began to run as fast as I could up the trail, away
from them. My strategy was to keep running until they fell
behind from exhaustion. Since they were undoubtedly sick
and malnourished and drugged out, this strategy seemed
sound.

However, the human body can tolerate an incredible
amount of abuse until age thirty-five or so. As I ran, I
guessed those guys still had a ways to go to reach that
magic number, because they not only kept up with me, it
sounded like they were gaining—not that I stopped to take
an exact measurement.

I cursed myself for being a thousand kinds of idiot, and
ran faster from sheer terror. I had assumed that because my
heart was broken, because I was suffering so much over
Li's death, that I had hit bottom. Further disaster could not
touch me. Well, it seemed I was wrong. Shortly I was going
to be mugged, gang-raped, and maybe killed, or if not
killed, at least beaten up and given a loathsome disease.

The race seemed to go on forever. If they'd been ordinary fit guys in their late twenties, they would have caught
me, no question about it.

The trail finally began to level off, just as I felt myself
beginning to really tire. I looked about for some sign of

other people—a camp of other homeless, even. As I was beginning to despair, I rounded a corner and caught a glimpse of a group of people ahead in a clearing. They had a big Weber grill that contained a great leaping fire. Evidently they were trying to start up a barbecue and had used too much lighter fluid.

I ran straight toward them, screaming at the top of my lungs. I realized distractedly that they had been singing, perhaps a campfire song, and fell silent when they heard me. No matter; I was too frightened to be embarrassed or feel stupid for screaming.

It slowly registered in my mind that they were standing in a great big, perfect circle around the Weber, and they all had on long, dark robes. A moment later, I burst through the circle, threw myself on the ground, and begged them to help me.

A woman broke out of the circle and ran toward me. She was younger than I, beautiful and striking, with long, jet-black hair that gleamed in the firelight. She was wearing a simple gown of what looked like black velvet—and several necklaces. The sight of one of them turned my blood to ice water—dangling from a black cord was a large, five-pointed star, surrounded by a circle, gleaming like molten silver in the moonlight and firelight. A pentacle.

After being chased by the ruffians in the park, I was ready to believe anything. I felt sure my luck had turned so sour, there really were Satanists in San Francisco, and I'd managed to run straight into one of their secret dark rituals. I'd given new meaning to the phrase "Out of the frying pan, into the fire."

I was so frightened I totally forgot that long ago, in England, I'd observed a gathering much like this one.

"Gray Wolf, Sea Otter, get those guys!" cried the woman. Two of the men hiked up their robes, revealing legs clad in blue jeans, and took off running, straight toward the thugs who had been chasing me. I had a glimpse of said baddies standing rooted to the spot, mouths open, probably as terrified as I was. As the running men bore down on them, they turned and fled like rabbits.

I was so totally frightened and demoralized, I broke into hysterical tears. The woman crouched down beside me and put her arms around me. "Hush, it's all right now. There are plenty of us to protect you. Did they hurt you, or are you just scared?"

I muttered something that approximated "Scared."

"Do you want us to call the police? We have a cellular phone in one of the cars."

The thought of Satanists having a cellular phone struck me as so utterly bizarre that I started to laugh and couldn't stop. "Are you kidding?" I managed to say. "*You* don't want me calling the police, are you out of your mind?"

The woman gave me a long, studied look. "Just what do you think we're doing?" she finally asked.

I opened my mouth, shut it, and gave a shrug. I sure didn't want to piss them off.

"You think we're devil-worshipers, or something like that?" the woman persisted.

I couldn't cope with it. I resumed my hysterical crying. As long as I had hysterics, they couldn't expect me to talk.

"Oh, for Goddess' sake," she said. "We're members of a Wiccan coven. We don't even believe in the devil. We're celebrating what's called an Esbat—a full moon."

"Oh," I said.

"This is a worship service. We'll be glad to call the police, if you want us to. We don't have to worry, because we're not doing anything illegal."

I nodded, for lack of anything better. "Oh, for pity's sake," said the woman, "would you like to see our permit from the parks and recreation department? Will that make you feel better?"

"Surely you jest," I said in a small voice.

"No, I don't. We come here a lot. For example, we gathered here last May Day, to celebrate the Beltane Sabbat. We wore green robes and flowers, and had a May Pole. We'll be back next Thursday for another Sabbat celebration, the Summer Solstice. There's no need to be afraid of us. We try our best not to harm anyone in any way. It's against our religion.''

A few of the neuroconnectors in my brain resumed functioning, and in a flash of memory, I remembered Arthur at The Green Man in the Haight; and, better late than never, the Druids at Avebury.

The two men who had gone chasing my thugs returned to the circle. ''We couldn't catch them. They ran into the forest, and they evidently know the terrain pretty well,'' one said. ''Is she okay? Should we call the cops?''

''I think she'll be fine,'' said the woman with the pentacle. She looked at me again and said, ''Do you have a car?''

''Yes. Parked a long way back, at the other end of the trail.''

''One of us can drive you there. Or if you'd feel more comfortable walking, we can escort you. There are so many of us, those guys won't dare come near you.''

I began to think I might come out of this alive. ''What about your—celebration? What about the Weber? You don't want to leave the Weber, somebody might steal it.''

She laughed out loud. ''The Weber's the least of our worries just now. So's the ritual. Look, we'll take you back to your car now, if you feel like driving. Or we can wait a little while, until you feel better.''

One of the guys who had gone on the chase came over with a large ornate clay goblet. I guessed he was the one called Sea Otter, because he wore a striking pewter pin of a Monterey Bay otter, probably purchased at one of those tourist traps down in Carmel. ''D'you drink wine?'' he asked, holding out the goblet.

The drollness of the situation began to get the better of

me. "Hell, yes," I said. My hysteria was trying to reassert itself in the form of giggles, and I was fighting for all I was worth.

"Here," he said, "drink up."

I looked at it suspiciously, and my woman friend gave a little sigh. "It's Cakebread Cellars Sauvignon Blanc, 1987," she whispered. "Twelve dollars a bottle."

I had been to Cakebread, up in Napa, and they truly made very fine wines. I sipped it, and knew at once she wasn't woofing me. "I'll buy you a replacement bottle," I said, and took a big gulp.

Sea Otter came back carrying a big tall plastic picnic glass that also appeared to be full of wine. "Sorry," he said, "I wasn't thinking. We need the chalice back for the ritual. Is this okay?"

"Free wine, following rescue from certain death? S'okay."

The woman patted my shoulder. "Why don't you sit here, drink your wine, and pull yourself together? We'll go on with our ritual, and then we'll take you to your car. And don't worry. There's nothing to be afraid of."

"What's your name?" I asked.

"Rhiannon."

Memories of Avebury were coming back big-time now. "Oh, I get it! Like the Celtic goddess," I said, showing off a bit.

"Or witch, depending on your point of view," she said. Then she glided off toward the Weber, where her companions were already reassembling in a circle.

Judging from the size of the plastic picnic glass, my strange companions had given me most of their bottle of wine, reserving only a little for their chalice. I did not wish to slight their hospitality, so I drank deeply. The wine landed in a totally empty stomach housed inside a woman in the last stages of major adrenaline withdrawal, and in no time I was tight as a tick.

So there I was, around ten o'clock on a beautiful San Francisco night, sitting in the middle of a forest that smelled of fresh pine-type needles and ocean air, looking at the most gorgeous full moon I had ever seen. I had drunk fine wine, and was now entertained by superb live theater. With great drama, my Wiccans called upon the four elements of Earth, Air, Fire, and Water to attend their ceremony. That done, they invoked the presence of a Goddess and God (in that order, I noted with smug satisfaction). They recited a lot of halfway decent poetry (though I must say that, considered as art, the old Episcopal liturgy had an edge . . . but give these guys another four hundred years, and who knows what they'd come up with). They danced and sang and chanted and generally carried on. By then I personally was in a mood to howl at the moon, but I knew that would spoil the mood, and restrained myself. They complimented the lovely orb on her beauty, and then they proceeded to work magic. Each member of the circle in turn produced a piece of paper, upon which was written a personal failing they wished to get rid of. Each failing was announced, and the paper tossed into the fire. (''Eating too much sugar'' . . . ''A bad temper'' . . . ''Being jealous of people who made more money'' . . . ''Being judgmental of others'' . . . ''Cutting corners when recycling'' . . . ''Not being patient with my clueless parents'' . . . ''Letting the Fundamentalists get to me'' . . . ''Can't stop lusting after a juicy steak'' . . . and so on.)

Next, the power of the moon at its waxing full was invoked, and prayers were offered up for things the group would like to see happen. Peace in the world; more caring for the environment; an end to animal testing; a plea for vegetarianism; et cetera, et cetera, et cetera. I was just eyeing my empty glass with regret when I heard one of them say, ''An end to repression in China, and never again a killing of students in Tiananmen Square.''

That brought me back to Earth in a big way. I gasped,

and quickly, with all my might, added my silent prayer to theirs, hoping no offense would be taken on account of my affiliation with the Episcopal Church.

Passing strange, the woman named Rhiannon paused, turned, and looked right at me, though I had said nothing. "Someone I love was just killed at Tiananmen Square," I said out loud.

She gave a slight nod. "May he rest in the arms of the Goddess," she intoned.

They wound it up after that, thanking the assorted deities for their attendance, and shut down the sacred circle. That was where the wine and a plate of Mrs. Fields cookies came in. Later Rhiannon told me that at the end of a ritual you were supposed to quaff a little wine and eat a cookie, some bread, or a piece of cake, to "ground" yourself after expending so much psychic energy.

It was time to go home and get ready for the Monday workday. Guys set to putting out the fire and dismantling the Weber, and Rhiannon came over to see how I was doing. I definitely decided that I was going to call in sick the next day.

"What part of town do you live in?" she asked. "You're clearly in no shape to drive."

"North Beach," I replied, "on Chestnut."

"Oh! We live in a condo on Union Street, at the top of the hill. Why don't you let me take you to your car? Then we can drive to your place, and I'll just walk home."

In North Beach, as festive and crowded as it was at all hours of the night, she would be perfectly safe, even dressed as she was. "Okay," I agreed.

We found my car, and Rhiannon offered to drive, earning my undying gratitude. We wended our way home without event. Rhiannon steered my car carefully into my tiny allotted parking space, and we got out and returned to the sidewalk.

"Well, thank you, Rhiannon," I said.

"What's your name?" she asked me.

"Moira," I said. I was trying to get up my nerve to ask her to go have coffee sometime. I knew I would have a lot of things to ask her about, once I sobered up and got some sleep.

"Oh, that's interesting."

"Why?"

"Your name is Irish or Gaelic for 'great one.' "

I laughed out loud. "My grandmother named my mom for the movie star, Moira Shearer, and unfortunately Mom passed it on. Well, that just goes to show there's nothing in a name."

One of the necklaces she wore was very beautiful. It consisted of alternating beads of golden amber and dark, glossy, carved beads that might have been made of wood. "That's lovely," I said. "The light-colored beads are amber, aren't they?"

"Yes, and the black ones are jet."

"Does it have a special meaning?"

"It does indeed. We wear necklaces of amber and jet to symbolize our struggle to keep the forces of light and darkness in balance."

When she said that, I wanted to gape at her, because I could swear I had heard them say something like that in the Robin Hood series. On second thought, add *Star Wars* to the list, too. I screwed up my courage and said, "Uh, Rhiannon, can I ask you something?"

Her expression suddenly became guarded. There was a slight pause before she answered. "Yes, certainly," she answered, her tone polite, distant, and very firm. "But I must say that if you are thinking of trying to convert me, please don't. I'm quite satisfied with my religion and have no wish to change."

"Oh. I was afraid you might try to convert me," I said in a small voice.

She laughed. "No, no," she replied, "we don't do that sort of thing.

We're not interested in growing, just in following our own path. What was it you wanted to ask?"

I was full of Cakebread Sauvignon Blanc, exhausted, and on the edge of a crying jag. "There are so many stereotypes about you guys. Do you ever perform your rituals naked?"

Rhiannon suddenly looked as if she were going to explode with laughter. "In this climate?"

"Oh, I see your point," I said.

"It's important to us to be outdoors, but here in San Francisco, we'd freeze our tails off. Some covens in Southern California work in the nude—actually, the correct word is 'skyclad'—but it's a trifle warmer down there!"

"Um, I heard one of the men refer to you as a priestess; was he a priest?"

"Gray Wolf? You could call him that."

"Do you have to sleep with him?"

Rhiannon stared at me as if I'd goosed her, and this time did break out laughing. "Well, yes, I guess so."

"Oh," I replied. "Wow."

"But we never do it during rituals, only at home."

"Why?"

"Have you ever tried screwing on the hard ground, like on a camping trip, perhaps? One's own bed is much more comfortable."

"What if you refused to, uh, do it with him?"

Her eyes danced. "In the olden days, I'm told, he could have divorced me."

That took a minute to sink in, but when it did, I felt like a complete and total idiot. "There are covens that do celebrate the Great Rite," she added, "but it involves consenting adults, and harms none, so I can have no ethical objection to it. It wouldn't be my cup of tea, but I shouldn't tell others how to worship."

I cast about for something else to say. "Oh, I was just

wondering, don't you guys ever get bothered, harassed, that sort of thing?''

"Occasionally. There are still plenty of people who think we sacrifice babies. You almost thought so, didn't you?''

She had me. I could feel my face coloring. "Yeah, and I had reason to know better.''

"Well, I'm even a volunteer at the Oakland Children's Hospital when I'm not at work.''

"Wow!'' I said. "You're a regular paragon.''

"Of something,'' she replied, ruefully. "Moira, you want to know what really gets to me? In general?''

"Sure,'' I said.

"I'm not ragging on you, understand. But sometimes I feel like the most unfairly misunderstood pagan in the world.''

This was getting really interesting. "Tell all,'' I prompted.

"Most people's stereotypes of witches get formed when they see *The Wizard of Oz,* and then by Halloween decorations every year after that. They never seem to remember Glinda, the good witch.''

"Well, I don't suppose good witches sell many newspapers.''

"You're so right,'' she said. "I've gotten to where I don't talk about my religion at work, or to people I meet casually, and certainly not when those door-to-door Bible thumpers come by. I'm tired of being reviled all the time, or having to spend three hours educating them before I can draw a free breath.''

"I can understand that,'' I replied. "I've gotten to where I sometimes don't tell people I'm a lawyer.''

She broke out laughing. "*Touché!* Now, Moira, what really chaps me is the static I get from other pagans. As if it weren't bad enough to be stereotyped by the general public, people who ought to be my own brothers and sisters give me hell.''

"No pun intended," I said.

She had a sense of humor, and so she grinned. "There are a gazillion different groups of pagans, just as there are many Christian sects. There are the ceremonial magicians, who practice magic with no religious overtones—they tend to be young, male, and rather full of themselves. There are those who insist that Gaia is both a light and a dark goddess, because she not only nurtures us, she also sends us earthquakes and hurricanes. Others insist that gods and goddesses who embody destruction should be recognized and even venerated, because death is a part of life—hence people who include Kali, Shiva, and the Morrigan in their rituals. There are those who say we should toss overboard our "Harm None" motto, because it's impossible to achieve. Well, I think one should emphasize the beauty of creation, while acknowledging its less pleasant aspects. There are danger and evil in the world, but you should live in spite of them. An earthquake could destroy the life I've built here in San Francisco in an instant, but that doesn't mean I should give up and go home."

"So you're not from here? Not that anybody I know is!"

"Nope. Detroit."

I almost broke out laughing, but Rhiannon wasn't through. "There's no justice. On Usenet, I'm the one who gets called names. A very pedantic, British traditional witch recently referred to me in a newsgroup posting as a 'white-light fluffy-bunny New Age Wicca-babbler.' "

"Ewww, ouch," I replied. "Well, at least they were creative. Rhiannon, what sort of work do you do? In real life, I mean."

"Real life? Let me think." She smiled and admitted, "I'm a computer programmer. Moira, enough chitchat. You look exhausted. Is it safe to say good-bye? Will you be all right?"

I nodded. "Yeah. Thanks, from the bottom of my heart. You guys probably saved my life."

"You're welcome." She put out her hand, and we shook. She smiled and said, "Many blessings."

"Would you do something for me?" I asked.

"Certainly."

It took me a long time to draw the right words together. "I'm coming up on forty," I said. "When I look back at my life, I can't tell that it follows any pattern, but I feel that it must, or else there's no meaning to anything. I can't tell that the world is getting any better, but it must—or else—"

"Or else you are simply gazing into a void, and that is terrifying," Rhiannon said, finishing my sentence for me.

I nodded. She continued, "You want to know that there is a Pattern. You want to know what it looks like. And you want to know your place in it."

"That's about the sum of it," I replied.

"I'll work a spell and ask that all this knowledge be given to you, if it be proper, and for the good of all people."

Then she took off down Chestnut Street like a black shadow. I was too looped, and also too chicken, to call after her, though I wanted to. She lived somewhere nearby, and we could have gotten to be friends.

I was not to meet her again for forty years.

PART FOUR

Men at some times are masters of their fates:
The fault, dear Brutus, is not in our stars,
But in ourselves . . .

—William Shakespeare, *Julius Caesar,* Act I,
Scene 2

Man . . . the first creature in all the immensities of time
and space whose evolution is self-directed. The first
creature, in any spiritual sense, to create his own environment.

—Aldo Leopold, "The River of the Mother
of God," 1924

Hamlet: . . . What news?
Rosencrantz: None my lord but that the world's
grown honest.
Hamlet: Then is doomsday near.

—William Shakespeare, *Hamlet,* Act II,
Scene 2

TWENTY

1989–1991

AFTER TIANANMEN SQUARE, I SET THE TORCH TO ANY hopes I might have harbored of a life with a husband. Until then, though I was nearing forty, girlish dreams of the perfect man and the perfect marriage had still lurked in the nethermost regions of my psyche. Those regions were cleverly camouflaged and highly fortified, given the inroads cynicism had made on my natural idealism, but they were there. Until Li disappeared. Then they did, too.

Like most yuppies in the 1980s, I had made a shitload of money while employed. Unlike most yuppies in the 1980s, I had saved much of it. Comes from being lower-middle-class when you're young, I suppose. True, I bought a lot of toys in my time, but I must have drawn the line somewhere. By the time Li was killed, I had more than fifty thou piled up in savings accounts, mutual funds, and retirement plans. For my golden years, of course.

Screw the golden years, I said in a fit of pique, and bought a copy of *Final Exit*. I'll off myself, and then they'll all be sorry. Or maybe they won't, but I won't have to stick around and suffer anymore.

That phase did not last for long, because first of all I was afraid suicide would hurt, and in the second place, I have never been good at pouting for long. What I did then

sounds so sixties, so counterculture, I can hardly bring myself to describe it now.

I didn't kill myself. I killed my job. I sold my vintage
Pantera and bought a sensible Toyota Corolla with only
seventy thousand miles on it. I said *hasta la vista* to my
terminally chic *Cosmo*-girl apartment. I took all my cash
and moved up to Mendocino to regenerate. I became a
"duppie," a downwardly mobile urban professional.

I stayed there for almost two years. It was great, for a
small burg. Unfortunately, I couldn't really make a bunch
of new out-of-town friends over the Internet, because the
era was only 1989–91. The Net hadn't turned into the social
whirl it would become by the mid-1990s, and besides, in
those days it was murder finding a good ISP up there in
Mendocino-Humboldt land. Still, the place was pretty cool.
I acted out my long-lost Texas hippie youth and became a
fixture at all the local happenings that were the least bit
artsy, literary, or leftist. Considering that I was living in
Mendocino, that meant most of them. I walked along the
ever-present seashore a great deal—and, trite as it sounds,
began to heal. I also amassed an impressive seashell and
driftwood collection.

I did not date, let alone shack up with anyone. I just
concentrated on getting over Li, and trying to stop having
nightmares about what must have happened to him after
Tiananmen Square.

Alas, by early 1991 my money started to run out. Since
the notion of dying had long since begun to bore me, I
knew I had to do something constructive. I would gladly
have stayed in little Mendocino for the rest of my life,
chomping croissants and downing lattes and smiling indulgently at the tourists who came there to relax for forty-
eight hours before diving back into the pressure cooker of
the San Francisco financial district. But reality beckoned,
so with great reluctance, I followed.

My sophisticated strategy to reenter the legal profession

centered around a single attempt: to approach my old firm, make them sorry for me because of what I had undergone, and get them to rehire me at my old salary.

By accident or design, the partner assigned to interview me was Roger. Remember him? The moment I laid eyes on him, I could tell he still cared about me, and crossed my fingers that it would help me land a job.

It did.

The job was not the one I had had in mind, however. Roger informed me, with genuine regret, that the firm had only granted me an interview out of courtesy. It was now the nineties, and the recession had slugged California but hard. Times were lean. The firm could hire an associate only a few years out of law school for much less money who could perform at the same level at which I had performed two years ago, so why should they hire me?

I swallowed my disappointment with what I hoped was good grace. Then Roger dropped the bomb. He said he hoped with all his heart that I had overcome the loss of the man I loved. He said he still hoped to marry again, if not to someone who loved him passionately and romantically (an unlikely prospect, given his advancing age), at least to a congenial grown-up woman who cared about him and would enjoy sharing life's little pleasures—such as his summer house in Gualala, the many fine restaurants in the San Francisco Bay Area, theater and museum trips to London and New York, shopping and dining trips to Paris, and a beautiful home on a full acre in the Berkeley hills.

He meant someone like me. In fact, preferably me.

For once, I did not act like a complete idiot. I did not reject him outright; I only asked for a little time to think. He hailed a taxi, which took us to Masa's (the best restaurant in San Francisco), and we had a lovely, tasty, wine-filled, nonpressured dinner.

The core of my being—my soul, if you will—was at that time totaled. Cauterized dead away by powers beyond my control, you might say. After some reflection, I accepted Roger's offer.

In later years, people took no end of pleasure in giving Jane Fonda all sorts of static for renouncing her political activism, marrying media mogul Ted, and kicking back and enjoying life for a change. Me, I always got mad and took her side. Anyone with a brain could see the poor woman was burned out. Even Joan Baez sat out the Persian Gulf War. Hell, at the end of a lifetime of fruitless struggle against Darth Vader and the Empire, a girl *deserves* Ted Turner.

Our marriage was a good deal for Roger, too. He was significantly older than I, and had nursed his first wife until her death. He was hoping, much like me, to wring a last little drop of sweetness from life after a nasty turn through the fire.

We had a very comfortable, bland, and happy life together. We had a small garden. I participated in charities and did lots of good works. Our beautiful home was nestled high up in the Berkeley hills, and had a stunning view of San Francisco, the bay, and the Golden Gate Bridge. We entertained, and we vacationed.

There was an early dreadful setback I should mention, only because it would have such a major impact on my life forty years hence. On October 20, 1991, a beautiful Sunday, we decided to go hiking on Mount Tamalpais, over in Marin. We told Professor Kingsfield, our little pedigreed Jack Russell terrier, to guard the house, and left—taking with us only the hiking outfits we were wearing, and a backpack containing identification, a couple of credit cards, some snacks, and water.

We hiked for several hours before we made it all the way up to a Mount Tam ridgetop. There we decided to stop and take a rest. Surprisingly, given the season, the day had turned out to be blistering. There was a hot breeze blowing toward us from the East Bay hills and the Central Valley; the Bay Area's usual cooling sea breeze from the west had been routed.

At one point during the hike Roger pointed out that there was a plume of smoke spouting up from what appeared to be the East Bay hills, but we were not sure of our bearings, and in any case we were not sure the plume was anywhere near our house. We fretted a bit, but told ourselves there was nothing we could do about it from the top of Mount Tam, and continued on our hike for another hour.

By then the pillar of smoke had grown to significant proportions, and we had begun to be so worried we could no longer enjoy our hike. We started hurrying back down the mountain, growing more and more frightened as we went. Halfway to the spot where we had left our car, we came across another couple heading pell-mell down the trail, their faces the color of ash. They had heard from another hiker about the fire in the East Bay, and that the unusual offshore winds were whipping it into a frenzy. People thought as many as a thousand homes might go up in flames; the news media were already referring to the event as a "hellfire."

We ran faster than we should have. Roger slipped on a patch of stones and dry dirt and fell, cutting his leg open. By the time we reached the trail head and our car, the sky over Oakland and Berkeley had turned black as night, and little bits of ash, blown hither by the wind out of the east, were covering our shiny new BMW like so many snowflakes.

As it turned out, in those flakes were tiny lost bits of many lives, including our own home and possessions and our feisty dog—all that was left, when the fire was finally put out, of three thousand other homes and the memories they contained.

• • •

We went about rebuilding. We spent the next year and a half in a constant battle with architects, contractors, our insurance company, and the City of Berkeley. Phoenix-like, our house was one of the first to arise from the ashes of the East Bay fire, and when it was finished it was bigger and more beautiful than the first.

And—pay attention here—it was new.

As time went on, Roger got this bright idea of buying up the half-dozen big empty lots that now surrounded our house. They were empty because many of our former neighbors just weren't up to the gargantuan task of starting over.

I can only conclude that Roger had a first-rate guardian angel, who worked for both of us; he couldn't have foreseen how important those extra lots would be to my future survival, yet he bought them anyway, just because they were such a bargain.

He was so good at making lucky guesses—I suppose he paid that guardian angel overtime. Though he was more than sixty and should not have been liquidating one damn thing in his portfolio to buy real estate with little prospect of appreciation, he still bought all those empty lots for us. Why? Because he wanted to install a gorgeous, sumptuous, expanded garden to enjoy when he finally retired.

Roger had no idea that in several years he would be dead of a heart attack and would never get to have that garden. He certainly hadn't a clue that by the third millennium, our rebuilt house and those six vacant lots would mean the difference between life and death for me and a bevy of desperate, aging companions. Yet he made the right move at the right time.

Rest in peace, Roger.

TWENTY-ONE

<<Thud, Thud, Thud>>

1992 AND AFTERWARD

ONCE MORE, I WAS ALONE.

I was well provided for financially and did not have to contemplate resuming the practice of law in middle age, with my craft rusty and my battery starting to die. Roger had left so many good investments behind him that I was able to pay off the balance owing on our house and all the empty lots and could have done absolutely nothing for the rest of my life, had I been so inclined.

That was the good part. On the downside, I was forced to admit that forty-plus years of my life had somehow disappeared down the tube when I wasn't looking, and I had no family, children, or noteworthy achievements of any kind to show for them.

This was a major trauma for someone who had been a charter member of the immortal Pepsi Generation. I couldn't be getting old. I had been too young to hitch to Woodstock, too young to experience the flower child scene in the Haight, too young to hitch to San Francisco to see the Beatles in their last live performance, too young to catch the really impressive sit-ins of the sixties—you name it. So it was simply unthinkable I could ever be . . . old.

There were the numbers in black and white, though: The year was 1995 and I was forty-three. That was when I started asking those middle-of-the-night, middle-of-your-life-span questions. I started searching for the meaning of it all.

I wasn't sure where to begin. I did know I was no longer content to give money to worthy causes from behind the scenes, or to dress up and organize charity benefits. And I knew I had to start somewhere. So I took the bit in my teeth and accepted a series of activist volunteer jobs, some of them heartbreaking, others downright frightening.

It's one thing to give money to fight AIDS and wear a nifty red ribbon to society functions—but another thing entirely to actually deliver free meals to people dying of the scourge. You don't feel like Lady Bountiful at all. You cannot help finding the victims repulsive, in all their bodily misery, and their dreary, impoverished surroundings. You are revolted because you find them repulsive. You cannot decide whether to put on a fake, cheery face or to break into tears. If you are trying to discover the meaning of life, you do not find it; you leave with more questions than you arrived with.

I had always given money to a center out in Marin County that rescued sea lions and seals and other marine animals from various perils. This time around I volunteered for the dirty work. I cleaned and scrubbed a lot. I helped out when the vets had to put down a sea lion that somebody had shot and left to die. Gulls with eyes put out by rocks, seals blinded by BB guns—it was all in a day's work. After one of those sessions, I was no closer to understanding my fellow man. The animals at the center must have thought us an utterly schizophrenic and unpredictable species. They had been injured in the first place by humans, only to be rescued by others—no consistency there. For my part, I could weather-vane between hating the whole of humanity when the maimed and dying animals were brought in, to positively loving my own species when I saw how the other volunteers struggled to save them. On especially bad days, I could make the round trip several times.

I joined brigades to pick up trash on the beaches up in Marin. Though such efforts were generally less dramatic than tending dying humans or other animals, the puzzle was always the same. People with time on their hands came out to the beach for a reason, presumably to enjoy nature in all her beauty. They brought all sorts of junk with them and left a lot of it behind, marring that beauty. Other people with time on their hands came out to the beach with bags and litter-pickers, and strove to restore that beauty. They were all members of the same species; go figure.

After some time spent in the trenches, I figured out I wasn't ever going to discover what it all meant. Perhaps there was no meaning. Nature was cruel and heartless in her own way—"red in tooth and claw," as Tennyson put it—and we were just part of nature. If we were inimical to ourselves and the other living creatures on the planet, so what? We were just another predator species, tilting toward imminent extinction.

Yet whenever I finished making that argument to myself (and I did so a lot, in futile attempts to reduce the great emotional discomfort I felt on behalf of the helpless while performing my good works), it rang hollow somehow.

If we were just another predator species, why did some of us *care* what we did to other creatures? Did *T. rex* ever agonize over his own cruelty as he chowed down on some hapless veggie-eating dinosaur? Did the neighborhood stray tomcat suffer qualms of conscience as it tortured the occasional bird it managed to nab at my Droll Yankee feeder? I thought not.

If we were just another predator species, why were some of us seemingly intent upon exterminating every whale we could get our hands on, while others of us were willing to band together in packs to push beached whales back into the sea? Or commit expensive, high-tech icebreaker ships to freeing other whales trapped in polar ice? You always knew what to expect from a *T. rex,* but you couldn't say the same for us.

Back in my soul-searching days, the good people of Hegins, Pennsylvania sponsored a "pigeon shoot" each Labor Day, in the course of which the participants observed a curious ritual. On a shooting field, young children were taught to line up boxes, each containing a pigeon. The boxes were designed to then propel the dazed birds into the air, at which point the participants, young and old, proceeded to blaze away with their guns and blow the pigeons to bits. However, it was estimated that approximately 77% of the birds were not killed immediately. When the volley died down, animal rescue workers (who had been waiting on the sidelines all the time) ran onto the field and attempted to save the pigeons that their fellows had just wounded. Pigeon shoot participants were known to body-slam rescue workers into pickup trucks, and then bite or rip the heads off injured pigeons to further provoke them. Afterward, you could count on there being much talk among the libertarian-minded about the legal rights of the individual, and much talk among the empathetic about the rights of all living things. When all the dust settled, it is true the pigeon was no worse off than a Tyson chicken, wrapped in plastic. But as we lawyers said, "Intent is everything."

It came down to this: Whenever I got good and ready to take out my *Homo sapiens* membership card and burn it, somebody would go and do something absolutely self-sacrificing or thoughtful or noble, and I would have no choice but to stuff the damn thing back in my wallet.

It made absolutely no sense unless you concluded that we weren't just another predator.

And that opened up a whole new ball game.

I quit trying to understand it all. I just decided to continue giving my time and money where I could. I wasn't being noble, understand. I had a very selfish reason for

doing all this. As long as I kept myself busy playing Luke
Skywalker with a light saber, I wouldn't have time to give
in to the feelings of futility and despair that lurked around
every corner.

Eventually, of course, my own situation grew so desperate—as did most people's—that I had to spend all my spare
time ensuring my own survival and that of my commune.
But that all happened much later.

When I married Roger and became a woman of relative
leisure, my life changed. Despite all my social and mon-
eyed-wife charitable activities and my considerable number
of friends, I still had a lot of free time to sit around, study,
and think, since I was not forced to resume billing more
than two thousand hours a year at the law firm. Magically,
I had time to read various and sundry newspapers and magazines.

So it was, in the early nineties, that I started maintaining
in earnest a file of articles I had been keeping in a desultory
fashion for quite some years. These articles, which I found
particularly distressing, were generally about the environment. Curiously, they rarely made the front page of the
newspaper in question, or appeared on the front cover of
the magazine.

At length I came to refer to this as my <<THUD>>
file.

After Roger died, despite my frenetic volunteering schedule, I had even more time to spend on my file. By late 1996
I could look back on almost a decade's worth of clippings
and discern a rather disturbing sequence of events.

Here are a few of them.

In the first week of November 1987, the *Los Angeles
Times* ran a story in which the National Science Foundation
made a most interesting report. Apparently a "monstrous"
iceberg, nearly a hundred miles long and twenty-five miles
wide, characterized as twice the size of Rhode Island, had

broken loose from Antarctica's Ross Ice Shelf, dramatically altering the shape of the shoreline where Richard E. Byrd had established his "Little America" base camp more than sixty years before. (In case you are wondering, the Ross Ice Shelf itself is about the size of Texas.) The NSF opined that if the berg could be transported to my beloved California, it could supply the water needs of Los Angeles for the next 675 years.

I was suitably impressed until the next week, when the *San Jose Mercury News* ran a follow-up story, pointing out that the previous year an iceberg three times as large had broken off Antarctica's Larsen Ice Shelf.

Only the *Mercury News* article mentioned the possibility that the giant icebergs of the past two years were an early sign of global warming.

The next year, in 1988, a blistering heat wave helped make the greenhouse effect front-page news across the country; as corn withered in fields across the nation that summer, news reports asked whether 1988 was a first taste of a time yet to come.

I can answer that question: Yes.

In 1994 a most curious story came to light. In the 1960s and 1970s, desperate to get at the region's oil, gold, diamonds, and other minerals, the Soviets had launched a mass settlement drive across Siberia. One town, Yakutsk, exploded into a showpiece city in a few years. In Yakutsk, the permafrost layer of perpetually frozen ground lay approximately five feet below the surface of the city. Large, modern buildings could not be erected on traditional foundations laid flat on the upper five feet of soil, the "active layer," which froze in winter and thawed in summer; they would have collapsed. So the Soviet engineers, faced with the problem of seasonally sagging ground, devised an elegant solution. They set concrete piles deep enough into the ground to penetrate into the permafrost, which was effectively like bedrock.

They hadn't counted on climate change, however. As the climate warmed, the permafrost layer retreated deeper into the Earth, and slowly, ominously, Siberia's new buildings began to tilt. The dismayed engineers revisited their calculations and concluded that by the middle of the next century, the permafrost layer would have receded to sixteen feet.

Actually, it receded that far by 2020, which is why the Russians, with plenty of other problems on their hands, never rebuilt Yakutsk. Ignoring the toppled buildings, it is once again a little hamlet of log cabins and wooden huts, riding the ups and downs of the slow seasonal earthquakes like little bobbing ships on the water.

Nineteen ninety-five turned into a real kick of a year. Here in California, nasty storms beat us up in January; then in February we baked. The "heat wave" broke records throughout California, with Los Angeles reaching an all-time high of ninety-four degrees. By March we were back in the soup again, drenching wet. Even the bees went on strike; it was too damn cold and rainy that spring to work, they said, and so the Central Valley fruit growers resigned themselves to a sharp decline in tree fruit crops that year.

This all caught the National Weather Service by surprise; the Service said it had never seen anything like that weather pattern, and furthermore, could not look back into history and find anything like it either.

In April it was reported that world temperatures were once again climbing, after briefly cooling under the shade of volcanic dust spewed into the atmosphere in 1991 by Mount Pinatubo. In May satellite data told us that sea levels were rising at more than a tenth of an inch a year, or twice the established historical rate. It was projected that most U.S. beaches would be under water within thirty years.

As they were.

In May torrential rains left seventy thousand homeless in Bangladesh. In June I read that eastern China was bracing for its worst flooding disaster of the century. A Reuters dispatch from Shanghai stated that global warming was melting the snows on the Tibet-Qinghai plateau, the source of the Yangtze River in western China; this had sharply raised water levels in rivers and lakes along the Yangtze's lower reaches, threatening dikes that had been in place for centuries. Chagrined, I remembered Li talking about the same plateau, and the Yangtze, that time we had wandered into the Green Man shop in the Haight.

July broke existing heat records across the United States. By mid-July there were more than five hundred deaths in Chicago alone. By the end of July another hundred had died. Tempers boiled over in New York City as the temperature soared past a hundred, and even San Francisco reached ninety-six degrees.

The U.N. Intergovernmental Panel on Climate Change, a body famous for being unable to make up its mind what to order for lunch, bit the bullet and stated that there was a warming trend, it was at least partly caused by human activity, and it would raise average temperatures around the world from two to six degrees Fahrenheit in the next century. They were conservative; in fact the temperature reached the midpoint of their predicted range in less than 40 years.

In August, in the aftermath of Hurricane Felix, experts predicted that in the coming decades, climate change would spawn far more hurricanes as the waters of the tropics grew warmer. Fifty-eight international insurance companies went to Geneva to demand early and substantial reductions in greenhouse-gas emissions. They were understandably upset. From 1990 to 1995 they had already paid out forty-eight billion dollars for storm damage, or three times the amount they were socked for in the entire decade of the 1980s.

In December paleoanthropologist Richard Leakey, son of the famed Louis and Mary Leakey, observed that human beings were likely to drive half of all living species to extinction within the next few decades, thereby causing the sixth mass extinction in the history of life on the planet. This catastrophe, he concluded, would destroy us as well as most other living things on Earth.

I had myself a merry little Christmas.

In January of 1996 I learned that in 1995 the Earth's average surface temperature had climbed to an all-time record high the previous year—1995 was the warmest year globally since records first were kept, in 1856. New Yorkers had scarcely had time to digest this news when the Blizzard of 1996 dropped twenty inches of snow on Central Park. California, however, enjoyed record warmth—as it had the previous January. All in all, the weather was sensational enough to make the cover of *Newsweek,* which proclaimed: ''Blizzards, Floods, and Hurricanes: Blame Global Warming.''

Come February, subzero temperatures smote towns and cities across the nation and stayed. We were okay in California, but we had an interesting news report to ponder: During the 1990s we had seen an average of thirteen tornadoes a year in the Golden State. That was up from six a year in the 1980s, four per year in the 1970s, three per year in the 1960s, and two per year in the 1950s.

Hmm . . . I thought, eyeballing the data, it looks kinda exponential to me.

As I was chewing that over, the *New York Times* said in March that eighty-eight reservoirs built across the temperate regions of the Earth since the early 1950s each contained at least 10 billion metric tons of water. This shift in the distribution of Earth's water tended to speed up the planet's rate of spin. Moreover, the weight of all that water collected close to the Earth's axis was slightly tilting that axis, and the shape of the Earth's gravitational field had been altered. The *Times* quoted experts who said these effects posed no danger to people or the global environment. I didn't know whether to be reassured or to take a Valium; you mean a bunch of dam builders could actually affect the Earth's spin, the tilt of its axis, and its gravitational field?

In April we baked again in record-breaking heat, even in San Francisco. In May the local paper reported that waters along the West Coast from Alaska to Mexico were warming in unprecedented fashion, even without the contribution of the infamous El Niño. That summer scientists announced that around the world the springtime blooming of trees and plants was shifting earlier and earlier with each passing year. In July *Time* magazine gave a pithy report on the Mississippi's killer flood in the Midwest, and the heat wave grilling the South and East—"A Season in Hell," the article was called.

We broke more heat records in San Francisco, in July, while a world conference on climate change adopted a declaration calling for compulsory reductions in the burning of fossil fuels. The major oil-producing nations, however, protested that such a move would devastate their economies.

In September, scientists reported that temperatures were higher in the tropics than they had been for thousands of years, and the average sea surface temperatures in the tropical Pacific had risen by a full degree in the past few decades. They recalled that the cautious Intergovernmental Panel on Climate Change had fretted in 1995 that a global warming of two to six degrees could cause up to a third of the world's glaciers to melt, and sea levels to rise as much as three feet.

I'll stop now. It was all there in print for anybody who cared to look at it. We just didn't do enough about it in time, because we wanted to wait until we were absolutely positive bad things were going to happen before we did anything.

So we went on pumping six billion tons of carbon dioxide into the atmosphere each year, until bad things actually did happen. The only problem was, by that point we were stuck with the brave new world we had made, because once carbon dioxide gets up there, it doesn't go away. It stays—for five hundred years.

The way I figured it, since the collapse of our civilization seemed pretty imminent, around the year 2550 things ought to really start looking up.

To be fair, there were occasional signs of hope. In the 1990s, a political candidate's greenness began to play a role in how he or she fared at the ballot box. Attempts on the national level to roll back a quarter century of environmental legislation were defeated. It was possible for the sort of man who wrote *Earth in the Balance* to be vice president for most of that decade, a state of affairs that would have been inconceivable in the 1970s. At frequent intervals, scientists sounded dire environmental warnings, which were useful except that they sometimes had the unfortunate effect of scaring people and sending them into big-time denial.

Eventually the mainstream religions began to champion environmentalism, bestowing on it the same moral legitimacy they had given to civil rights and other causes years earlier. Now other clergy, as well as scientists, urged religious leaders to embrace the environment and organize on its behalf. The Earth and all creation was sacred, they said; since anything recognized as sacred was more likely to be cherished and safeguarded, the various denominations should throw their weight behind attempts to imbue the environment with an aspect of the sacred.

Pretty soon you had groups forming such as the National Religious Partnership for the Environment the Evangelical Environmental Network. When the Texas moneyman Charles Hurwitz was on the point of logging California's Headwaters Forest in 1996, you had rabbis aplenty begging "Woodman, spare that tree!" on religious grounds.

All this was nice, but it was a classic case of too little,

too late. And the delay was due, in part, to a most curious phenomenon.

In many cases it was not just the clergy who were slow to acknowledge that attempts to save the natural world might have spiritual dimension to them. Not that this notion was all that radical—since most religions posited that one or more gods had created the Earth, it did not take a huge intellectual leap to conclude that the creation of a sacred being might itself be somewhat sacred. But in many cases, the most passionate advocates of environmental preservation resisted any linking of it to matters sacred.

Why? It was a matter of public relations.

In spite of the fact that the vast majority of environmentalists were plain-vanilla Christians, the folks who found environmentalism to be hazardous to their personal agendas figured out early on that a promising way to discredit environmentalists was to paint them as sinister pagans. (Remember the Dominionists? They traced their roots back to the 1980s and the "war against the Greens.")

Pat Robertson wrote in 1991 that government could not operate successfully unless "led by godly men and women operating under the laws of the God of Jacob." Environmentalists were "animist tree worshipers" and "New Age worshipers of Satan" and so presumably did not operate under those laws. In 1995 Pat Buchanan, under the impression that environmentalists were believers in a malevolent non-Christian faith, charged that they had turned Easter into Earth Day and worshiped dirt.

In 1992 the Wise Use Movement declared that environmentalism was "the new paganism." The movement reported that "trees are worshiped and humans sacrificed at its altar. It is evil. And we intend to destroy it." The next year they declared a spiritual war, a genuine home-grown American Jihad, against environmentalists.

In 1993 the *New York Times* reported that the Roman Catholic establishment was perturbed by the worship of the earth goddess by certain feminist American Catholics, because the practice created an unacceptable blend of Catholicism with animist faith that veered toward witchcraft.

Also in 1993, a *Wall Street Journal* editorial charged that environmentalists promoted "a pagan fanaticism that now worships such Gods as Nature with a reverence formerly accorded real religions."

In 1995 the Pope denounced the election of Lech Walesa in Poland on the grounds that the former Communist was a proponent of a Neopagan philosophy. (No, I never did figure that one out.)

And in 1996, an elderly western congresswoman said it better than any of them, testifying to Congress that "environmental policies are driven by a kind of emotional spiritualism that threatens the very foundation of our society. There is increasing evidence of a government-sponsored religion in America. This religion, a cloudy mixture of New Age mysticism, Native American folklore, and primitive Earth worship, is being promoted and enforced by the Clinton administration in violation of our rights and freedoms."

I was always certain that the president, a dyed-in-the-wool, grits-fed, hymn-singing good ol' Southern Baptist boy, at whose inauguration none other than the Reverend Billy Graham had officiated, must have dropped his rocks in sheer amazement when he heard that one.

You get the picture. In fact, there was a spiritual dimension to the environmental movement, because there is a spiritual dimension to a sentient race's efforts to escape destruction. No atheists in foxholes, as it goes. But for years, the very people who could have used morality as an argument against our wholesale destruction of our terrestrial life support system refused to do so—for fear of being branded as pagans. As if the sky would thereupon have immediately fallen.

Anyway, things definitely went downhill the last part of my life. Actually, they went to hell in a handbasket. Starting around the year 2010, the disruptions we had wrought in the Earth's natural balance gained momentum, and had increasingly unpleasant effects on our daily life, even in the United States. Climate disruptions led to floods, droughts and massive famine in Africa, the Indian subcontinent, and other parts of Asia; the collapse of regimes and governments followed, not to mention the reemergence of ancient tribal grudges. These led to the displacement of record numbers of refugees, who could not be fed, and who spread disease among their fellows like wildfire. As countries collapsed, so did financial markets and regional economies. When those countries could not afford to produce and sell their own goods, buy foreign goods, or pay back foreign debt, foreigners suffered.

Slowly, at home and abroad, the web of our highly sensitive, highly technical civilization began to unravel, one thread at a time.

The United States fell into a depression more severe than the Great Depression of the 1930s. In California, daily urban life became progressively more unpleasant as unemployment skyrocketed and as the social safety net that had kept so many of us from the fear of starvation began to fray. On my sixtieth birthday, in 2012, I had grown old and nervous enough to surround my property with a security fence and spend thousands of dollars on a state-of-the-art home protection system. When I turned sixty-two, I opened my doors to a succession of friends, and people referred by friends. My old office pal Aleta was the first to join me at the top of my Berkeley hill; others followed, and over the years the final members of the commune came and stayed, one by one. Aleta, then Loki, then George for safety, then Rhiannon, then Lorenzo, and last of all Lyla Ann. Aleta was also the first to die, in a drive-by shooting at the hands of a stranger.

It just got worse and worse. My second forty years

passed by as slowly and inexorably as my first, and so I
came at last to age eighty, and resolved to put some of my
rage and despair into a book—as if I presumed there would
be posterity to read it, or care about our misery if they did.

TWENTY-TWO

OCTOBER 15, 2032

WE WERE WITHIN A FEW WEEKS OF THE ELECTION, AND Julian Imber had still another fireside chat scheduled. He was speaking from Ann Arbor, Michigan, where he had gone to school. Like Rhiannon, he was originally from Detroit; for some reason she was inordinately proud of this fact.

He was going to speak at 6:00 P.M. our time. As the appointed hour drew near, we gathered around the tube, even though it was still wretchedly hot inside the house. We gritted our teeth and endured it, hoping against hope he would say something that would lift our spirits.

He came onscreen right at six, quickly thanked the University of Michigan for hosting the talk, and turned to face the cameras, his expression sober.

"We all know that our planet is in crisis," he stated, wasting no time on chit-chat. By our careless intervention, we have altered the life-sustaining atmosphere of the Earth and disrupted climate patterns across the entire world. We have already begun to pay the price for our folly; every one of us has already suffered greatly from the devastation we have brought upon ourselves.

"Our situation is critical, yet so far the government of the United States has failed to do what has to be done—

for fear of political repercussions from powerful special interests. In short, out of cowardice.

"I've come here tonight to acknowledge to you that we are in great danger. Unlike other candidates, I refuse to downplay any longer the peril in which we now find ourselves. We have reached a point in our nation's history where we have very few options left to us and very little time in which to act.

"We are like passengers on a ship that is headed in the wrong direction. If you send me to the White House a few short weeks from now, I won't be afraid to make a controversial move for fear you won't reelect me in 2036. Instead, I will do everything within my power to turn the ship around.

"If you don't want me to turn the ship around, then don't vote for me. I don't want to be president unless I have your mandate to do what needs to be done, before it's too late for everyone.

"I was recently reminded of a conversation that Franklin Delano Roosevelt had with a close friend when he was first elected to office. America was in the depths of the Great Depression, and the republic was in serious danger of disintegration. Roosevelt, however, believed his New Deal would turn the country around. One day a friend said to him, 'If the New Deal is a success, you will be remembered as the greatest American president.' Roosevelt thought carefully and then replied, 'If I fail, I will be remembered as the last one.'

"If you choose me as your president, I will be in the same position as Franklin Roosevelt. If the sweeping changes and reforms I intend to implement are successful, then I will have been able to render my country as great a service as Roosevelt. If I fail, or if you elect a president who continues to do nothing—then you will have elected the last president of the United States."

Here his expression grew stern. "It is difficult to believe

that we have come so close to the Apocalypse, and yet still can count within our society groups of people who would complete—for their own selfish, short-lived gain—the destruction of the delicate planetary balance upon which all our lives depend. The Earth is our own personal life support system, entrusted to us by a generous God—and it is failing. Yet these people seem to believe that if they can only make more money, if they can only build stronger and higher walls around their gated communities, if they can only double or triple the power of their air-conditioning systems, that the collapse of the planet will somehow not hurt them. Or they shrug and say, as did a cynic some years before the French Revolution, 'After us, the deluge.'

"These groups not only exist, they are very powerful. If I am elected president, and do what I must do, be warned— I will incur the hatred and militant opposition of each and every one of these groups. I will need your support every step of the way.

"Accordingly, I ask you to stand by me, and work with me to save our country and our planet while there is still time. If we do not put aside our differences and turn our back on selfishness now, we will be destroyed.

"Over the past months, I have tried to describe in my speeches the sacrifices that will be required of us in coming years. I won't repeat them here and now. Instead, I will stress the single, overarching principle that must guide us all. We must renounce our differences and act as one, for the good of all people. We are facing the gravest threat in human history, and this is the only way we will overcome it.

We must draw together to defeat a common enemy of our own making. We must defeat the impulses of greed and selfishness, and the blind eye we have cast toward the welfare of all living things upon the Earth, which have led us to this grave impasse.

"We are a great nation. Time after time in our history,

we have reinvented and reinvigorated ourselves, and emerged from adversity stronger than ever. My friends, until this latest catastrophe brought us to our knees, *we were winning*!

"For many, many years we did not see this new demon standing ahead of us in the road, waiting to fall on us. We did not realize we would have to grapple with it. We feel outraged that it has poisoned our lives; we feel angry and resentful, for it seems to have crept up on us by stealth. Its very existence is still a shock and surprise to many of us. The environment has become like a hostile power in its own right, an enemy every bit as menacing as Nazi Germany was a hundred years ago. But *we* have made it so. We have set the stage for our own destruction. In this desperate hour, *we*—and our own failings and weaknesses—are the enemy.

"This is the greatest threat and the greatest challenge that we have ever faced. Yet we have changed our beliefs before, when we had to. We have reinvented our very ways of thought, when we were forced to. We have been in situations like this before, and come through them to a better life. We can do it again.

"We must transform ourselves one more time. We must give our love and understanding not only to the whole of humanity, but to the Earth and all its creatures as well. We must believe with all our mind and heart that we are part of creation, not apart from it. When we look at the poisoned air, the rising water, the degraded Earth, the displaced men and women dying by the millions, we must see ourselves mirrored there.

We believed in the equality of human beings and made that dream a reality. We must bring that same fervor to this, our new battle. We must see as one the Earth, all her peoples, and all creatures that still survive. We must do whatever is necessary to cure her—and ourselves. In the past, when we have carried within us a passionate belief in a moral truth, nothing could stop us. Let us prove that we are still capable of change.

"My fellow Americans, *this* is World War III. I call on all of you to put aside your differences, and sacrifice individually so that we all may live. When we act as one, nothing has ever been able to stop us. We are at war—and this is your call to arms. My friends, let us overcome the demon within ourselves."

He stood back from the podium. He let a few seconds of silence tick past. Then he simply said "Thank you" and left the stage.

Rhiannon was weeping openly. "Well," I said, "let us march!"

"*Homo sapiens,*" said Lorenzo, "you're up at bat. Don't blow it."

Beto seemed bewildered, but Ciel stared at the television screen as if she had understood every word of it.

George kept shaking his head. From the look of him, he couldn't decide whether to cheer or cry. "Long-winded son of a bitch," he said under his breath. "You sure he's not related to Bill Clinton?"

"Oh, hush up!" I said. "You just saw history made."

George continued to shake his head, and his look turned woeful. "They're going to nail him now for sure, after this! God almighty, the Secret Service had better know what it's doing."

"Don't say that!" Rhiannon cried. "You'll make it come true!" She got to her feet and set off determinedly in the direction of her room, no doubt to work a protection spell on Julian's behalf.

I felt sick to my stomach, as if I could read the future.

Julian went back to his hotel, escorted by said Secret Service, leaving the nation boiling like a hill of ants in his wake. His uninteresting Democratic opponent sputtered and hissed but couldn't come up with one damning thing to say about the speech. The commentators just babbled. Over and over, by those with more than a passing acquaintance with history, Julian was compared to Theodore Roosevelt—that crusading, reforming, icon-busting young Republican from more than a century in the past.

His killers were ready for him. They sent a suicide bomber to masquerade as a portly bellhop at the hotel where Julian was staying. The man was not in fact fat, but was wearing enough of that undetectable plastic explosive stuff under his clothing—you remember, the junk they started using to blow up airplanes in the mid-twentieth century—to bring down the whole hotel, and most of the surrounding city block. This happened barely an hour after his speech, when the pundits had just gotten up to speed dissecting and digesting and rehashing his speech. The Blue Northers and the Dommies took credit for it, but I had a feeling they were just the first ones in line to actually get to him.

We had all halfway expected it—just not quite so goddamn soon. We turned off the television, and each of us trudged off to our own room. I went to see Rhiannon; she was shut up in her room meditating and spellworking, and didn't know.

She took one look at my red face and puffy eyes and guessed what had happened. All the spirit went out of her, and she lay down on her bed, seeming to diminish and shrink into it before my very eyes.

When she was all wept out, she sat up. "So much for the political system," she said in a dull voice. "We're done for. This was our last chance—not that I really expected us to take it."

"It's not the last chance," I replied, lying to myself for all I was worth. "Get on-line and tell your Green Man friends it's their turn."

She looked at me with tired, empty eyes. "Yeah, right, they can pull a rabbit out of a hat and save us at the last minute. I think not."

"It's not a rabbit out of a hat if they've been working on it a hell of a long time," I replied. "Based on everything you've told me, it sounds like they've been cooking up this magic bullet for many, many years. Get on the Net and find out what they intend to do now that Julian's dead."

She shook her head. "It's false hope, Moira. I'm not going to put myself through that tonight. Right now, I'm just going to lie here and try to sleep."

I left her alone, closing the door quietly behind me.

TWENTY-THREE

Not Single Spies, but in Battalions

OCTOBER 16, 2032

WELL, THE PREVIOUS DAY'S TURN OF EVENTS PRETTY much knocked the stuffing out of us. While much can be said for the power of positive thinking and the importance of attitude, there are times when your team is just plain losing and you have to admit it.

When it was dark and the air had begun to cool, Rhiannon, Lorenzo, Beto, and I headed for the oak tree as usual. Ciel, who was due to have the baby any minute, was sleeping like a log upstairs, a beeper beside her in case the pains started. Rhiannon was a trained midwife; in spite of her current despair, there was still no way she was going to miss that gig.

Fortunately for me, as it soon turned out, Hillary had taken a real shine to Ciel recently—or perhaps to Ciel's nice, warm bed, and the fact that Ciel was usually in it. Hillary was upstairs, too, as zonked out asleep as the girl.

Nobody said much of anything. We hadn't gotten a rat's ass worth of work done that day, in shock as we were over the killing of Julian, and worried sick about what else might happen while everyone in Washington was running around like chickens with their heads cut off.

We plopped down on the bench and I, for one, just stared glumly at the garden and all the work that had to be done: cleanup, preparing the terraced beds for planting next spring, last-minute harvesting of late fruit and winter squash—it never ended. As soon as we ticked off one item on our to-do list, another climbed on board. Sure, it just goes with being a farmer, but try leading that kind of life sometime when you're eighty.

I was simply bummed out, no two ways about it. Lorenzo was so dog tired he could barely keep from nodding off. However, it slowly began to dawn on me that Beto and Rhiannon were as nervous as cats. Beto couldn't sit still, and he didn't seem to want to meet anybody's eyes. Rhiannon looked preoccupied and kept glancing at him, as if bedeviled by a worry she couldn't shake.

"You have to help me," Beto finally said. Rhiannon's head snapped up, and she gazed at him intently. "I don't know what to do. Some guys are going to hurt my grandmother."

Now it made sense. Beto was freaked out, and Rhiannon had been picking up on it. "Why, Beto?" I asked.

"They found out I was living here, and they want me to let them in. But I can't do that. They'd kill Rhiannon."

Not to mention the rest of us, I said to myself.

"Beto, are you sure these guys would really hurt your grandmother? Is it possible they're bluffing?" I pressed.

Beto just looked at me like I was the stupidest old woman he had ever met, who knew nothing about the streets. A relic of a bygone era—which in fact I was.

Lorenzo sighed. "God please damn that selfish asshole George. If he'd only been halfway generous, we wouldn't be in this bind, but no, he was worried you'd want to let *all* your relatives in."

"No way," said Beto. "My grandmother's the only one I care about. They can kill all the others if they want."

Rhiannon shot me a look of chagrin.

Suddenly she sat bolt upright. In the faint light, her face was suddenly drawn and pale. "Somebody's coming!"

Beto let out a gasp of fear. We saw three figures emerge from the shadows that lay across the street. Two carried a big cloth sack, full of something heavy, that they had strung on a pole between them. The third one carried a smaller sack, which also appeared full.

I stood behind the bench and dragged Rhiannon after me. "Lorenzo, get down!" I said with a hiss. "Beto, offer them money. Offer to give them a thousand dollars cash if they'll bring your grandmother here unharmed. We can get it."

I couldn't tell whether he heard me. He went running toward the gate, and only stopped when the third figure, a boy his age who was carrying the small sack, waved him back with a gun.

The other two dropped their burden on the ground and opened the sack. There was a little old woman inside, who sat where they had put her. She was sick, or dazed, or perhaps just half dead with terror.

For an awful second I couldn't decide what to do. I couldn't make up my mind—I was paralyzed. If I called George, he would come out with guns blazing; Beto might be killed, and we might lose the chance to get his grandmother away from those little beasts. But if I hesitated, to give Beto time to negotiate with them, I might be the ruin of us all.

Beto said something to them. I thought I heard the word "thousand." The three of them broke out laughing, and the one with the gun said, "No, you let us in, man, that's the only reason we're here."

I beeped George. Beto hesitated, and with a quick motion, the one who had spoken took a short ax out of the small bag, stretched out the old woman's arm on the pavement, and chopped it off below the elbow. She screamed, a horrible, wailing sound I could never banish from my dreams after that. "Open it, now!" the boy ordered, pointing to the gate.

There was no sign of George. Beto shrieked, and looked back at us. Savagely, the boy bent down and hacked off half of the old woman's other arm. Beto broke, and began to work at the gate.

I raised my gun to shoot him in the back, before he could let them in. The other boy saw me, and quick as a snake striking, fired at me first. His aim was bad, and he only grazed my shoulder, but I dropped the gun.

Rhiannon and I ducked behind the bench as the boy kept firing. We heard Lorenzo cry out in pain as he was hit, and then I heard the gate scrape open.

"Lorenzo!" Rhiannon cried, and dared a quick glance over the top of the bench. "Oh, God," she gasped. "His head . . ."

Then she transformed into a person I had never seen before—I could feel her anger turn cold and vengeful, and I remember noticing in the dim light that her hand did not shake the least little bit as she picked up the gun. She peered around the side of the bench, took careful aim, and shot the leader dead.

Then there were three sharp, crackling noises from the direction of the house. In quick succession, the two other invading boys, and Beto, dropped to the ground.

George had made a wise investment in that high-tech rifle.

I stumbled out to the gate and dragged the old woman into the compound. Needless to say, she had lost a horrendous amount of blood, and I was pretty sure she was in shock and dying right before my eyes. But I couldn't leave her out on the street.

Then I closed the gate and reactivated the security system.

His wheelchair whirring like an angry insect, George descended on us. He ignored the three boys, Beto, and the grandmother. He went up to Rhiannon instead and demanded to look at Lorenzo.

"Shut up," she said. "He's dead. The bullet went right through his forehead."

"I warned you people about the kid," said George.

Rhiannon's face contorted. She called him a heartless son of a bitch, drew back her arm, and slapped him across the face with all her might. Then she dropped my gun like it had bitten her, and ran for the house.

At Withering Heights, somebody always managed to rise to the occasion and pick up the pieces when disaster struck. Once again, it was my turn. First I went back to check on the old lady, and determined that now she was indeed dead. I went back to the bench and tried to prop up Lorenzo's body in a halfway dignified fashion. Then I sat down on the ground and wept, ignoring George, wondering how on Earth Rhiannon and I were going to bury Lorenzo, as old as we were, and with my shoulder starting to hurt like hell. I knew I could get the City to come and dispose of the other bodies, but Lorenzo was family—we couldn't throw him away like a dead cat.

George said nothing; he didn't dare. At length I got up and hobbled back to the house in search of our first-aid kit. It was only a flesh wound, as John Wayne would have said, but it needed tending to. Somehow I had to play Kitty to my own Matt Dillon.

I fixed my wounded arm all by my goddamn lonesome. Then I went to see Rhiannon. Her door was closed; through it, I could hear her sobbing. Worse, I could hear Ciel calling out, frightened and upset, from her own room. "Rhiannon? Is somebody there? Beto?" I was sure that when she found out what had happened, the shock would send her into labor.

I figured Rhiannon was going through a serious crisis of faith, since she had just killed somebody, and her religion was not keen on her doing things like that. However, she would have to deal with it later.

"Go away!" she cried when I walked into her room.

"No, girlfriend," I said, trying to sound firm. "You have to help me bury Lorenzo, but likely before that, you have to deliver a baby. Pull yourself together."

"It's not Lorenzo anymore, it's just a body. Let the City take it," she said. She was lying face down on the bed and did not appear to have any intention of moving.

"What about a funeral pyre? He'd have liked the style."

Rhiannon made a shrugging motion. I was so numbed myself, I started to make a joke about what a change it would be for a witch to burn a Catholic priest on a pile of wood, but somehow managed to think better of it. "All right, the City it is," I replied. "Just tell me as long as we're chatting: Do you plan to take care of Ciel or not? You're the one she's close to, not me. She's screaming her head off in there, she's scared to death, and for all I know the baby's on the way. Or do you even care anymore?"

After a couple of minutes Rhiannon hauled herself to a sitting position and rubbed her face. "Yes, I have to think of the baby," she said, "even though I'd probably be doing it a favor by letting it die. Who could bring a child into this world, in good conscience?"

"Good point. Are you going to let it die?"

"For crying out loud, Moira! Of course not! What a dumb thing to say. Can you help me get all the supplies together? I'm having trouble thinking straight."

"Yes, ma'am."

We consumed the last of my current stash of rotgut to calm our nerves, and went in to break the news to Ciel. She'd heard the gunfire and the shouting, and she wasn't stupid—she had an inkling some very bad things had happened.

We told her the state of things, as best we could. She took it bravely. I don't know whether there was a connection or not, but early the next morning she went into labor. The gods of good fortune smiled on us briefly; it was quick and easy, and she delivered a baby girl before the sun had set. She was even well fixed with a goodly supply of milk, so we didn't have to figure out immediately how we were going to feed the poor little thing.

Ciel named her Madonna. I asked whether she was thinking of the famous pop star of the past century, but she didn't know who I was talking about. Rhiannon took me aside and reminded me that some people were still Catholic, even in this godforsaken era, and Ciel was clearly thinking of the original Madonna, who was—after all—just another incarnation of the Great Goddess.

Whatever.

I resolved to call her Donna. Less work.

TWENTY-FOUR

The Destroyer of Worlds

OCTOBER 20–29, 2032

WE WERE IN SHOCK FOR SEVERAL DAYS AFTERWARD. THEN reality came knocking, and Rhiannon and I realized that we were running very low on certain supplies. Less than a week before, there had been no particular urgency to making a grocery run to Mad Mac's; Beto could do it anytime. Of course, he should have gone the day after Julian was killed. Any fool could put two and two together and figure out that the country was going to turn topsy-turvy in the wake of the assassination, which would mean supplies would be even harder to get than they usually were. Yet we were so stunned, we weren't thinking straight. Then Beto and Lorenzo were murdered, and any prospect for rational strategic household planning went straight out the door.

By the twentieth we were sufficiently out of shock to start taking care of business. Somehow Rhiannon and I were going to have to take the scooter to Mac's, get the supplies, and make it back to Withering Heights in one piece. George couldn't help us. Mean as he was, he had no legs, and would be more of a liability than an asset at the store. Ciel was hopeless. So that left me and my witchy friend.

At length we resolved to dress up like the meanest couple of old butches you ever saw. We didn't care about political correctness; we wanted to invoke any badass stereotype available and make it work for us. I had worn my hair long, braided, and coiled on top of my head all these years, but now I cut it real short and macho. It really should have been steely gray for the best effect, but I had always been a blonde, so that was that. I put on dark sunglasses, got Loki's dirty, roughneck blue jean jacket, stuck a pack of old cigarettes in the front pocket, scraped grease under my fingernails, and took off every last piece of jewelry. I also put on extra sweaters under the jacket, to bulk me up, and I exchanged my own tiny little gun for George's Uzi. Rhiannon would not cut her hair, but put it under an old redneck Leer cap that belonged to George, and appropriated Loki's black leather jacket. We both borrowed pairs of heavy leather boots from Loki's estate, and practiced looking like nasty old junkyard dogs.

I'm not sure how much good it did, but we did get back alive.

We blew in there and stalked around, loading up on all the stuff we needed. Understand, we had a lot of preserved food socked away at Withering Heights, enough for months. We needed to stock up on things we couldn't grow: medicine, lightbulbs, tools, batteries, soap and detergent, booze, matches. We did get some awfully scrutinizing looks, but nobody actually hassled us, ripped us off, or tried to follow us, so I counted the trip as a success.

Sure enough, prices had skyrocketed, and the amount I entered into my debiter made my stomach hurt. I felt the beginnings of true desperation; at this rate, our savings would melt away but fast, and then—impossible as it seemed—we would be even more screwed than we already were.

Then, of all things, this teenage kid came up and said, "Ma'am, a free sample?"

Free sample? In this day and age? And him so polite

besides? "What kind of a joke is this, sonny?" I demanded, glaring at him.

"Air freshener, ma'am."

For a moment I was absolutely speechless. Struck dumb. "The hell you say," I finally squeaked. "Can I see that?"

He handed me a little cylinder. It was about the size of one of those little travel-size hair sprays you used to buy at the drugstore in my youth. I tried to read the manufacturer's name, but the print was so fine, or my eyes were so bad, I couldn't do it. "In this day and age," I said querulously, "what damn fool company thinks it can sell air freshener, when everybody's poor?"

He just shrugged. "Lots of things smell bad these days, so it'll come in real handy. It's not supposed to cost much when they start selling it for real—the marketing strategy is to sell people a little treat that will really brighten up their day, that they can still afford."

I studied the kid—he sounded way too smart. "This your dad's company or something? You sound like you actually give a shit."

He looked startled and then said, "Yes, ma'am, something like that. Here, take a whiff, it's delicious." He spritzed a little in the general direction of my nose and waited.

It was *lovely*. There was no cheesy, artificial, chemical smell about it at all. It was like the potpourri of good smells you'd get in a kitchen on Christmas Day, with bottles of spices and vanilla uncapped, bread and cookies baking, a turkey roasting, tea brewing—and a fresh, woodsy overlay, as if all this Grandma's-house cooking activity was taking place in a cabin in the woods.

"Here, take another," said the boy. "Give it to a friend."

"Sure," I said. Right then Rhiannon came over, and I sprayed a nice glob of the stuff into the air and told her to smell it. Me, I inhaled deeply.

"I think you've got a winner," I said to the boy. "I'd buy it, provided it wasn't too expensive."

He just smiled.

"Come on," I said to Rhiannon, "let's get out of here while we're still ahead."

That pleasant interlude behind, reality returned to roost as soon as we got home. We unpacked our haul, sat down and had some hot coffee substitute, showed off the air freshener to George and Ciel, and turned on the television.

Much had happened in the outside world while we were busy coping with our latest private trauma. Things had gotten really, really ugly.

Our neighbors to the south took full advantage of all the confusion that swept the country in the wake of Julian's assassination. The people of Mexico had become desperately poor and hungry. Well, by the time Julian had been killed, they were about to explode with that desperation. They had nothing to lose.

Mexican president Lopez-Iglesias had feared for a long time that his starving countrymen were about to go into French Revolution mode. With the United States in crisis, he took advantage of what must have seemed like the opportunity of a lifetime. He cleverly turned his citizens' desperation and fury against us—the rich gangsters to the north who refused to share their great wealth with the *campesinos* of Mexico, whom they regarded as no better than dirt.

In fact, Texas, New Mexico, Arizona, and California were a paradise of security and prosperity in comparison to Mexico. So Lopez-Iglesias exhorted his starving masses (most of whom he was glad to get rid of, before they overthrew him) to storm the gates of the Colossus of the North. They listened. Within a matter of days, a tidal wave of human beings began to move toward the United States border, intent on crossing to the land where a bit of milk and honey could still reputedly be found.

Lopez-Iglesias had little to lose. He bluffed for all he

was worth, calling on the international community to sit in judgment on the United States as events unfolded. Would the Norteamericanos massacre his wretched multitudes as they swarmed into the southwestern states, or would they give his people shelter? Would the army mow them down like so much ripe sorghum, or offer them food and water?

Our American equivalents of Lopez-Iglesias pointed out that if the Mexicans crossed the border and were not mowed down like ripe sorghum, they would devour everything in their path, like a plague of locusts, and we would all starve to death, not just some of us. These folks happened to be well-represented in the Pentagon, and our befuddled old President couldn't begin to oppose them.

The international community paid no attention, being occupied with its own problems. Right after Julian was killed, the Brits had had a copycat plastic-explosives bombing which took out the Prime Minister. Then all hell broke loose, with everybody figuring that given all the chaos, this was their chance to grab stuff they wanted, or settle old grudges. The Algerians had an old peeve about the French, and blew up a lot of famous public places and monuments in Paris. The Arabs got real serious and did Tel Aviv with a smuggled-in nuke—Kiev all over again. The Israelis went ballistic, literally, and lashed out with the cumulative crazed fury of a hundred years of Chinese water-torture clashes with their neighbors. Before long, Cairo and Damascus were nuclear history. Amman, too close to home to merit that kind of nonsense, got the Dresden firestorm treatment.

Iran went for Iraq. Iraq swatted Iran like a fly, and went for Kuwait and Saudi Arabia with a vengeance. These countries could not match the onslaught of Iraqi firepower, and torched what remained of their oil wells, as Iraq had done to Kuwait in the Persian Gulf War so long ago. The whole Middle East flared into an environmental disaster of unprecedented proportions.

Therefore, the international community basically didn't

give a shit what was happening on the Texas-Mexican border.

The decision was made in Washington to stem the tide of human bodies pouring into the American Southwest by every means possible, including the use of battlefield nuclear weapons. As the army and air force deployed their vast potpourri of antipersonnel devices at the Mexican border, planes dropped short-range nukes on refugee staging camps deep within Mexico.

The brass in Washington knew that Lopez-Iglesias had a collection of aging Slavic nukes, but apparently they were under the impression that he couldn't deliver them properly, or that the plutonium had degraded too far to be useful in any case.

Wrong.

Lopez-Iglesias had gotten hold of some antiquated, souped-up SCUD technology, and trained a couple of nuclear warheads on Oklahoma City—specially chosen because it was the hometown of our poor old tired president. He ordered the president to cease exterminating the hordes of hungry people attempting to sweep into the United States, or he'd launch.

Apparently the guys at the Pentagon crossed their fingers, hoped against hope that they could intercept any missiles that Mexico managed to lob toward the great state of Oklahoma, and kept on killing Mexicans.

Lopez-Iglesias realized we weren't buying the nuclear blackmail. Or maybe the East Coast Power Establishment, the president excepted, just couldn't get that exercised about losing Oklahoma City. So Lopez-Iglesias, still having nothing to lose, found himself standing there with his macho up and his bluff called, looking stupid in front of the Yankees. The humiliation was more than his proud, hot blood could take, so he fired up his wretched missile-delivery system and went for the Okies.

Rhiannon and I watched these events transpire on television in absolute, quaking terror. When the missiles launched, we sobbed and prayed and clung to each other for what poor comfort it would give us. George, of course, played the steely-jawed veteran to the hilt, even though he sure seemed to go to the bathroom a lot during the whole episode.

Then word came that Lopez-Iglesias had apparently missed. The minutes ticked by, and Oklahoma City remained absolutely unharmed.

"If that isn't just like a Mexican," George said with a snarl. "To put us through all this, and then he can't even hit the frigging target."

"Oh, stop it," I said weakly. I was on the verge of fainting with shock and relief, and didn't appreciate the racist comment.

"But where did the bombs GO?" whispered Rhiannon.

We found out soon enough. One fell to Earth in a part of eastern Oklahoma known as Tornado Alley. It was a dud. The other wasn't, however. It undershot Oklahoma City and did its thing right over the Austin College campus in Sherman, Texas, a town sixty miles north of Dallas.

In retaliation, we launched nuclear missiles at every single major Mexican city.

We didn't miss.

I began to ask myself, in a state of semihysteria, whether all the dust and debris in the air would cause a minor nuclear winter. If so, it might temporarily offset the greenhouse effect—and if we were really lucky, for the next couple of years it might not be so goddamn hot.

Who says there's no such thing as a silver lining?

At this point we had every right to hope for a lull in the festivities. Silly us. The party was just getting started. The truly horrible stuff had not even begun to hit. When it did, on the twenty-ninth, it all happened so fast it left me breath-less.

Rhiannon stayed on duty all day, checking the Net for developments. About seven in the evening, she started screaming in absolute terror, calling my name.

I ran up and actually grabbed her by the shoulders and shook her, just like they used to do in the movies. She was scaring me to death. "What is it?" I cried. "What hap-pened?"

She pointed toward her computer screen and kept jabbing her finger at it, all the while crying hysterically. I figured out that I should read it, so I let go of her and went over and sat down.

What I saw made me feel like my blood had frozen in my veins. Literally—when you get such a bad shock, your capillaries constrict, and you feel like you're freezing to death.

"This is a message to everyone on the Internet?" I de-manded. "Who are these people? Why are they calling this stuff Shiva?"

"Shiva, in one of his aspects, is the Destroyer."

I read and reread the message on the screen, my heart racing so hard it was a miracle I didn't drop dead then and there.

"Greetings," it said. "Recent events have at last proven a great truth to a doubting world—that human beings are a blight upon the face of holy creation, a cancer devouring the body of our mother Gaia. We are a planetary calamity like the meteor that destroyed most life on Earth sixty-five million years ago. *Homo sapiens* cannot be allowed to work further destruction on the biosphere that first gave it life.

"The human race is a criminal race and must be exe-cuted. We, the Guardians of Gaia, the Great Goddess, have created a highly contagious swine flu mutation, which is fatal in nine out of ten cases of exposure. We Guardians have a thousand eyes and a thousand arms. Five days ago, a thousand emissaries were positioned in the world's largest population centers. Each emissary was infected with the virus, and made his way among the people of his chosen location. As you read this, most of the human beings infesting the Earth are about to fall ill—and 90 percent of them will die within the week.

"This is the only way. So mote it be!"

When I could breathe again, I said to Rhiannon, "Surely this is a joke. These people are mad."

"By the Goddess, *I'm* mad," she whispered. Her voice trembled, and her dark eyes were full of anger. "They're nothing but mass murderers. How dare they call themselves the protectors of Gaia, and kill in Her name? They are no better than the members of the Inquisition, who killed in the name of God."

At that moment, I felt utterly devoid of any hope for the human race. "All this proves," I said, "is that there are fanatics of every religious persuasion, but we knew that anyway. This is not news. Christians, Muslims, Jews, Buddhists, Pagans—they've all got their nut cases. Unfortunately, these idiot pagans are apparently well educated, and know how to make use of sophisticated technology. Unless I'm mistaken, of course, and they're just a bunch of cranks making noise. Are you sure they're on the level? Can they do what they say they can do?"

"There are a lot of documentation links at the end of the message," she replied, sounding sick. "I read some of them. They're telling the truth. I can feel it."

"Oh, God. You and your hunches. Anything about it on TV?"

"I haven't checked in several hours. Let's see."

She flipped over to the venerable CNN, which was already sporting a story-line logo of four dark-clad horsemen, evidently supposed to represent the Four Horsemen of the Apocalypse. One of them, undoubtedly Mr. Pestilence, was highlighted by a red halo. It was too bad James Earl Jones was dead; if they'd been able to add his Darth Vader tones as a voice-over, the effect would have been perfect. As it was, they just had a written legend underneath the picture that read, "The Coming Plague."

People were getting very, very sick and dying unpleasantly all over the globe, and everywhere there was absolute chaos. I had the feeling of falling through space. "Tell your Green Man saviors they waited too long to shoot."

Rhiannon gave me a look that was passing strange. "Oh, we have a message from them, too," she said.

I stared at her in stupefaction. "Say *what*?"

"They want to come here. They're already on their way."

"Whatever for?" I cried.

"They want to talk to you."

"*ME?* What's going on? They know you, not me!"

"They say they know you," she said, and just looked at me.

"What?" I yelped. "I thought way back months ago, back when this was all getting started, you tried to throw them off the track. Didn't you say something like the Internet account came with the house?"

"Yes, I did, but do you really think they're that stupid? They figured out you're still alive and kicking, and they want to see you."

For a long time, I didn't move. Then I simply lost all self-control. I ran away, up to my room, and slammed and locked the door.

I pawed through my chest of drawers and looked in my closet, but I had no drugs of any kind, no booze, nothing at all to blot out my consciousness.

Then I remembered the *kehft*. I had hidden it from Loki months before, in a concealed compartment in my desk— a doddering antique I had inherited from my grandmother. Without hesitation, I got it out, opened it up, and drank the contents in a single gulp.

TWENTY-FIVE

OCTOBER 30, 2032

I LAY ON MY BED FOR ABOUT A HALF AN HOUR, WONDER-ing anxiously if the *kehft* was going to do anything to me at all. Then worrying about what was going to happen seemed to slip my mind altogether. I lost track of time; my thoughts drifted, directionless, in the grip of a very pleasant high.

My mind cut loose its moorings to the here and now. It browsed through memories, picking up one gratifying rec-ollection after another. It would sniff each one like a rose, enjoy the scent, and then toss it away and move on in search of another.

For a short while I was a child in the 1950s again, perched in my treetop hideaway, safely distant from all the terrible news emanating from my parents' black-and-white television set. I watched night fall over San Antonio, saw the lights of downtown wink on one by one, and marveled at how fresh and soft and gentle the evening air had been in those years.

My mind skipped around, cherry-picking, choosing at whim from a whole table piled high with tempting tidbits. I remembered swimming with college friends in one of the myriad crystal springs that gushed out of the limestone rock of the Texas hill country. The sky was an agonizingly bright, perfect blue, the weather was hot, the beer was plen-

tiful, and the springs icy cold. I frolicked away that entire
summer like a careless grasshopper, never dreaming that
the world could ever change.

My mind replayed many of the little moments of pure
happiness in my past—they were strung out across the
backdrop of my eighty years like so many tiny white
Christmas lights entwining the branches of a leafless tree
in the darkness. Again, I saw the hummingbird dance in
the spray of my garden hose shortly after Roger and I
bought our house. I remembered my first sight of San Francisco's financial district, and how utterly thrilled I was to
know I would be working in such a wonderland. I remembered all my strolls by the ocean during my years in Mendocino, and the delight I had taken in the whimsy of Aunt
Cecilia's cottage at Avebury when Miles had taken me
there to visit.

Some indefinite time later, one single memory fastened
on my wandering consciousness and drew me to it. Early
on in my relationship with Li, he had suggested a camping
trip in the redwoods north of San Francisco. Since that description covered a lot of territory, I asked him to be more
specific, and helped him research the possible places we
could go. After a lot of reading and asking around, we
settled on a spot in the middle of Redwood National Park,
a thin strip of magnificent coastal redwood parkland in the
northernmost part of the state.

It was called the Prairie Creek Unit, and it boasted your
usual plug-in campground for trailers and gas-guzzling mo-
torized homes. What was unusual was its crown jewel of a
hiking trail, one that marched from the main highway
straight west through mile after mile of virgin redwood forest, until it emerged into a magnificent deep canyon covered
with ferns, and finally met up with the sea.

Li was at that time in a slightly more advanced state of
redwood tree-huggerism than I—but only slightly. After all,
being Chinese, he could claim to have come from the land

of the fabled Dawn Redwoods, while I was merely a denizen of the Johnny-come-lately New World. Anyway, he was in seventh heaven as we took off into the wild, our backpacks bravely shouldered, leaving all the sounds and smells of civilization behind us.

We passed all sorts of wonders on our hike. For a bit of background, let me explain here that a virgin redwood forest is dramatically different from a second-growth one. Most of the redwoods I had seen in parks around San Francisco were second-growth, except for specially preserved stands of virgin trees in places such as Muir Woods. A second-growth forest has regrown in an area that was once clear-cut; in the case of the San Francisco Peninsula forests, around the turn of the century. In a second-growth forest, the trees have come back, but the new forest is nothing like the old one that was cut down.

When a redwood is logged, the plant does not die. Redwoods are ancient, primitive life forms, and very vigorous. The stump and root system, shocked into sudden growth, can send out as many as a dozen new sprouts around the circumference of the severed trunk. But because the mother tree was logged, a problem arises. So much organic matter was removed from the forest when the logged trunk was hauled away—wood that would have eventually died, decayed, and literally turned into food—that none of the puny, hydralike sprouts that spring up around the stump can ever become as big as the original tree. I saw them all over the place in peninsula parks, standing in tight little constricted circles around decaying, logged-off stumps, the forest a shadow of its former self.

Li and I, however, stumbled across an extraordinary spot on the Prairie Creek trail. Thousands of years before, an enormous mother tree must have begun to die back naturally—slowly, with plenty of warning. The redwood was not shocked by the sudden severing of a logger's saw. Knowing it was dying, the mother tree had plenty of time to react. Slowly, over a long period of years, it signaled many shoots to emerge from the soil and sprout in a huge circle at the outermost tips of the tree's enormous root system. As the mother tree died back and decayed, the circle of new trees fed on its body. A couple thousand years more, and they had grown into an enormous, Stonehenge-like circle of gigantic trees, each as large as the original. In the center of the circle, where the mother tree had been, there was nothing but flat, needle-covered earth. But the newer trees, each as mighty as their ancestor, could have put the stones at Avebury to shame.

We hiked deeper into the forest, planning to camp by the sea when night fell. As the *kehft* guided me through this memory, I kept wondering what was so special about this moment in my past, that the *kehft* had chosen it to illuminate. It had been pleasant enough, but that was all.

As the memory unfolded, I began to suspect its goal. The *kehft* had not only given me a vision of my past, it also wanted to open a doorway of perception that was closed in my present life. But why the *kehft* wished to do so, I did not know.

I watched the memory play out and relived it fully, all the while knowing in one part of my mind what was going to happen.

Li and I had been hiking so long, we were giddy. The hours of constant physical effort had given me an excellent case of runner's high; my endorphins were in fine working order. I was high as a kite, without a single drop of booze. As we trudged on toward the nearing ocean, the skin on the back of my neck began to prickle, as if I were being watched—or, more accurately—as if there were a great breathing presence at my back.

Finally something made me stop in the path and slowly pivot to face the direction from which we'd come. We were now several hundred feet beyond *It*—far enough away to see the giant in all its grandeur.

Puny ants, we had walked right by it and paid no attention. Rising out of the ground to the east was the biggest living thing I had ever seen, and that included the whales at Sea World and the elephants in San Diego. Had it been a *T. rex,* I would have been only slightly more impressed.

It was a single giant redwood, whose bulk split a third of the way up its length into a candelabra of multiple trunks. Me, I was used to big things, like my office building in the Embarcadero Center; but this was a tree as big as my office building, as big as a Cape Canaveral rocket.

"Good Lord!" I said to Li.

Those many years ago, I had certainly not meant the words as an invocation of any kind. It was just the kind of thing I said when overwhelmed. But now the connection was made. The memory and my past vanished. My mind whirled with smoke, and the *kehft* parted curtains to reveal a new stage.

I was standing in a sweet-smelling forest as old as time. It was unfamiliar to me—it certainly was not in California—and I sensed power and presence all around me. "Who's there?" I called. My voice sounded neither young nor old; it seemed to have no age.

I heard a noise, a crackling sound, and saw a figure approaching me through the glade. It was a beautiful man, young and strong, with hair like the sun. He was dressed in muddy green clothes and carried a longbow. "Don't you know me?" he said, and grinned as if he wished to share a joke.

For some reason, my heart felt light, and I joked back. "I must say you resemble a certain television Robin Hood of my youth," I replied.

"Then to you I am Robin Hood," he said, and grinned again.

Then, in the depths of my heart, I realized what he really was—an ancient spirit, as old as the Earth itself. I knew this being had come to pay me a visit the moment the gates of my mind were thrown open by the *kehft,* and I was finally able to admit him. He must have an important message for me.

"Herne, Cernunnos, Green Man," I said, drawing back. "Welcome."

"Thank you, my lady," he said, and gave me a most courtly bow. Though he was as old as the Earth, he chose to wear a young and merry mask today, and the bow suited him.

"You were my teacher," I said to him, "that day I walked into my garden in the depth of winter and learned to read the signs of coming spring. You were by my side when I slept beneath the giant redwoods with Li. Even now, when I force food to grow from the blasted earth in my garden, I feel your hands guiding me."

He smiled again, and it warmed me like the sun. "Of course. You have always known me."

"Yes." I drew a tentative breath. "What message do you have for me? One of hope, though surely that is impossible?"

He gave a sweet, sad smile. "Not impossible. I'm hope itself. In legends, there is always hope."

"In legends," I replied, and felt my spirits sink. "But not in real life. Old one, you well know what we've done to the world out there. How can there be any hope for it?"

"Hope endures, even now. Wait for it; be prepared, it is coming, though not in a form you might expect. Remember the story of Pandora."

"I will believe this, but only because you say it," I said, forcing back tears.

"Very well," he said. "Know this: The Earth you love is truly near death, but the struggle is not yet over. Many are coming to her aid."

"Who?" I demanded. "Men? Ancient beings such as yourself?"

"Many are coming," he repeated softly.

Though his image did not waver in the slightest, I could sense that he was preparing to take his leave. "Wait!" I cried on impulse. "Before you go, show me what you really look like. Show me your true face."

He paused and then replied, "I have no form that is real and absolute, in the sense you mean. Each living thing would see me through a lens of its own making; in the eyes of an eagle or a hawk I would wear one guise; for a bear, another; and still others for a tiger or a deer."

"Show me only how would you appear to a human being if you put aside your mask!"

He was silent for a moment, as if lost in thought. "Very well. Like this," he said.

The forest grew dark around me, yet shortly I saw him. His image took shape with every beat of my heart. He was like the oak tree in my garden, like the great redwood I had seen with Li, but immeasurably grander and more magnificent. He was possessed of dizzying height, with roots descending to the very center of the Earth, and branches flung wide like arms to embrace the sky, that sheltered a hundred forms of life. Images whirled in my brain from old pictures of the Saxon Tree of Life and the Norse Yggdrasil. The next moment he was a fierce, magnificent bird of prey, like those that had finally died out in the present century, drifting on thermal currents above his domain the Earth, watching over it and protecting it, and the moment after that, a jewel of a hummingbird, darting across my garden in the utter joy of life and movement.

In my childhood I had read *The Wind in the Willows*. In that book there was a passage where Rat and Mole rowed to an island and came upon the ancient god Pan, sitting among wild cherry and crab apple trees. The animals trembled with fear, even as they were overcome by reverence and adoration. That was exactly how I felt, looking on the faces of the Green Man.

Then the images dissolved, and he again put on his human form. The young man stooped, reached for my hand, and kissed it. "Fare thee well, my lady. One day we shall meet again."

With that, he vanished, and I fell dead asleep.

TWENTY-SIX

OCTOBER 31, 2032

WHEN I FINALLY WOKE UP, IT WAS FOUR O'CLOCK IN THE morning. Of Halloween; of Samhain. I didn't seem to have a hangover. In fact I felt very rested and very hungry.

I summoned all my strength and hauled my stiff old bones into a sitting position. I sat there for a short while, remembering the dream—or rather the vision—that the *kehft* had given me. None of it had faded; in my memory it was still as clear as crystal. It had been thrilling and beautiful, and I would treasure it for the rest of my life, however long or short that might be.

My mind and heart felt temporarily at peace, despite the minor consideration that Rhiannon and I, safe for the moment in our eyrie in the hills, might soon be privileged to witness the wholesale destruction of human civilization. So I decided to do something constructive, such as go to the kitchen and find some food for my rumbling belly.

As I walked, I noticed with one part of my mind that my eyes felt dry, my throat felt scratchy, I was sweating, and I was feeling alternately too hot and too cold. My nose itched, too, and I was a wee bit giddy. However, since my main physical sensation was one of overpowering hunger, I paid little attention to the other signals my body was giving me.

When I got to the doorway, I stopped dead in my tracks.

Rhiannon had every light in the kitchen and family room blazing away, expense be damned, as well as a bunch of hoarded candles she'd put on the breakfast table as part of a makeshift altar. The room smelled fabulous, so that at first I thought she'd used up the last of that wonderful air freshener I'd gotten at Mad Mac's—it took a moment for me to realize she'd really baked bread, and had prepared a large pot of soup, which was bubbling away on the stove. Heaven alone knew how many cans of vegetables she'd used from our precious stash in the basement.

She had gotten her ratty old guitar out of the basement, too, and was sitting on a chair in front of the jerry-rigged altar, singing softly to herself. I thought she'd lost her mind. I started to sound off like a screech owl and ask her what on Earth she thought she was up to, but something intuitive stopped me.

It dawned on me what she was doing. She was faced with total despair, and she was spitting in its eye. She was Cleopatra, donning her best gown and jewels before taking up the asp. I smiled with grim appreciation. I liked her attitude; Fate wasn't going to get me without a fight, either.

After a moment I recognized what she was singing— "The Bells of Norwich," which I had learned long, long ago at church camp. She must have learned it back when she was a kid, too, going to the Methodist church. I remembered it had to do with Julian of Norwich, a woman, a Christian mystic born in the fourteenth century soon after the Black Death had swept through Europe. Ah-ha! I said to myself—there was the connection.

I stayed where I was and listened to her sing, enjoying the familiar old melody.

> Loud are the Bells of Norwich
> And the people come and go.
> Here by the tower of Julian
> I tell them what I know.

> Ring out, bells of Norwich,
> And let the winter come and go
> All shall be well again, I know.
>
> All shall be well, I'm telling you
> Let the winter come and go
> All shall be well again, I know.

My eyes filled with tears as I listened. Even after my encounter with the Green Man, I was afraid to believe completely in that song of hope—that all would be well again. And so, as beautiful as the song was, it broke my heart to listen to it. She resumed, tempting me sorely to run back to my room before I started bawling, but still I stayed, hearing the familiar words.

> Love, like the yellow daffodil
> Is coming through the snow
> Love, like the yellow daffodil
> Is Lord of all I know.

Then she began to sing words that were unfamiliar to me. My skin crawled as she sang a new verse over and over again. I had never heard it before. She must have written it, or perhaps one of her friends had. The candles were on the table, the altar was prepared, and she was singing, spellweaving.

> Some say the fire and slaughter
> Are the end of all we know.
> I say the fire and slaughter
> Shall be healed by winter's
> snow.

I did start sobbing, but forced myself to do it quietly. If there was the slightest chance in the world this spell would work, I wouldn't have interrupted it to save my life.

Again and again she sang this last, strange verse. Then, when she was spent, she put down the guitar, got to her feet in a single, sweeping motion, raised her arms to the sky, and whispered, "So mote it be."

I saw then that the big paned windows in the family room were open, and a waning, setting moon was visible through them.

As I was almost on the verge of stepping forward, the strangest thing of all happened. There was a flutter of beating wings at the window, and suddenly, on the sill, there appeared a most unearthly-looking creature, backlit with moonlight. It was a large white bird, with black eyes rimmed with blue skin, a dark beak, and a great, snowy, erect crest of feathers that framed its head and made me think of an Aztec emperor. It lifted and spread its wings in full display, showing underfeathers of a glorious lemon-yellow color. It hissed, but it seemed to me that it was calling Rhiannon to it, not warning her away.

Calmly, she walked up to it and put out her forearm, as if it were a falcon and she a medieval lady. "Step up," she said softly, as she always did to Tweety Bird.

To my astonishment, the bird did so. It lowered its crest, folded its wings close to its body, and let Rhiannon cuddle it like a baby. In a hoarse, throaty voice, it said, "Hello."

Rhiannon turned and saw me. There was a smile of utter happiness on her face. Me, I had begun to shake like a leaf.

I shambled forward, went past her, and closed the window. "What has happened here, Rhiannon?" I asked wonderingly.

She looked down at the creature in her arms and said quietly, "Faith is the bird that feels the light and sings when the dawn is still dark."

"What?" My voice was very faint.

"Rabindranath Tagore," she said absently.

I looked around. "I see. Yes, this is all an exercise in

faith. That I can understand. But it's madness."

"No," she said, and looked down at the bird. "See here: This is what I've always wanted, and now I have him." She scratched its head gently and said, "Hi there."

The creature piped up again. "Hello," it said in that throaty voice, "my name is Sheena."

"Now I have *her*," Rhiannon amended with a grin.

"This is no spirit—it must be someone's pet!"

Rhiannon examined the creature and found a little plastic vial attached to one leg, above a closed metal band. I stepped forward and, since my hands were free, opened it and unrolled the small scrap of paper I found inside. "I live in Berkeley. I am dying of the plague and there is no one to take my Sheena," I read aloud. "I have to turn her loose. Please, if anyone is still alive and finds her, take good care of her. A Neighbor." I paused and looked Rhiannon in the eye. "The bird saw the open window and the lights and probably smelled your cooking."

"And felt the call of the spell I cast," she said.

"That also," I conceded. "Rhiannon—what is this thing?"

"This is a cockatoo," she said. It lifted its wings an inch away from its body, and she slid her hand underneath them and proceeded to give it a full-body massage. "Remember years ago when I searched so hard for one, and only found Tweety Bird?"

"Yes, and now you have one. Rhiannon, it's awfully tame."

"These are the most affectionate parrots on Earth," she said, her voice reverent. "Here—hold her yourself."

I put out one arm hesitantly, but the bird stepped right up on it. I ventured to stroke the snowy head, and looked into the creature's eyes. The pupils were the color of obsidian, and the irises a dark, rich brown.

For an instant I felt as if a camera had flashed, illuminating the whole scene before me so that it appeared strangely different. For a brief moment it was as if I looked out at the warm, comforting room through the bird's eyes. The tableau was disconcerting, for my eyes were placed differently in my skull than a human's; yet I saw Rhiannon and her companion, recognized the love and fascination in their faces as they gazed at me, and knew with the intelligence of a very young child that I had found a new haven.

Then, with a snap, my perspective shifted, and I was back in my own mind again. "Jesus," I said under my breath. The *kehft* sure had some weird aftereffects.

"Are you all right?" Rhiannon asked.

I suddenly focused on the sound of her voice and felt a wave of apprehension sweep through me. "You sound like you're getting a cold, Rhiannon."

"Am I?" she asked. "Oh, great!"

"I am definitely getting one, too." I covered my mouth and coughed.

Our eyes met over the cockatoo in sudden horror.

"No, it absolutely cannot be Shiva," I said. "We haven't been anywhere but to Mad Mac's, and we went there *before* they released it. It's impossible for us to have it."

"Then we don't have it," replied Rhiannon. "We just have colds. We're both run-down—not a surprising state of affairs, under the circumstances."

I looked at her curiously. "You're awfully blasé, considering what deep dung we'd be in if we had Shiva."

"You're right," she replied. "I just don't feel worried about it. In fact, I feel pretty damn good."

"That must have been one mojo spell!"

She regarded me for a moment and then said matter-of-factly, "Yes, it was."

I changed the subject. "You know, the Shiva people were awfully stupid to go on-line and announce what they did, and when they had done it. They're not going to get their ninety percent kill rate this way. Maybe sixty, seventy percent, max. Everybody who can stay indoors like you and me will do so—and in a short while, the people who are going to die will have died, and those few who were able to survive the flu will have done so and not be contagious anymore. It'll be safe to come out again. The survivors may go tribal for a while, but they'll keep on surviving. So Shiva didn't get rid of the cancer at all.''

''Nope,'' she replied. ''Those guys were real amateurs.''

''You realize,'' I said, ''that we are still in a mess of trouble. I read a science fiction book one time where half the people on Earth agreed to kill themselves to take a load off the planet, but the hero figured out that all those decaying, unburied bodies would generate so much methane—a greenhouse gas far more potent than carbon dioxide—that the sacrifice would all be for nothing.

Rhiannon looked very thoughtful. ''Yes, objectively it does appear that we are in—as you put it—a mess of trouble. Even when Shiva's through with us, the climate will still be screwed up. Civilization is likely to break up into tiny bands of people just like in every postapocalypse movie you can think of. After Shiva has run its course, there are going to be plenty of nasty people left alive. They will be desperate in the extreme. The first time we venture outside the compound, they might nail us. But . . .''

''But what?''

''Nothing is written in stone,'' Rhiannon replied. ''My spell is not yet finished. And, frankly, I'm just not—afraid.''

I wished I could feel reassured. ''What's gotten into you?'' I demanded. ''You sound like Little Mary Sunshine.''

She shrugged, smiled, and let loose with a great big honker of a sneeze.

''Ick,'' I said, looking around for a tissue to reuse or an old cloth. ''Rhiannon, where on Earth did you get that different verse of 'Bells of Norwich'?'' I asked.

''I went to a pagan festival years ago, in Seattle. A

woman by the name of Greenleaf sang it. I was never able to find out whether she'd recorded it, but the words just etched themselves into my brain, and to me, they've been part of the song ever since.''

"Greenleaf, huh? Rhiannon, listen, I have got to have some of your hot soup. My throat is really starting to hurt, and I don't feel so good,'' I said.

I walked to the kitchen sink to get a clean bowl from the drainer. Suddenly a dark shadow passed across the moon, and I heard a loud, whirring sound, like 'copter blades. I scurried outside to the deck, with Rhiannon behind me, bird in arms. To our mutual astonishment, we saw what appeared to be a small, sleek black chopper trying to set down in the road in front of our place.

George, ever-vigilant, appeared in the doorway. "What in the name of . . .'' he exclaimed. I noted distractedly that his voice had a distinctly nasal sound, like he, too, was coming down with a whopper of a cold.

Rhiannon actually laughed. "Let's see, it's the Feds—or maybe the U.N.—in one of their infamous black helicopters. Call out the militia boys!''

"That is one hell of a nice-looking machine,'' George said appreciatively. "I'd be amazed if the Feds could afford something like that nowadays. Besides, they're all tied up in Mexico. And how long has the U.N. been bankrupt, anyway?''

"Then we must be gazing on the fruit of private enterprise,'' I said. "They can't be space aliens, because space aliens fly saucers, not sexy 'copters.''

"Somebody's getting out,'' George announced, peering through his binoculars.

"Well, what do they look like?'' I cried.

"Hold it . . . they're moving pretty slow. Now they're waving at the house. Looks like they're two old geezers.''

"They'll fit right in with this crowd,'' murmured Rhiannon.

"This is all too weird for me," I said. "Spells, moons, big white birds, big black choppers—I must still be lying in my bed, zonked out with the *kehft*."

As I finished my sentence, Ciel padded up from somewhere. "Is something bad happening?" she asked. Her nasal passages were all stuffed up and I could barely understand her.

"Oh, man, in the name of all that's holy, what is going on?" I cried. "She's got a cold, too? What is this, a *Twilight Zone* story? A lost episode of *Laugh-In*?"

Abruptly, a loud buzzing sound filled the house. It had been so very long since I'd heard it, at first I didn't realize what it was. My stupefaction must have been painfully evident, for Rhiannon said quietly, "They're ringing the doorbell down by the fence. They must want to come in."

"What the . . ." I said with a gasp. I snatched the binoculars away from George and had a peek at the visitors myself.

I looked at them for a long time, while the buzzing continued. The binoculars didn't really help all that much, but in my most buried heart of hearts, I think I guessed—and longed for, and dreaded—what was waiting for me at the gate.

I drew a slow, full breath. I tried to keep my voice from shaking, and it came out all deep and hoarse. "I'll be back," I said, and I walked toward our gate and the two silent figures who waited for me on the other side.

TWENTY-SEVEN

The Green Man

OCTOBER 31, 2032

As I neared the fence that separated me from our visitors, I was filled with so many conflicting emotions I could barely maintain my composure. I was nervous and just a little scared. These people were, after all, at the heart of the enigmatic Green Man conspiracy—irrelevant as it had surely become once the Guardians launched Shiva.

Also, I had a feeling who one of the men was, and if that feeling turned out to be right, I didn't know whether I'd want to throw my arms around him and never let him go, or kill him. By the time I got to the gate, I was so giddy, I knew one good, hard shock was all it would take to send me into a dead faint.

A figure stepped forward and looked me in the face, leaving only a few feet of space and a bit of nasty electrified fence separating us. "Hello, Moira," he said. "Recognize me?"

It had been fifty-five years. There were few similarities between the white-haired man before me and the very young man I had known for only a day. "Miles," he said, "Miles Earnshaw."

Wait a minute! I had not anticipated this at all. I shook my head, speechless, and tried to figure out how and why he could possibly be standing there in front of me, after all these years.

A taller, thinner figure, slightly stooped, came forward from the shadow of the copter. "It's Li," he said.

I gasped. So my intuition had been right—Li *was* part of it! Swiftly, I opened the gate. "Excuse me," I managed to say at last, my voice quavering, "but exactly what the hell are you two doing here—and how come you're together?"

They came inside, and I closed the gate and secured it again. "Long ago, you gave me Miles's e-mail address," said Li. "Don't you remember? The rest of the story will take a long time to tell."

"Li and I have just completed—what shall I call it?— an extended business trip," said Miles. "The Bay Area was our last stop. We both wanted to see you again. Whether or not you realize it, Moira, you played an important role in both our lives—in the development of the Green Man. In fact, we hoped we could wait out Shiva here with you. I assure you, we've not been exposed."

I nodded. Then I walked up to Li, looked into his eyes, and burst into furious tears. "You're a lousy son of a bitch!" I cried. "I had nightmares for years, picturing in my mind's eye over and over again what must have happened to you in Tiananmen Square—and all the time you were alive! Why didn't you get word to me? Even if you couldn't come back and be with me, how could you let me go on thinking you'd gotten crushed under a tank or shot or God knows what? You could have contacted me, you could have put my mind at rest! If I still had the strength, I'd slap you."

Li, his face suddenly full of misery, looked down at the ground. "When I got back to Beijing, I did all I could to help the students who had survived the massacre in the square. I saw them hunted; then I myself was hunted, for aiding them. Many of them were imprisoned and tortured— as was I, in the end. Before too long I escaped, and continued my efforts to help the students; you may recall that their persecution went on for years. Then I was captured again, and was imprisoned for more than five years, until I was able to escape a second time.''

''And so? And then what? What stopped you from at least getting a letter out to me?'' I cried.

''It is difficult to explain quickly, Moira.''

''We've got all the time in the world,'' I retorted. ''You won't get off the hook that easily.''

''I will tell you more in the coming days. Briefly, I will say that I suffered things in prison that, even now, I cannot bear to speak of to others. After my second escape, I spent several years convalescing in France, cared for by my mother's family. While I recovered, I had a great deal of time to think and plan. At last I came to two conclusions.''

He paused, as if marshaling his strength to go on. ''Do you remember how you and I used to talk about the nature of mankind—about how there seemed to be something fundamentally wrong with us as a species? As if we were the product of poor engineering?''

''Yes,'' I said, ''I particularly remember that conversation we had after going to that shop called 'The Green Man' and meeting Arthur.'' Then I caught my breath; I had an inkling how he, with input from Miles, might have chosen the name for their project.

''After the brutality I experienced in prison, I came to believe in my heart that that assumption was correct. But more importantly, I also developed a working theory about *why* we were so flawed, one I hoped I could prove. You should guess what I am talking about; you were the one who put the first pieces together for me when we shared a bottle of wine after visiting Arthur and his shop.

''I knew that once I had a valid theory, I would be well on the road toward testing it. If my theory held up under testing, I could begin to search for a way to fix the flaw. So, around the turn of the millennium, I began to draw together a group of people from all over the globe who possessed the knowledge to perform those tests. I had enough money from my family to get the project started. I also had the ability and the drive to 'network,' as you always used to put it, and get much more money from sources all over the world. There are many, many people who have suffered as I did and are willing to assist an endeavor such as mine, in secret. Just as there are many men of principle—scientists, educators, and scholars—who are willing to help.''

''Why was it necessary to be so secretive?''

He seemed quite startled, and looked at me as if he could not believe his ears. ''Moira, how can you be so naive? If any government on the planet had gotten wind of this project, yours included, it would have done everything in its power to stop me. What I have done is create a method to radically alter human nature itself. Governments exist to protect the status quo, and the Green Man would overturn it forever.''

He said this so calmly, I could only gape at him.

''Furthermore, I never planned to ask for permission to carry out the project,'' he added. ''What government would not have tried to stop me, had it learned of Green Man?''

''I see,'' I replied, though my mind was whirling.

Then, knowing full well I sounded like a twit who thought only of herself, I said, ''Li, I still don't understand why you couldn't contact me once you had recovered in France. That just doesn't wash. You could have gotten in touch if you really wanted to.''

I just couldn't help myself. I had to say it.

''Moira,'' he said, ''it is true, you do not understand, but I will try to tell you. When I was sane and whole again, many years had gone by. I learned you had married, and then been widowed. Yes, I could have reached out to you, but by then your life had greatly changed. And I had dedicated the rest of my own life to my project. For more than thirty years I have done little else but pour the entirety of my mind and soul and heart into the Green Man. It is the child I never had. For three decades I had no life of my own, no life apart from the project that I could have offered you.''

I didn't say anything. I just felt like my heart was breaking, all over again, at age eighty.

"I am sorry, Moira," he said.

"Hey, listen, guys," I said, feeling suddenly rather weak in the knees, "let's go sit down on that bench by the tree. I shouldn't stand much longer. I'm getting a horrible cold, and at my age, they can be pretty debilitating. Be warned, you may catch it, too.''

I went to the bench, making them follow me. "Don't worry, Moira," said Miles. "We've already had our colds.''

That remark didn't make any sense to me, but so far not much else had. Maybe he was trying to be funny—whatever. I just blew it off. Silly me.

"I have so many questions, I don't know where to start," I said to them. "I know how Rhiannon stumbled across you guys on the Net. Despite her trying to throw you off my trail, it must have been a piece of cake for you to figure out I was still around. My bank accounts are active, my bills get paid, my signature is on file everywhere. But I can't figure out for the life of me what you're doing here now. All you ever did on the Net was agonize with Rhiannon over whether you should move ahead with the Green Man. Seems like that's all moot now, thanks to the guys who thought up Shiva. Whatever it is you were going to do, it seems you got preempted.''

Miles sighed. "We did spend a lot of time talking with Rhiannon about ethics and moral issues. I felt intuitively from the start that she was a safe contact, and when I realized she was your friend, I was sure of it. Call it 'agonizing' if you like. Each of us does have a conscience. Because of moral doubts, we were very indecisive; we stayed our hand over and over again, long after we could have released the Green Man. Most recently, we held back because we hoped desperately that your President Imber would be able to save humanity through more—conventional means.''

"Saving humanity? Listen to yourself, Miles,'' I said drily. "If I didn't think you two were rather remarkable men, I'd think you were suffering from delusions of grandeur.''

Li just laughed. "A group of bumbling fools has just managed to destroy much of the human race. Why do you think it so unlikely that men of more ability could devise a way to save humanity?''

Miles hurried to his own defense. "Moira, by creating Green Man, we were playing with fire. By releasing it, we knew we would be playing God. It's not a comfortable position to be in. So we waited. Then Julian Imber was killed, the world began to go up in flames, and we no longer had any convincing arguments left for hiding in the wings and letting events take their natural course—''

"Hello, hello,'' I interrupted, "perhaps I'm just stupid, but get a clue—whatever you were planning to do, those Guardians of Gaia idiots beat you to the punch.''

Li regarded me with his old inscrutable Chinese scholar look, much enhanced by his advanced age. "The Guardians were indeed idiots,'' he said. "Irresponsible, posturing fools, terrorists, bungling dilettantes, misguided murderers. The few of them who survive their own scourge will soon suffer a fitting punishment. They will learn that the evil they did was completely unnecessary.''

"I don't understand.''

Miles cleared his throat. "They thought they were saving the world in the only way possible. Well, they were dead wrong. As you Yanks would put it, by the time the Guardians released Shiva, the cavalry was already on the way.''

"Because,'' said Li, his tones clipped, "the Guardians did *not* beat us to the punch.''

I stared at them. It was still not coming together for me. At that moment, my beeper went off. I answered it. George, yelling, demanded to know what was going on down there.

"Shut up," I said to him, "I'll tell you when I'm good and ready. Everything's okay, so go away."

"Moira," said Miles, "we released the Green Man first. We just used a slower-acting virus than Shiva. Worldwide, people are only now beginning to show symptoms of infection."

I stared at him. *"What?"*

"How much do you know about gene therapy?" he asked.

"Absolutely nothing," I replied.

"Damn," he said. "I'll try to make this simple. It is possible to create something called a 'retrovirus.' Once it infects a cell, it makes a DNA copy of its genes, which then goes into the chromosome of the host cell. HIV is an example of a naturally occurring retrovirus; once you have its genes in your DNA, you have it for life. Such a virus can be designed to go into targeted cells—say, in a crucial gland—and literally rewrite some of the genes there. Delivery is not difficult. As early as the 1990s, new methods had been developed using viruses developed from cold viruses to infect the nasal tissues, usually through a nasal spray. We constructed a highly contagious rhinovirus—a cold virus—which is a carrier for the important retrovirus that we named Green Man. Unfortunately, the rhinovirus has annoying side effects that do not show up for approximately ten days, although it was highly contagious from the first."

I digested that. "Oh, God, speak English, please," I replied.

Miles sighed in frustration. "A retrovirus can be engineered to invade the cells of a crucial organ, or a gland—perhaps one that releases, or inhibits the release, of a key neurochemical. Genetic therapy is nothing new, Moira, it simply has not been used on this scale before.''

"What was that you said about a 'worldwide' infection?'' I asked.

Miles gave a grim smile. "Moira, we had many, many years to plan the Green Man's release. Over the years we set up a multitude of global distribution channels. We have achieved far, far greater penetration with Green Man than those bloody Shiva fools with their amateur, homegrown swine flu.''

"Exactly what sort of channels?'' I asked. I was beginning to harbor a deep, dark suspicion.

"People, to start with. Many, many people. The Guardians of Gaia bragged about having a thousand eyes and a thousand arms, but from what we've been able to tell, they never had more than a hundred kamikaze blockheads at their disposal. They even bungled the effectiveness of those poor deluded fools, because they could not resist taunting the world with what they'd done to it. We, on the other hand, had literally thousands of people willing to spread the Green Man—and we did not announce our plans.''

"How on Earth could you get so many to help, and keep their mouths shut?'' I asked, bewildered.

"For one thing,'' he said, his voice wry, "because Green Man is designed to save mankind, not to exterminate it. It is much easier to find people who are passionately dedicated to achieving that sort of goal.''

"How could you keep such a thing secret for so long?'' I cried.

"It's possible to keep large projects secret if you plan carefully—ask your government. It's even easier if no one has any reason to suspect that you're up to something. It's not like we were the Manhattan Project.''

"So you used people who already had the virus and were contagious,'' I pressed. "That's one channel. What else did you use?''

"The people were very effective by themselves, but we

still made use of supplementary methods for those populations that were harder to reach—your isolated household is a prime example. To give you just a few examples, we injected it into the air circulation system of sealed buildings, we used small aircraft to 'crop dust' selected areas, we packaged the virus in marketable aerosol containers, we—''

"Stop right there!" I cried, and looked at each of them in turn. "Air freshener! Air freshener, in free samples, right?"

Li nodded. "In selected markets all over the world."

I began to feel distinctly light-headed. "So I've got Green Man. And so does everyone else in my house!"

Li nodded again. "Regrettably, you will all suffer from a rather vexatious cold for the next few days."

I heard footsteps on the path that led to the house. Most appropriately, I heard Rhiannon sneeze. She paused, blew her nose, and then the footsteps resumed. In a moment she appeared on the steps above us, her black nightgown moving in the breeze, and her long white hair catching the light of the setting moon.

"All right," she said, "enough of this, Moira. Bring our guests inside so we can know what's going on, too."

"This is Rhiannon, whom you already know," I said, stating the obvious. "Rhiannon, this guy is an old acquaintance of mine from London, Miles Earnshaw, while this other is someone I've told you a great deal about—Li, my long-lost China love. As you have no doubt concluded for yourself, they are the Green Man folks."

She came down and stood beside us. "I am very pleased to meet you," said Li, at his polite and formal best.

There was a significant halt in the proceedings while she and Miles gazed at each other. They shook hands. "So you're Rhiannon!" I heard Miles say. "It is such a delight to meet you at last, after getting to know you so well over the Net."

They kept staring at each other. Normally I would have found this extremely droll, for I could almost hear the violin music beginning to play in the background. But I was far too overwhelmed to give much attention to this whimsical little development.

"Please," I said, "do come up to the house. Rhiannon has just made some hot soup." I beckoned to them to follow me, and started back up the path.

"Li," I said sternly when he caught up with me, "start thinking how you're going to explain Green Man to the rest of us up at the house—what it is, and what it's going to do to us. As soon as she's poured the soup, you're on."

"Gladly," said Li. "Moira, your estate is lovely."

"Glad you think so," I replied. "After you disappeared and I finally stopped grieving, you selfish bastard, I married rich."

When we got to the house I went straight to George and had a heart-to-heart talk with him. Under no circumstances was he to go ballistic and threaten our guests, I said, or he really would have to go live with Mr. McClelland. I took his Uzi away from him and stowed it in the closet for good measure.

So, there we all were clustered in the living room, slurping down bowls of hot soup and staring at our remarkable visitors: George, sullen but unable to go to his room and sulk because otherwise he'd miss the soup, not to mention the drama; Ciel, who was totally overwhelmed, and baby Donna, who was sound asleep; Hillary, looking wistfully at Ciel, as if wondering when she would go back to her nice, warm bed; the cockatoo Sheena, looking pleased with herself; and Rhiannon, myself, and our honored guests.

"It can't hurt if you tell me everything," said Rhiannon. "Or if the others know. So start from the top, old friends. What is the Green Man, and can it do any good now?"

I spoke up hurriedly. "And please don't forget that none

of us has an advanced degree in any branch of the sciences. None of us talks the talk or walks the walk, you know? Just pretend you're talking to a few bright eleven-year-olds. No technospeak.''

"You are familiar with the old Human Genome Project, are you not?" asked Li for starters. Rhiannon and I nodded. "They almost finished it. But around the year 2015, the global economy began its catastrophic decline, and the project was discontinued. It soon became possible for people like us to hire the brightest stars in the biological sciences for a very reasonable price—not only Americans, but also scientists from all over the world.

"The situation was quite similar to that which prevailed in Russia after the collapse of the old Soviet Union. In that era, you may recall, the most brilliant Russian nuclear scientists were desperate to find employment—even with rogue states such as Iraq or Libya.

"As I said, we collected money from donors who shared our views, and invested it in various profitable enterprises, many of which could be characterized as black market.''

"You sound like Rhett Butler," Rhiannon said. "He told Scarlett O'Hara that there was as much money to be made in the collapse of a civilization as in the building of one.''

"Oh, be quiet," I said to her. "He won't get it. Li, it's a literary reference. Just go on.''

"We hired some of the best scientists in the world for a single purpose—to determine whether a faulty gene, or a set of them, was responsible for the sad, bloody history of the human race. And what if we found that gene? If we did so, and learned what mechanisms in the brain it suppressed, or enhanced, we resolved to engineer a virus capable of rewriting its DNA and fixing it.''

The room was very quiet. "So you *did* find it? Or them?" I said at last.

"Yes. We called them 'the Kurgan Genes.' ''

"What on Earth does that mean?" I said.

"We chose the term to commemorate an obscure body of research and speculation dating from the past century," replied Li.

A hesitant smile began to spread over Rhiannon's face. "I think I get it—there was that professor emeritus at UCLA who died back in the nineties, Dr. Gimbutas. She studied Neolithic cultures in ancient Anatolia, I think, that appeared to have existed without warfare for hundreds upon hundreds of years. Then horsemen swept down from an area that would one day be part of Russia and overran them. The horsemen were called Kurgans, am I right?"

"Indeed you are," said Li. He grinned, pleased with his own cleverness, and for a moment looked just like the Chinese imp I remembered from our days together at the firm.

"Wait, wait," I pleaded. "Pull all this together for me. What does the set of genes do—or not do?"

"Remember our discussion over that bottle of wine?" Li asked me. "Many behaviors, and many perceptual flaws, are genetically based. A person's habitual level of anxiety has been linked to genetic factors. Similarly, when one particular set of genes is faulty, the bearer is color-blind," Li replied. "But there are many kinds of blindness—blindness to things that are far more important than color."

I was so tired, and I felt so wretched from my cold, that I could hardly keep my eyes open. Yet I drove myself to stay awake. "You always said that you sensed, you *felt*, that you were part of a greater whole. You felt a community with other people, with animals, with the Earth. Remember my saying how one man could walk into a beautiful forest and see the hand of God at work, but another could see only board feet there for the cutting. You're saying this is controlled by a set of genes?"

Miles spoke up. "It is a form of perception. A sixth sense, if you will. It seems to contain elements of empathy, perhaps even of limited telepathy. The interesting thing is that at no time in history has the gene been completely disabled in all members of the human race. Think of a man like Gandhi, or a woman like Mother Teresa. In such individuals, the disablement must have been very minor. I am sure you can think of other men and women in whom the disablement must have been close to complete. Throughout the ages you come upon thinkers and writers clamoring about the unity of man and nature. They clamored so because they could literally *see* that it was true, and they despaired because others could not.''

"So all of us probably had the right genes to start with, but something went wrong?'' I asked.

"Yes,'' put in Li. "That's one likely answer. Think, Moira—if you were God, would you create beings like us, with all our intellect and cleverness, without including a mechanism to govern and restrain our more destructive tendencies? It would be like constructing an automobile without a set of brakes, or a government without a set of checks and balances. It would be utter folly.''

Miles nodded. "I am only theorizing, but here is one scenario that might approximate what really happened. Assume that at the dawn of time, we were endowed with the sort of mechanism Li described. For countless years human beings lived in small groups, and there is provocative evidence that warfare was simply unknown to some of them.

"But genes mutate incessantly. In the Neolithic era, suppose that the Earth's population grew large enough so that for the first time in history, in certain areas, scarcity of food and desirable areas in which to live became a problem. Suppose you were a member of a hungry tribe of mounted horsemen to the north of fertile lands such as ancient Anatolia, and wished to take them for yourself.

"If your genetic inhibiting mechanism were still functioning as originally designed, you would not ride south and take that land by force. The welfare of those people would be, to you, as real as your own welfare, or that of your children. But if your genetic brake had become disabled through mutation, you would overrun your peaceful neighbors and take what you wanted by force. In the short run, your defective gene would be quite adaptive, in an evolutionary sense. Survival of the most ruthless, as it were. You would have plenty of descendants who carried your defective gene, while the people you had slaughtered would have none.

"In other words, over the short term, aggression and a blind eye to the pain of others are a powerful and successful combination of traits. But if you consider the long-term survival of the species, that same combination is deadly. We see its handiwork all around us, as we speak. Given our current genetic makeup, we don't have a prayer of surviving as long as the dinosaurs did."

I mulled that over for a while. "I'm almost buying it. So, Li and Miles, what is the virus going to do to us? Are we going to turn into worker bees in a hive? Ants in a hill? Mindless cogs in a machine? The Borg?"

Miles threw back his head and broke out laughing. It had been a very long time since anyone had laughed like that in our poor house. "Do I look like the Borg to you? Does Li?"

"You mean you took it?"

"Of course we did. Mad scientists always experiment on themselves first. It goes with the territory."

"Moira," Li broke in, "do you remember all those days and nights that we worked and studied side by side in my apartment in San Francisco? You would bring home work from the firm, and I would be buried in my latest favorite line of research. Often we would not speak for hours, or even be in the same room together. But I always knew I was not alone. I knew that there was someone in the apartment with me. And so I was never lonely. We might not speak for hours, but I knew you were there, and took comfort in the fact. The way one experiences the world after the Green Man is similar. You are conscious of the presence of other people, of animals, of the world turning beneath your feet, to a degree formerly unknown to you. You are independent. You have free will. But you act on that free will with more perfect knowledge.''

I drew in my breath. ''That's the key,'' I said.

''Yes. The Green Man does not strip away our individuality. It does not make us into zombies. All it does is restore a perceptual faculty that has been damaged for thousands of years. It restores to us a source of information about the world around us that has been missing throughout recorded history.

''If you were to do something that would harm another, once you had been infected with Green Man, you would no longer be able to blind yourself to the reality of that fact. You would not be able to twist your perception of reality to persuade yourself you were doing no wrong. You would act for the greater good of all, because you would now have firsthand experience of the existence of that greater good.''

To my amazement, George spoke up. He seemed very excited. ''When I was a kid I went to this evangelical school. We had a history book—what was it called? Well, hell, I can't remember, but I know that Bob Jones University published it. At the time I was struck by this passage. It said that Christians were able to understand spiritual things, while people who weren't saved could not. Specifically, it said that Christians had 'spiritual receptors' that unsaved people didn't have. The unsaved weren't sensitive to spiritual things, because they didn't have those receptors.''

The rest of us stared at him. ''Spiritual receptors?'' Miles said. ''That's amazing. Some of your conservative Christian thinkers were following the same conceptual path as Li and I. But the book said only Christians had these receptors?''

''Yeah, that bothered me,'' replied George.

"Li and Miles," broke in Rhiannon, "to change focus a bit, are you implying that even with two-thirds of the world's population dead from Shiva, the survivors will not fall back into barbarism? The Green Man will connect them, prevent that? You mean we will finally pull together and act as one, for the good of all?"

"We fervently hope so," replied Li.

Rhiannon sank back against the couch. "Blessed be!" she whispered, and closed her eyes.

"Oh, man," I said. "*The Day the Earth Stood Still. The Abyss,* uncut version. *Independence Day.* I feel like I'm in a movie."

"As we've said, the disablement of this crucial gene varies from person to person," Miles added. "Environmental factors are certain to play a part in determining a person's behavior, too. I suspect that people who carry a less-disabled gene to begin with would notice less of a perceptual shift than others who were not so fortunate. When Li first infected himself, he was afraid that the virus didn't work, because he did not experience a dramatically altered state of consciousness. I myself, however, experienced quite a change. I would wager that Rhiannon will undergo the spiritual equivalent of going to the eye doctor and getting her prescription bumped up a notch."

"Don't count on it," Rhiannon said, her voice suddenly bitter. "I kill people. You must be thinking of someone like Lorenzo. He was truly a saint."

Miles tried to look sympathetic. "You, Moira," he said to me, "may experience more of a jolt."

I was rather taken aback. "If I wasn't already so blown away, I might think I was being insulted," I replied.

Miles shrugged. "But you are not responsible for the genes you carry."

"Miles," said Rhiannon, "what would the Green Man do to someone like Saddam Hussein?"

"Who's that?" asked Ciel.

"Dead guy," I said quickly. "Twentieth-century generic badass dictator."

"That's a very good question," he replied. "It is possible that the perceptual shift would be so dramatic for such an individual, they could not assimilate the change. I wouldn't be surprised if we see people like Hussein or Lopez-Iglesias throwing themselves off bridges."

"Big fat loss," I said. "Well, so much for 'Harm none.'"

"There you have it," replied Miles. "The core of the ethical dilemma. If you could go back in time and kill Hitler, would you?"

I pondered on that for a moment. "I think the answer would be yes. You were infected with Green Man first, and had access to more perfect knowledge. You held back time and time again from releasing the virus, hoping we'd find another way out of the pickle we were in. And then, when we were going down for the third time, you did release it, because you knew that course of action would best further the common good."

"That's about the sum of it," Miles said. "Still, there is no denying that we made a certain decision on behalf of the rest of humanity, without their knowledge or consent. We can't escape that responsibility, whatever we do."

"For crying out loud," I said, feeling a bit annoyed by all this high-mindedness, "it's not like we had anything left to lose when you finally released Green Man! Get real!"

"Plato's cave," said Rhiannon thoughtfully. "Remember that story? It was about enlightenment. These men were living in an underground den, chained so that all they could ever see were their own shadows, and the shadows of others, thrown by a bonfire on the wall of the cave before them. If one of those men had ever been able to break his chains, leave the cave, and see the world outside, how could he have ever described it to his fellows still in captivity? If he had the chance to bring them out of the cave, wouldn't he do it, even without their consent?''

Miles beamed at her. ''I never thought of using that example. I've never heard our dilemma stated better.''

She beamed back.

''Excuse me, people, when will the shift take place for those of us in this house?'' I interrupted. ''We brought home your cleverly packaged air freshener on the twentieth of this month.''

''Anytime now,'' Miles said.

I surveyed the others gathered in the room. ''I don't know about you all, but I am about to collapse of exhaustion. There are a couple of empty bedrooms for our visitors, or the couch if they prefer. It folds out into a queen-size sleeper.''

''Yes, I'm going to turn in,'' said Rhiannon.

''Me, too,'' said George with a grunt.

''The couch is fine for me,'' Li said. ''Please, everyone, get some rest. I have some work to do first.''

Rhiannon started to go, but stopped and turned to Miles. ''It is so wonderful to meet you at last,'' she said. They shook hands, and it was clear he was agreeing with her fervently. I could almost hear the violins start up again. Normally I would have been delighted to see young love blossom under my very eyes, but I had a mother of a headache, and I was still mad at Li.

He had pulled a computer out of his briefcase that must have been worth as much as my house. ''What are you doing?'' I asked him. ''Surely your work is done, and you can kick back.''

He shook his head. ''I'm telling everyone on the Internet about Green Man.''

''Why?'' I asked, baffled. ''What's the need?''

''People are dying from Shiva all over the world. Once the Green Man takes full effect, the survivors will wish with all their hearts to go out into the streets and help the dying. Yet they can do nothing for the dying; there has been no time to develop a way to combat Shiva. They must stay inside and let the pestilence run its course. I must explain to everyone why they will find themselves afflicted by such sudden altruistic urges, and tell them to restrain those urges, so that the race may survive.''

I shivered; I hadn't thought of that turn of events. I stood there and watched Li tapping the keys on his computer, oblivious to my presence.

"So," I said querulously, "I'm going to go to bed with a bad cold, and wake up with a full-blown case of enlightenment, huh?''

Li didn't answer. But Miles was there. "I'm afraid so," he answered.

I did my best to grunt like George. "I can't wait," I said. With that, I pulled my aching body up the stairs to my bedroom and fell into an exhausted, dreamless sleep.

I slept all through the following day and half the following night. When I awoke, my room was dark, and there was the faintest murmur of voices downstairs. The shrinking moon must have been high in the sky, for the deck outside my room was bathed in the cold brilliance of its light.

Pulling on an extra sweatshirt for warmth, I got up and went over to the French doors, intending to open them and go out onto the deck. Then the memory of Miles, Li, and the Green Man returned, and my hands stiffened on the door handles. I froze, unaccountably certain that the moment I let in the night air and the moonlight, my own Green Man change would manifest itself.

For a second I felt sick with terror. Then I called on all the courage I possessed and threw open the doors.

My first impression was that the world outside my room was far larger, more mysterious, and more beautiful than I

remembered. The waning moon was radiant, and the play
of its light on the waters of San Francisco Bay was a thing
of heart-stopping splendor. I took a deep breath. Despite
the ever-present pollution, the air had an undertone of life
and sweetness I had never noticed before.

I turned my head and looked at the great oak by the road.
As I studied it and focused on it, I thought I could sense,
in a ghostly fashion, its roots descending deep into the
Earth, and its branches reaching toward the sky. If I listened
very carefully with my newfound sense, I could feel the
presence of small animals and birds in the tree, and
throughout my garden.

I could feel the nearness of all the other people in my
house, and the neighbors surrounding us. It was not intru-
sive; it was a quiet, steadying feeling, very comforting—I
guessed it was rather how a trapeze artist might feel, knowing there was a safety net beneath her. If I tried in the least,
I could sense great pulsing clusters of life across the bay
in San Francisco, and beneath my hilltop perch in Berkeley
and Oakland.

The night before, I had seemed, for a moment, to see the
world through the eyes of Rhiannon's new bird. Now I
knew that had been no caprice of my mind, but one of the
first symptoms of the Green Man lifting the blinders from
my eyes.

Only three times before, by chance, had I been able to
see past the veil that lay across everyday consciousness,
and catch a glimpse of the greater world whose existence
must soon become common knowledge to the human race.
One was when, as an artless child in a San Antonio park
with crystal streams, I had fancied there were dryads in the
trees and sprites in the pools. The second time was at Avebury, for all the vision had been terrifying. The last time
had been when I took the *kehft*.

Now I thought I could lift the veil by myself, without

special help, so honed were my faculties of perception. But did I dare?

I had to try. I walked down the steps of the deck, sat down, and buried my hands in the dirt of a garden terrace. I called into consciousness all I could remember of the experience at Avebury and tried to open my mind to the fullest, to see, to *really* see.

The perception came slowly but gradually. I became aware of the presence of the Earth I touched. Again, it seemed much like a creature, a thing of rock and fire and soil and trees and animals and people that, taken as a whole, as a dynamic system, almost lived. This time, with unerring precision, I sensed the great web of which I was a part. Again I thought I sensed something almost like consciousness.

At Avebury my experience of the Earth had been like touching a dying creature. I had felt fear and anger and revulsion. But this time, much had changed. *It* was not alone anymore. Care and love and energy were pouring into its veins from the three billion people who yet lived, despite Shiva. It was no longer a thing to be exploited, ignored, held as a chattel, and brought to the point of death by its own children. The link between it and us had been restored. It would live. We would live, though the going would be rough for a while. We were all on the same team now, and that was enough to overcome all obstacles that lay in our path.

Slowly, I withdrew my mind from the contact. I didn't want to go too far, too fast. This was a mind-wrenching turn of events, and I wanted to keep my balance while I still pushed ahead.

When my mind was back inside its tiny human shell, I took inventory. Was I still myself? To answer that question I ran a logical spot check. I still had a childish fondness for playing Monopoly, and I hated caraway seeds on anything. I still liked the Brontës, and thought William Burroughs sucked. I loved the Beatles and couldn't stand Rap, even though both were cultural antiques. Yes, post-Green Man, I was still definitely me.

For the first time I became aware of a sensation of hunger. I would have to find some food in the kitchen. Thinking of food directed my thoughts into another channel: what I could and could not eat.

Since time immemorial, my idea of paradise had been a perfectly cooked, medium-rare filet mignon. I had always thought I should become a vegetarian out of principle, but my carnivorous instincts were too deeply ingrained. Now I realized that eating pieces of dead animals was no longer my idea of a good time.

I felt some significant sorrow at this turn of events, but it was not like my philosophical change of heart was going to make any real difference in the course of my daily life. I'd last had a filet mignon steak around the year 2011. You couldn't get meat now, unless you were willing to pay more for it, ounce per ounce, than for dope, and that was sheer madness. Get real.

We had engineered our plant crops to produce a balanced, complete protein diet. We had subsisted on such a nutritious diet for longer than I cared to contemplate. Still, once upon a time, for me, there had been nothing better than a BLT with lots of really crisp greasy bacon made from dead pigs.

I heaved a sigh. Then a new thought occurred to me. I still lived on a planet where all creatures had to eat something to survive. And that something was inevitably other living things. That much had not changed, Green Man or no Green Man. All the virus had done was repair human consciousness, not redesign the basic characteristics of Earth's biosystem.

So I started testing myself. Eating any kind of plant food felt perfectly acceptable to me. I didn't break out in a rash at the thought of eating shrimp, either, or fried oysters the way they used to cook them at Scholz Garten back in Austin, Texas. Yum! Fish were okay food. So were eggs. Only as I began to move up the scale of animal intelligence did the feeling of revulsion begin.

I decided to go inside to see Rhiannon and the others. Also, I particularly wanted to see how the Green Man had affected that cussed old fart George.

I touched the knob of one of the French doors and started to go back into my house. But I was beginning to sense something very disturbing, so I stopped.

Moments before, I had experienced great euphoria as I explored all the new perceptions that Green Man had made possible for me. In my excitement, in my intoxication with the beauty I saw unfolding before me, I had been able to overlook a troubling undertone that echoed in the recesses of my mind.

It was true—across the bay I could feel the presence of a great pulsing cluster of life. But now, as I listened more carefully with my newfound sense, I knew that much of that cluster was dying. The undercurrent of pain and distress was like the drumbeat of distant music—steady, incessant, a refrain that pervaded everything.

Sickened, I felt as if that undercurrent were seeping into the very cells that made up my body. I had truly become part of the family of man. I could sense the presence of my fellows all around me, like so many tiny bonfires dotting the hills and mountains surrounding San Francisco Bay. But now two out of three members of my family were dying, and the distress of their passing left the rest of us in agony.

I tried as best I could to shutter my mind from that pain, and stumbled downstairs to find the others. They were all watching the television, which was tuned to CNN. The whites of their eyes were showing; each appeared to be exerting great control to keep from shattering into a thousand pieces. I didn't have to ask Rhiannon what was happening.

When she saw me, she burst into tears.

"We must wait this out somehow," I said. "There's nothing we can do right now."

She nodded. "But how? I can feel them dying, and it hurts so much!"

Until then I had not fully understood, in my flesh and bones, just why this restored sense, this wonderful, heightened ability to feel and see and experience, was also a deadly curb on the darker side of our nature. Few of us could willfully kill any longer. We were all members of one another, so when one of us died, the rest of us suffered, too.

A wave of pure fear washed over me. I looked at Miles. "Do you have the answer, you and Li? How are we going to get through this?" I asked, my traitor voice turning hoarse.

"With courage," said Miles. "Put your head down and wait, like an animal in a storm."

"If we can live through this week until Shiva is done," Li said, "then we can all begin to rebuild."

There was a long silence. My feeling of nausea and unease steadily deepened. I glanced at Li and then back at Miles, whose face was gray and covered with sweat. "You could not have foreseen this," I said.

Li did not answer. Miles whispered, "I am sure there will be many effects of the virus we couldn't foresee."

"Such as?" I asked.

"Well, we have a good idea how Green Man will affect ordinary people, but as we discussed the other night, none of us is sure how certain other—*types* will respond. Think of a Hitler, or even a Lopez-Iglesias. How would it affect such a man? Would he come to his senses, recognize his kinship with his fellow man, and do his utmost to help repair the damage he'd done? Or would he kill himself when the realization of all the suffering he'd caused was brought home to him? Would he deny the changes within himself, and intensify his worst behavior to compensate for it?''

I nodded. ''You could ask the same questions about a street thug, or a soldier who killed others under orders, or a good man who took evil actions to achieve a goal he believed was good.''

''We could go on like this forever,'' spoke up Rhiannon, her voice on the point of breaking. ''They still make cigarettes and sell them to people who want them. What do you think the chief executive officer of a tobacco company is feeling right now? Or the guys down south who produce all our cocaine? Or the head of a firm that makes assault weapons? Or psychopaths—the Green Man won't even touch them, not if they had no empathic sense to be corrected in the first place.''

Li, ever a sucker for a good workout of the intellect, rose to the bait. ''Psychopaths are very rare. They will simply be more easily identifiable when Green Man has run its course—as will any so-called thug who strives to deny his new perceptions.''

Miles still looked awful. ''Are you having second thoughts about this?'' I asked him. ''It's too late now.''

He shook his head again. ''We certainly did not count on there being a wild card in the design like Shiva. Of course, a greater empathy with the living would imply greater empathy with the dying, and consequent suffering. We had no idea that a group of maniacs would succeed in putting to death much of the human race—right after Green Man had taken effect globally and changed people's ability to be conscious of such a calamity! That many people have never died at once in the history of mankind; the weight of all those deaths, taken at once, will surely traumatize the survivors.''

''Well, if we live over this,'' I replied, ''one thing is sure: The survivors cannot possibly be tempted ever to go to war.''

Ciel stood up slowly and walked over to my side. "I know what would make *me* feel a lot better." Rhiannon's head jerked up and she stared at Ciel intently. I suddenly got the feeling that there was a lot more depth to Ciel than we'd so far realized.

"What is it? Tell us!" I said.

"There are people in the bushes across the street."

"Yes, of course," I replied, "there always are."

"I saw a woman with a baby go in there while it was still light. They don't dare go looking for food, because of Shiva. Let's give them some of our canned goods."

Rhiannon turned and stared at the jungle of dark on the other side of Alvarado Road, as if listening. At length she said, "Ciel senses their presence, intensely. I think we can do the same if we try. Everyone, focus all your attention on that spot of land over there. Close your eyes and listen with everything you've got. The presence of those people will become—quite real to you."

I did as she said. After a minute, it seemed to me that I could sense the presence of half a dozen other people in that direction—little dots of burning life and energy and thought in the blackness.

"Go for it, Ciel," I replied.

She hurried down to the basement, Rhiannon at her heels. They soon returned quickly, each carrying a cardboard box loaded with cans.

"Spam?" I said to them. "You're giving them all our Spam?" Yes, even in the fourth decade of the twenty-first century, Spam was still on the shelves. It cost as much as real Italian prosciutto did back in the good old days, but when you needed a big dose of calories to keep going, Spam was still the ticket.

"They should still be able to eat it," Rhiannon said thoughtfully. "A loaf of Spam certainly doesn't bear much resemblance to an animal anymore. Besides, it's not like eating that stuff would cause any new harm. The animal's long dead.''

"Yea, sister," I said. "Long, *long* dead."

In addition to the Spam, they had pulled a potpourri of various foodstuffs off our pantry shelves: canned chili, beef stew, macaroni and cheese, tuna—all stuff that we had been hoarding for a very rainy day, or a disaster.

"This certainly qualifies as a disaster," I said, leaning toward the philosophical. I got a can opener—one of two remaining in the house—and wrote a note asking the people across the street to return it when they had eaten all the food. Rhiannon, Ciel, and I went down to the road, opened the gate, and put out the boxes in plain view. That done, we locked up again and went inside.

I found our binoculars, sat down in a darkened room, and peered down at the road. We didn't have long to wait; no sooner was I settled than a tall man emerged from the tangle of bushes and greenery and approached the boxes.

There, before my eyes, I saw a most curious little drama play out. The moment he was out of hiding, he struck a pose of seeming indifference, but all the while looked up and down the road to either side of him, antennae on full alert for any lurking danger. Then he began a leisurely walk toward the boxes, his body language conveying a wealth of information to whoever might be watching. He was streetwise, he was strong, he was tough, he wasn't afraid of anything, he was macho macho macho, and nobody in his or her right mind would dare make any trouble for him. All the while his eyes and ears were scanning his surroundings like radar, and his body was poised for instant action.

Halfway across the street he came to a sudden halt and looked downright confused. The theatrical display of body language stopped, as if someone had turned off a switch. He stood there in the middle of the road, looking around as if he were seeing his surroundings for the first time. As if mesmerized, he put his head back and looked up at the moon for a very long time.

Then the tension suddenly broke, his body relaxed, and he started laughing. He said something to himself, shook his head, and then simply walked across the street in a businesslike fashion, picked up the boxes, and carried them back into the bushes.

I wasn't entirely sure yet just what I'd just seen, but whatever it was, I knew it was very revealing.

I went back into the family room. "They're eating," announced Ciel. "I feel a whole lot better now."

I could not entirely banish the clamor of the dying from my mind, but amazingly, I felt better, too.

"I think we're on to something. Ciel, you deserve a medal."

We watched, powerless to intervene, as Shiva swept across the planet, devastating the human race. Everywhere, the poor and powerless were most greatly affected. We were typical of those who survived Shiva's onslaught—the richest in wealth, in housing, in land and space, and in access to information. People like us learned early about the virus and were in a position to isolate themselves from their fellows. The billions of people who died were largely those who could not get out of the virus's way in time: the great masses of poor in cities across the world, and their rural cousins, who died when they came in contact with refugees fleeing those cities. There were exceptions, of course, such as Sheena the cockatoo's unknown owner, who had been our neighbor. But for the most part, Shiva only destroyed the poor and helpless of the Earth. We might have been living in the time of the Black Death, when the wealthy could flee to their houses in the country, and the poor remained in the cities and died.

The privileged remnant of the human race who had access to information soon learned from Li's announcement on the Internet that a second virus, the Green Man, had altered their empathic and perceptual abilities. They learned that they must hold in check their benevolent impulses to help the dying, lest they die themselves and the human race be completely destroyed, as the makers of Shiva had intended. The rest of our species, lacking this cold knowledge, did as their hearts bid them and tried to help their dying neighbors, even as they themselves were stricken. And died for their pains.

In the end, Shiva did not come near its makers' goal of exterminating humanity. Furthermore, the irony of its selective pattern of killing was exquisite. The Shiva virus, far from obliterating the so-called human cancer that was ravaging the Earth, left alive the very people who—save for the advent of the Green Man—would have been most capable of rebuilding our deadly, flawed civilization, and continuing to destroy the planet.

Three wretched days later, the Centers for Disease Control announced that it was probably safe to approach strangers who showed no signs of illness. All over the country, the Army and state National Guard units began setting up temporary stations to distribute emergency food rations; for the near future, there was a surplus of these, as so few people were left alive to demand them. The Army was also distributing biohazard masks for those willing to volunteer to collect and bury the many dead. The Internet buzzed, for people were turning out in droves, not just for the food, but also to help each other.

"Look!" cried Ciel, from one of the family room windows that overlooked the street. "There's a man at the gate!"

I grabbed the binoculars. "He's from across the street."

Rhiannon tugged on her shoes and made for the door.

"Wait, wait!" I cried. "Don't go alone, wait for me."

"And me!" said Ciel.

"Please, the rest of you stay here!" I cried. "We don't want to scare him off."

As we made our way down the steps toward the road, I thought my heart was going to pound out of my chest. "I swear he's returning the boxes," I said to Rhiannon, "and probably the goddamn can opener!"

He saw us all scurrying down to meet him, and despite the distance, I was sure I saw him grin. "We are in a science fiction movie," I said, gasping, "and it's about first contact with aliens."

"You can say that again," replied Rhiannon.

We arrived at the gate, flustered and out of breath. "Hi," said our mysterious neighbor. "How you people doin'?"

Or something approximating that. He spoke the same street language in which Beto had been so fluent. Again, I'm translating.

Before we could reply, he set down the boxes and held out a bright, shiny can opener. "This is for you," he said to me. "It's brand-new. I stole it myself last month."

"Um, well, thank you," I replied.

"You know, we would have starved this week without your food," he said.

"We knew that. We simply couldn't let it happen. On top of everything else that's happened, you think we wanted somebody right next door dying of hunger? Give me a break."

He mulled over my reply, clearly intrigued. "Say, have you heard the story that there is supposed to be a *second* virus? Not the one that's killing everybody—one that makes people get along?"

Rhiannon nodded. "Everybody's got it."

"The hell you say!" he exclaimed. "That explains it— why you gave us the food, why we've been acting so weird."

I grinned, too, in spite of myself. "Weird? How so?" I asked.

"I got ready to take your stuff back to you, and my girlfriend said I should give you the new can opener to say thank you."

"Say, are *all* of you acting 'weird'?" Rhiannon put in.

"Yeah," he said, "all except this fucked-up kid that's been holed up with us. He's always been a mean little shit, and now he's turned into the biggest pain in the ass this side of the bay."

"Look!" Ciel broke in. "There's the woman I saw with the baby."

"Oh," said the man, "that's my girlfriend, Letitia."

A woman carrying an infant came out of the greenery, followed by half a dozen other motley men and women. Bringing up the rear was a teenage kid who looked just plain—well, mean, that was the only word for it.

"What's your name?" I said to the tall man.

"Will."

"Will, I am Moira, this is Rhiannon, and this is Ciel. We have other friends who are still in the house."

The woman with the baby approached cautiously. "It's all right," called Ciel.

"Oh, hell," I said to myself, "what am I doing?" I opened the gate and shook hands with Will. Seeing this, the woman broke into a hesitant smile. Pretty soon everyone else was smiling, except the kid. He was wound up like a spring; his eyes darted from face to face, up to the house, down to the road, incessantly.

"We have been thinking all the time since you brought us the food," began Will. "We have been wondering if we could team up somehow. You people in the house have all the stuff, but you are pretty old and you can't work hard. We don't have anything, but we're young and we can work. We were wondering whether you could show us how to put up some cabins or a house across the street. There's wood all over the place up here, if you know where to look. And maybe you could show us how you grow all that food.

We could help you out whenever you need it.''

''I think that could be arranged,'' I replied.

He pointed down the road to Mr. McClelland's property. ''That old man's got a lot of space, but he doesn't grow much. Maybe we could talk him into letting us use his yard, too. There's got to be something he could use help with.''

''Oh, fuck it, man,'' cried the kid, no longer able to contain himself. ''Why don't you just waste 'em and take the shit?''

Will turned on the boy with a look of controlled fury. He took the boy by the shoulders and shook him. ''Because that's a stupid idea, can't you see? What's the matter, are you blind?''

''Just waste the old fuckers and get 'em out of the way,'' the kid said. ''They're good for nothing.''

Will shook him again. ''Don't you get it?'' he cried. ''Don't you see why that's so stupid?'' I felt icy tingles run up and down my neck to hear the utter frustration in his voice and the way he worded the last question.

''Let me spell it out to you,'' Will whispered to the boy. ''They know stuff we don't. How are they going to teach it to us if they're dead? They teach us stuff, we do stuff for them, we all have a roof over our heads and something to eat. We don't have to live on the street anymore. We don't have to waste time anymore stealing things, getting shot, fuckin' with people, all that shit. It's *easier* this way, don't you get it?''

The boy did not reply but only glared at him. ''They gave us the food, man,'' cried Will, ''so how could we waste them? Tell me, what part of this do you not understand?''

The boy shook like a leaf, and tears began to run from his eyes. ''Fuck you,'' he said to Will, and to us, over and over.

''They helped us!'' Will yelled. ''We can't kill them. Can't you see? Can't you *see*?''

"Let go of me! Get off me, motherfucker!" With a wrench, the boy tore himself free of Will's grasp and backed away down the road. Safely distant, he shot the finger at Will—a gesture that provoked a little ripple of laughter among the watchers—and then tore off running down the hill toward the Berkeley flats.

"He's going to crash and burn," I said.

"Yeah," said Will, "big-time." He regarded Rhiannon and me thoughtfully and added, "You folks sure understand a lot about what's going on."

"Well, we hear a lot from TV and the Internet," replied Rhiannon.

"Yeah," said Will. "We only know what we hear from other people."

"About the boy," Rhiannon said quietly to Will. "He is beginning to 'see,' as you put it, but he doesn't want to. That's the key. Will, there is a virus that's changing things, but in his case, it's changing him so much he can't bear it. Nothing he knows is any good anymore; none of the ways that he has always behaved seem to work anymore. He can't handle it."

"What if he didn't have the gene at all?" I whispered to her. "Maybe there are a few people in whom the gene is just plain missing, like the psychopaths you spoke of. Or what if he has the gene but is able to turn his back on the Green Man change? He might become very dangerous. In that case, would you call him—one of the new Kurgans?"

"I don't think so," she whispered back. "There won't be that many of him, and the rest of us are not fools. We're not unprepared for violence, like the original tribes that fell prey to the Kurgan horsemen. People like that boy are going to stand out like a sore thumb from now on; I for one would have no qualms about restraining him. I wouldn't hurt him—I just wouldn't allow him to go on hurting others."

"Could you kill him?"

She looked thoughtful. "If I absolutely had to, to protect myself or others. But I could not initiate violence, nor could most of us—that's what has changed."

I turned to Will. "Hey, listen," I said, "we heard they're giving away emergency food down in the city. They're also asking people to pitch in and start cleaning up bodies."

Will glanced at the others in his group and then faced me again. "Most of us can go. Letitia here should stay here with the baby, and then we've got the Screecher, who's crazy as it gets."

"The what?" I asked.

"The Screecher—you've heard of him, huh?"

"No, I don't think so. Is he mentally ill?"

Will nodded. "I guess so. He's an old guy. Years ago, they say, he used to have money that his family left him. He'd go into San Francisco every day and sit at the cable car stop by Embarcadero Four and the Hyatt and yell crazy things all day long. He never hurt anybody—in fact, they told me a lot of San Francisco book writers used to put him in their stories. I don't know about that, I can't read much."

"Holy Jesus!" I said with a shock of recognition. "I remember him, from back when I worked at the law firm. It was in Embarcadero Four! That cable car stop was right next to my BART station!"

"Is it old home week or what?" replied Will, laughing. "So, see here, Moira, we'll bring back as much food as we can carry. Why don't you women write down on a piece of paper how many of us there are, so I can show it to the man—so he knows we're not asking for more than we should. I'd do it, but see, I can't write much either."

"I'll get some paper," said Ciel, and sped up the stairs toward the house.

"It's going to take a long, long time to put everything right again," I said to Will. "You realize that, don't you?"

He sighed and gave a shrug, then grinned. "It shouldn't

take as long as it did to ruin everything, now, should it?''

I felt like grinning myself. "You do have a point there."

Suddenly Rhiannon let out a gasp. "McClelland?" she said incredulously.

Startled, I looked past her to see the old geezer himself approaching, shotgun in hand. He looked faintly embarrassed. "Hello," he said. "I just wondered what you folks were cooking up down here."

"We're drafting a mutual assistance treaty," I replied.

Will introduced himself and stuck out his hand. Looking as freaked out as the punk kid, Mr. McClelland shook it. "We're going to help them pull together the stuff to build some shelters across the street and to start farming," I added. "Then we can figure out how to get an actual house built over there. We were thinking about pooling all this land here and getting some really good crops going."

McClelland got a funny look on his face, as if he desperately wanted to say something but was wondering what on Earth he could be thinking of. "Uh," he said, "forget the shelters. I've got extra room at my place, it's only me there, not a whole group like you girls have got. Look, I've even got a huge mobile home covered up back there if you want it. It hasn't been on the road in thirty years, but it's a beauty—cost a hundred thousand dollars back in the eighties. We could haul it across the street so you folks could use it. We'd have to figure out how to put in water and power somehow, and maybe a chemical toilet."

"A hundred thousand dollars!" I exclaimed. "Jeez, and to think I remember when people had things like that."

"Well, none of us knew the collapse was coming," he replied, looking faintly hurt.

"I wasn't trying to upset you. I think you're being very generous," I said quickly.

"Yeah," he said, sounding puzzled. "I am."

Ciel came hurrying down the steps with paper and pencil. I wrote down all our names, plus Mr. McClelland's, and took dictation while Will rolled off the names of his companions.

"All right," said Will when I was finished, "we'll go on down to Berkeley now. I don't know if they'll want us to do anything today, but if they do, we may not get back until dark. But we are coming back, don't worry."

"We won't," said Rhiannon.

When they were gone, the three of us collapsed onto the concrete bench. "If I didn't know about Green Man," I said, "I'd be so bewildered now. Thank God Li got on the Net and told everybody he could. I'm not completely sure McClelland had heard the news—here he was, trying to be a nice guy, and it was really blowing his mind."

"I heard some news when I was up at the house," said Ciel. "Things are starting to happen."

"Like what?" I asked.

"The president of Mexico went on television down in Argentina. He must have escaped from Mexico before the bombs hit. He said he was sorry for what he'd done and then shot himself, right on TV. Then there was a news story about our president. He's resigned because of the part he played in the Mexican crisis. They swore in the vice president, and he signed into law all of Julian Imber's reforms, which just passed Congress. A group of people has confessed to killing Imber and turned themselves in. The Red Cross is very optimistic about us getting through this crisis, since everybody is staying calm and helping everybody else get by."

There was a significant pause while Rhiannon and I assimilated this information. "Well, gee whiz, is that *all*?" I asked.

Rhiannon smiled and then looked thoughtful. "You know, that's just how people acted after the big 1989 quake in San Francisco. We all helped each other, and we got by. The crisis of the quake brought about a temporary state of

'Green Man.' Maybe we weren't so hopeless, even back then.''

''Oh, be realistic,'' I replied. ''What good is getting it up if you can't keep it up? We *were* hopeless, admit it.''

Rhiannon stared at me for a moment and then burst out laughing. ''Green Man's doing you a world of good, dear. Your girlish sense of humor is even returning.''

With that, we all went back into the house for a bracing cup of hot instant milk, imitation chocolate flavoring, and rotgut.

APPENDIX

April 2042

ORIGINALLY, I HAD WOUND UP THE LAST CHAPTER OF THIS little account by listing all my tremblingly held hopes for the future, and lamenting that I would never get to see the dawning of that Golden Age.

However, as the above date would indicate, I managed to make it through another ten years and got to see a nice little chunk of the new beginning—and, in fact, at this point I seem to be still going strong, a regular old Energizer Bunny.

Miles married Rhiannon in a Wiccan handfasting ceremony and lives with us. Li asked me to marry him, but I turned him down. I could forgive him for dedicating his life to saving the world, even if that cut me out of the picture. But I could never forgive him for letting me think he was dead all those years, and keep on grieving.

Even so, we are still close friends. He lives in San Francisco and visits all the time. Both of the guys have been on my case to put the finishing touches on this story so they can publish it on the Net, so I figured I'd better dust it off and give it an ending that reflects the events of the past decade, not just my gooey hopes as of New Year's Eve 2032.

In late 2032 the survivors of Shiva faced a new world full of heady possibilities and many vexing problems.

For one thing, the climate of our home world was still shot to bloody hell, and would be for hundreds of years; that had not changed. Then there was most of the human race to bury or otherwise dispose of, and quickly—so that a new pestilence did not descend up on the survivors of the plague, and large amounts of the powerful greenhouse gas methane were not released into the atmosphere as the bodies decayed. Even so, some cities were left with so many millions of dead bodies that there was no choice but to abandon those cities altogether, and wait until scavenging animals and the passage of time had made them safe to enter again. The climate suffered of course from all those rotting methane-filled corpses, and we suffered along with it.

Those of us who still lived had to determine what stores of food and medical supplies we had left, and then distribute them swiftly across the globe to those burying the dead, and to those struggling to restart the machinery of food production and the manufacture of essential goods.

Everywhere, small groups of people began to pull together—as in our neighborhood—to rebuild their lives and our civilization. Wherever possible, we had to figure out how to supply these groups with tools, food, seeds for growing crops, and information—for it was clear their success would hasten society's recovery from the scourge of Shiva.

To this end, that pesky little institution known as the nation-state had to be thoroughly reinvented. Now that people were no longer interested in killing their neighbors and taking their cookies, functions such as making war, or defending the nation's citizenry from the wars of others, were simply obsolete.

Governments, possessing stores of food and medical supplies, and having the ability to coordinate actions and communication, ended up in charge of Marshall Plan–type mercy missions to areas where famine threatened. They made those essentials available where famine did not threaten so that survivors like us could get back on our feet and begin to rebuild.

When the Green Man rewrote our Kurgan genes, the very ways in which we organized our communities and our civilization were transformed. Heightened empathy and a sense of connection to our fellows led to the disappearance of many human attributes that had once been thought immutable. The intense loneliness and alienation that had plagued modern society became things of the past; everyone lived with the knowledge that family was near. The destructive aspect of selfishness, the desire for power and status, even greed dwindled away—as did any impulse to advance oneself at the expense of others.

With them vanished the drive to amass great quantities of wealth and possessions, beyond what one needed to prosper and enjoy being alive. Certainly the denizens of Withering Heights and Mr. McClelland's growing commune looked forward to acquiring a new wall-size color television, or a state-of-the-art computer, once the economy had really picked up. But the new century would see no more Donald Trumps, or solid gold bathroom fixtures in the ancient style of Jim and Tammy Faye Bakker. After 2032, an acquisitive personality such as Imelda Marcos, she of the many shoes, would have been as hard to find as a triceratops.

When the tempest of Shiva had passed, the world found itself in a strangely fortuitous situation. There was an enormous amount of work to do—a global community to rebuild, food to grow, things to make—and just barely enough able people left to do it. Our situation resembled that of Japan or Germany after the Second World War. There was work enough for everyone, and as the years began to tick by, we actually prospered.

In the early years there was so much catch-up to be done, we worked our ever-loving tails off. Yet from the start, it was unthinkable that we would rebuild our new economy in the image of the old. We worked, we put our house in order, we provided first the basics for everyone, and only then moved on to some neat-o, keen-o frills. This was feasible, you understand, since there were only a couple of billion consumers left on the planet, after Shiva had finished with us.

At that point, with everybody in passable shape, we purposefully slowed the economic engine. We held further needless growth in check, and allowed production and consumption to reach equilibrium at a level we knew was sustainable.

We practiced every method of conservation we could think of, we got into alternative sources of energy big-time, we wasted little, we built goods to last, and we did not overconsume. We didn't squander precious time, money, and energy on stupid investments such as wars. So when all was said and done, there was enough to go around for everyone.

We had babies, in moderation; along with the usual childhood inoculations, they got their own dose of Green Man. We had houses, built to last like a Roman road. We had cars. We also built them to last, and did not power them by burning what little fossil fuels the Earth had left. We repaired roads and highways, but put most of our energies into building short-range and long-range mass transit systems. We made all sorts of appliances, stoves and washers and dryers and stuff like that, designed to be serviceable for a lifetime, and to be recycled when they finally bit the dust.

We had fewer clothes and shoes, but that was no deprivation, because our game plan was to copy the superbly crafted goods available in places such as Paris during the past century. As a woman who was formerly one of the most accomplished shoppers in North America, I can attest that this strategy was sound. You see, there is no joy like the hardship of owning a teeny-tiny wardrobe of well-made

clothes and shoes from Paris, just as there is no joy like
being poor in Paris and being forced to subsist on all that
(sigh) cheap French bread and cheese.

After I had been practicing law at the firm in San Francisco a few years, Aleta Mahoney and I had jumped on a
plane to Paris to see some museums, but mainly to go shopping. Until then, I had frequently plunked down hundreds
of bucks for successive pairs of shoes at Macy's or the
Emporium—shoes that barely lasted a season. Then Aleta
and I blundered into those two side-by-side department
store shopping meccas in Paris, Printemps and Galeries La-
fayette. Several days later we emerged, groggy and blinking
our eyes at the unaccustomed sunlight, carrying several
very large packages of wearables.

Back in the United States, I wore my lovely Parisian
pumps to work day after day after day. After about eighteen
months, the black patent leather ones looked like they could
use a resole, so I took them to the shoe doctor. Another
eighteen months, another resole, and so on. I must have
worn those things for twenty years, and by the time they
wore out, I had no more need for fancy lawyer shoes. Plus,
all that time they looked great, felt great, and were so classic they never went out of style. They had cost a little more
than a single pair of my poorly made, quick-turnover American shoes, but considering they lasted as long as a dozen
American pairs, they were dirt cheap.

Same with the couple of Hermès scarves I got in Paris.
There was a saying that a Frenchwoman with a simple skirt,
blouse, jacket, and Hermès scarf is always well dressed,
and based on what I saw in Gay Paree, that was true. After
Paris I no longer spent my money on an endless procession
of slimpsy little silk scarves from Macy's that looked
wasted after a dry cleaning or two. With just a couple of
Hermès scarves, I was elegantly dressed for life.

Our new society basically embraced the Paris shopping
strategy on a global scale. We made good stuff, and when

we got to a point where everybody on Earth was well stocked with it, we stopped. We went home and smelled the roses and played with the kids. Other, more talented people went home and wrote books and plays and poetry, composed music, made lots of movies, dreamed up lots of cool art and a great deal of new entertaining stuff to do with computers, built new hiking trails all over the place, restored wildlife habitats, and did other very cool things. An army of terminally mundane folks even restored Las Vegas. Don't knock 'em; it could be a kick if you were in the mood.

In short, there was never a shortage of stuff to do, even though the chugging economies of the past, and the sixty-hour workweek that went with them, gradually faded into our collective memory.

I meant to close here, but I must make one final contribution to this story.

As my ninetieth birthday approached, I had every reason in the world to be happy. But strangely I found myself becoming increasingly subject to painful bouts of remorse and bitterness whenever I thought back on all the waste of the world that used to be.

I couldn't seem to stop the episodes no matter how desperately I tried. There is a downside even to something as benign as a heightened empathic faculty; now that the crises of the past decades had subsided, I was finally beginning to encounter it.

I kept remembering the wasted years, lives, and opportunities of the past; the needless suffering, killing, and destruction. I would dwell on all the people who died, especially the children; the animals pushed to extinction, the forests cut down, the landscapes ruined, the misery felt and endured throughout the ages of human history. I would think of how pointless it all was.

If only we had been able to see clearly back in those

days, we could have avoided such tragedy. In the final analysis, it was all completely unnecessary—if only we had been able to get our heads screwed on right. That fact is what burned in my heart and mind.

My friend Will said it better than anyone, that day ten years ago when he yelled at the boy outside the gate to Withering Heights—we didn't have to waste time anymore doing the stupid things we used to do; it was easier this way.

This irony galled me more than words can say. I wanted to go back in time and scream at people to make them understand. Yet, back then, nothing would make us see reason. Even when our species was on the point of death, we wouldn't do it.

At last I thought I had guessed what was wrong with me. I was reminded of the title of a science fiction book I read when I was young, by the one and only Robert Anton Wilson, called *The Universe Next Door*. The bitterness I felt during these mood swings was so strong, I almost felt as if its source was not within me—that my empathic sense was picking up transmissions, so to speak, from a neighboring universe in which we had not been so lucky.

Next door to us, perhaps in another dimension, or an alternate timeline, there was a world in which we really did crash and burn. And somehow I was tuning into its anguish.

Occasionally I even wondered if my own world were still a living nightmare from which, dreaming, I had briefly escaped—and that when I woke, it would once again be there in all its ugliness, waiting for me.

But I told myself this was nonsense. I might be very old, but feebleminded I was not.

Today, the twenty-third of April, one of these bouts hit me again. I called an electric cab, went to the newly reopened BART station, and trekked over to San Francisco to see Li. He has a little apartment in the Marina with a view of the Golden Gate Bridge, which always sends me into a Zen-like state of serenity. For comfort and companionship, I took Sheena along for the ride. She has a lovely little travel cage Will built for her, and loves to go on trips.

When I arrived, I put Sheena on a perch Li keeps for her. As she contentedly began to preen, I told him about the feelings that had been plaguing me. He did his best to console me, and said he did not think I was losing my grip on reality, or anything like that.

"Moira," he said with a sigh, "in the past ten years the world has undergone a frenzy of rebuilding, rethinking, and remaking. Now we have achieved a secure foothold on the mountain we are climbing, and for the first time can catch our breath and look back at the path we have taken.

"I understand how you must feel. At the eleventh hour, and not a moment before, mankind finally managed to undertake a course of action that would ensure its survival. You are asking yourself, 'Why did we have to wait until the hour was so late? Why couldn't we have made up our minds to act long, long before?' Moira, I can't answer that. When I die, if I find there is a God, I will certainly pose that question to him."

I lowered my head, pulling my eyes away from the mesmerizing view. "Li, you speak of *mankind* finally taking action to ensure its survival. But it wasn't 'mankind.' It was a very small group of people. You were the brains behind Green Man, with a bit of synergy from your partnership with Miles. Your helpers were merely that—helpers. What if you really had been killed at Tiananmen Square? What would have become of us?"

He made comforting sounds and tried to get me to hush. "I believe there are points in history when an idea is ripe to be born—when its time has come. We saw many currents of change gaining strength and intensifying during our lifetimes. Think how many times a scientific discovery has been made all but simultaneously by two or more teams of scientists, working in ignorance of each other. If I had not

lived, and had not developed Green Man, there would have
been someone else.''

I shook my head. ''But there wasn't someone else. There
was Shiva—but not someone else doing what you did. Take
you out of the picture, and nothing would have saved us.
It's not graven in stone anywhere that the course of history
can't turn on the actions of one man. I can give you a
million examples where it did!''

He clasped his hands together. ''Moira,'' he said intently,
''in the past fifty years, we had many warnings, many opportunities to change—to stop our self-destructive behavior
while there was still time. If Julian Imber hadn't been
killed, who knows what would have happened? I think most
Americans were ready to follow him and do what had to
be done. I also think most of the other countries in the
world would have followed the lead of an America united
by the kind of purpose Imber was ready to give us.''

''But he was killed, Li,'' I whispered, breaking into tears.
''It all came down to this: Except for one fabulous stroke
of luck, the fact that you survived Tiananmen Square, and
had the time and resources to develop the Green Man—we
would have been done for.''

Li gave a very nervous laugh. ''I'm only trying to say
that I believe there were many strokes of luck in the running. At any point in time, a different lucky break might
have finished the course and won the race instead. It was
only chance that I happened to be the arrow that hit the
target.''

I stood up to go. He had not put my heart at rest; I
doubted if anything could. ''Don't misunderstand, Li,'' I
said. ''My life has been a great adventure. I'm going to be
ninety years old next week. I've lived to see the world I
loved dragged back from the brink of destruction. I've lived
long enough to have a look at the new world that is going
to replace it. But when I think how close we came to losing
everything, I get to feeling very shaky. The fact remains

that by the time the year 2032 arrived only one man, one single thread of hope, stood between humanity and destruction. If you'd been killed at Tiananmen Square, we'd be— well, you know where we'd be.''

Li looked thoughtful, and was silent for quite a while. "You may think me a fool, but I believe that there was more than one chance out there for us to survive, because I believe we're here for an important reason. I'm not sure what it is—I don't know if any human being is capable of comprehending it—but I believe it exists. If you asked me to 'go wild' and speculate, I might surprise you.''

"Go for it," I replied.

"Here's one idea. I know I could think of others, given a little time. Do you remember when the Guardians of Gaia compared us to the meteor that struck the Earth sixty-five million years ago?''

"Of course. How could I ever forget?''

"That's what they said, but I don't think they ever stopped to ask Gaia what *she* actually thought.''

I gave him what felt like a stupid look. "What?''

"I'll anthropomorphize to an unforgivable extent. Suppose you were a spirit called Gaia and that you had labored for millions of years to bring forth life on the surface of a new planet. Even by your frame of reference, it seemed to take forever. Then, finally, one day you had everything up and running. You had oceans full of life, and land masses teeming with vegetation—magnificent trees, ferns the size of an office building, you name it. You had created a hundred varieties of dinosaur, from the mighty *Tyrannosaurus rex,* to flying creatures who were the ancestors of the first birds, perhaps earmarked to evolve into the planet's first truly sentient creatures. You were quite pleased with the way things were going. And then, one day, the meteor came and destroyed most life on Earth. You probably suffered great pain. Perhaps you lost hope, seeing the ruin of all you had worked for, and wondered how you would ever recover from this setback.''

He paused. I felt distinctly creepy, because, on one level, I could almost buy it.

''Suppose you said, 'Never again.' Suppose you would rather have died than see another meteor destroy all you had labored to build. Suppose you were ready to gamble for big stakes.''

He stopped again and I said, ''Li! Finish!''

''You selected a tiny mammalian survivor of the meteor strike. You arranged for it to evolve a great, powerful brain. Perhaps you were frightened and desperate; perhaps this time you forced it to evolve more quickly than was entirely prudent, for fear another meteor might come before the creature was ready. Perhaps, because of your haste, it evolved with certain systemic and genetic flaws it would not have otherwise possessed.

''You knew that you might be releasing a genie from a bottle that you could not control, but you were willing to take that risk. Anything was better than another meteor. You knew that the genie, once released, might itself destroy you—but it also might come to love you, and use its great big brain to protect you. Now, if the genie species were to go through a stormy adolescence, wouldn't you try to plant opportunities to help it grow up—everywhere you could? Wouldn't you try to load the dice? When things got especially rocky for your new species, wouldn't you arrange for many more safety nets than little old Li and his Green Man virus?''

I looked at him sharply. ''I see where you're going! You're talking about that tiny asteroid we nuked back in 2019!''

''It was only a hundred yards across,'' Li admitted. ''It was nothing like the meteor sixty-five million years ago. It would have devastated the local area where it impacted the Earth, but it couldn't have caused even a mild nuclear winter. However, there are plenty of other asteroids out there, and we still have the technology in place to deal with them.''

"So you think all this is about protecting the Earth from wandering *asteroids*?'' I broke out laughing. "Li, you are a master of bullshit.''

He laughed, too. "It is only an idea, Moira. None of us knows yet why we're here. We may not know for millions of years, if ever. It's only a fanciful notion.''

We kissed each other and said good-bye. Li promised that he'd be at my birthday party the next week. He said he had found a delightful gift for me, a bit of nostalgia from the late 1980s, but despite all my wiles he adamantly refused to tell me what it was ahead of time.

Sheena and travel cage in hand, I made my way back to the BART station. I still could not keep from thinking how very slender and fragile had been the thread upon which our survival had depended such a short time ago.

Ten years before, our world had balanced on the razor's edge between survival and destruction. It certainly seemed to me that we had thrown away all the chances Fate had given us to save ourselves, except one. Ten years ago, only a single man had been left who could tip that balance toward life and away from death.

I boarded the train that would take me to Berkeley and sat back in my seat, grateful for the chance to rest. Once we were settled, I let Sheena out to perch on my arm and cuddle against my chest for the ride.

The train began to move, picked up speed, and with a loud rattle of doors hurtled into the TransBay Tube that rested on the floor of San Francisco Bay. I stared into the darkness rushing past my window. The thread of hope that Li represented had been far too slender to give me any lasting peace of mind; I was still afraid that someday soon the tormented world next door would begin to appear in my dreams.

Sheena, sensing my distress, made a comforting little noise that sounded like ''Uh uh!'' I rubbed her under her wings and rested my head against the window of the train, still gazing into the darkness that surrounded us.

Then I began to feel very, very strange. I would have gasped, but it seemed as if a pair of hands were clasped around my lungs, preventing me from drawing breath. Slowly I was overcome by a powerful sensation of dread and wonder and delight; I was both Rat and Mole, trembling with awe in *The Wind in the Willows*. I shivered, and watched spellbound as a window opened in the darkness. Just as if I had taken a new dose of the *kehft*, I began to have a vision of another world.

Yet it was not the dead and blasted world next door which I had feared to meet in my dreams. This was quite a different neighboring world, and it, unlike my nightmare, was very beautiful.

The gooseflesh stood out on my arms as the vision took shape. In this other world that might have been, Gaia's original plans for our planet had never been destroyed by a thunderbolt from the black of space. Another race was master of the Earth in our stead.

But what race? My skin prickled, and an unseen hand turned my gaze away from the window a moment, to look into Sheena's obsidian, intelligent eyes. Sheena. A bird, one of the only remaining descendants of the dinosaurs on Earth.

''Oh, my God,'' I whispered, ''it would have been *your* world.'' I read assent and understanding in her shadowy eyes, and turned back to gaze again through the window between the worlds.

Though not mammalian, the masters of that other world were warm-blooded. Perhaps they were covered with scales; then again, perhaps not. Long ago I had seen a beautiful artist's conception of how *Archaeopteryx*, the dinosaur who was also the first bird, might have looked. If the artist was right, the lords of that world would have been adorned with glorious feathers in every color of the rainbow. And the longer I gazed into the dark, into the heart of my vision, the more I came to discover this was true.

My spirit took flight, watching the vision unfold like a flower in the morning sun. Rhiannon's birds could speak; these creatures that should have been could speak and sing like the angels. Sheena used her feet and claws like hands, to hold and examine and fling about items of interest; these creatures, given the millions of years of evolution denied them in my timeline, could write, design magnificent musical instruments, and play haunting melodies upon them. They could even split the atom. But they—brought to maturity in the fullness of time, with great prudence and care—had always known to do no harm.

I had no trouble imagining Gaia's anguish and sorrow when the meteor hit and snuffed out that bright and lovely future. Of course she had taken a desperate gamble by creating us to catch up the fallen torch. And she had won that gamble.

I held Sheena next to my heart, as birds so love for us to do, and tried not to weep. Perhaps Li's story about the meteor was nothing but fanciful nonsense. But as the train sped toward Berkeley, I discovered to my great joy that if my thoughts began to dwell on the dark and destroyed world that hovered just beyond my perception, I could reach out and turn them back toward that bright other world, full of life and beauty and song, that should have been.

Had Sheena's world not died, we would never have enjoyed our moment in the sun. Now that the moment was ours, it was our purpose, our duty, and our birthright to create a new Earth, equally beautiful, to take the place of the one that had been lost.

The train burst out of the Tube, and a rush of light filled the car. I suddenly felt very pleased with the state of things. In fact, I felt so hopeful, I began speculating on the chances of making it to my hundredth birthday, and wondered where I was going to throw the damn party.